C000063625

My Perfect Daughter

Sarah A. Denzil

CHAPTER ONE
THEN

I met my daughter under unusual circumstances.

To say I wasn't prepared for what happened to me, and my daughter, would be an understatement. No one could predict waking up one day to endure the events I endured. But I lived through them, and in return for my suffering, the universe gave me a child.

Everything started on a cold January day. A Saturday. I'd had a stressful start to the morning, with two awkward and unpleasant phone calls. My husband, Simon, insistent on keeping the house in the divorce, took pleasure in reminding me that he'd paid the full deposit and over half of the mortgage payments.

His clipped voice muttered, "It's only fair."

Rolling my eyes, I listened as he gave me more reasons, but I didn't argue.

Ten minutes after I'd hung up with Simon, my mum called to tell me I should under no circumstances let Simon keep the house and that I was weak and stupid for marrying him at all.

"The man is a narcissist. He's going to say whatever works to make you give up *everything*. Don't allow him to take everything, Zoe. He doesn't deserve it," she ranted. "Fight back."

"Sure," I lied.

And as she carried on, I stopped listening, because she wasn't telling me anything I didn't know. Then I *did* feel weak and stupid—which made me agitated. The four walls of that much-contested house closed in on me until I had to get out. So I hung up, grabbed my car keys, and drove out to the one place I felt alive and alone.

My fingernails drummed against the steering wheel as I ventured into the Peak District, passing the popular beauty spots like Stanage Edge, until there were no more walkers striding across the landscape. It took thirty minutes or so to find the place I loved. But as soon as I saw my hidden parking spot in the middle of a seemingly forgotten valley, I exhaled with relief.

The January wind bit deep into my body, taking a chunk out of my lungs when I tried to breathe. I set off jogging up the long, shallow hill, forcing my muscles to work hard. As I warmed, I tried to push the voices of my husband and my mother out of my mind. Mum's tuts and staccato-quick judgements. Simon's nasally whine, the one that made my ovaries shrivel into raisins. Three years earlier, a few months after our wedding, I'd suggested that I come off the pill so we could try for a baby. He'd disagreed. Now the thought of bearing his child made me want to vomit.

And in the back of my mind were those words from my mum: "weak and stupid." My feet pounded the tarmac, left foot weak, right foot stupid. Holding on to the house meant keeping Simon in my life for longer. It meant putting up with his gaslighting, whining, and passive aggression. It meant listening to him talk about how much he loved his new girlfriend, the twenty-year-old administrative assistant he'd sweet-talked into afternoon delights between meetings. It meant fighting a man I never wanted to see ever again.

I breathed, letting it all out, and slowly, my rounded shoulders moved up and back as the coil of my muscles unfurled. All around me stretched the moorland with its dead, burnt-brown heather and scrubby grass. I remained vaguely aware of a farm about half a mile behind me. Its presence made me feel less alone. I'd often considered the fact that it might be dangerous to jog in such a secluded spot, but then I reminded myself that I could run to the farm to get help. It seemed like the best of both worlds: I got to see the untouched parts of the landscape. I got to be alone. But I always had a place to ask for help.

I wore bright running gear, even in the early afternoon like today. I kept my keys in my pocket and planned to poke them through my knuckles if anything bad happened. I never listened to music, always aware of my surroundings, paying close attention to the sound of passing cars or other people. But those who want to do others harm will always find away, no matter what.

And then it happened.

In an empty field, the little girl appeared from behind an oak tree like a fairy-tale nymph. Dressed in shorts so ill-fitting they cut into her waist and a T-shirt that rode up her torso to reveal her belly button, she shivered and clutched her tiny body for warmth. My heart could hardly take it all in. I let out a muted yelp when I saw her. It was the strangest feeling, like I'd stepped into a movie or a television show. My brain told me that it wasn't possible for a child to be standing alone in a field in January. And yet, she was there.

"Hello," she said.

Finally, my body leapt into action. I hurried over to the wall, searching for a jutting stone to help me climb. She pointed to a stile a few metres down the road. I sprinted over to it and ran into the field to get to her.

"Hello," she said again, a bright, if quivering, grin on her face. "What's your name?"

She shivered violently, her poor skinny knees knocking together. She clearly hadn't had a bath in days. Her fingernails were filthy and her ankles black. I slipped out of my jacket and wrapped it around her shoulders.

"I'm Zoe," I said. "Wh...What are you doing out here alone?"

"I ran away. But now I'd like to go home to my mummy, please. Can you take me?"

"Of course, I can. Where do you live?"

She sounded it out carefully, her eyebrows rising and her chin bobbing up and down in concentration. "Eye. Vee. Cwoss."

While I thought about what she meant, I rubbed her fingers with my hands, desperately trying to warm her up. "Eye. Vee. Oh, Ivycross. You live at the farm?"

She nodded enthusiastically.

"Is it okay if I pick you up?"

"Yes," she said, and her face lit up. Genuinely happy to be lifted into my arms, she even nestled her head into my neck. "Thank you, Zoe."

The earnestness in her tone made my scalp tingle. What had happened here? Why wasn't she wearing clothes that fit her? Or a coat and boots? She had on scruffy trainers with the stitching falling apart. A squirming, uncomfortable horror crept up inside me as I carried her back to the place that had allowed this to happen. I was tempted to put her in my car and drive her straight to the nearest police station. Fear stopped me from doing that because... would it be kidnapping? Would I be convicted of a crime? Would it make everything worse for the child in my arms?

My thoughts looped around until I settled on a compromise. I decided to take her back to the farm and call the police while I waited in my car for them to arrive.

"What's your name?" I asked her, realising I didn't know.

"Maddie."

"That's so pretty."

"Yes," she said. "I think so too."

Her response made me chuckle. She wasn't afraid of strangers at all.

"How long have you been out here, Maddie?"

"Not long," she said.

"Why were you behind the tree?"

"I was playing a game."

"Like hide-and-seek?"

"Yes!" She laughed. "I was playing it with you."

I shook my head. "But you don't know me."

"I saw you."

"But how could I find you if I didn't know I was playing?"

Maddie slapped her head like I was stupid.

Wow, rough crowd. First my mum and now this kid.

"I was *seeking*," she said. "I had to find *you*."

I stepped onto the farm with Maddie in my arms, and a sense of dread lay cold and hard at the bottom of my belly. I'd never seen the place close up. A dead body had more life in it than the farm. No livestock brayed or cooed. I passed a beaten-up Land Rover. Facing the house, my gaze trailed up to the windows. Every curtain was drawn shut, blocking the view within. There were no ornaments or vases on the windowsills, just the dirty fabric of those old curtains. To my left, I noticed several sunken and decaying outbuildings and a long barn. No one used those buildings. No one had bothered to fix the broken window or brush away the crumbling brick. I approached the door with reticence, my heart beating hard.

"Zoe," Maddie said, pulling me from my fears. She wasn't smiling anymore. "Can you put me down now please?"

I gently placed her down on those broken shoes.

"You're very nice," she said.

At first, I thought I'd imagined the sadness in her voice. But when a pair of strong arms grabbed me by the neck, I realised I had not imagined it.

CHAPTER TWO
NOW

I blanket a chilled macaroni-cheese bake with a layer of cling film. I place it in my sensible Volvo alongside a bag of brand-new underwear and socks. I get in and drive down the coastal road towards Penry, a small Cornish village, over three hundred miles from the wild Peak District moors. As I take a left turn, sea air drifts in through the open window. I pull in three lungfuls to help calm my pattering heart. Taking my time, I drive towards Parvati and Dev Shah's house. They are my friends who are going through the kind of pain I hope to never experience.

On the outside, I appear normal. Here I am, a suburban mum doing suburban mum things. Inside, I'm screaming, fearing the worst. At a traffic light, I see a torn poster flapping and fluttering against a lamppost. A few tourists pass it, their eyes skimming the image of the smiling teenage girl. Tremors dance across my skin. My heart aches for the Shahs. Then I can't stop thinking about him, the man who choked me until I passed out. The man who dragged me to his barn and tied me up.

All around the world, women are being killed. What if Riya Shah is one of those women? She's a girl, really. At sixteen years old, she's still a child. And she's been missing for two weeks. A week before that, I shared a bottle of Rosé with Parvati in the Black Swan. We sat in the window, watching a hen party stumble by. They waved, and we waved back, grinning at the young woman dressed in a veil and white stilettos. Now Parvati's daughter is missing, and everything has changed. Beautiful Riya. My daughter's best friend. I wish I weren't thinking about what happened to me in that barn.

The Shahs live in a beautiful home overlooking the Celtic Sea. Their lawn swoops down towards the coast, met first by the outer edge of a holiday park. I can hear the distant sound of music from the caravans. Sweet, early-summer air throws up the scent of Parvati's gorgeous, magenta honeysuckle. I park on the drive and pick up the things from the boot.

Dev answers the door, glassy-eyed and stiff. He notices the casserole dish in my arms and waves me into the house. "You didn't have to, but thank you."

"It's just macaroni cheese. Gabe mentioned that Sadiq liked it at school."

"He does," Dev says. "Here, I'll take it."

He leads me through to the kitchen and places the dish inside the fridge. I notice several other dishes there too. At least they have food.

"I also brought..." I regard the bag in my hands. "Sorry, I hope this isn't taken the wrong way, but I thought you might need some fresh clothes."

"We do. Thank you." He takes it from my hands and places it on the kitchen counter. "Would you like a cup of tea?" His motions are robotic, his voice soft monotone. There are half-moon bruises beneath his bloodshot eyes. The Dev I know is always smiling. This is a different version, a stranger.

"No. I won't keep you long." I find myself giving him *that* smile— the patronising one I remember from all those years ago. The smile of journalists and police officers that I found to be nothing more than performative. I hate myself for it. "Have you heard anything?"

He shakes his head. "False information mostly. A witness thought they saw her in Aberdeen, but it was someone else."

Pain emanates from him like a swelling storm cloud, from the slope of his shoulders to the tight set of his jaw. I remember the haggard expression on my parents' faces when they came to visit me in the hospital that first time. They'd both aged ten years in one week.

"If there's anything I can do to help," I say, the words stilted and lame. I can't find their girl for them. All I can do is imagine what a man might be doing to her right now.

"You've done so much already, Zoe. Thank you. I hope Maddie is okay."

"She misses her friend, but she's okay."

"Good. She's a good girl."

Hearing him say that releases a tightness in my body that I hadn't noticed.

"Zoe."

I pull my gaze away from Dev to see Parvati standing in the doorway.

"What are you doing here?"

The words and her tone of voice—it all stings. Since Riya disappeared, Parvati's demeanour with me has changed. And I don't think it's to do with her fear and grief. I think it's *me*. I take her in, the way she vibrates with rage. Her hair, usually full of volume, is unwashed and clogged with grease. Her skin is blotchy and dust grey. Her arms are clamped tightly across her body, and she hovers far away from me like we're enemies.

"I brought some... um... food. And I'm going now. I..." My mouth hangs open, trying to find the words. After what I've been through, I should know what to say, but I don't. "We're all thinking of you. We know she'll come home safe—"

"No, you don't," Parvati snaps. "You don't know that at all."

"You're right." I back up, grab my handbag from the counter, and make my way towards the door. "You're completely right. I'm so sorry, I know how—"

"You know from your own experience? Yeah, you've mentioned that," Parvati says bitterly. "Thank you for coming here to remind us of what happened to you."

Dev raises a hand to calm her. "That's unkind. Zoe came to help."

"No one can help us," Parvati says, her voice breaking. "Our child is gone. Can't you see that?"

I linger by the doorway, desperate to cross the space between us and comfort my friend. But I don't. She doesn't need to say what she means, because it's written across her face. She stares at the scar on my hand, no doubt remembering what happened to me and imagining the same thing happening to her child. I'm a reminder of all the horrible things that can happen to girls like Riya. I shouldn't have come.

EVERY NARROW ROAD feels like it's pressing down on me as I drive home. The past has a weight to it.

I'm lucky to have what I have. Justin, the rock I need on the bad days, a man who holds me when I shake at night. Gabe, my seven-year-old boy, hilarious and silly. Maddie, the daughter I found on that countryside road all those years ago. She's now sixteen, and I wouldn't change her. We're messed up together. I love her dry sarcastic humour. I worry for her, though. I worry for us both, but I love her, and to me she's perfect. I'm also lucky to have money, which bought the house that makes me feel safe.

That money came with a price. About nine years ago, I sold a book to a publisher for a six-figure advance. I wrote about my experiences as a victim of the notorious serial killer Peter McKenna and as someone who had adopted a daughter through difficult circumstances. I wrote about my relationship with Maddie, the highs and the lows, the lack of support from my family, and the way we both struggled to move on. That book was a phenomenal bestseller that completely changed my world. It was adapted into a movie, and all of a sudden, I had money and options.

Even now, after living in this house for seven years, I'm amazed it's mine. I drive down into the underground garage and park the car. Then I take the hidden staircase into the house. Right next to this entrance is a control panel that allows me to lock doors, lower shutters, and check security cameras. We have them in all the rooms, but the cameras in the bedrooms are switched off unless there's an intruder alert. Maddie and Gabe deserve their privacy.

It's a smart home with a built-in panic room, shutters that encase the entire building at night, air conditioning controlled in each room, and an alarm that alerts the police of any suspicious activity. There's even an outlet that produces steam to frighten away anyone who *can* get into the house. Because you can't be too careful. You can never be safe enough.

I have the house to myself today. Justin, Maddie, and Gabe are all at school. Gabe is at the tiny Penry primary school in the village. I check the time. I have a few hours before I need to pick him up. Justin and Maddie are both at Bartholomew's Secondary School, but Justin isn't a student, obviously. He's a counsellor for kids with mental health problems or issues they don't want to discuss with a teacher.

After a quick shower to wash away the anxiety sweat, I leave the house and walk along the coast, enjoying the breeze on my damp hair. The house is a five-minute walk from a quiet beach, one missed out by most tourists because of the turbulent tide and scattering of stones mixed in with the sand. I kick them around as I walk, breathing in fresh sea air. My agent thinks I'm writing the sequel to my first book, but I'm not. I haven't been since Riya went missing. I'm trying not to think about *why* my daughter's best friend went missing.

I enjoy my days, even though they can stretch. Since we moved to Penry, I've focused on being a mum. But now Maddie is almost seventeen, Gabe is seven and I have more time to myself. It's taken me years of therapy to appreciate my own company, and after what happened at the farm, I will never again take my freedom for granted.

In almost no time at all, I've spent most of the afternoon walking up and down the beach. I need to collect Gabe from primary school. My legs burn as I hurry back up to the house to get the car. But luckily, I make it to school on time.

Parvati is standing by the gates, waiting to collect her youngest, Sadiq. I wave shyly, but she pretends not to see.

"Did you know that the average dinosaur is the size of a car?"

I hadn't even noticed Gabe running over. He walks straight past me towards the Volvo.

"I did not know that."

"Yep. And the smallest one was like... like a chicken." He mimes the size of a chicken with his hands before yanking open the door.

"So, I guess you learned about dinosaurs today." I check his seatbelt is fastened correctly.

"Yep. Can I show Maddie my pictures?"

"She's going camping after school today, bud. How about tomorrow?"

"Fine. When can we go camping?"

I grimace. "Let's see when your dad can take you."

"What about you?"

"Me and tents don't mix. Too many spiders." I exaggerate a shudder, and he boos me.

"Booooring."

"Erm, watch it, you." I flash him a stern look, but I only half mean it. Then I close the door and make my way around to the other side of the car. As usual, the road outside the school is chock full of parents in large cars, and it takes me a while to back out of my space.

"Dad's not even going to be in tonight, is he?" Gabe asks from the backseat.

"No, sweetie, not tonight." But in truth, I'd completely forgotten Justin was going to the pub to watch football. Then again, he often has things going on in the evenings. My husband is the kind of person who's never still. We have our movie nights, and he knows that I'm a homebody, but he needs more. He needs nights out with other men and sports. Lots of sports.

"He'll be home late, won't he?"

"Yup," I said.

"Booooring."

"Oh, I see. I'm not good enough for you, am I?"

He doesn't answer. He ends up distracted by playing his game counting the lampposts on our drive home. Gabe loves numbers and cars. The two together is his idea of heaven. If one day, he managed to add in dinosaurs, he'd be entertained for days on end.

After parking the car back in our garage, I clutch my heart as though wounded by his words. "It hurts!" I exclaim dramatically as Gabe laughs.

We actually have a pretty fun evening. I make spaghetti with the kind of tomato sauce he likes—one packed full of hidden blended veggies. He finishes his homework while I watch my favourite soaps and sip a nice Merlot. Both of us end up in bed at nine, Gabe with his nightlight on and a book about dinosaurs on his lap—he tells me he's too old for me to read him a story now—and me with my Kindle, the screen brightening the space around me.

I'm not sure what time I wake up, but there are hands on my thighs working their way up my body. The air smells like stale beer, the sourness worming up my nostrils. I freeze. That's how my body works. It shuts down.

"You awake?" His hands travel up towards my chest.

"No," I say.

"You feel nice."

He's drunk. I don't like drunk men, not even my husband, the sweetest man I know. They scare me. They have to be *handled*, either through ego stroking or mothering. How do you get out of sex with either of those options?

"Babe, I was asleep."

"Yeah, but I'm wide awake." He laughs and pretends to bite my side.

I'm making the decision whether to throw him off me or give in when my phone rings. I grab it, grateful for the interruption, and hear Justin swear under his breath. I don't have time to feel disturbed that he didn't pick up on my pretty big clues that I wasn't into it.

"Mum."

With that one word I'm sitting bolt upright, spine tingling, stomach sinking. Her tone is *off*. Maddie isn't an emotional person, so when there's any kind of distress in her voice, I'm immediately terrified.

"Are you okay?"

"I'm fine, but something happened."

"What is it?"

"One of the girls died."

CHAPTER THREE
THEN

My right hand throbbed. Even half asleep, I knew not to move it. Blinking open sticky, sleep-encrusted eyes, I wondered why my hand throbbed, why my throat ached, and why I was freezing cold and groggy. I saw the nail sticking out of my skin. A Halloween prop, surely. And yet I didn't move. I didn't *dare* move because my instinct told me it would hurt. The air around me smelled like old keys. The sweet scent of rust. My stomach lurched, and bile filled my mouth like saliva. I tilted forward, dizzy.

The nail was real. My hand throbbed because someone had hammered a nail into my hand. I smelled sweet rust because I'd bled all over the desk in front of me.

"Take it out."

His voice washed over me like a bucket of cold water. I sat up, breathing heavily. And there he was, sitting in front of me on a plastic chair, the kind found in most schools.

He hunched over that damn chair like a gorilla on a kiddie-sized stool. Tall and broad, he was intimidatingly enormous, with long legs that he struggled to fold beneath the seat. He leaned towards me, a dark moustache sitting starkly against his pale, flaky skin. His long fingers wrapped tightly around his knee. I found myself drawn to them... and the blood on his knuckles. *My* blood.

"Take it out," he said again. "I left you enough room to do it." He gestured to the nail.

Quelling the desire to scream, I focused on my surroundings. My arms rested on an old school desk, wooden and stained. And I could tell that my seat was made out of plastic by the shape of it underneath me. Another school chair similar to the one he slouched over. The desk appeared to be made from good quality wood, but there were many marks along the grain. Marks from other nails. Blood from other women.

He clicked his fingers, bringing my attention back to him. "Are you deaf, dumb, or stupid? Take the fucking nail out of your fucking hand."

I whimpered. I didn't want to, but the sound slipped from my shivering lips. When had he done this to me? Had I been conscious or unconscious? I had no idea of that or the answer to many questions, like how long had I been there? But my not doing anything only made him angrier, and that was bad news for me. I bit my lip and gently tested my restraints, starting with my feet. Cold metal encircled my ankles. The chair didn't move, and I realised, with yet more dread seeping over my skin, that it was bolted to the concrete floor. Then I checked my hands. Both were in cuffs attached to a bar that had been drilled onto the desk. I could slide one hand across to the other, giving me enough room to remove the nail. A tight rope cut into my abdomen, pinning me to the chair.

He stood. I winced, sliding down in my seat to make myself smaller, cowering like a submissive cat. I wanted to close my eyes and pretend he wasn't there, like a child in trouble. Instead, I screamed. I'd never screamed before, not like this, not this throaty, desperate screech. *Help me!*

He laughed, but after the second scream, he clamped his hand over my mouth. I tasted my own blood mingled with his sweat. He leaned over me and whispered into my ear. "Why do they always make this hard? Huh? Every last one of you. I get a woman in here, and I ask her one simple thing—to pull that nail out. And every one of you screams at the top of your lungs instead. Well, you know what? That's it. Shut your pretty little mouth." His breath tickled the tiny hairs by my ear.

Repulsion shuddered through me.

He produced a rag from his pocket, removed his hand, and wrapped it around my mouth before tying it hard around the back of my head. He forced it between my teeth, and my tongue got all twisted in the material. It tasted like his hands. Once he was done, I hated myself for not clamping my teeth over his flesh. That was what the feisty woman in a movie would've done. My mind went straight back to the phone call with my mum and the rhythm of my feet pounding the tarmac: left foot weak, right foot stupid.

Self-pity flooded through me. I didn't deserve to escape. I deserved this, whatever it was he wanted to do to me. Rape. Torture. Whatever. I deserved it. The shame of it, the fucking *shame*. I'd been alone, far from home, with hardly anyone around me. I'd been asking for it. I'd given up my rights to safety as soon as I'd started thinking like a man, thinking I could do what men do—go somewhere without expecting to be abducted.

"I think maybe you're shy and perhaps you'd do better on your own. So, I tell you what I'm going to do. I'm going to give you one hour. When I come back, I expect that nail to be out of your hand. Do you understand?" He grabbed my hair and wrenched my head back. A searing pain shot across my scalp.

He loosened his grip so that I could nod my head back and forth.

"Good girl," he said. His voice changed. He sounded like a farmer calming a cow before it gave birth. "Good lass." He stroked my hair. One finger trailed down the side of my jaw.

I trembled. Then I wondered if he assumed that meant I was aroused, which brought bile to my throat. He leaned in as though to kiss me, but his attention drifted to the nail, and he leaned away. He glanced down at his own hand. It was quick, furtive. An act I shouldn't have seen. But I had seen it, and I noticed the scars dotting the back of his hand. So that was the reason. Someone had hurt him a long time ago, and now he wanted revenge. A new emotion shot through me. Triumph? Hope? I wasn't sure. But at the same time, I understood his hatred and how it could fuel everything that came next.

I let out a sigh of relief as his hulking back disappeared through the large double door. Of course, it was temporary, but I allowed myself a second to appreciate it. Then I made myself concentrate.

Without his presence in the barn, I noticed new things. Firstly, the freezing cold penetrated down to my bones. Yet sweat somehow covered my skin, from adrenaline or pain, I don't know. Secondly, the barn had two doors, both bolted shut on the outside. If I managed to get out of the chair, I'd have those doors to deal with.

I checked the chair legs. They wobbled slightly. Perhaps the screws he'd used to keep the chair in place could be rocked out of their fixings. But when I tried to tip the chair, it jolted my injured hand. A second, or maybe third, dizzy spell washed over me. That nail needed to come out of my hand. Now.

Calm, Zoe. Calm.

Zoe Carter, née Osbourne. No. Zoe Osbourne, definitely not Carter, had never been described as a tough woman. I winced at paper-cuts. I swore at a stubbed toe. I was a normal, pain-avoidant woman whose eyes watered at a skinned knee. And now I had to pull a nail out of wood and drag it through my broken flesh... I almost laughed.

One swift motion. Do it, Zoe.

I stared at it. I wondered how much time I had left. Around fifty minutes, perhaps? Or more?

My teeth chattered together. I inched the fingers of my good hand towards the nail. I allowed them to stroke my thumb, but even that motion brought me pain. Tears flowed down my cheeks, and I hated every one of them.

Do it, Zoe. Fucking do it.

The barn door opened, and my body tensed. But it wasn't him. The child walked in. Maddie.

She slipped what I assumed was a key into the pocket of her shorts and hurried over to me. She had on a thicker jumper and rubber boots. They were warmer at least, but still old and dirty. My heart soared.

Help at last. But she was so tiny. What if he hurt her? What if he hurt her because of me?

She placed a finger over her lips in a gesture far too mature for a girl her age. She'd done this before, I realised. She'd seen her father take women so often that she had a system. The thought filled me with a horror that sharpened my senses. This man, this murderer, had forced a child out into the cold to lure the women back to his farm. Then he killed them.

"I'll do it." She pointed at the nail. "If you scream, Daddy will come. Don't." She shook her heard earnestly.

The astonishment of watching this child helped to distract me from the pain when she furrowed her brow in concentration, placed her small hand around the protruding nail, and yanked it hard enough to pull the thing out of the desk and my hand. I screwed my eyes shut and let out a low moan. Then I opened them again and watched her place the nail down on the wooden surface.

"He'll be back soon," she said.

"Please let me go." My words came out muffled through the gag. "I'll take you with me, I swear."

Her gaze lowered to the ground. She knelt on the concrete, and hot tears washed down my face. I couldn't bear to examine my hand even though I knew I needed to address the severity of my wound. A rattling sound came from the floor, where Maddie was fiddling with something. I couldn't see exactly what she was doing, but I imagined she was working on loosening a bolt. A moment later, she stood, a triumphant grin stretched across her face.

"It's loose," she said.

I tried to smile through my gag. She was helping me escape. But she did it in such a clever way that her father wouldn't realise it was her.

"I'll get you out," I mumbled. "I promise."

CHAPTER FOUR
NOW

To Justin's credit, he sobers up as soon as he hears me ask Maddie if she's okay. And when I launch myself out of bed, he does the same thing.

"What's happened?" His voice sounds sharp and focused.

"A girl at the sleepover died." I can barely believe the words are coming out of my mouth. A seventeen-year-old girl is dead.

"What?" The disbelief in his voice echoes mine. "I'll get my keys."

"You can't drive." I grab a jacket and pull it on over my pyjama top. Then I pull on jeans. "And you need to stay here with Gabe."

"Is Maddie all right? What happened to the girl?"

"Maddie's fine. The police are there with an ambulance." I take a deep breath to steady myself. "Phoebe Thompson fell over a cliff."

"They were camping next to a cliff?"

"No, they were at the campsite. I guess Phoebe walked off in the night and..." I rub my tired eyes, trying not to picture it.

"Jesus."

"She'll have to give a statement, and I should be there for her when she gives it. I can't believe it. First Riya disappears, and now *this*?"

He runs a hand though his short blond hair. "Yeah, it's... it's awful. It's unbelievable even." He crosses the space between us and rubs my shoulders. "Are you sure you're okay to drive? We could get you an Uber."

I glance at the time—nearly one o'clock in the morning—and shake my head. "It's too late. They won't be operating around here. I'll be fine."

"Be careful, Zo. Take it steady, all right? And call me as soon as you know what's going on."

"I will." We peck on the lips, a standard goodbye that feels more autopilot than anything, then I'm running through the house towards the garage. I stop at the control panel and punch in the number to open the door, resisting the urge to lock the entire house down.

There is a *before* and an *after* in my life. The before is me living without any real restrictions or inhibitions, going about my day like a regular person. After is me living my life in fear, waking up in the middle of the night and imagining Peter McKenna's sour breath tickling the hairs along my neck. It's the scar on the back of my hand and the stiff index finger that throbs in the cold. It's the sudden public interest that messed with my head and the online stalkers who came after. It's me living in a state of paranoia with the one person who understands any of it: the little girl who pulled the nail from my hand.

I think of her like that as I drive the car out of the garage. Every therapist, every doctor, and every police officer struggled to come to terms with the extent of the violence that Maddie witnessed when she lived with Peter McKenna. A child walked over to me when I was strapped to a chair and pulled a nail through my hand without flinching. "Brave," they said when we told our story.

Yes, Maddie is the bravest person I know. But they don't know how *normal* that was for her. And for years since then, I've worked with Maddie on changing what she considers to be normal. From the way she should handle animals, to the way she handles her temper and the way she treats her brother. I've had to teach her that pain is not an everyday occurrence. Inflicting pain on other people is not normal.

After winding through some of the narrow, coastal roads, I pull over, realising I'm not sure where to go next. It's pitch-black beyond the scope of my headlights. I wonder how many other parents are frantically driving up to the site as I type the address into my satnav and let it guide me there. Are they already there? Or did they take a better route?

Maddie isn't generally the girl who gets invited to parties. In fact, I had to persuade her to go. With Riya missing, I thought it might be a good distraction for her. I thought it might finally help Maddie socialise with her school friends. They don't like her, but they don't know her. Maddie has sharp edges that make her tricky to get on with. Teenage girls like to fish for compliments, but Maddie doesn't care about that kind of social custom. Maddie isn't quick to reassure like most girls. If a dress is unflattering on a friend, she'll say so. If a boy isn't interested, she'll bluntly tell it like it is. Maddie doesn't understand diplomacy. She'll talk about how she performed better in an exam or how her family is richer. It's not her being mean; she simply doesn't care what other people think about her.

But Phoebe Thompson's mother, Connie, invited all the girls in the class, including Maddie. I try to imagine what Connie is going through right now, and my heart aches for her. My nose tickles with the threat of tears, but it's too dark to allow myself to cry. I need to get to Maddie in one piece. She needs me.

THE CARPARK IS full when I arrive at the campsite. I manage to squeeze into a spot on grass with the help of a police officer directing me in.

"I'm here for Maddie Osbourne," I say, climbing out of the car. "She was at the sleepover."

"Right, well, most of the girls are all clustered around." He points to a group of five or six girls, but I don't see Maddie.

"Thanks," I say then head along the damp grass towards the main campsite.

There's no ambulance. Perhaps they've already taken Phoebe away. But there are several police officers around. One passes a crying teenage girl a cup of water. Others are scribbling in notebooks. I see parents holding their children, tears glittering under the moonlight. Some of the girls are wearing blankets.

Where is Maddie? My gaze travels over the scene, finally finding her standing far away from the others. She's on her own in her tracksuit bottoms and the soft long-sleeve top I bought her to wear while lounging around the house. She isn't crying or sipping water. An image flashes through my mind of her when she was five years old. She had messy, long hair then, and she does now. But now she's almost grown and beautiful in the way that terrifies a mother. Tall and slender, she's also serious and pale, with shoulders that slope into graceful arms, and hips wider than I'd realised.

"Maddie," I say, not too loud, not wanting to attract attention.

She sees me, and a small half-smile appears on her face. Prickles work their way across my scalp. Maddie isn't reacting to what's happened like the other girls. As I close the gap between us, I cast a quick glance across at the police. Have any of them noticed her? That's when I lock eyes with a plain-clothes policeman in a shirt and tie. He's short, stocky, and around fifty, maybe older. His analytical gaze is fixated on Maddie. That isn't good.

He walks over.

My heart starts to bounce. I glance at Maddie and whisper beneath my breath, "You're upset. Okay? You're upset she died."

"Of course I am," she replies, but she sounds flat.

The officer's mouth is set into grim line, drilling down the seriousness of the situation. "I'm sorry to meet under such terrible circumstances. My name is DS Rosen, and I need to take your names." He lifts his notebook and pen to scribble them down.

"Zoe and Maddie Osbourne," I say. "Maddie was here at the sleepover."

"Right. Have you given a statement to any of the other police officers?"

"No," she says quietly. Her voice always has a smooth-honey texture to it. She can turn on the charm quite easily. The problem is, many can tell after getting to know her better that it's a shallow kind of charm. Beneath the surface, she's messy, and not many people have the patience for messy.

"Would you like to give me your statement?"

She glances at me first, and I nod to tell her it's okay.

"Absolutely, officer," she says politely.

A cold sweat breaks out on the back of my neck. This man is watching her closely and taking in every single red flag Maddie signals. She isn't upset, she isn't nervous, her teeth aren't chattering, and she isn't draped around me like the other girls are with their mothers. She's as self-possessed and calm as always.

He starts off by asking her regular questions, such as what time she arrived and what the girls did at the campsite—they went hiking in the day and had a barbecue in the evening.

"Where was your tent, Maddie?" he asks.

She points to the single-berth purple tent she'd packed before leaving.

"Is that a single-person tent?"

"Yes," she says.

"You weren't sharing?"

"No."

"Why is that?"

Maddie shrugs. "I like my own space."

When I clock the expression on his face, I want to blurt out something defensive. *It isn't a crime to want to be alone. It isn't a crime to not be tearful and dramatic.* Instead, I clear my throat and say, "Maddie is an introvert. She gets easily drained by being around people, so she likes a space she can be alone in."

It's not exactly true. Maddie likes her own company, but people don't tend to drain her. Sometimes she thrives on attention from others.

He ignores me and carries on with his questions. "Did you hear anything in the night?"

"Laughing," Maddie says. "And whispers. I think some of them started singing songs at one point. They played music. Rihanna, Taylor Swift, Drake. That kind of thing."

"Did you leave your tent in the night?"

"I went to the toilet," she says.

"Do you know what time that was?"

"Um, about eleven?"

"Okay." He glances up from his notebook. "Did you see Phoebe when you went to the toilet?"

"No," she replies.

"Did you see anyone?"

"No."

"Did you go straight to the toilet and back?"

"Yes."

"Okay. How well did you know Phoebe?"

"We were in the same form at school."

"They had been since year seven," I add.

"Right, so you're good friends?"

Maddie shrugs. "Not really."

I wish she'd said something more effusive. She sounded so cold.

"But you were still invited to her seventeenth birthday party?"

"Her mum invited girls from the whole form," Maddie explained. "Otherwise, Phoebe wouldn't have asked me. She doesn't like me very much."

I'm convinced that I'm pale in the moonlight, my face masklike as I try not to let my anxiety show. Maddie was alone in her own tent, she admitted to leaving it to go to the toilet, and I'm guessing none of the other girls will be able to provide her an alibi.

"Detective, I hope you don't mind, but I really ought to get Maddie home for the night. She's been through a lot, and I can tell she's in shock—"

"She doesn't seem as though she's in shock to me. She's done very well answering my questions." He offers me a smooth smile.

"I understand how it might look to someone who doesn't know Maddie, but I do, and I know that my daughter is still processing what happened in her own way. She's been through a lot tonight—"

"And in the past," he says.

"Excuse me?"

"And in the past too. My wife owns your book."

Shit. I glance up at the sky, expecting to see rain, because I feel like I've been drenched in ice-cold water. "Then you'll understand why Maddie doesn't react to trauma in the same way as other people. We're both different because of what happened to us. In fact, what happened tonight was triggering to us both. I'd be grateful if you could let us go home."

He closes his notebook and places it back in his pocket. "Of course. Thank you, Maddie, for answering all my questions. I'll be in touch soon."

I walk my daughter slowly towards the car, trying not to notice the way I see faces angle towards us. Hate gleams from the eyes of a dozen or more teenage girls, suspicion coming off them in waves. From the mothers too. My step quickens, and I grasp Maddie's wrist, hurrying her along.

CHAPTER FIVE
THEN

I counted two bolts on each chair leg and four small screws fixing the metal bar to the wooden desk. I needed to loosen all of them if I had any hope of getting out. Maddie had helped me. Now I needed to work on the rest myself, and there wasn't a moment to lose.

I rocked the chair back and forth by throwing my weight against the seat then toward the desk, feeling it move a few millimetres forward and a few millimetres back each time. It would be better to have my hands free before he returned, but I didn't have anything to loosen the screws, and if I fiddled with the desk too much, the nail might roll away and implicate Maddie. I didn't want anything to happen to her because of me. So I rocked carefully, trying not to knock the desk, feeling on instinct as to whether the bolts were loosening.

I had a plan, or at least the bare bones of one, and that tiny bit of action helped me focus. I pictured how an escape could play out, running through the possible scenarios in my mind. If I loosened the bolts securing the chair, then I could tip it over. Then I could work the shackle down the leg, and my feet would be free. But my hands would still be cuffed to the desk, which was also fixed to the concrete floor. Loosening the bar on the desk would take more time without my hands free. Perhaps I could do it with my feet somehow? No, I couldn't see that working.

Right, I thought. *Get the chair free first. But don't remove the shackles. Let the psycho man come back to check on the nail situation and then fuck off again so I can work on the desk screw.*

What if he doesn't leave me alone?

The meticulousness of this setup made me believe he had a system to work through. It began with the nail in my hand. Then what? Another test? A staple gun to the knee? An arrow through the shoulder? Torture? Rape? Whatever it was, I had to survive it.

I tested the desk screws with my fingers. They were tight, and I had a wounded hand that throbbed with every movement. Without a screwdriver, it could take hours... days—if I could remove any at all.

Rocking the chair, I focused on the cold to stay alert. I assessed everything I saw in the barn. Two doors. Both locked. Maddie had come through the smaller door on the right side of the barn. *He* came through the larger door, the kind used for livestock. A double door with a bolt in the centre. I thought about him moving out of the door, his back disappearing. What had I heard? Chains? A key scraping against metal?

The roof stretched above me, fifteen, twenty feet high. I saw the remnants of stalls used for housing animals. A long metal bar lay on the cement floor, probably a barrier for cattle once. I didn't see much that I could use as a weapon. Strands of hay littered the stained concrete. My stomach lurched when I realised the mud-brown stains weren't from cattle, rather old blood that had seeped into the surface. My teeth chattered together. *Whymewhymewhymewhyme* rushed through my brain with a big dose of self-pity that almost erupted into tears. I swallowed it down and forced myself to feel anger instead.

It lasted until I heard the scrape of the bolt, but no chains, and one half of the wide doorway swung open. He swaggered back into the barn, his boots scuffing, a thoroughly delighted grin on his face. He barked out a laugh as soon as he entered. "What do you know? The bitch has some spirit after all. Good for you." He dragged the chair closer to my desk and hunched over it. "Are you cold?"

I said nothing. No doubt he could hear my teeth chattering against the gag.

"I asked you a question."

I mumbled purposefully quietly. He walked over, yanked the gag down, and went back to his chair.

"Yes." I hated myself for being obedient, but it wouldn't be smart to anger the person with all the power. Though I had to admit, I wasn't exactly sure what would be smart. Too much submission could risk exciting him into killing me faster. Too much spirit could do the same. I needed to distract him. "What's your name?"

He brushed his moustache thoughtfully with his fingers. "Peter."

"I'm Zoe."

"I know," he said. "The kid told me."

"Maddie, right? Your daughter?"

"Yeah." He didn't come across as particularly proud or interested, so I decided Maddie wasn't a good line of questioning. But he did want to talk, which was good.

"Have you always lived here, Peter? The barn is beautiful." My body sat rigidly on that chair. But every so often, my fingers inched across to the nearest screw, covered from view with my other arm.

"My parents ran the farm here. Good people, my parents. You know, this isn't like the movies, Zoe. Nothing you say is going to make this process any easier for you." I hated the grin that spread across his lips. I hated the sharp edge of his incisors and the way they touched his bottom lip.

"I know," I said. "Didn't you talk to the other girls?"

"Yes. They all do it. They ask me about my ma, and they tell me they'll do anything... anything I want." His tongue dashed out to taste his lips, and I made a mental note never to beg. "It doesn't work, Zoe. Not for them and not for you."

"You mean you don't want to tell me about your tragic childhood? About how your ma hammered a nail into your hand. And how she forced you to pull it out on your own to prove you were a real man. Over and over. Did you kill her first, or were you too much of a coward then?"

When he directed his dark, stone-cold expression at me, I knew I'd pissed him off. I knew I'd hit a nerve. It terrified and thrilled me in equal measure.

"A lot of things go on out here in the places no one notices." He stood and took a step forward. His black eyes widened until I saw the blood vessels at the edges, red veins reaching to two empty pits. "You'll find that out soon."

I fiddled with the screw while I cringed away from him, filled with panic. But as he came closer, my fingers groped for the nail Maddie had pulled from my hand. He moved around the desk, and I tried to stab his arm with the nail, but the cuffs restricted my movement. Peter swatted my hand away, and the nail tumbled from my fingers. My wrist slammed against the cuffs and hit the desk. But I hardly had time to react before he grabbed me by the throat.

"Now, then, boy. Where I come from, sneaky-snakes are punished. Do you understand what that means?"

I said nothing. I cowered down in my chair, a low whimpering noise emitting from between my lips.

He positioned his face closer to mine. He squeezed my throat, and I gurgled in panic.

"Shut up, boy! Shut up! Stop that snivelling."

He kept calling me boy, and I was convinced he was back in the past, reliving scenes from his childhood. But that thought didn't have time to linger, because he let go of my throat and slapped me so hard, I heard a ringing in my ear. Then he did it again but on the other side. His breathing started to rasp out of his chest. He was red skinned, like a flayed man. All the blood rushed to his face in the excitement. He dropped his hands, and they balled into fists.

Then I begged.

I DIDN'T REMEMBER PASSING out, but at some point, I woke up shivering, the blood cold and dry on my face. I sensed the wetness between my legs and glanced down in horror, but it was urine, not blood. My chest heaved with painful breaths. I felt like every bone in my face had been broken. My vision blurred, and a heavy exhaustion settled through me.

The moment stretched because he'd beaten the fight out of me. I knew I was going to die. The question was when? Or how?

I thought about my ex-husband and the years I'd wasted believing he would change. I thought about our wedding. We'd been all smiles, even though I'd had doubts about Simon, and we'd already had a few arguments. I'd ignored all the red flags as people in their twenties often did. It'd rained, and Simon had complained during the ceremony, but I loved our photographs with the storm clouds gathering behind us.

Then I thought about the fight I'd had with my mum. I thought about all the times I'd rolled my eyes and every time she'd thrown one of her barbs in my direction. I thought about the children I'd never had. Chestnut-haired twins, perhaps, or one girl with blonde hair that gradually darkened as she aged. Hot tears rolled down my torn face. Tiredness seeped into every wound, and I lost consciousness again.

When I woke for the second time, the dizziness had abated, and I could concentrate again. I leaned my head back and clapped a dry tongue against a dry mouth. *Stay awake, Zoe. Stay fucking awake.*

The barn door creaked open, and I flinched. But it was Maddie, who tiptoed in. She hurried over to me with a rag and a bottle of what appeared to be antiseptic liquid. She had a backpack with her, too, and my heart soared. Was she going to let me go?

"Daddy's asleep. He likes to sleep after. He dreams less."

It sounded like something she'd heard him tell her. And I was horrified that it took beating women for Peter McKenna to get a good kip.

"How long does he sleep for?"

She shrugged. "Depends."

I had to lower my face to her so she could press the soaked rag on my cuts. I winced, hissing through my teeth, but the pain wasn't half as bad as I'd thought it would be.

Once Maddie had cleaned my cuts, she produced a bottle of water from her backpack and held it to my lips. I thanked her and told her again that I would help her escape. A thought popped into my mind—what if Peter made Maddie come in here and help me? What if he did that to prolong my agony, to make me believe I might actually live?

"Please, Maddie. Please help me."

She hesitated. "I am."

I whispered breathlessly, "Thank you."

She stared at me then, biting her lip, thinking.

"Where's your mother? Do you have one?"

"Daddy says she's dead."

"I'm so sorry, Maddie," I said, hoping she heard the genuine sadness in my voice. "Did he hurt her like he's hurting me?"

"I don't know," she replied.

"Okay. I'm sorry you don't know your mummy. That must be hard."

She blinked again, like she didn't know how to respond. I understood. She didn't know any other way. "I'm so grateful for you bringing me water. Is there anything else you can do to help me get out of this chair? I've loosened the legs, but I need to get my hands free. Can you get my hands free, Maddie?"

She reached back into her bag and pulled out a screwdriver. All the pain in my bones and skin left my body at that moment, and my heart soared so high, I wondered if I'd ever get it back. Maddie was my saviour. My angel.

CHAPTER SIX
NOW

I find Justin pacing the kitchen. Relief passes over his face, and he envelopes Maddie with his arms. I stand back, happy to see her return the hug, albeit tentatively.

"Kiddo. I can't believe it. Are you all right?" He pulls back and places both hands on either side of her face, as though examining her for injuries.

"I'm fine!" Maddie drags out the word *fine* in that quintessential teenage way and removes Justin's hands from her face. "I didn't see anything. I didn't even see the body."

Justin's blue eyes flash worry like a train signal. I can't deny that I noticed it too—how easily Maddie referred to her former school friend as a "body."

"How's Gabe?" I ask, trying to break the tension.

"Fast asleep." Justin leans against the back of a chair. His hair is dishevelled and his jaw tense. He has a habit of caring too much at times, almost the opposite of Maddie. "You know how he is. Could sleep through a bomb, that kid."

I put my car keys down on the table and let out a long breath.

"Jesus, you look exhausted. Sit down, love." Justin moves away and picks up the kettle to fill. "Tea for us and hot chocolate for Maddie?"

"Sure," I say. "Mads?"

"Yeah, okay."

She slumps down on one of the dining chairs, and I do the same next to her. We didn't talk much on the drive home, though I did give her some advice about the police. I told her to be honest, but cautious about what she said. I wanted to tell her to pretend to be sad, to pretend to cry, to fake who she was, but I couldn't bring myself to do it.

After Justin passes us our drinks, we sit at the table as a family, me and Justin exchanging worried glances, both hesitating. In the end, Justin breaks the silence.

"Do you want to talk about what happened to Phoebe?" He directs his words towards Maddie, but his flickering eyes keep landing on me.

"I didn't see it happen, so I don't know," Maddie says.

I clear my throat and add, "It sounds like Phoebe Thompson went for a walk in the night and fell off the cliff."

He shakes his head. "It's just... awful. Her poor parents."

I nod, watching Maddie. She sips her hot chocolate, her face the picture of serenity. No frown. No sign of tension.

"What I don't understand is why Phoebe would walk away from the camp like that," I say. "You'd think she'd stay around her friends at her own seventeenth birthday party. The campsite doesn't spread to the edge of the cliff. It stops over a hundred feet from there. So, she left the site, climbed a barrier, and..." I stop. Am I implying that Phoebe Thompson killed herself? Or am I implying more? That she was pushed?

"What do you think happened, Maddie?" Justin asks gently.

I worry we're pushing her too hard so soon after the event, but I stay quiet and let her speak.

"Who knows?" Maddie shrugs. "I don't get those girls, and I never have. Some spotty rugby player tells them they're fat, and they have a mental breakdown." She laughs.

"Maddie!" I say, horrified.

"Well, it's true, Mum, and no one wants to admit it. She probably wanted to take a selfie or a video or something."

"In the dark?"

"Yeah. I don't know. Maybe she was sleepwalking." She takes another sip of hot chocolate. "Look, don't get mad, but I didn't like her, and I don't care that she died. I just don't."

Justin opens his mouth to speak, but I shake my head to stop him. This is the side of Maddie that only I understand.

"I know," I say softly. "We don't always like people. But it's always a sad event when a life is lost, because that girl you didn't like never had an opportunity to grow into someone you could like or someone who could've made a difference to the world. Do you understand that?"

She sighs. "Yes."

"It doesn't mean we'll always mourn those who pass away too soon, but it does mean we'll never wish someone dead, and we'll always be respectful."

"Okay, I get it, Mum."

Justin gives me the barest nod, showing me I did a good job. I let out a long sigh.

"They're going to think I killed her," Maddie says, her words provoking a rush of tension to flood my limbs. "The police, those other girls, Phoebe's parents. They think I'm some devil child because of who my dad was."

"Well, we'll prove them wrong," Justin says, his voice slightly higher than usual, as though he's trying to hide his nerves.

"That's right," I say. "We know you didn't do it, and you know too."

"It doesn't matter," Maddie says. "First Riya and now Phoebe. They'll think I'm a serial killer like Peter."

Goosebumps erupt along my forearms. I hate hearing his name. Maddie can talk about him with emotional detachment, but I can't. I lean back in my chair as though bracing myself against the power of that name.

"We're going to protect you," I say. "At all costs."

"Like in the barn?" she asks.

"Exactly like then."

Justin's eyebrows bunch together, and I shake my head once to indicate that I don't want to explain right now. We've talked about what happened in the barn before, but I've always avoided the worst details.

"Can I go to bed now?" Maddie asks. "I'm tired."

I place my hand on her arm. "Of course you can, sweetheart. Sorry we kept you up so late."

"It's okay," she says. "Thank you for the hot chocolate, Justin."

He pulls her into an awkward hug that she barely reciprocates. "That's okay, Mads."

Her lips are thin when she says goodnight and leaves the kitchen. Once we're alone, Justin places his head in his hands.

"God, what a shitshow," he says. "What's going to happen?"

"I don't know," I mutter. I dread to think.

INTRODUCING Justin into my life proved to be tricky at first. We met when Maddie was nearly seven years old, us both still living in the Peaks. The adoption process had been long and arduous, with the authorities doubtful I could care for Maddie. But she wanted to live with me. She'd made that clear from the start.

Maddie used temper tantrums to get her own way. She didn't respond to discipline. She reacted badly to cold parenting styles, those that relied on punishments to correct behaviour. But we had a connection. I understood exactly what she'd been through, and it gave me an endless supply of patience with her. When she beat the ground with her fists in the park, I got on my back and wriggled my legs in the air until we started laughing. She whispered her secrets to me in the dark, about how she'd actually loved her father despite everything he did. I told her that was okay. I wasn't horrified by it.

I met Justin while trying to find a school for Maddie. He helped smooth the process by sitting with her in the classroom or taking her out of the classroom when she became overwhelmed. Justin was the first man Maddie enjoyed spending time with. He was the first man she bonded with after leaving Ivycross Farm. But when my relationship became romantic with Justin, Maddie's behaviour changed drastically. He was my boyfriend, and Maddie hated it.

When Justin and I talked to each other rather than to her, she played up. Once, she even hit another child with a doll at a children's party simply because she'd seen me kiss Justin on the cheek in the hallway outside the play area. I had to apologise profusely to the mother of the crying child and take Maddie home. Another time, she screamed in a supermarket and told a customer that Justin was trying to abduct her. It took months of therapy for Maddie to accept Justin in our lives. And from there, it had been a rocky road. Even now, she could be very cool towards him, even though he loved her like his own daughter.

I love Justin even more for immediately believing Maddie and for not even considering the thought that Maddie might have pushed Phoebe off that cliff. We finish our drinks, talking for a short time about the tragedy, then we make our way to bed. I ensure the shutters are down first. My body is riddled with the hypervigilance of anxiety. One of my therapists told me that hypervigilance leads to burnout. Thoughts consumed by paranoia, playing havoc on my body. All those muscles pulled tight. My heart working harder, driving my blood pressure up. Anxiety puts the body in fight-or-flight mode, something I know a lot about.

"Babe," Justin says as I climb into bed. "I'm so sorry about earlier. If I hadn't been drunk, I could've gone with you."

"It's not your fault," I reply, almost unconsciously. My thoughts are with Maddie and Phoebe at that campsite. *What happened?*

He swats the light switch and pulls me into his arms. At first, I tense, but then I realise he's just holding me.

"It's all going to be okay," he says. We're silent for a moment, then he adds, "The poor Thompsons."

"I know." I shake my head. "How could this happen? Two girls in Maddie's year both gone."

"We still don't know what's happened to Riya," he reminds me. "She could've run off to London or something."

"I hope you're right."

"So do I." He sighs. "Come on. We should get some sleep. The next few days are going to be tough."

"They already think it was Maddie. I saw it. I saw their anger."

"Who? The Thompsons?"

I shake my head. "No, all of them. The kids, the parents, the police. You should've heard the way DS Rosen spoke to her, like she was a suspect already. They all think Maddie's inherited Peter's psychopath traits."

"We know that's not true," he points out.

"Does it matter? We're her parents. We can't convince all those people. She has no alibi. God, they're going to come for her, aren't they?"

"Hey. Zo, you're spiralling. Don't do that, not until we know what's going on. They can figure all kinds of stuff out with forensics these days. I bet they can prove Phoebe fell and wasn't pushed."

"Yeah, but what if she was pushed?" I blurt out.

"Then we find a way to prove it wasn't Maddie."

I can't see his expression in the dark, only the profile of his face when I angle my body towards him. He sounds so convinced, but perhaps he's doing the same thing I am—pushing down every doubt I can. The problem is, I'm starting to choke on them.

CHAPTER SEVEN
THEN

Maddie concentrated as she placed the screwdriver into the grooves on the screwhead. She poked her tongue out from between her teeth.

"You have to twist it anti-clockwise, sweetheart," I said, bobbing my head up and down with encouragement.

But she paused and frowned at me. "What does that mean?"

"Turn the screwdriver to the left, away from your body. That's it. Nice and slow. Good girl."

She grinned, giggling. But the screwdriver kept spinning inside the grooves because she wasn't able to press down hard enough.

"Maddie, hun, I think you might need to pass it to me. I think it needs a bit more force." I twisted my wrist so that I could grip the metal of the screwdriver, but I couldn't reach the handle with my cuffed hands. "You know what? Let's work together. I want you to push down on it as hard as you can, and I'm going to turn it, okay?"

It moved agonisingly slowly, but with patience and Maddie's body weight on the screwdriver, we managed to loosen the fixing. Every slight notch to the left made her giggle. She wasn't scared, not for a moment. But I was alert and on edge, expecting him to barge in, full of rage, spittle flying from his mouth. We dropped the screwdriver more than once, stumbling fingers making the work cumbersome. Sweat beaded across my forehead from concentration and effort. When the first screw finally fell out of its fixing, Maddie performed a little dance for me, her tiny feet shuffling across the concrete. Despite everything, I laughed. But the lightness didn't linger. We continued on to the next screw, the mission not over.

"Do you go to school, Maddie?" I asked as we worked. I wanted to know how this child had become so lost to society.

She shook her head.

"Is your daddy kind to you?"

She shook her head, and my stomach dropped.

"He makes me cereal," she said suddenly. "And lets me watch TV."

Well, that was better than nothing, I decided. Not much better, though.

"I get to talk to the ladies," she said again. "But most can't talk. They keep screaming."

Everything she said tinged this horrifying situation with another layer of repulsiveness. "How many times have you pulled out the nail for the ladies?"

She shrugged. "One asked me. I didn't want to, but..."

"You're a good girl," I said. "You wanted to help her."

"Uh-huh. Then I did for all the others."

I wondered then if she could count, or perhaps it had happened so often she'd lost count. It was hard to ascertain whether Peter McKenna had tried at all with her development. She was a chatty little thing, but I had no idea if she could read or write. But she was young. If I got her to safety now, perhaps it wouldn't have too much of an effect on her in the long run.

"Okay, Maddie, I think these screws are loose enough now. Maybe you should go and hide. When your daddy comes back, I'll try and break free."

She picked up the bloodied, six-inch nail from where it had dropped earlier and placed it on the desk. I palmed it, thanking her. Every part of my body trembled with fear. Pain pulsated through my broken face. Whenever I shifted my tongue, I tasted rusted pennies and had probably lost a tooth. How the hell was I going to pull this off?

Maddie backed away from me, her brow knitted with worry, carrying her small Pokémon bag with her. She waved once as she disappeared out of the barn.

"There are two lives at stake," I muttered to myself while fumbling through the last few turns of the screw. "Don't fuck this up. No hesitation. No chickening out. Stab that fucker and get out."

Stab that fucker and get out.

My breath rattled through my ribs. With a sense of alarm, I noticed the heaviness of my lungs for the first time. Did I have a fluid build-up? It could be the cold. The start of pneumonia perhaps. I felt thinner, as ridiculous as it sounded. Judging by the light in the barn, I was pretty sure I'd been cuffed for longer than a day. I gazed at the orange rays filtering through the barn windows. The tail end of the sunrise, perhaps.

The circumstances hit me all at once. I had no fuel in my body. I was weak from injuries and possibly sick. Meanwhile, Peter the Psycho looked like he could pick me up and hurl me like a rugby ball.

Stab that fucker and get out. Simple. Right?

I had two things going for me—surprise and hunger. If I wanted to live more than he wanted to kill me, I could use that. No, it didn't guarantee my safety. I couldn't materialise my own survival. I couldn't make it happen through will alone. There was no way I was going to victim blame all of those poor women who hadn't made it out, but I knew I could ride the wave of adrenaline as it coursed through me.

The last screw tumbled from its position, and the bar shifted. I slid the cuffs from the bar and worked on the rope around my waist. The nail helped. I poked it into the knots, wiggled it around, and prised them loose. Sweat poured down my forehead as I twisted the bolts holding the chair to the ground. I rocked the chair legs back and forth, back and forth. I found myself convinced that we'd taken too long, that my conversations with Maddie as we worked on the screw had eaten up precious time. He'd be back any minute. Any second. Those bolts held on, surprisingly robust. I leaned down and twiddled them with my fingers, and drops of blood hit the concrete.

With a heavy clink, the first bolt fell from its fixing. I rattled and rattled my shackles, scraping the skin from my shins. Frustrated, grunting, and frantic.

Clink.

The next bolt fell. The chair came away from the ground. I slid the shackles away from the chair legs. I didn't have the key to get them off my ankles, but at least I could move now. And luckily, they weren't chained to each other. That meant I could...

Run, Zoe.

The voice came from nowhere. Running was not an option, not with Maddie here alone with that man. *Run and get help. Come back for her.*

I had to be ill now, because I was hearing things. That voice sounded exactly like my ex-husband telling me what to do again. If I got caught by the psycho while trying to rescue Maddie from this murder farm, no doubt he'd be the first in line telling me "I told you so." Even if he had to wait until the afterlife to do it. The thought almost made me laugh out loud. I clamped a hand over my mouth and forced myself to focus.

Hide.

I needed to surprise him when he came back. I could hide behind the door he always used, but there was a slim chance he might use a different door this time then see me right away. I needed to hide somewhere I could jump out from, because he knew I couldn't get out of this locked barn.

Damnit, Maddie, why didn't you leave the door open for me? But I knew why. If I failed, he'd know. Escaping from the chair could be blamed on resourcefulness or a rogue loose screw. But an open door? He'd know.

It had to be one of the old animal stalls. I hurried through the barn, ducking into each one. But none of them had enough cover. Could I time my reveal perfectly enough to catch him off guard? Because as soon as he checked any of these stalls, he'd see me right away. But what else was I going to do? I stepped into the final stall, the one with the least amount of light. I manoeuvred an old bale of straw over to the wall next to the entrance. I stood on it then crouched down. I gripped the nail in my good hand, one thumb over the head, ready to thrust it into whatever soft part of Peter McKenna's body I could reach.

Stab the fucker and get out. I replayed that one thought in my mind over and over again as my muscles ached from the crouching position. As plans went, it wasn't the best, but it was simple.

The light changed as I waited. The warm yellow transformed into a pale blue. Between the barn slats, I saw bright white. Snow? Clouds? The winter light? I wasn't sure. I huddled there with my arms folded across my body, head tucked in so I could breathe against my skin for warmth. Luckily, I was pretty sure my nose hadn't been broken in the beating. I breathed through it okay, but it whistled. I had to breathe through my mouth instead.

Metal against metal. *Chiiiinkshh.* Wood scraped the concrete floor. As soon as that barn door opened, a level of adrenaline flooded my veins that I'd never experienced before and probably never would again. My mouth opened. Baring my teeth, I lifted my arm with the long nail clutched in my hand. I tilted my head, listening.

"Shit. Fucking bitch." I heard the door slam shut. A gravelly, frustrated roar croaked through his throat. "Why did you have to do that? Huh? Why? Now you've made things so much worse for yourself. Stupid…"

I stopped listening to his words, filtering them out of my mind. Instead, I listened to his footsteps.

He carried on with his tirade, unable to control his anger. It didn't frighten me, because I knew that if he did find me, he'd kill me much faster than he would've done before. I knew this because of how frustrated he sounded. Peter McKenna at least knew himself enough to know he wouldn't be able to check his impulse and draw it out as he'd planned to do.

Suddenly, his diatribe ended. His footsteps quietened. Now he was listening for me, trying to work out where I'd hidden. His boots scuffed and shuffled, a tell-tale sound of him speeding up. I imagined him jumping into one of the stalls, ready to grab me. The first stall. Everything went quiet. Then I heard him moving again, with the same scuff of his boots in the second stall. Each time, he let out a frustrated breath, hissing through his nose like an old-fashioned kettle about to boil. Two more then me. I flexed my fingers, waiting. *Stab the fucker and run the fuck away.*

I'd never felt so ready in all my life. The fear vanished, like I'd never been abducted and brutalised at all. My body shut it all down because I think it knew, instinctively, that I wasn't getting out of that barn alive unless I suddenly developed the overconfidence of some mediocre middle manager dominating an office meeting. Or the overconfidence of a man like Peter McKenna, who liked to dominate *me*.

Shuffle, scuff, stomp. I flew off that straw bale like a lion pouncing on an antelope, throwing my body at his chest. My arm, already raised and in position, slammed down, driving the nail right into his eye. I'd imagined driving it up, hoping to penetrate the brain. Instead, it angled down. I hit some bone, and it stalled three inches into his face.

He screamed and screeched, high-pitched and terrifying, then staggered backwards, his hands groping his face. I didn't waste a single second. I pitched away from him, my trainers pounding. But he had such long arms. One of them caught the back of my top, tugging it right up to my throat. I pushed on, but it started to strangle me. The tough polyester fabric refused to tear. I ducked down, squirming out of the top, bending my arms at odd angles, trying to get out of the sleeves as quickly as I could. He managed to take hold of my arm, bending it behind my back until I shrieked. I lifted a heel and kicked out, hitting him somewhere, likely in the thigh. He made an *oof* sound, but his grip never faltered.

"I'm going to flay the skin from your bones." His spit hit the back of my neck.

Ignoring the searing pain coming from my shoulder, I reached behind me with my free arm, grabbed the nail and yanked it free. He screamed twice as loud as any of my own screams, and he finally let go of my arm, falling backwards. I didn't want to look. But I did. His clutched his eye, the socket bleeding profusely. The nail was still in my hand. I lifted it again, and this time, I jammed it straight into his throat. His cries became choking gurgles as the blood gushed from the wound.

I stepped back, watching him squirm and scream and babble through the blood, to find Maddie standing in the entrance of the barn. I instinctively hurried over to try and shield her from the sight, but she pushed me back towards her father.

"You need to make sure he goes to sleep and never wakes up." Her voice was calm, collected, and deadly serious. And most of all, she was right.

I tucked her behind me so that she couldn't see her father dying, and I stood there, watching him bleed out on the barn floor. Once he was still for sixty seconds—I counted each one—Maddie placed the screwdriver back in my hand and gave me a shove. I walked over to him and forced myself to pick up his lifeless wrist. I felt for a pulse. There was none.

CHAPTER EIGHT
NOW

I wake up late. Sunlight streams into the room, and it takes me a moment to remember the events from the night before. The lights of the campsite come back to me, dreamlike at first, like a distant memory. Then I remember Phoebe. I remember DS Rosen's cool blue eyes examining Maddie.

When I hurry downstairs, I find Justin and Maddie on the sofa in front of the television, watching cartoons. Gabe is on the carpet by Maddie's feet, giggling away and shovelling Cheerios into his mouth. I make my way cautiously over to them. Justin sips his cup of tea. Maddie nibbles on a piece of toast. She's not one to giggle at cartoons, but she doesn't seem particularly tense either.

"Hey, babe," Justin says. "Kettle's boiled if you want a cup." He lifted his mug to show me the tea.

"Thanks," I reply, still nervously scanning the room. "Maybe we could all have a chat after breakfast?" My voice sounds unnaturally high.

Justin's smile gradually disappears. "Sure."

I glance across at Gabe and lower my voice. "Have you told him?"

"No," Justin says. "I thought it best to wait for you."

I head into the kitchen, pour myself a tea, and contemplate eating.

It's impossible while my stomach is swirling. That's one anxiety symptom I can't stand—the unpredictability of my digestive system. Not long after returning home from the rural hellscape that was Ivycross Farm, my stomach issues led to disordered eating. At first, I comfort ate. Before I was abducted, I'd thought it was important to be slim in the right places because society tells women that's what men want. So, I thought, *If that's what men want, I'll take it away, and they'll leave me alone.* I gained forty-five pounds in a short space of time by binge eating chocolate, cake, crisps, and whatever else I wanted.

In a way, I was healing. After sobbing during one of my therapy sessions, that particular doctor hit me with a truth that has stayed with me: *You did what you needed to survive.* If overeating kept me alive, then so be it. But it wasn't a healthy coping mechanism in the long term. Unfortunately, I replaced it with a toxic loop of binging at home —where I felt safe—but starving myself before I had any sort of stressful event to deal with. Breaking that cycle and reclaiming my body and my health for *me* proved harder than pushing a nail into Peter McKenna's eyeball. But today, when I stare at the cereal cupboard, there's a gurgle in my belly that scares me too much to eat. I just drink the tea.

"Maddie won't let me watch *Paw Patrol*." Gabe slams his bowl down on the kitchen counter.

"Well, why don't we watch it in here on the kitchen TV?" I suggest.

"It's still not fair. Maddie always gets to watch what she wants!"

"Well, we're going to have a family chat now, so why don't you watch *Paw Patrol* later? Okay?"

His tiny nose wrinkles up as he scowls, brightening my morning. I ruffle his curls, and he pulls his head away. But it's all an exaggeration, because there's a twinkle in his eyes, as though he's about to laugh. I tickle under his arms, and sure enough that squeaky little-boy laugh bounces through the kitchen. I become the tickle monster, and he's howling with laughter as I chase him around the table. It's only when Maddie walks in with her plate that it ends.

"Are you done, sweetheart?" I ask, taking the plate from her. "Or do you want some more?"

"I'm done." She turns to leave, but I catch her on the shoulder.

"One sec, Mads. We need to all have a chat." I call Justin in from the living room and get the two kids into chairs.

"Is Maddie in trouble?" Gabe asks.

The question takes me by surprise. It amazes me sometimes that even young kids are so perceptive to the world around them. I didn't think I was treating Maddie any differently, but he'd picked up on the atmosphere right away.

"No," I say. "She's not, because she hasn't done anything wrong. But something very sad happened last night, and we need to talk about it."

Maddie folds her arms across her chest. She does that when she's about to shut down emotionally. I reach across and touch her lightly on the arm, hoping to bring her back.

"A girl died at the sleepover Maddie went to last night," Justin says, keeping his voice steady and calm. "There was a horrible accident, and Phoebe Thompson fell off a cliff."

"Oh," Gabe says, his face pale. "That's sad."

"It is, honey." I glance at Gabe then Maddie. "Which means I'd like you to be extra nice to your sister today. She's upset about what happened last night, and we need to make sure she's okay."

Gabe thinks for a moment then says to his sister, "You can watch whatever you like. I'll watch *Paw Patrol* tomorrow."

"Thanks," Maddie mutters.

My heart swells with love for them both.

"That's very nice, Gabe." Justin grins. "Right! What shall we do today? Go down to the beach? Put on a movie?"

"Beach!" Gabe slaps his palms on the table in excitement.

"Can I go to my room?" Maddie asks.

"Don't you want to spend the day with us?" I tuck a lock of her dark hair behind her ear, and she ducks her head away. She used to love that when she was younger.

"I'm tired." Her arms tighten around her body as she stares down at the table. Perhaps I misjudged how upset she is about Phoebe's death.

"Sure, if that's what you want to do. Would you like some company?"

She shakes her head, stands, and quietly leaves the room.

"She's upset," I say to no one in particular. "You take Gabe to the beach. I need to do something for Connie and David Thompson. Maybe I should drop off some food."

"I don't think that's a good idea, Zo," Justin warns. "Not considering... everything."

My throat thickens with impending tears. I can't shield Maddie from the inevitable accusations that will come, and it kills me.

"What about a condolence card? Or... I could send them flowers? I don't know what to do!"

Justin rubs my shoulder and says softly, "I know. I think a card is a nice idea. We should let them know we're thinking of them."

"Could you pick one up on the way home? I think I should stay with Maddie."

"Absolutely." He stands and plants a kiss on my forehead. "Right then, fella. You, me, frisbee action on the beach?"

Gabe roars, lifting his arms in excitement. I'm jealous of him. I want that freedom to feel excitement again.

AFTER THEY LEAVE, I check my social media accounts to see what people are saying about Phoebe. I don't use them often. Maddie and I have never quite managed to escape the attention of the general public, and every now and then either an internet troll or true crime stalker filters into my direct messages. They tend to target me rather than Maddie, but I set up Maddie's accounts with filters to keep out the worst of it.

My deep dive into social media is a big mistake. I discover so many opinions on what happened that it makes my head spin. It starts off fairly innocuous, with lots of condolences on Phoebe's Facebook page, but the deeper I go, the more insidious the comments become. I find my way onto the local forum for parents, where there's a thread about the incident. Many users comment about how Maddie is the obvious culprit. Some of them pull quotes from my book as examples of why she has to be violent now. Five comments into the thread, they're already calling her L'il Psycho like it's her rapper name.

But none of them know her. None of them know the hours of therapy she's been through or the time I've taken to give her the upbringing she both needed and deserved. Maddie is not an average kid, but it doesn't make her a killer.

It's not right. She shouldn't be roaming the streets. She wants locking up.

Did the police ever investigate this woman? Zoe? How do we know she was the 'final girl'? What if she was secretly PM's girlfriend?

I noticed how easily they attributed derogatory nicknames to me and Maddie but simply shortened Peter's name to PM. He was the serial killer. He was the misogynist, and yet these women wanted to dehumanise us instead.

Maddie could be reading these comments right now, alone in her room. I put down my phone and make my way through the house to her most sacred place. I rarely go into Maddie's bedroom. Teenage girls protect their space like lions over prey.

"Mads?"

"What?" She sounds like a regular teenager then, her voice monotone, slightly annoyed but lacking emotion.

"Can I come in?"

She sighs. "If you want."

I open the door. "Make me feel welcome, why don't you?"

I find her sitting in her purple armchair, staring out of the window. When we moved into the house, Maddie fell in love with this room. She has an ocean view, with seagulls squawking and the waves crashing below. If I linger too long, a sensation of insignificance washes over me. I feel it now, watching the sea stretch beyond the horizon.

"Can we chat?"

"If you want."

"Maddie."

She pulls her attention away from the window because I used my "mum voice," the one that signals for everyone to stop their nonsense. I sit down on her bed and fold my legs underneath my body, knees complaining. God, have I become the woman trying to be the "cool mum"?

"I think we should go and see Dr Boateng this week. Perhaps we should have two sessions a week for a while to work through what happened."

She picks at a fingernail and doesn't say a word.

"I know you said you didn't feel traumatised by what happened, and I understand why, but sometimes these things creep up when you least expect it. So I think we should see Dr Boateng and talk it all out. But until we make an appointment, we can talk about it together."

"What is there to talk about? Phoebe wandered off in the dark and fell." She shrugs. "It's sad, but the world moves on."

"No. There's a lot more than that. First of all, you were there, and you were woken up to the news that someone had died. Second of all, you had to talk to the police like you did after your father died. And I know that was a tough time for you—"

"This isn't the same."

"I know."

"You're making this into something it's not."

"No, Maddie. *You're* not seeing the dangers here." I check myself, remembering my warm parenting. "Hun, it's hard, I know, to see the relevance. But remember, I went through that week with you, and I know how tough it was. I know what you saw and experienced. Sweetheart, I'm really upset by this. I didn't know Phoebe very well, but simply hearing about another young woman losing her life is pulling me right back to Ivycross Farm."

She's quiet, but I see her listening.

"Your best friend is missing, and now someone your age died in extreme circumstances. You've been through a lot recently, and we can't ignore it," I say.

"Okay, well, if you think it's a good idea, we'll do it."

"I'll make an appointment. We're going to get through this together, okay?"

"Oh my God, Mum. You sound like those mad journos." She laughs.

It makes me chuckle too. For years, we were asked inane questions from journalists and listened to their repetitive statements about us. "At least you had each other." We quote that one to each other at least every month.

"Hey, and don't spend much time online, okay?"

"I don't care what people think," she says, quickly enough to make me think she's already read a lot of the comments.

"I know. But these things can stick in your head. 'At least you had each other.'"

She laughs. "You're so brave."

"It must have been terrible," I quip.

"But how did it *feel*?"

I laugh.

"How did it *feel* when you drove that six-inch nail into my father's eyeball? Did you hear it pop?" He dark eyes flash with mischief.

This doesn't shock me. When she's feeling vulnerable, she tries to shock.

"How did it feel pulling that nail from my hand?"

"Like pulling a sharp object out of a raw steak," she says without missing a beat.

"Okay, now *that* is the kind of talk you need to rein in."

"What? So they don't think I'm a 'l'il psycho'?" The sardonic smile on her face makes my blood run cold. "Yep, I saw that too."

"This is what I mean about staying offline."

"Like I said—"

"Yeah, I know. But, Maddie, you need to be careful. Not just about what you read, but about what you say."

"Do you think they'll arrest me?" she asks.

"Would that scare you if they did?"

"No, because I didn't do it."

"Well, it scares me, because I want to keep you safe. Now come here and give me a hug. Don't make that face."

She moves onto the bed and lets me wrap my arms around her. Maddie isn't one for human contact, but she melts into me today. A moment later, her arms envelop my rib cage, and she buries her head in my shoulder.

CHAPTER NINE
THEN

For five minutes, we stood stock-still. The barn's freezing-cold air bit down to the marrow of my bones. My face throbbed. The place stank of the blood that pooled around the corpse. One more stain to add to the rest, except now it was *his*.

I ached painfully, and yet I waited, convinced he would rise, zombielike, from the concrete. Every time the barn creaked, I flinched, expecting his limbs to twitch. They never did. I held Maddie close to my side, one hand lingering protectively on her soft hair.

"What's your last name, sweetheart?" I asked.

"McKenna." Her face tilted upwards, the dim light bouncing off the end of her button nose. "Are we going away from here now?"

I bent down so we were on the same level. "Well, now we call the police. Or we drive out to the nearest police station."

"Okay," she said.

For the first time in about forty-eight hours, I swung open the barn door. But as soon as I put one foot outside, I stopped. A snowstorm had laid a good foot of snow over everything. We trudged through it, slipping on the slushy patches already worn down by Peter's boots.

Maddie swung open the farmhouse door, excited to be showing me around. I held my body, numbly aware of the dwindling adrenaline allowing me to feel all the pain I'd blocked out. My face, my ribs, and my throat—everywhere he'd touched—seared, like meat dropped into a hot pan. I started to cough, which rattled through my body, angering those blistering wounds.

"Can you show me where the house phone is?" I asked. I flexed my good hand, feeling the weight of the cuffs around my wrist. If I'd been thinking clearly, I would've searched McKenna's body for the keys.

Then my attention drifted to the house. I wasn't sure what I'd expected from a serial killer's home, but it wasn't this chintzy, shabby-chic farmhouse. Clearly, he hadn't redecorated since his mother died, but he had kept it tidy. Then again, I supposed that made sense for a man who'd had an organised plan to abduct and murder me. It made me wonder where all the bodies were hidden. He'd have a plan for that too. Would the police even find them? The responsibility hit me. My voice could bring closure to families missing their children.

"Daddy has a phone," she said.

"Do you have one inside the house?"

She blinked, not understanding. I guessed from her reaction that McKenna had a mobile phone, but there was no house phone.

Then I remembered the phone I'd kept in my jacket pocket during the run. "What did your daddy do with my things?"

She took my hand and led me up the stairs, following old-fashioned wood-panelled walls with a dado rail. Above the rail, I saw photographs of a family, and it took me a moment to realise it was Peter McKenna with his parents. Peter was never older than about ten years old in the photographs, always positioned in front of his mother, where her wide hands settled on his shoulders. I saw nothing but a regular family, posing and smiling. I stopped and stared at one taken in front of the farmhouse, searching for clues, but of what I wasn't sure. I leaned towards that woman's portrait, trying to find evidence of evil or malice. But she reminded me of many women I'd seen photographed in the early nineties. She had soft, fluffy hair above a round face and plastic-framed glasses around her eyes. Her pink-painted lips stretched far enough to reveal teeth.

But I noticed two strange things about Mrs McKenna. She was missing her little finger on her right hand, and in the centre of her left hand was a scar.

"That's Grandma," Maddie said, pointing at her.

"I know, sweetie. Did you know her?"

Maddie shook her head. "No. Daddy said she died."

"Do you know anything about her hand? She has an ouchie there."

Maddie nodded, as solemn as a funeral director. "Like what Daddy does to the ladies."

"The nail?"

"Yes. And that finger too." Maddie jabbed her index finger at Grandma McKenna's hand.

I shuddered, wondering who'd done that to Peter's mother. Surely Peter was too young, considering he was a child in the photograph. It had to be someone related or close to the mother. Perhaps Peter's father or grandparents. Perhaps Peter had seen it or Peter's mother had repeated the process on her son. I didn't want to think about it anymore.

"Let's find that phone," I said, moving on before I lost my composure.

Maddie toddled at a spritely pace through the house, taking me to a bedroom at the end of the corridor. By this point, my entire body throbbed with pain. I stumbled, stooped over and shivering. Once I called the police, I needed to change out of my clothes and turn on the heating in the house, or better yet, make a fire. She opened the door and gestured to a bundle of clothes on top of a neatly made bed. My jacket lay crumpled with my phone on top. I grabbed it and tried to unlock the screen, but it was dead. Of course it was. I'd been here for days, and I'd come out with my battery on thirty percent.

"Shit." I checked through the pockets of my jacket, searching for my keys, but they were gone. "Do you know what your daddy did with my car keys?"

"Drove it," she said.

So he got rid of my car. I had wondered if someone would find it. There had to be a search going on by now. The problem was, no one knew about my solo excursions up here. Not my ex. Not my parents. No one. They'd search local areas, not out here in the middle of nowhere. I had hoped that the police could track my car travelling out to the moors, but the countryside wasn't exactly a CCTV hotspot.

"Okay, never mind. Do you know where your daddy keeps his mobile phone?"

"In his jeans," she said, patting the pocket of her own.

"The ones he's wearing right now?" I asked.

She nodded enthusiastically.

My heart sank. I didn't want to go back out there. The thought of seeing that man again, even knowing he was dead, filled me with a terror that would wake me up at night for many years to come. I'd never experienced the sensation of crawling skin, not properly, but I checked my arms and legs to make sure a cockroach hadn't burrowed beneath my flesh.

"What about a car? Has Daddy got one?"

"Yes."

"Do you know where the keys are?"

She shrugged.

I guessed they were either in the kitchen or on Peter's corpse. Either way, I was too weak to drive, and we'd have snow to dig away first anyway.

"Let's warm up first, shall we?"

She regarded me with an open face, so trusting and sweet. I wondered how long it had been since she'd been around a woman not being tortured by her father. She raised her hand towards mine as though she wanted me to hold it again, and I took it gently then led her over to the door. But before we left, I got a glimpse of the room in its entirety. I'd been focused on my clothes, ignoring the rest of the place. Now I saw it.

"Oh my God," I mumbled.

There were neatly folded piles of women's clothes inside plastic storage containers. I saw high-heeled shoes, hiking boots, and trainers. There had to be half a dozen piles, each in its own storage box. I clasped a hand over my mouth, biting down on my finger to stop the bile rising. They hadn't made it out. They were gone.

"Come on," I said, my voice shaking. "Let's make a fire and warm up. Then we can try and find a phone charger, or... or your father's phone."

"Cool!" Maddie said brightly, squeezing my hand.

CHAPTER TEN
NOW

Justin comes home with a card that says "with sympathy" underneath an illustration of bleach-white lilies. It takes me thirty minutes to come up with a few lines to write inside the card. I settle on: *We are here if you need us. We all miss Phoebe and send you our love.*

I close the card with a sense of nauseating finality. Before I change my mind, I seal the envelope and scribble the Thompsons' address on the front cover. Then I check the news before I leave for group therapy. I go every week to talk through the events in my past.

Aside from the usual speculation, there's no news regarding Phoebe's death, and I'm not sure how to feel about that. One the one hand, the police haven't announced that they're considering her death to be suspicious. On the other hand, they haven't ruled Phoebe's death as an accident. Does that mean they're keeping their options open? There is one request for any witnesses to come forward and a reminder for people to contact the police if they remember anything further.

I exhale as I close the laptop. Every time I think about what happened to Phoebe, my chest tightens. Group therapy will be good for me today.

It's a Monday, but Maddie's school has closed for one day to allow students some time to process their classmate's untimely death. Gabe is back at primary school, but Justin is home, seeing as he works at Maddie's school. I nip into the living room and find him rearranging the bookshelf.

"Hey, babe." He waves a duster in my direction and grins. "You off to therapy?"

"Yeah. Is Maddie in her room?"

"She's catching up on some coursework." He lifts the bust of Shakespeare he bought me after my book release. "I'm thinking of putting him on the third shelf. What do you reckon?"

"Sure. Go for it. You'll keep an eye on Maddie while I'm gone, right?"

"I'm here if she needs me. Everything's going to be fine." He places Shakespeare down, walks over to me, and rests his hands on my shoulders. "Are you okay? I know this is a lot for you."

He's not wrong, but I don't have time to let it out right now. I reach up and squeeze his hand. "I'm fine. A little... you know, upset about everything, but I'm holding it together."

He pulls me in for a hug. "I'm here if you need me too. You know that."

"I do."

His embrace tightens for a second before he lets me go. "I know we're all feeling a bit raw and sad, but it's a beautiful day outside, and everything is going to be fine."

I glance over at the sunshine streaming in through the window. He's not wrong about the weather.

"Darkness makes the light shine brighter," he says. Then, when he notices my expression, he shakes his head and lets out a short laugh. "Sorry, I can't help it. Sometimes I say that to the kids at school when they're going through a tough time. They think I'm cheesy, but it's true."

"I think it's nice." I kiss him on the cheek. As much as I love his positivity, there are times when I need to lean into the pain, and right now, I'm relieved to be going to a place where I can do that. It's remarkable that I married a man who deals with difficulties in such an opposite way. Perhaps it helps.

He tucks a strand of hair behind my ear. "I'll see you later. Maybe I can cook a roast tonight."

I shake my head. "Let's have something lighter." I can't face a big meal; my stomach is churning.

He hugs me one last time, and I head out of the house.

ASIDE FROM THE PSYCHOLOGICAL BENEFITS, the best thing about group therapy in Penry is that it takes place in an adorable small library with a traditional café at the front. I grab a latte on my way into the back room and take a seat in the circle. Our group rents the stock room amongst stacks of old books resting against the walls. I like to arrive early so that I can read the spines. It's one of my favourite ways to the pass the time before the stressful part begins.

Usually, group therapy sessions run for a maximum number of sessions and work towards a goal. But this trauma session is a recurring one for people to dip in and out of, like an Alcoholics Anonymous meeting. For some reason I prefer the group setting. I like to know I'm not alone, even though none of the others have a story like mine. We're interconnected by trauma. We're survivors. We know the guilt of having survived. We know the lasting, physical scars from emotional pain. We know the DNA of it, of ourselves.

As people filter in, we exchange a few hellos and nods. I've never made any close friends from the group, but sometimes a few of us stay later and grab a coffee together. Our therapist, Susannah, is very gentle. She allows us to tell our stories and rarely sets up any formal group activities that I hate.

Today, I notice two new people in the group—a red-haired woman a couple of years younger than me, perhaps in her late-thirties, and a tall, broad-shouldered man with grey in his beard. A shock of sudden anxiety sends me an adrenaline spike. Bulky, tall men remind me of Peter McKenna.

"Hi, everyone." Susannah settles into her chair and rearranges her long skirt. "Welcome to group therapy for emotional trauma. Regulars will know that we take a relaxed and loose approach. Everyone gets a chance to speak, but there's no pressure. Now, it appears we have two new members joining us today."

We all glance over at the broad-shouldered man and red-haired woman.

"As always, I'll give them the floor to introduce themselves. You don't have to tell us why you're here right away. Whatever you feel comfortable saying."

I watch the nervous glances between the two newbies. After a slight pause, the man clears his throat.

"Okay, well, I don't mind going first." He lifts his palm for a quick greeting. "I'm David. I'm new to therapy. I'm not from Penry, but this is the closest group I could find. I, well, I suppose I'm here to work through some issues I should've worked on a long time ago."

A murmur passes through the circle. There are plenty of us who have pushed down our problems for too long.

"I had a brother who died a long time ago now. And I'm not sure I've processed his death. Not yet." He lifts his head, and I see the shiny film of tears coating his eyes. He lets out a quiet, self-conscious laugh. "Which is why I'm here."

"Well, you're in the right place, David. And you've taken the first step. That's important," Susannah says, and the people in the group murmur in agreement.

After the mumbled encouragements die down, attention moves to the woman sitting across from me. She flips her auburn hair over one shoulder and fiddles nervously with a gold band around her wrist.

"I guess it's me next." Her fingers slide the metal band up and down her arm. "My name is Cecilia, and I'm not from Penry, but I have moved here recently. If any of you know a good place for bottomless brunch, let me know." She grins but then shakes her head. "Sorry, bad joke. I'm... Well, I'm actually getting over some substance abuse, so I'm staying away from Prosecco for a while."

"Thanks for sharing that," Susannah says. "You're not alone.

Substance abuse is an issue that many people in the group have been through too. Why did you decide to come today, Cecilia?"

Cecilia sighs. "I'm here because of my ex. AKA the bastard who tried to grind me down. I'm pleased to report that he failed. That I live, breathe, forget to floss, and put too much butter on my toast." She laughs. "When I don't spend the day in bed sobbing, I actually get up and go to work and live my *fucking* life. He hasn't broken me, and never sodding will."

A ripple of applause breaks out around the room.

"Oh, thanks." She hides her face in her hands, charmingly embarrassed.

"Well said," Susannah says. "We're all still here. That's an achievement. Being in this room is worth celebrating."

Sometimes, when Susannah celebrates tiny achievements, such as coming to therapy, I quell a strong desire to roll my eyes. But the genuine emotion in Cecilia's voice moves me, and I find myself nodding along.

After the introductions, the group spends some time on individuals. People get an opportunity to talk about their challenges since the last meeting. When it comes to me, I semi-consciously grip hold of the chair seat beneath my thighs.

"You must know about the local girl who died this week. Phoebe Thompson. She was, um, she was in my daughter's class at school. No one knows how it happened because it seems likely she was alone. She may have fallen over the edge of a cliff, or she may have jumped, or—" I stop myself from uttering that last option. "My daughter, Maddie, was there at the campsite. She didn't see anything, but I'm worried about how this might be triggering for her, after everything we've been through." An image flashes in my mind of tiny Maddie standing next to me, staring at her father's corpse. *You need to make sure he goes to sleep and never wakes up.*

"And what about you, Zoe?" Susannah asks. "What about your triggers?"

My grip tightens. The mottled pattern on the plastic seat presses into my skin. "I can't allow myself to go there. If I do, I fall apart. And if I fall apart, Maddie will have no one around to make sure she stays together." I think about Justin. Yes, he'd pick up any slack I dropped, but Maddie only trusts me completely. She isn't close to him in the same way she's close to me.

"That's a lot to deal with," Cecilia says quietly, then she clamps her hand over her mouth. "Sorry, I wasn't supposed to speak then, was I?"

"That's okay," Susannah says. "This is a safe space, and you didn't do any harm."

"Oh, good." Cecilia turns to me. "I know we don't know each other, but I think maybe you're putting a lot of pressure on yourself. I have a teenage daughter. She's pretty wayward. For a long time I tried to control the world around her. But there comes a time when you can't do it anymore." She lowers her head and lets out a sigh. "It drove a wedge between us."

I nod, understanding the balancing act we take on as parents.

"I wish I could've stopped what happened to us," Cecilia continues. "After I left my ex, I spent so long pretending it never happened, creating this fake, happy life that isn't ours. It didn't work." She shakes her head. "One day I realised I'd never dealt with what he did to me, because like you, I couldn't go there. I forgot that I'm more than just a mother. So are you. You're a human being, and you deserve time to deal with your own shit. You know?"

I can't think of the words to respond, so we exchange shy, tentative smiles. It's difficult to say or even admit how wonderful it is to hear my worries spoken by another person. Another mother.

"Cecilia raises a great point, Zoe. How do you feel about that?"

My throat feels thick, but somehow, I manage to speak. "Like I have worth beyond being a mother to two kids and a wife to one husband."

"And what about your triggers?" she asks gently.

"I can't stop seeing his face." Then I say something I never expected to say today. "I see his face when I look at her, and it terrifies me." When I break down, Cecilia walks across the circle and wraps her arm around my shoulders.

Chapter Eleven
THEN

We coaxed a fire to life in the large brick fireplace. By the time the flames crackled and spat, I had no energy left in my body. I slumped in an armchair next to the fire, with a fleece blanket draped over me, the handcuffs still around my wrist, shackles dangling from each ankle. Shivers juddered through my body, as did the chesty coughs. I asked Maddie to find me some food, and she brought over a packet of crisps and a Mars bar, which my trembling fingers struggled to open. My mouth watered as soon as I smelled the salt and vinegar, but I reminded myself to eat slowly, so as not to throw it back up.

"I could make you some toast," she said brightly.

"That's okay." Black spots danced across my vision. "I think I need to sleep for a while. I'm so tired. Do you know what a phone charger looks like?"

She nodded.

"Could you search for one while I rest? We need to call the police." My eyelids drooped, and the world sounded as though it were underwater.

When Peter McKenna's face appeared, one eye missing, the other bloodshot and angry, I screamed and screamed. Someone shushed me, and I drifted into the third or fourth unsettled sleep I'd had since being abducted. As I drifted, I thought to myself, *A computer. Surely Peter has a computer with the internet.*

I didn't remember much about the hours after we built the fire. Perhaps a fever worked its way through me, and dreams and reality merged. Maddie's face appeared next to mine a few times. At one point, she crawled onto my lap and fell asleep with her head against my chest. I had a vague memory of showing her how to stoke the fire so she could keep it going. There were times when I woke up screaming, convinced that Peter was still alive. Once, I even dreamed that Maddie stood over me with a sharp knife in her hand. But I was sure I was projecting my fears onto her.

As I finally woke from hours of troubled slumber, I coughed up phlegm onto the carpet.

Maddie stared at it then at me. "Are you going to die?"

I laughed. "I hope not." But for the first time since watching her father bleed out on the barn floor, I wondered if she might be right. "Could I have that toast now? And a glass of water." I needed to get my strength back. "Did you find a phone charger."

Maddie grabbed a wire from the coffee table and held it up triumphantly, her tongue poking out between her teeth. I saw that it was a charger for an Android phone. I had an iPhone. But it might still prove useful.

"Oh, well done, sweetheart."

She beamed. "Am I a good girl?"

"You really are."

She hugged me, and I hugged her back. Then she trotted off to the kitchen to make toast and pour water. I heard her dragging a chair around the room. She'd obviously done this before.

My brain was still foggy, but I had the wherewithal to assess everything going on. The farmhouse was warm and comfy, but we needed help. If there was no landline, we needed to find either Peter's phone or his computer. Surely he had both. Maddie appeared to be physically healthy, though I imagined she'd been through an ordeal living here with a serial killer. But she didn't appear to have bruises, and she walked around with ease. She was skinnier than most of the children I knew, but she obviously knew how to fend for herself. She wasn't wearing a nappy, and while I hadn't seen her use the bathroom, I had to conclude by now that she was potty-trained. Whether Peter had abused her, I didn't know. She'd been nothing but sweet to me. I liked her a lot. Without her, I couldn't say if I would have had the strength to fight my way out of the barn.

"Zoe! Toast!" Maddie skipped in with two slices of bread bouncing on the plate. She'd buttered it for me too. "I'll be back."

This time, I demolished the food, which was under toasted but still the best meal I'd had in my life. Maddie then returned with the best glass of water I'd ever tasted.

"Are you okay, honey? Do you need something to eat?"

"I had choc-choc." She grinned.

"Good," I said. "Okay, so now we need to get help, because I think I need to go to the hospital. I'm not sure I can get up yet. Do you know if your daddy had a computer?"

"Um, yes."

"Can you get it for me, Maddie?"

Eager to please, as always, she hurried out of the room. I heard her small feet stomping up the stairs and along the corridor. Imagining her entering her father's bedroom alone made me shudder. As I waited for her to come back, I sipped the last of the water and rested my head against the chair. Now I needed the bathroom, and I hadn't yet changed out of my urine-soaked running tights.

Maddie returned a few minutes later, cradling the laptop to her chest. I beckoned her over, and she passed it to me. Excitement flooded through my veins until I opened the lid and came across the password request.

"Do you know Daddy's password?"

Maddie shook her head.

I groaned and tipped my head back. "Okay, here's what we're going to do. Could you get me another glass of water and a chocolate bar? And while you do that, can you think of everything you know about

Daddy. His birthday, the name of his mummy—your grandma, or the names of any pets you've had."

"Like Chalkie?"

"Yes!" I said, matching her enthusiasm. "Who's Chalkie?"

"He was my puppy. He was white."

"That's right. Good girl!"

She beamed. As she walked off with the empty glass, I tried the name, while refusing to focus on the way Maddie had referred to her puppy in the past tense. I did not want to know what Peter McKenna did to animals.

Chalkie didn't work, and neither did several variations in spelling. Maddie sloshed a third of the water on the carpet as she returned with a Twix and a packet of Maltesers. She handed me the Twix and opened her Maltesers.

"You have a lot of chocolate in the house," I noted.

"Daddy likes it. But I'm not allowed to eat this much."

"You can have as much as you like now," I said brightly, then added, "As long as you don't rot your teeth." I shook my head, feeling like my mother. "Anyway, honey, I've tried *Chalkie*, but it doesn't work. Can you remember Daddy's birthday?"

"Ummm." She bit her lip. "Berf-day." She mouthed the word as though it were new to her.

"You don't... You don't know what a birthday is?"

For the first time since I'd met her, she started to cry.

"Oh no. Oh, Maddie, I'm so sorry. Come here." I pulled her onto my lap and rocked her back and forth as she sobbed into the fleece blanket. "It's okay. It doesn't matter, sweetie. It's not important. But would you like to know what a birthday is?"

Her head bobbed up and down against my chest.

"It's a day where we eat cake and buy balloons and sing songs."

She blinked her big brown eyes. "Why?"

"Because we're a year older. Do you know how old you are?"

Her face scrunched again, and she shook her head.

"That's okay. We'll figure it out. So, every year, we celebrate the day we were born. Do you know what being born means?"

"Yes." She pulled on a few strands of hair and avoided my gaze. "No."

"It's like waking up for the first time."

"Oh," she said.

"So whatever date you were born, we celebrate that every year. And when you're safe and settled, I'm going to personally make sure you always have a birthday celebration, okay? I promise."

"Promise?" I noticed she knew that word because of how her eyes lit up.

"I promise."

She stayed on my lap as I tried to think up more password ideas. Maddie didn't know her grandmother's first name. She couldn't think of any more pets either. I was at a loss, and I couldn't put it off any longer. Either I had to dig Peter's phone out of his jeans pocket, or I had to send Maddie up to the piles of women's belongings in the man's bedroom. Perhaps one of them had owned an Android phone we could charge. But I didn't like the idea of messing with evidence. I thought about it for a minute and decided to go out to the barn first. Peter's phone was the most likely to be charged and ready to go. Plus, it meant not having to disturb the victims' belongings, which felt sacred.

However, getting out of the chair proved to be harder than expected. I had to stop and cough more than once. Dizziness washed over me. My limbs and swollen face throbbed. Still, I refused to send Maddie to the barn. Little children shouldn't be forced to search a corpse.

She brought me some of her grandma's clothes—I specifically requested they not come from her father's room—and I changed by the fire, trying to soak up as much warmth as I could before going out into the snow again.

The clothes were three sizes too big, but I layered up, wrapped a scarf around my neck, and pulled on a pair of boots over the ankle shackles, tucking the chains in as best I could. I made my way to the front door, using furniture as a crutch.

"Wait," Maddie said, running out of the corridor. She returned breathless, a minute later, carrying a walking stick.

"Oh, clever girl." I wanted to bend down and hug her, but I was worried I'd never get back up. "Okay, Maddie, you wait here. I won't be long."

She thrust her tiny hand into mine and let out a whimper.

"I won't be long, I promise."

Tears welled in her eyes, making them shiny and bright. Her skin was still blotchy red from when she'd been upset before. And soon, I was crying with her.

I reached down for her, despite my weakened body, and I touched her cheek. "I'm coming right back. I promise."

"Promise?"

"Yes."

She pulled away from me, and her hands balled into fists. "No! No!" she screamed. Then she twisted around and started beating the wall with her tightly wound fingers. "No! No!"

Even though the intensity scared me, I remained calm and allowed her tantrum to play out. Someone had broken an important promise to her, and she was scared. I understood that. The world had broken its promise to Maddie. Every child should know love, warmth, and stability, but she'd never known any of those things. She had a right to be angry.

"Maddie, I swear I'm coming back. Why don't you climb up onto the kitchen counter and watch me through the window? That way, you'll see me walking there, and you'll see me walking back. Is that all right? Do you think that'll help?"

"Guess so."

I wiped the snot away from her nose and planted a kiss upon her head. "I keep my promises, Maddie. You'll learn that about me."

She scowled as I opened the door, then she sprinted to the kitchen. When I walked out of the warm house into the frigid cold, I saw her pressed against the glass, watching cautiously.

Chapter Twelve
NOW

Justin has the house clean and tidy when I get home. It's his love language. Whenever I'm overwhelmed, he takes up the helm of the household chores because he knows I can't handle it. Maddie and I lived through some slobby periods following the adoption. Justin straightened all of that out. Sometimes he takes it too far, throwing out things I'd like to keep or moving everything so that I can't find it. Still, I love it about him, that he needs to be useful.

"I thought we might order in for lunch. What do you reckon? I know it's a bit cheeky, but if we order extra, it'll double up as tea later." He grins, a feather duster tucked under his arm.

Before I can answer, the phone rings, and Justin lifts a finger in a "hold that thought" gesture. I head over to the kitchen sink to pour a glass of water. I've gulped half of it down by the time he returns.

"That was DS Rosen. He said he took Maddie's statement at the campsite."

My spine immediately straightens. I place the glass down on the kitchen counter, harder than intended, and it chinks against the marble surface.

"What did he want?"

"He's coming over with a colleague." Justin shuffles from one foot to the other, his gaze travelling over kitchen cupboards and to the window. "They want to ask Maddie some more questions so they can put together a statement."

I fold my arms and lean my weight against the counter. "I don't like that guy."

"You don't? Why?"

"The way he looked at Maddie. I dunno. It was like he was assessing her. This is the last thing we need." As I walk through to the lounge, Justin follows. Rather than sit on the sofa in the centre of the room, I head over to the large bay window, hoping the sea in the distance will soothe me. It doesn't. "He knew about my book. Which means he's probably read it. He certainly knows about mine and Maddie's background with Peter McKenna, and I'm worried he's going to use it against her."

"Against me?"

I twist my body around to find Maddie standing in a doorway. "Yes." I purse my lips together. "I mean, we don't know that for sure. But..."

"But there's a load of incriminating shit in there that they could twist," Maddie finishes.

"Well, I wasn't going to put it quite like that—"

"The thing is, Mads, your mum's book talks about your diagnosis when you were little and—" Justin starts.

"Yeah, I get it." Maddie strides across the room and slumps down on the sofa. She curls her legs underneath her body, grabs the remote, and switches on the TV.

I want to tell her I'm sorry, that I wish I hadn't written so much about our relationship. When it came to writing that book, I'd opened a vein and allowed the blood to spill onto the page. I did it to survive, just like my stress eating. And perhaps I shouldn't have sold our story, but the process didn't feel complete until others had read it too. Yes, the money was good, and it'd set us up for life, but those emails from readers telling *me* I'd saved *their* life meant more to me than any special house I could buy.

Maddie was assessed a lot as a child, and while she was never diagnosed with a conduct disorder, therapists identified the callous and unemotional traits associated with a conduct disorder. I remember at the time that those words felt cold and made her sound like a robot. A person without a soul. But people are complicated, and as the experts explained to me, Maddie wouldn't necessarily grow up to be a callous person. Her lack of emotion came from difficulties bonding with people. Crucially, they believed she could change. Discovering all of this early on became a good thing so that I could adapt my parenting style to help her.

Writing about the pressure to bring Maddie up the right way helped lighten the load. It was good for me to talk about the ways her behaviour frightened me. There are many other parents dealing with children—biological or adopted—with similar problems, and my book helped them as well as me. There hasn't been one single second in the last eleven years that I haven't loved Maddie just as she is, but I'd be lying if I said there hadn't been moments of pure desperation.

We let her sit and chill before the interview. Justin makes himself busy again, folding clothes and ironing. I finish my water and pick up Gabe from school. After he's settled at the dining room table with his homework, there's a knock at the door. It's game on. I take a moment to compose myself and head into the hallway to let the detective in.

DS Rosen flashes me a breezy smile that doesn't quite reach his eyes. I find them penetrating as we exchange pleasantries, and I invite him in. A younger officer who introduces herself as PC Morton follows. She's short, but stocky, her hair pulled into a bun, exposing her undercut.

"Good afternoon, young man!" Rosen says brightly to Gabe, who sits up and grins. "Excellent work there. Keep it up."

Gabe absolutely loves praise, especially from strangers. He positively beams.

I lean over and give him a peck on the crown of his head. "Wait in here while we chat, okay?"

He grumbles but stays put.

We settle on the sofas in the living room. Justin offers the police drinks, which they refuse. DS Rosen remarks on the pleasant weather we're having. It's all typically British, stalling the main event, everyone on edge except, perhaps, for Maddie. Finally, we get down to business.

"Maddie, I wanted to come and see you today so that we could get a bit more information from you about the night Phoebe died. Is that okay?"

Maddie is on guard. I notice the little things, the impassive expression on her face, the straightness of her back, and the way her hands are folded on her lap. I wonder if she's taken to heart the things we discussed. She nods cautiously.

"Great stuff. Let's run over that timeline again." DS Rosen proceeds to read out the events as Maddie told him at the campsite. I don't like the way he glances at PC Morton as he speaks. She's very quiet, sitting there with her notebook on her knees.

Maddie confirms every time, location, and detail. She answers questions quietly and calmly.

"There is something else I'd like to talk about," Rosen says. "A few of the other girls have mentioned an argument that occurred earlier on in the day. Could you tell me about that?"

Maddie lets out a short breath through her nose—a sure sign of her irritation.

I flash her a glance to tell her to hold it back.

"It was stupid," she says. "Girl stuff."

"What sort of girl stuff? Go into as much detail as you can. Everything helps us."

Maddie moves her attention to me. "Am I in trouble?"

I open my mouth to answer, but DS Rosen gets there first. "Not at all."

I pray that Maddie is smart enough not to trust that statement.

"Well, Nina Patel, one of Phoebe's best friends, wanted to play truth or dare after the barbecue. So we sat in a circle and spun this bottle around. It landed on Ellie Oaksmith. She had to do the dare. And then it landed on me."

"Right. What does that mean?" Rosen asks.

"That I give Ellie a dare."

Oh no.

"What kind of dare did you give Ellie?" Rosen is poised, waiting for the answer, leaning towards my child. Meanwhile, my heart jumps around in my chest.

"I dared Ellie to throw her arm over the cliff."

My heart sinks. Justin gasps. PC Morton lifts her eyebrows. Only DS Rosen has no reaction. He's probably already heard this from the other girls. He must also know that Ellie has a prosthetic arm.

"It was a joke," Maddie clarifies. "I wasn't going to make her to do it or anything. But she started crying before I could tell her it was a joke."

"What happened after that?" DS Rosen asks, even though I'm sure he already knows.

"Phoebe yelled at me. She told me to go home."

"But you didn't?"

"No, I stayed. She can't tell me what to do. Besides, I wanted to tell Ellie that I was joking. So I went over to Ellie and told her. I told her that my real dare was for her to eat twenty marshmallows in one go." Maddie's expression is pale and tight when her focus moves to me. "See? I'm not mean. She just didn't understand."

"I know, hun," I say. I turn to DS Rosen. "Maddie and I both have a dark sense of humour. It's a coping mechanism we developed to help us deal with what we went through in the past. The thing is, Maddie doesn't always recognise that other people don't find that sort of humour funny. Ellie is quite self-conscious of her prosthetic, so it was an unfortunate occurrence."

"I told her I was joking," Maddie says desperately.

"You mentioned that Phoebe yelled at you. Did you shout back?"

"Not really. I mean, I said her party was shit. And I pointed out that her mum only invited everyone to flex their wealth. But I didn't yell." Maddie shrugs.

"Is there anything else you'd like to tell me, Maddie?" Rosen asks.

She's quiet for a moment. "I don't think so. After Phoebe told me to go, I went to my tent and chilled out there for the rest of the night."

My heart breaks for my daughter spending a birthday party in a tent alone. I don't want to think ill of the dead, but Phoebe and her close-knit friendship group have always given me mean-girl vibes. Yes, Maddie said a terrible thing—a horribly insensitive thing that her woke schoolmates would find unforgiveable. I didn't support what she said to Ellie, but I did *understand* how she'd ended up blurting out that dare. When the girls around her hadn't ever shown her kindness, Maddie, with her blunted emotional awareness, wouldn't feel the need to show *them* any kindness either. And to me, their unkindness is just as horrible. Maddie is different to them. It isn't her fault. They shunned her because of her differences.

"All right, Maddie. Thank you for talking to us today." He regards PC Morton, who gives him a nod to say she's made notes. "We'll let you get on with your day."

I show them to the door with a thick sensation at the back of my throat, like I'm close to being sick. Maddie and Phoebe fell out hours before Phoebe's death. And I'm not sure how I feel about that.

CHAPTER THIRTEEN
THEN

Numbness spread through my toes as I hobbled towards the barn. A fresh layer of snow had topped the last snowfall. As my boots slipped on the ice below the surface, I threw my weight onto the walking stick, which somehow found purchase, keeping me upright.

My sense of smell had dulled since the beating I'd received from McKenna, but the place smelled fresh. Cold. Ice had its own scent, and I breathed in a lungful of it. My breath came out vapourised, like the hot steam expelled from an engine.

I stepped towards the barn, glancing back to see Maddie still pressed against the glass. I waved at her and smiled. She waved back. Her presence helped motivate me. I had no desire to collapse and die in the snow, but knowing that child had been brought up *here* by that monster made me want to give her a new life.

The barn door was still open, and I caught my first glimpse of the body. As soon as I saw him, my hands started to shake. Panic surged through me. I wanted to scream until my lungs were raw, but I knew it would hurt. Instead, I let out a whimper and carried on, limping towards him, trying not to stare at the hulking body on the floor. I focused on the desk, remembering Maddie's expression of concentration as she worked the screwdriver. *One step at a time. Get the phone and get out.*

Ten paces in the door, I was right by him. I had to admit, despite facing the lifeless form of my torturer, it was a relief to be out of the snow for a moment. In the barn, the icy chill wasn't quite so bad, and my feet didn't slip. Breathing into my fingers to bring them back to life, I gently lowered myself to the hard floor, careful not to kneel in the bloodstain that haloed out around the body.

As I searched him, I kept my fingers on the denim of his jeans, unwilling to feel the temperature of his body. Repulsed by his freezing cold, blue skin, I closed my eyes as I slipped my fingers into his pocket and groped.

First, I found his key to the barn, and with some relief, the keys to the cuffs around my wrists and ankles. I pulled off my boots and unlocked them immediately, relieved not to have the metal jangling around me any longer. Then I forced myself to reach around his hip to his other pocket. It was empty. I steadied my hand and forced it underneath his body to feel in both back pockets, and with a jolt of revulsion, I realised he was both freezing cold and extremely stiff. Rigor mortis or frozen, I didn't know, and I didn't want to know.

Where the fuck is his phone?

Next, I tried both jacket pockets. Both were empty.

I staggered away from him and sat down on the same chair he'd intimidated me from. Now I thought about it, I figured his decision not to carry a phone into the barn was more than likely calculated. If his victim managed to get free and injure him in some way—or kill him like I had—he wanted it to be as difficult as possible for that victim to get help. But he'd needed his key to open the padlock on the outside of the barn. And I assumed he needed to carry the keys to the restraints in order to move me whenever he wanted. But perhaps he'd hidden his phone and his car key somewhere inside the house. I wondered if Maddie had noticed this behaviour, but surely if she had, she would've said something.

Feeling exhausted and stupid, I heaved myself back onto the walking stick and made my way slowly back to the farmhouse, trying not to dwell on the image of blue-mottled grey skin or the feel of his stiff body.

Maddie ran to meet me, grabbing hold of my legs. I gently prised her from me so I could move into the kitchen and half collapse on a chair.

After a hearty cough, I took both of her hands in mine. "I want you to think very hard. Did Daddy have a special hiding place for his things?"

She stared at me for a moment. "His phone was in his pocket."

"No," I said. "It wasn't there."

"Oh." Her forehead screwed up in concentration. "He'd take it out of his pocket."

"When he was in the house. But not when he went to the barn."

Her eyes lit up. "The box!"

"Box? What box?"

Maddie pulled me by the hand, and I staggered onto my numb feet. Still in the boots, she dragged me through the house to the hallway. I hadn't noticed it before, but next to the shoe cabinet was a small metal safe.

"He puts his phone and car keys in here before he goes out to the barn," I said. "Shit! What about the phones of the other ladies? Are they in his bedroom?"

Maddie shrugged.

Slowly, we made our way back to Peter's room. I gently searched each pile of clothing for a phone. I found one dead flip phone that we wouldn't be able to charge. Uncovering my phone had turned out to be a fluke. Peter had made sure it was virtually impossible for his victims to get to safety.

"I bet they're in the safe," I mumbled. "Maddie, do you know the code to the safe?"

She shook her head. I'd known she wouldn't, but I had to ask.

I sat down on Peter McKenna's bed. My need for support was greater than the disgust I felt knowing he'd once slept there. I had no phone and no key for his old Land Rover, and I was in the middle of nowhere, surrounded by snow. I was pretty sure I had pneumonia. My body was battered and bruised. I was weak and tired. Maybe I was even dying. *What the hell am I going to do?*

"We'll have to wait until the snow melts," I said. "And then try and flag down someone driving along the road."

"Okay," Maddie said.

"Unless we can get into the safe. We may as well try. Right?"

She grinned, fully energised with the idea of being helpful again. "Okay!"

FOR TWO DAYS we searched the house. I thought Peter might have kept the safe code scribbled down somewhere. But I was weak, my chest leaden with fluid, and I spent a lot of that time sleeping on my stomach by the fire. We even tried to *guess* the four-digit code, but it was no use. All the time the snow slowly thawed, too gradually to make much difference to us though. Maddie made toast, but I saw the mould on the crust before I took a bite. We ran out of Peter's chocolate supply and ended up eating dry cereal whenever my appetite came back. Luckily, the central heating prevented the pipes from freezing, and we had a steady supply of heat and water.

I sweated and coughed as I stumbled through to the garage at the side of the house. A scrapped car took up most of the space, but I eyed the shelves of tools and shuffled my way through stacks of old boxes and abandoned car parts to get to them.

Maddie, always by my side, scrambled up onto the car and sat cross-legged on the bonnet. "What're you doing?"

"We need some tools, Maddie. A crowbar, a hammer, screwdrivers. Can you help?"

She skidded her way down the bonnet of the old car, stepped on top of a box labelled "magazines," and clambered onto the workbench next to the shelves.

"You can climb like a monkey," I said.

She exploded into a fit of giggles. "A monkey?"

"Yes!"

"Like *ooh-ooh-aah-aah*?" She danced and wiggled with her hands stuck under her armpits.

"Yes," I said, laughing. "But be careful. Don't fall."

Maddie let out a "tut" sound. "I won't fall."

"Go super steady, okay? Now, try and pass me that screwdriver. The one with the flat head. That's it. And the crowbar." I guided her gently towards the tools we needed, gathered them up, and left the garage.

Back at the safe, I tried hammering the screwdriver into the thin seam connecting the door to the base. But I'd seen these kinds of safes in hotels and knew there were two large bolts keeping the door closed. It was going to take more than a screwdriver to get the door open. After jimmying the seam open slightly, I forced in the crowbar, pinning the safe to the floor with my feet. It exposed half of one bolt, at least a centimetre thick, and I knew my exertions would be fruitless. There was no way I could get into that thing without the code. I grabbed hold of the notepad by my feet and skimmed all the combinations of numbers that I'd tried so far.

Defeated, I lay back against the wall and closed my eyes. Not long after, her small body leaned against my shoulder.

"We can't stay here any longer," I said. "I need to go to the hospital."

Soon I heard her sniffs and felt the wetness of her tears on my chest.

I briefly considered our options. The thought of walking in the snow made me shudder. I couldn't bring myself to send Maddie alone either.

I opened my eyes and stared at the dented safe. That was all I'd managed to do—dent it.

"Maddie, do you know any important dates? Anything. Doesn't have to be a birthday. It could be anything that you've heard your father mention. Please think as hard as you can, because we really, really need help."

"The day you came," she said softly.

I stroked her hair and was about to tell her how sweet she was for saying that, when I thought, *Why not try the date?* Perhaps he changed the code for every woman he kidnapped. It'd stop Maddie from learning the code, but also be memorable enough to stick in his mind. I tapped the keypad, entering the date I was abducted.

The door sprang open.

Maddie jumped to her feet, dancing frantically. Then I pulled her back to the floor, holding her tight.

"Well done, Maddie. Well done!"

She gleamed like a lightbulb had lit up beneath her skin.

"Come on, let's see what's inside."

Along with McKenna's car keys, I found seven phones—three Android smart phones to match the charger, one ancient Blackberry, and three iPhones of varying ages. I spread them out along the corridor.

"Some of these are old models," I said to myself. "This is the newest." I picked up a Samsung phone. "I bet it's his." All of them were out of battery, but it wouldn't take long to charge them. However, I had his car keys and the sudden need to get out of this place. I dragged myself to my feet, checking the snow situation.

"I think we can get out. The Land Rover isn't in a drift anymore. Do you want to leave, Maddie?"

"Yeah!"

"Then let's get out of here."

"Okay!" she said brightly.

We both wrapped up in coats found in the farmhouse. I used the cane Maddie had found for me, and she ran ahead down the driveway. My hands trembled. In my weakened state, I wasn't sure I could even do this.

I heaved myself up into the driver's seat, and Maddie pushed the door closed for me. She hopped into the passenger's side with ease.

"I've never driven a Land Rover before," I mumbled. "Can't be too hard, right?"

I eased the clutch out slowly, and the car rolled forward, tyres crunching over snow and gravel. But before we could go farther, we had to wait for the icy windscreen to melt. I revved the engine and switched all the heaters onto high, still edging slowly down the driveway because I could barely wait to leave this place.

Maddie sat quietly next to me, some of her usual energy depleted.

I tapped her on the knee. "Are you okay?"

She glanced back at the house and pressed her hand to the window.

"Have you left the farm before?" I asked.

"Yes," she said.

But before, I thought, she was always coming back. This was different, and she felt it.

The screen cleared, the petrol gage showed me half a tank, and the engine chugged along well enough. I pressed the accelerator and guided the car to the end of the drive. When we hit the road, my heart skipped a beat. Ivycross Farm lay behind us, already like a memory. Perhaps I might have taken in one last look if I hadn't been concentrating.

On the tarmac, the snow lay in patches. Every time the Land Rover hit a patch of snow, my fingers gripped the steering wheel. My vision blurred at times, and sweat poured down my back despite the cold. At one point, I thought the car was making a chattering sound until I realised it was my teeth. Despite my jangling nerves and the thundering of my pulse, waves of exhaustion kept washing over me.

"Okay, kid," I said. "You're going to have to keep me awake here. I'm struggling, and I don't want to drive this car into a ditch."

Dutifully, she flicked my shoulder.

"Ow!" I exclaimed, hamming up my reaction. "I was thinking more about a conversation." I took a left, vaguely remembering my way home. The road distorted and blurred. "Maybe we need to talk about what's going to happen now. This is a big step for you, isn't it? Okay, well, I'm going to try and get us to a hospital. And then, once the doctors make sure we're okay"—I was not, but I didn't say that— "we'll have to talk to the police."

"Oh," she whispered. Her skin grew pale, like the moon on a wintery night. "I don't like them."

"I know it might seem scary," I said, swerving around a tight corner, "but they're going to help you. I promise. I'm quite poorly,

Maddie, so I might go into a hospital bed. But if I can be with you, I will."

"Daddy said the police are fucking pigs."

"Hun, that's a grown-up word."

"Which one?"

"The F word."

Her eyebrows bunched together again. I steered wildly around another corner until finally arriving back in civilisation. As soon as I saw another car, my body tingled all over. I started to doubt the situation I was driving from. Had I truly left a dead body at a farm? Had I watched a child pull a nail from my hand? I couldn't quite keep my foot on the accelerator. The car kept shuddering forwards and slowing. Someone behind me blasted his horn as he almost drove straight into me. I realised then that I couldn't drive any farther.

As soon as I saw houses lining the street, I pulled over.

"Come with me," I said, motioning for Maddie to slide across to my side. She did as she was told, and we staggered over to one of the houses.

I made it almost to the gate before collapsing. To this day, I'm not sure if it was the pneumonia or a kind of agoraphobia seizing my body in a tight grip. Then I saw feet running towards me. But I kept my attention on Maddie. I didn't want her to get scared and run away.

"Stay with me," I muttered.

She knew what I'd said. She slipped her tiny hand into mine.

Chapter Fourteen
NOW

In my rearview mirror are a pair of blue eyes as light as ice, penetrating as the cold. I blink the image away and focus back on the road. DS Rosen is on my mind, and somewhere, in the depths of my imagination, he has become as menacing a figure as Peter McKenna. It isn't fair, of course. As far as I know, he's just doing his job.

Maddie never mentioned anything to me about the argument with Phoebe. Hearing that in front of the police blindsided me in the worst way. Maddie doesn't keep secrets for no reason.

I glance up at the mirror and smile at the two kids in the back seat. Gabe gives me a thumbs-up. Maddie stares out of the window. Either she hasn't seen me, or she's ignoring me.

There could be a few different explanations for why she didn't say anything. Either she wanted to hide it because she's worried it implicates her in Phoebe's death, or the events of the night pushed the argument out of her mind. Maddie isn't stupid. She knew she couldn't hide the argument from the police. There were witnesses. Ordinarily, Maddie would tell me about an incident like that, though she wouldn't express much emotion about it. Perhaps she was ashamed about what she'd said to Ellie.

Maddie tends to understand consequences extremely well. Once, during a group coursework assignment, she planted seeds of her own incompetence to the rest of her group while nudging the others in the wrong direction for the presentation. She then gleefully informed me about how she'd twisted their presentation into a debate. Her arguments won because she'd manipulated the others into getting it wrong. The group all got As—the teacher saw the debate as a theatrical example of playing Devil's Advocate—but Maddie figured out a way to shine. I'd told her to be careful, that manipulating people like that was not only mean, but would also get her into trouble. She's never mentioned another such occasion, but it's possible she simply stopped telling me. And that scares me.

Justin unclips his seatbelt as I pull into the school carpark. It jolts me out of my thoughts. I hadn't spoken a word throughout the journey.

"Have a good day, hun." He leans across and kisses me on the cheek.

"Sure, you too."

Maddie is a blur in the rearview mirror, leaping out of the car and striding silently towards the school building. No goodbye. Not even a wave.

Justin grabs hold of the door handle, but I place a hand on his arm to stop him from leaving. "Keep an eye on her today. The other kids might go after her."

"I will." He frowns. "Though I think she can take care of herself."

That's something else I'm worried about.

"Want a lift home too?" I ask.

"I think I'll walk," Justin says. "Mads can join me if she likes."

"All right."

"See you later, Zo." He grins and plants a kiss on my lips.

As he leaves, I wonder why I can't deal with stress in his typically breezy way. Then I notice someone waiting for my space, and I manoeuvre back onto the road, ducking in and out of the parked cars clustered around the school. Today I'm less patient than usual, muttering under my breath as the large four-wheel-drive vehicles take up the road.

For some reason, it bothers me that I won't be collecting Maddie from school. Justin and Maddie usually walk—separately, of course; no teenage girl wants to walk with her dad—to and from school, but we all overslept this morning. It was a hot night, and I tossed and turned thinking about Phoebe Thompson tumbling over the cliff, her slim bones smashing against the rocks. Letting Maddie out of my sight for even a second feels wrong. But what am I afraid of? That someone will hurt my daughter? Or the opposite?

"Mum, you missed the turn!"

I'd completely forgotten about Gabe in the backseat. I flash him a guilty smile. "I was testing you!"

"No, you weren't. You forgot!" Then he starts singing, "Mum forgot, and she's a big stupid head!"

I roll my eyes but can't deny his squeaky voice coaxes out a laugh.

Once I've corrected my route and dropped Gabe off at his primary school, I head back to the house.

Since moving to Cornwall, I have to admit that my days can be quite empty. They drift. After writing six chapters of a follow-up to *Maddie and Me*, I hit a wall. Now most mornings, I walk along the beach or the cliffs, potter around the house, try to meditate—which usually helps my anxiety—and find other inconsequential things to waste time between dropping Gabe off at primary school and picking him up again at three.

The beginnings of a headache stroke at my temples. I settle into the sofa and scroll through social media posts about Phoebe until an Instagram photo catches my eye. White lilies are tied to a fence, the ash-grey sea in the distance. I pinch my phone and make the picture as large as I can, trying to read the condolence cards underneath the flowers. I haven't seen the area where Phoebe fell before.

I grab my car keys and run out of the house. A few moments later, I'm heading up the coastal road towards the site. I have a vague idea of where the photograph was taken. And now I want to see it for myself.

Not wanting to be noticed, I continue on past the carpark and pull into a tiny spot for hikers to park. It's a beautiful day. A fresh breeze coming off the sea has replaced the suffocating heat from the night before. Some days, I can taste the salt as it hits me, and feel it coating my skin. I like the texture and the way it transforms my limp, wavy hair into wild curls. It's taken me a long time to enjoy being in the countryside alone again, but now I can appreciate it once more.

I march past the campsite and follow a footpath along the cliff. Most of the coastline is open, but there are a few fences here and there. The spot where Phoebe fell is on the outskirts of the campsite grounds. To fall, she had to climb over the camp's boundary then walk over to the cliff.

There are the white lilies settled amidst red roses, yellow carnations, and a few teddy bears. I lean closer to read the cards. *Your smile lit up a room. You will be missed. You were perfect.* But I can't read on. Instead, I check the area. Unlike I suspected, there are no floodlights attached to the fences. It's possible Phoebe wanted to leave the site but had gone too far in the dark and stumbled close to the cliff.

But why would she leave via this route and not walk through the carpark? Why would she go for a walk in the middle of the night in a dangerous area? Maybe she did sleepwalk. Unless she was meeting someone. Or she was with someone. And if she was, that person is now lying. Either they saw her fall, or they pushed her.

Below the edge, choppy water breaks against jagged rocks. I picture myself lying like a broken doll on those rocks. Then I picture Phoebe. Finally, my mind rests on Maddie's lifeless figure beneath me. I gasp, realising how close I've come to the edge. The call of the void pulls deep here.

On my way into Penry, it surprises me how Phoebe's death already leaves me cold. I'm not sure whether it's the involvement of my own child or knowing for a fact that Phoebe wasn't always a pleasant young woman, but I've already disassociated in a way I couldn't when Riya went missing. Then again, I knew Riya. She came to our house, spent time with my daughter, and played with Gabe on the beach at the weekends.

I pull into the carpark next to the bank and get out, unsure why I'm here or where I'm going, knowing only that I can't go home. I thought about sending Susannah a text to see if she'd meet me for a one-to-one therapy session, but then I changed my mind. Instead, I walk aimlessly towards the pier.

"Zoe."

The sound of my name surprises me. I turn back, pulling windswept hair from my face. Parvati stands five feet away, her body held stiff and tall.

"Hi," I say, taking a few cautious steps towards her.

"You need to tell me where she is," Parvati says.

I shake my head. "Who?"

"My daughter." Her voice trembles.

"You know I don't know where Riya is. What are you—"

"Maddie," Parvati replies. "Maddie did this." The wind blows tears down her cheeks. She rubs them away angrily.

"No. She wouldn't—"

But before I can say more, Parvati runs away. She actually sprints, like a someone fleeing from an enemy. Even though I reach out as though to catch her, I'm pinned to the spot. I sense my mouth flapping open like a trout's.

"Are you all right?"

I retract my hand, quickly swipe a tear from my eye, and notice that the red-haired woman from group therapy is now standing next to me.

"Cecilia," she says. "I hope it's not too forward, but we met in group therapy. I... I was at the bank, and I saw you across the street. That looked... intense."

"Yeah." I lift my eyebrows. "I guess that's one way to put it." I watch people across the street as they make a hasty exit. It's obvious to me that people were staring. Perhaps they even overheard Parvati's accusations. *Great, more fodder for the Penry rumour mill.*

"Feel free to tell me to get lost, but I'm gasping for a cuppa, and I think you might be too. Fancy one?"

"Why not." I can think of many reasons not to join her, but getting inside, away from prying eyes, feels pretty good.

"Well, lead the way, missus," she says. "You're the local."

"Oh, hardly," I say. "I'm from up north."

"Thought I heard a touch of it in your accent."

I start walking, grateful for the change in subject. Then I steer her towards a tea shop on a side street between the bank and the pier. The bell above the door chimes cheerily, and we grab the last table in the window. We both order a tea and settle in.

"So," she says. "Do you want to talk about it? I know we don't know each other, but... Well, I can be a mate, if you want. I'm new, remember. I have no friends. I take what I can get." Her smile is warm, genuine, and chips away at a wall I didn't know I'd raised.

"That was my best friend," I say.

"Wow, some best friend, yelling at you in the street like that."

"It's not like that," I reply, wincing. "Her daughter went missing about three weeks ago. She's in pain."

"Oh, God. I feel terrible."

"Don't be silly. It's not your fault. She's lashing out. Our daughters were good friends and... Well, like I said, she's lashing out, trying to find someone to blame." I sigh. "God, what a day. I started it by visiting the place Phoebe Thompson died. And I stood there on the cliff edge and stared out into the distance. It was like invisible fingers, reaching for me." I shake my head. "Ugh, it sounds so stupid."

"No, I get it." Cecilia wraps her hands around the tea. "It's not stupid at all. But do you think... It couldn't be suicidal ideation?"

"No, nothing like that. More like the call of the void."

"Oh, like intrusive thoughts," she says. "I'm no therapist, but you're stressed. I bet it's making your brain do some weird shit right now." She reaches across the table and grabs my hand. I'm so taken aback that I just let her. "How's your daughter doing?" She lets go of me relatively quickly and sips her tea.

"She seems fine." I consider leaving the topic there, but I have an urge to get more off my chest. It's not like I can voice my concerns inside the house. Justin would worry, and Gabe is too young to understand. "She takes this kind of thing in her stride. She's not the most... emotional person. Which can be... frightening, I suppose, in a way. Other people jump to conclusions about her because of her background, and it's tough to see that happen, but I also understand it, and that's the..."

"The what?"

"The part I can't say."

"You can say." Cecilia nods, encouraging me to speak. "You're safe here."

"I don't know you," I blurt out. "Sorry, that was rude."

"No, you're right. I'm prying. It's my fault." She eyes the door of the tearoom, and I can tell I've hurt her feelings. "Maybe I should go."

"No, don't. This is nice. Since Riya went missing, I haven't had anyone to meet outside the house. I don't have a job in an office, and most of the mums at Maddie's school are in a clique, you know? They play badminton and go to karaoke."

Cecilia makes a face. "Damn. It's posh here."

"I'm not much one for badminton, to be honest."

"I get it," she says. "If it makes you feel any better, I'm having a hell of a time with my daughter too."

"Right," I say. "You mentioned in therapy."

She nods. "We're not speaking to each other right now. She moved out as soon as she hit eighteen and started living her own life. I don't blame her. Okay, I blame her a little. I was still bruised from my relationship with her father, you know? When she left, it felt like she was being selfish, and maybe that's unfair, but maybe teenagers *are* selfish, by definition. You know?"

"I can relate."

"I think you're holding something in, Zoe," she says. "It might feel better if you let it out."

I laugh. "It's that obvious, is it?"

"No. But we met in group therapy, remember?"

As I sip my tea, she waits patiently. Then it spills out of me. "Sometimes I agree with what people say about my daughter. I love her. I don't believe she's malicious, but she isn't like other people." I pause, gripping my mug, letting the heat burn my fingers. "I think she *is* a sociopath. But I don't believe she's the kind of sociopath you see in movies. She doesn't feel much emotion or have an attachment to people because of what happened to her when she was a child. Maddie's conscience needs to be trained and exercised like an athlete trains their body. And that frightens me, because what if, one day, she switches it off and stops using the conscience she's learned to use?" I let out a long breath. "I've been wanting to say that out loud for a while now."

"I don't think you have anything to feel guilty about," Cecilia says. "Putting your head in the sand wouldn't be useful either. You know who she is, and that must help, right?"

"In some ways," I admit.

"Are you afraid she pushed the girl?" Cecilia stares at me, no sign of judgement on her face, her expression as open as always. She bobs her head as though to encourage me to speak.

"No. No, that's too far for Maddie. I'm more concerned about her reaction to Phoebe's death and about her emotional attachments going forward."

Cecilia's eyes narrow. I get the impression she wants to say more, but then she sips her tea instead. At first, defensive hackles rise along the back of my neck, but I soon calm. I'm actually grateful for her bringing it up. Maybe I need to confront the darkest of my fears. If I don't, they'll fester, propagate, and consume me.

"You know her best," Cecilia says. "You should talk to her."

"Yeah, maybe you're right."

That ends our conversation about Maddie, and we move on to safer options—Cecilia's hopes and dreams of buying her own shop one day.

"We always came to the sea for holidays when I was a kid," she says. "And the gift shops were the best bit."

Soon after, our mugs are empty, and we get up to go. On my way out of the café, Cecilia taps me on the arm. "Sorry about what I said in there. It was rude. I have no filter, and it gets me in trouble."

I shake my head. "Don't worry about it. Thanks for being so kind today. I know I was rabbiting on about my problems when you have your own shit to deal with."

She lifts her eyebrows knowingly. "You'd be the first to know what a great fucking distraction it is to hear someone else complain for a while."

I laugh. "You're right."

"Do you fancy meeting again sometime? It's all yummy mummies around here. You're the first person I've met I can actually have a conversation with."

"Yeah, all right," I reply. "I'd like that."

We type our numbers into each other's phones and awkwardly say goodbye. I swear, making friends past the age of twenty-five never gets any easier.

For some reason, as I'm about to walk away, I stop. "I *am* scared she pushed that girl over the cliff. But a mother isn't supposed to think that, is she? So I must be a bad mother."

She shakes her head. "You're not a bad mother."

"Maddie can never know, though. And she never will, because I'd fight to the death for that girl."

"I'm sure you would," Cecilia says, slowly and fiercely.

I walk away. My chest feels lighter, but the nerves in my gut tingle. I've said the words out loud now. But admitting them isn't the worst part. The worst part is wondering if I'm right to be worried.

CHAPTER FIFTEEN
THEN

I woke up in a hospital bed with my parents sitting next to me. Mum's dry fingers squeezed mine and she let out a little gasp. Dad leapt to his feet and raised his hands, calling for a nurse. His voice sounded distorted in the thick fog of semi-consciousness. I blinked, the bright, flickering lights searing into my sore head. Then I stared down at my arms, noticing all the tubes for the first time. The room smelled like bleach and sickness.

"Oh, sweetheart! Everything's going to be all right now." Mum's cheeks were wet with tears, and her thin fingers gripped even harder until I winced.

"Where's Maddie?"

Her expression froze for a fraction of a second. Even in a drug-addled state, I noted the sense of disappointment on her face. She hadn't expected me to say that.

"You mean the child? A foster home, I suppose."

"What? How long have I been here?" I tried to push myself into a sitting position, but there was no strength in my arms.

"I don't know exactly. I'm so tired, I've barely slept." Her voice had a hard edge to it. "I didn't want to leave your side."

"Thanks, Mum." I squeezed her hand, and her face crumpled.

Dad stroked my hair as a nurse appeared to check on all the tubes sticking out of me. We all waited awkwardly, wanting to be alone again to speak. I sipped water and felt some of myself returning.

"Do you both know what happened?" I asked.

"We know some of it," Dad said. "While you were sleeping, the little girl talked to the police, and they went up to the farm." His expression darkened. "That was yesterday."

"So, I guess they found the body." I let out a long sigh. Did that mean the end? Was it over?

Mum started to cry. Dad wrapped an arm around her shoulder.

"To think this happened to our little girl," she said between sobs. "It's... You don't..."

"It's okay, Mum. I'm okay. I am okay, aren't I?"

"The doctor said you had pneumonia and an infection in the wound on your hand. You need to rest, now, until you're better," Dad said. His eyes crinkled. He reached out and stroked my cheek with the back of his finger.

Before we could chat any longer, there was a knock at the hospital room door. Two men popped their heads into the room. They wore plain clothes, but the cheap suits gave them away as police.

"Can we have a chat with Ms Osbourne?" The first man was tall and broad shouldered but moved with ease. Grey hairs peppered his dark hair and the pencil moustache above his full top lip. He walked in without asking for permission. "I'm DCI Cooper. This is DS Trent."

"Good morning," Trent said. He walked with a slight stoop, uncomfortable with his height in contrast to the way DCI Cooper owned it.

"I guess you're here to find out what happened at Ivycross."

"That's right," Cooper said. "And to find out how you are."

"I'm fine," I replied, aware of the tetchiness in my tone. "Let's get this over with. Is Maddie okay?"

He hovered by my feet. "She's absolutely fine. She's with temporary foster parents."

"I wanted to be with her when you questioned her. I promised her I'd make sure she's okay. Can I see her soon?"

"We'll have to run it by her appointed social worker, but we'll do everything we can," Cooper said.

"Okay." I steadied myself for the questions. Then I thought of my parents hearing my story, and it made my stomach flip over. How could I say what I needed to say in front of them? My dad didn't need to know how Peter McKenna had leaned into my ear to speak, his foul breath tickling the baby hairs along my neck. "I'm ready to answer questions. But I think my parents should go."

Mum's jaw dropped.

"It'll be easier," I said. "I can't give the police all the information they need if I'm worrying about how you guys will react."

"She's right, love," Dad said. "Let's give her some space. This is going to be hard."

My voice choked when I replied. "Thanks, Dad." I locked eyes with my mum. "Thank you."

She sniffed and walked away, holding her body in a stiff way that let me know she was still hurt.

"It's hard for them," Cooper said. "But harder for you, I'd imagine."

"Where do you want me to start?"

"From the beginning would be good," Cooper suggested, sitting down on the chair my dad had just vacated.

I went through it all in as much detail as possible, completely numb and emotionally detached, especially when it came to describing how I'd stabbed Peter in the neck.

"We've been to the crime scene," Cooper said. "There's a lot to process. But what I can tell you is that Peter McKenna has been living pretty much off the grid since his parents died. We don't know how many victims there might be yet. However, he kept trophies, which may help us with identification."

I scratched my arm, trying not to think about McKenna's bedroom. "The piles of clothes. The phones in the safe. I touched a lot of it. I had to search for a working phone."

A suffocating silence spread throughout the room. The realisation of what had happened landed on us in the same way dust gathered in an empty house.

"We'll need to search the rest of the farm. It's going to take time," Cooper said.

I figured he meant digging up the grounds, looking for human remains. "He must have kept some of them imprisoned for a long time," I said, more to myself.

"What makes you think that?" Cooper asked.

"Maddie. She didn't mention her mother. I guess she doesn't know her. I think Maddie's mother must be one of his victims. I think he kept her and impregnated her." Grimly, I wondered whether that might have been my eventual fate if Maddie hadn't helped me escape.

"That makes sense," Trent, who had been mostly quiet, added. "There were no photographs of a child in the property."

"Unless he kidnapped her," I blurted out.

"Let's not speculate," Cooper said. "It's going to take some time. Zoe, would you be willing to provide your DNA and fingerprints so that we can eliminate you from the crime scene?"

"Yes, whatever you need."

More poking and prodding. I'd never felt so relieved not to have been raped. Because if I had been, this process would have been even harder. I settled back on the bed, suddenly exhausted.

And then it hit me—if Maddie had been kidnapped, she might have parents out there searching for her. Or what if Maddie's mother was alive? If they could figure out who Maddie's mother was, then they could find an uncle, aunt, or grandparent. Then she'd be able to grow up with family. But was that the best course of action for Maddie? Selfishly, I thought about myself, too. Any relative of Maddie's could cut me out of her life forever. I couldn't bear the thought of that.

PETER MCKENNA'S body had been removed by the time I was released from hospital, but in my nightmares, it stalked the barn. I cowered in the animal stalls, listening to the dull thudding of his slow footsteps and the rasping of his lazy breathing. I sobbed and waited for that one good eye to find me in the dark, waiting for the moonlight to catch the grisly red hole of the adjacent empty socket.

Going home proved to be a transitional period for me, for many reasons. First of all, Simon, my soon-to-be ex-husband, visited with the divorce papers practically the moment I put the key in the door.

"How are you holding up?" he asked while pushing the document towards me with the pen.

I hadn't even offered him a coffee. I signed them, passed them back, and told him to lose my number. Honestly, he appeared relieved. And as he left, I watched the mousy-brown back of his head with complete disinterest. Simon had never been abusive, but he had some controlling tendencies he had no interest in working on, and whenever I noticed him manipulating me into wearing what he thought was best, making me worry about staying out too long, or discouraging me from veering too far from our home, he pretended like it never happened. Something about escaping from a serial killer had made me never want to deal with a man's shit ever again.

"Hey, Simon," I yelled from my downstairs window as he sat in his car, checking the signature.

He raised his head and rolled the window down, an annoyed expression on his face.

"You need therapy."

The annoyance morphed into puzzlement.

I shut the window, tugged the curtains closed, and laughed until I thought I might cry. What a childish and yet wholly satisfying thing to do. Still smiling, I plopped down on the sofa and put my feet up, taking in our beige décor. I'd already removed every wedding or holiday photo from the walls. This house wasn't my home anymore. He could have this place. I didn't want his memories as my memories anymore.

In the weeks that followed, I researched every rental property in the area, seeing as I didn't have a deposit saved up. I'd already mined the bank of Mum and Dad while buying the house in the first place. My boss called and tentatively suggested I come back part time for a while.

I could tell he wanted me back full time but didn't want to seem insensitive.

One of the small surprises I'd experienced during this time was the complete and utter lack of interest in my job. Before Peter McKenna had wrapped his meaty arm around my neck and choked me out, I'd been consumed by the prospect of receiving a promotion. Working in an HR department at a large accountancy firm wasn't exactly a vocation. I'd enjoyed it, though. And I'd hoped to take the next step up to assistant manager. Now I couldn't care less about the office. I didn't want to go at all. But part time was better than full time.

I changed my phone number to avoid reporters, but the barrage continued in my email inbox. When I left the house, I heard camera clicks, noticed strange cars on my street, and hoped they hadn't seen me yell at Simon through the window. There were days I didn't want to leave the house at all.

I wanted to talk to Maddie. I wanted to read stories to her. I wanted to make toast for her the way she had for me. I wanted to know she was safe, well, and loved, finally.

DCI Cooper called me into the police station for a "chat." I didn't like the sound of this chat. His deep voice, practised in neutrality, had an ominous ring over the phone. I wondered if he needed me to identify items from the farm. I'd seen enough blood for one lifetime, and I didn't need to see more.

He offered me a cup of tea and took me into an interview room. I decided to accept the tea, which was a good idea, considering the temperature in the room.

"How's the recovery going?" he asked.

I angled my hand to view the dressing over the wound. "It's fine. Minor face ache, fatigue, and no doubt a few scars, physical and not so physical."

"I can only imagine," he said.

I tapped the ceramic mug and sighed. "Okay, as much as I love a trip to the police station for small talk, I'm dying to know why I'm here."

"I wanted to update you about the case. There are a few things you should know."

"Okay."

He threaded his fingers together, resting his hands on the table between us. "McKenna's body was released, and his cremation is scheduled."

The words sent electricity shuddering through me. "Right. Okay."

"We tested Maddie's DNA. She's definitely Peter McKenna's daughter."

"So she wasn't abducted?"

"No. She's been appointed social workers and psychologists who are helping her talk about what life was like living with her father. You weren't the first woman she brought back to the farm."

"No, I figured that."

"He drove out to other remote areas, often in different counties, and used Maddie to lure away vulnerable women. Drug addicts, prostitutes, and so on."

"She told you that?"

"In her own way," he said. "As a child would put it. Plus, we've been matching up the items left at the farm with missing persons reports. It's going to be a long process because some of these women probably didn't have many people out there searching for them. Aside from you and another missing local woman, he was cautious about who he targeted."

"Do you know how many are dead?"

"No, we're still figuring it out."

"Have you found any bodies yet?"

"Yes," he said. "There's a paddock behind the farmhouse. He buried most of the bodies there."

It was like a punch to the gut. Under different circumstances, I'd be with them, beneath the dirt. I sniffed back tears.

"Don't forget Maddie helped me escape," I said. "She didn't want to lure any of those women away."

Cooper made a tight *mmhmm* noise. "She's a child who was

manipulated by a monster. But she did help him murder people *before* you, Zoe."

"So?"

"That has to affect a child's developing brain. Their sense of right and wrong."

"She had to wait until she learned the best way to help his victims. She'd already tried with some of the others, but they were too panicked, or they didn't have the strength to fight."

"I understand all of that," he said. "But Maddie is going to need specialised care."

"Is she getting that right now?"

"Yes. She's actually staying in a residential home specialised for dealing with children with behavioural problems."

"Can I visit her?"

"Let me get you the contact details for Maddie's social worker. Hold on."

I grabbed a pen and scribbled down the name and number of Maddie's social worker.

"Look, DCI Cooper, I know I didn't spend much time with Maddie, but in the time I did spend with her, she saved my life more than once. I don't know the law that well, but I know juvenile detention centres exist, and I don't want Maddie thrown in one. She has a kind heart. I don't know where it came from, obviously not her father, but she was either born with that emotional intelligence, or she learned it from someone else. Maybe her mother or TV, I don't know. So just... don't throw her away."

"I have absolutely no intention of doing that," he replied.

I wanted to believe him.

CHAPTER SIXTEEN
NOW

Justin places the local newspaper on my lap as I'm watching TV. He taps the page, and as I follow the placement of his finger, I tense.

"It's the funeral on Saturday," he says.

Phoebe's pretty face beams, perfect teeth peeking out from her mouth. The black-and-white print makes her timeless, like a fossil in amber. Her notice takes up almost a quarter of the page. Below her photograph, the box is filled with facts about Phoebe. She was the school hockey team captain, a member of the Penry drama company, and about to apply to Cambridge. She loved horses, K-pop, and all of her friends.

Justin leans back against the sofa and places an elbow on the back cushion. I sense what he's about to say simply by staring into those wide, plaintive eyes.

"We can't go," I say, aghast. "Not considering what they're saying about Maddie. We can't. Those people *hate* us. They think our daughter killed that girl." I find myself tapping beautiful Phoebe Thompson right on the nose.

He shakes his head. "We have to."

But I disagree, and we spend an evening at odds with each other, silently watching reality TV as Gabe sleeps and Maddie finishes her homework.

The next morning, I drag myself out of bed for a walk along the coast, desperate to clear my head. Seagulls squawk above me, and it's less peaceful than I'd pictured in my mind. Reluctantly, I head home to feed the kids before school.

"Why don't I take them today?" Justin says. "That way you can chill or go back to bed."

"Are you sure?"

He nods then kisses me on the forehead. "You've been wound tight these last few days. Take some time to yourself."

"Thanks. I really appreciate it. Sorry about last night."

He ruffles my hair. "A rare Zoe Osborne apology. Do I receive a plaque for this momentous occasion?"

"Don't push it."

I can tell he's about to say more, but Gabe comes bounding in before Justin opens his mouth. Justin grabs him by the arms and lifts him. "Morning, spaceman. Ready for school?" He turns his attention to me. "Where's Mads?"

"I don't want to go." Maddie stands by the kitchen door. She has her game face on: narrowed eyes, protruding bottom lip, arms folded tightly across her chest.

"Why not?" I ask.

"I just don't."

"You have to go to school," Justin says. "It's not optional."

"Are you having problems with the other students?" I ask. "Is it about Phoebe?"

She glares at the cliffs through the window, watching the waves crash on the beach below.

"Maddie, you have to talk to us. Come on, hun." I walk over to her and try to put my arm around her, but she pushes me—and not gently. I stagger back, almost tripping into a chair. "Maddie!"

Justin strides over, Gabe no longer in his arms, and grabs Maddie by the shoulder. "You don't do that to your mother. Say sorry. Now!"

"Justin, don't." I try to pry him away from her. From the tension in his arm, I can tell he's gripping her too hard. "I said stop!"

My heart pounds. Justin drops his hand. Maddie stares at him, her expression hardening into stone. I've seen her angry before, but I haven't seen it directed at Justin for many years. I thought we were past this, but apparently not.

"Get in the car," Justin snaps.

Silently, she grabs her school bag from the back of a dining chair and storms out.

Seeing as I have the day to myself, I decide to text Cecilia and ask her if she wants to go for a walk around Penry. While the weather isn't quite as glorious as it has been, we can still enjoy the tiny cafés and pubs near the beach. Maybe grab some ice cream and watch the surfers. Though it hits me that I don't know what she does for a living. She could be at work for all I know.

She replies straight away, and we meet in a café by the beach at ten. Cecilia suggests we grab coffees to go and walk around the bay to one of the viewing areas pointing out to sea. And on the way up to the benches, I start to learn a bit more about her. She grew up in the midlands and has floated in and out of mid-level management jobs for a while now.

"My last job was at a travel agent," she says. "I managed the office. But then they closed down. And I figured, if I'm going to be unemployed, it may as well be somewhere scenic. I had a bit of money saved up, so I took the plunge and came here."

"Wow. That's brave. So what are you going to do if you don't find a job?"

"I will." She lifts her eyebrows. "I'm very persuasive. But money is going to be tough for a while."

"How did your daughter react to you moving?"

Cecilia sips her coffee and lets out a humourless laugh. "She didn't. She's eighteen. She's at uni now, studying English lit at Warwick."

We settle on the benches and stare out at the Celtic Sea. Cecilia promptly changes the subject.

"I read your book," she says. "I thought you looked familiar, and then Susannah told me who you were. Bloody hell, Zoe. What a life you've lived!"

I shake my head. "I guess when you're in it, everything seems sort of normal."

"I completely understand what you were saying about your daughter now. I get it. You must worry about what she inherited from her father." She straightens her sunglasses and whips a fly-away lock of hair from her face. Cecilia gives off a carefully composed veneer that a lot of the mums around Penry share. Manicured nails, big sunglasses, and a nice bag. She's so open and down-to-earth in her mannerisms, though, that it's not as noticeable.

"I do," I admit. "But I also know that we're providing a loving home for her. Plus, she's been going to therapy since she was five years old."

"And what you said, about the girl who died." This time, she removes her glasses completely and meets my gaze. Her voice softens. "How does that fit in?"

"If she did it," I say carefully, "then I'll support her as best I can. I don't quite know what that means, but I know I'd do anything for her. But... I don't know. It would be out of character for her. Yes, she's had her problems, but she understands right and wrong. Phoebe Thompson, the girl who died, was not kind to Maddie, but it's never bothered Maddie before." I let out a long shuddering breath. "Why would the party trigger this sudden urge to do violence?"

Cecilia lips grow into a pretty but knowing smile, and I frown, confused.

"You're a good mother," she explains.

A puff of air whistles through my teeth. "Hardly. A good mother would never suspect her child of murder."

"That's not true. If you remained blind to exactly who she is, then you'd be doing her and yourself a disservice. What's the point in blind faith? What does it achieve? You can't help her if you don't know her."

"But how am I going to find out if she did it? How can I even broach it? I can't admit to *her* that I think there's a slim chance she's a murderer. If I did that, I'd lose her."

"I don't know." Cecilia leans back against the bench. "I just don't know."

I HATE TO ADMIT IT, but Justin wins the argument. He points out that if we don't go, DS Rosen might find that suspicious. In the end, we agree to a compromise—Justin and I attend the funeral, but Maddie stays at home babysitting Gabe.

"Do you think that's okay?" Justin asks, his voice low so that the kids don't hear. We're putting the clean dishes away after dinner. They're arguing over the Xbox controller in the living room.

"What do you mean?"

"Leaving Maddie with Gabe."

I pull my eyebrows together, confused as to why that would be an issue. "She's babysat for us loads of times."

"Yes, but..." He grimaces. "That was before."

I dump a pile of clean forks into the drawer. "Before what? Before Phoebe Thompson died?" I avoid his gaze. Admitting Maddie might be a murderer to someone who's basically a stranger is one thing, but to my husband is another. With Justin, my worries will be formed and complete. I'm not ready for that. "You don't think she'd hurt Gabe?"

He doesn't answer.

Now I'm annoyed. Yes, I have my worries, but not when it comes to Gabe. *No, she couldn't. She wouldn't...*

"She'll be fine," I snap, slamming the drawer shut and walking away.

ON OUR WAY out the next morning, Gabe throws my car keys on the kitchen tiles and screams. "I don't want to stay here! I want to go with you!"

But luckily, Justin has a great trick for ending a tantrum before it begins. He grabs Gabe under his arms and spins him around until Gabe snorts with laughter.

"Oh my God, Dad, I'm too old for this," he says, pink-cheeked and grinning.

"Mads." Justin beckons her over. "Let him watch cartoons, okay? And don't leave the house. We'll be back after lunch." His hands flex and release by his sides. "Your mum and I have agreed that you're to stay here today. No going into the village or down to the beach. Okay?"

"Yes, sir." A sardonic smile plays on Maddie's lips.

"I'm serious," Justin reiterates.

I can't stop staring at my husband, who is so uncharacteristically tense. But the funeral is affecting us all in different ways.

"I've left sandwiches in the fridge if you get hungry," I say. "There's plenty of chocolate milk and some snacks in the cupboards."

"Mum, we'll be fine. Just go," Maddie says.

I spontaneously pull her into a huge hug, one that she doesn't reciprocate. "I love you both." I plant a kiss on Gabe's forehead.

"Are you going to cry?" Maddie stares at me with a neutral expression on her face. She's even more closed off than normal today.

"Maybe," I say. "It's a sad day today. And I'm thinking about how much you both mean to me. I know, I'm a soppy mummy, but sometimes things like this put everything in perspective."

Justin drapes his arm over my shoulder, squeezing me tight, our disagreement momentarily forgotten. We leave our kids in the house alone, ready to go somewhere else and witness the burial of a different child. I drag my heavy limbs into the car, already tired even at the thought of it.

"Do you think Maddie will be okay?" Justin presses the ignition switch, and the car comes to life.

"I don't know. I think Phoebe's death is affecting her, but she's trying to hide it."

"I meant with Gabe," Justin says. "Do you think they'll be all right? Maddie will listen to us, right?"

I sigh. "Yes, I think she'll take care of her brother. Let's not argue about this again. We can't lose faith in her, can we? She's our *child*."

"Fine," he says. "I just... I guess I see her at school, whereas you don't. She's not always nice to people, and you're not the one witnessing that."

"I don't need to see her behaviour at school to know she always looks out for her brother." My tone is sharper than I intended it to be, and it results in an awkward drive to the church.

Despite the tension, Justin still holds my hand as we make our way to the back of the congregation. His fingers tighten and release. When I meet his eyes, I find mine awash with warm tears. We know this moment is bigger than our argument.

I don't want to attract much attention, so I keep my head down as the service begins. The coffin enters, and silence settles. My palms begin to sweat.

Connie and Malcolm Thompson sit on the front row, wiping away tears. The Thompsons' friends and family crowd around them, quietly weeping. Behind them, I notice teenagers sitting with heads bowed next to their parents. The service continues with the drone of the priest, the sniffs and whimpers coming from a devastated congregation. Funerals are always sombre, but here, the weight of loss hangs heavily, all the way up to the rafters. When Malcolm stands to read a eulogy, I hear Connie sobbing, then my own tears begin to fall.

But it's over quickly, and soon, people begin to filter out. I avoid seeing the Thompsons as they walk past us, but I do notice a few other mums I know. I also can't look Ellie's mum in the eye knowing what Maddie dared her daughter to do. But Maddie's headteacher, Mr Browning, smiles a hello. A few others, including Parvati, visibly direct their faces away. We're persona non grata to half the people here. My blood runs cold when I see DS Rosen and his partner heading out of the church.

"We should go home," I whisper.

"We're not going to the cemetery?"

"No, we're not welcome here."

We leave last, scuttling away like two unwanted cockroaches. I feel like the lowest of the low. I came to the funeral even though my daughter might somehow be responsible. I came for myself, not for them. The thought makes me feel sick.

CHAPTER SEVENTEEN
THEN

Sade, Maddie's social worker, visited the house while I was in the middle of packing boxes. We cleared a space on the kitchen table, and I made us each a cup of tea. I rustled up some stale biscuits from the back of a cupboard, and she politely declined. She placed her slouchy leather bag on the back of my chair and arranged a wide hoop earring that had caught in her curls.

"How's Maddie doing?" I'd opened a box to grab a mug, and unfortunately, all I had to hand were the llama-shaped mugs Simon hated. They were uncomfortable to use and super kitsch, with rainbows for eyebrows.

Sade thanked me for the tea and said nothing about the mug. "Honestly, it's been a tough transition for her. We can only imagine what her life has been like to this point." Idly, she traced the rainbow eyebrow on the mug. I saw the way talking about Maddie affected her. It gave me hope that she cared and that she'd remain honest with me. "As you know, her father never registered Maddie's birth, and she was kept isolated on the farm. She's never been around any other children before. And for that reason, the staff are mostly keeping her separated from them right now. They'll slowly introduce her to the other kids. It's like getting a second cat and monitoring them together." She smiled. "We've observed that her behaviour can become aggressive quite quickly. She has temper tantrums when she doesn't get her way, and sometimes she withdraws into herself and refuses to speak for long stretches of time."

I suppressed a shiver, sitting down deep in my chair. The way she described the place, it sounded more like a punishment, though I understood why they were cautious with Maddie. "That doesn't sound good. Are you sure this place is suitable for her?"

"She needs structure right now, and she'll get that where she is. Consistency and structure. The staff are excellent." Sade flashed me a reassuring smile, her skin creasing slightly around the eyes. I realised then that she was older than I'd originally assumed because her bright yellow-and-blue floral dress, red lipstick and lush curls hid her age. But then I saw the emerging grey roots contrasting with her dark hair. She had to be in her mid to late forties. "I see you connected deeply during your time together. Maddie asks about you too."

"She does?"

Sade lets out a quiet laugh. "It usually involves a tantrum. She demands to see you."

I shook my head. "I promised her I'd make sure she was okay."

"And you did."

"No, I promised her I'd be there. But it's been weeks, and I'm only now going to visit her."

Sade sighed and tapped the handle of her mug. "Yes, about that..."

"I am going to see her, right?"

"Yes, but I think it's best if we keep the visit supervised. I'll stay with you at all times."

I let out a relieved breath. "That's fine. That's sensible."

"I'm glad you're okay with that. You never quite know how people are going to react to being told what to do," she said. "Can I ask you about your time with Maddie?"

"Sure."

"Did she tell you much about her childhood?"

"No," I said. "I guess some of the things she said gave me some insight. Like how she'd tried to help other victims or the fact she knew her way around the kitchen. I think she was accustomed to fending for herself."

"We've made some observations similar to yours," Sade explained. "She's very capable, but she hasn't been taught to read or write properly. Her understanding of right and wrong is, as you can imagine, complex. But she's fully potty trained, and her speech is fantastic. Someone has spent time with her and done the basics at least."

"Her father, you think? I know he was a monster, but if he needed her as bait, then I suppose he took care of her."

"It's possible," Sade replied. "But something about the way she talks about him makes me wonder if there was someone else present."

"You think so? I got the impression she never knew her mother. But I suppose there's no way to know how long they spent together. Maybe she doesn't remember those years very clearly."

"Maddie never ever mentions her mother," Sade said. "I can't tell if it's as you say—she can't remember her—or if she doesn't feel comfortable talking about her yet."

SADE DROVE me to a pleasant house set behind a large gate that reminded me of the kind of posh private school my family could never afford. Tall grey walls clad with creeping ivy. Thick stone lintels beneath every window. I half-expected the cast of St Trinian's to come running out of the front door.

Things changed once we ventured inside. We had to show our visitor passes at the door and enter a secure area accessed by a staff swipe card. As we walked along a white corridor to a break room, I wondered how Maddie would react to seeing me again. Would she be happy to see me? Did she think I'd abandoned her at the hospital? I braced myself for a difficult encounter.

"Nervous?" Sade asked, pulling a seat out from a small table.

"Yeah. Stupid, isn't it?"

"Not at all. I'd be surprised if you weren't."

Someone had prepared the child-sized table by laying out a stack of white paper and two packs of crayons. I idly nudged the papers with my fingertips as we waited. Then I heard the sound of footsteps, both adult and child, and one of the staff members led Maddie in by the hand.

"Morning, ladies," said the staff member. I clocked the name tag—Jess. "I hear you've come to see someone special."

Sade and I stood so we could make a fuss of Maddie's arrival into the room. She stepped in with her head low and her dark hair pulled forward. Once she let go of Jess's hand, she folded her arms across her narrow chest.

"Hi, Maddie," I said. "Goodness, you've grown already."

Maddie lifted her face to glower at me, her beady eyes hard and dark as marbles.

"Are you mad at me?" I asked.

Jess cleared her throat and guided Maddie to the small chair next to the table. "Come on, love. Let's get you settled. Do you want to draw?"

But a fuming, visibly trembling Maddie swiped her arm across the table, knocking all the crayons and papers to the floor.

"Now, that wasn't very nice, was it?" Jess said.

"Maddie, do you want me to leave?" I asked. I bent down low, next to her.

She squirmed away, directing her chin back towards the door.

"Are you okay?" I asked again.

She shrugged.

"I've missed you," I said, leaning slightly closer.

Her gaze drifted towards me for a fraction of a second, revealing the tiniest glint of interest. But then she went back to pretending otherwise.

"I've been in the hospital," I said. "Don't you want to know if I'm okay?"

She shook her head vehemently.

"You don't care?"

More head shaking.

I reached down to the sick-green carpet and gathered up some of the papers and crayons. Then I sat down on the small chair and idly began to doodle while humming. "What shall I draw? Cat or dog?"

She stared at the paper, biting her lip. Then she blurted out, "Rabbit."

"All right." I wasn't an artist, but somehow that made the situation better. When Maddie began to laugh at my terrible rabbit sketch—and truthfully, it ended up more alien than bunny—the atmosphere finally changed. "It's good to see you smiling."

She took her hand and literally wiped the smile from her face. A childlike cartoonish scowl replaced it. Only this time, there was a hint of humour in it.

"Daddy once drew a bunny," Maddie said.

I noticed Sade's shuffle in her seat, immediately interested.

"Did he?" I asked.

She picked up a crayon and nodded.

"Did he teach you to draw?"

"Sometimes."

An emotion washed over me—one I didn't think had a name. Relief and horror in equal measure. Relief that her serial killer father had at least shown her kindness, and horror that she'd had to live with him at all. Sade and Jess both remained silent as Maddie scribbled on paper.

"But mostly, he was busy," Maddie said. "He had all his things to look at."

This time, pure horror hit me like a bucket of ice.

"What do you mean?"

"The things in his room. Their things."

Sade shuffled in her seat, and I noticed the way her fingers tightened against the table. I was sure I was as white as a sheet. Maddie was talking about her father spending time with the belongings he'd stolen from his victims. I supposed he liked to hold them in between kills to satiate his appetite. Every time I thought I'd become desensitised to what Peter McKenna had done, a new detail would floor me.

I wasn't sure whether to keep Maddie talking about her father or try to move on to happier things. In the end, I stayed quiet for a while and decided to let her lead.

"But I had to be good," she said.

"To get your picture?" I asked.

"Yes. Or a treat."

"What kind of treats did you get?"

"Strawberry."

"Oh, that's nice. Do you like strawberries?"

She nodded.

"Maybe she could have some here?" I asked Jess.

"We'll get some," Jess said. "Or you could bring some next time you visit."

Maddie's head snapped up. She'd detected the "next time," but she didn't say anything.

"Would you like it if I visited again?"

Maddie blushed then nodded again.

To my surprise, my throat thickened with emotion. The affection I felt for this child swelled inside me, exactly how I imagined love for my own child might bloom.

For another hour, I drew pictures for her, and she told me about life at Marigold House. There was another girl called Olivia, whom she didn't like at all. Apparently, Olivia stole her pudding once. Sade later told me that Maddie had hit Olivia right in the face without hesitation. Maddie certainly had some anger issues to deal with.

Sade glanced at her watch, and I realised my time with Maddie was coming to an end. So I reached across the table and took her hand. "Maddie, before I go today, I want to thank you for saving my life."

Maddie started to cry then. She stared up at me desperately, a high-pitched wail coming from her tiny body. I stood up, gathered her in my arms, and held her to me, crying with her.

She tried to speak, but it was difficult to understand her amidst the tears. I thought she asked me to take her with me.

"I'll be back soon, sweetheart." I placed her back on the chair, but Maddie latched herself to my leg.

"Come on now." Jess reached down and tried to pry her away, but Maddie gripped on, her fingernails pressing into my calf muscle.

"No!" Maddie screamed. "No!"

By now, there were tears streaming down my face. Sade and Jess both had to pry Maddie from me, and Jess carried her out of the room. I practically collapsed onto my chair then put my head in my hands.

Sade gave my shoulder a quick rub. "I know it's hard. She's been through a lot, and her behaviour is going to be tricky for a while. Believe it or not, I think you coming here was a good thing. I think the goodbyes will get easier."

I lifted my head and leaned back. "For her or me?"

She laughed. "Both of you. She really opened up to you today. You have a bond."

"We went through hell together," I said.

"Yes," Sade said. "You have a shared experience that only the two of you understand. I think she'll open up to you about her father and her life on that farm."

"Is here the right place for her?"

"I think so," Sade said. "She'll learn there are consequences to her actions. Her view of right and wrong is skewed at the moment. She leans towards violence in certain situations."

I sighed. "That's not surprising."

"No," Sade said. "No, it's not."

DURING MY NEXT visit a week later, Maddie showed me around her room. We ate strawberries and cream as she told me all about how she was learning to read. I promised to bring her books the week after. At the end of my visit, she threw herself on the ground and started to bash her head against the carpet. I watched in shock as Jess and another staff member restrained her and took her away.

On the drive home, Sade turned on the radio to drown out the silence. I wanted nothing more than to save that child from that place. I couldn't stop thinking about it.

In between meetings at work, I found myself daydreaming about my next visit to Marigold House. I nipped into the city centre at lunchtime and bought her all my favourite children's books: *The Very Hungry Caterpillar*, *The Tale of Peter the Rabbit*, and *Peter Pan*. I picked out comfy clothes for her, even though the home had already provided some for her.

When I next visited my parents, Mum asked if I was still seeing "the child." She couldn't bring herself to say Maddie's name. She saw her as Peter McKenna's spawn, and that was it. And she made her feelings about it very clear: she thought I was crazy, not solely because of who Maddie's father was, but also because in her mind, every time I saw Maddie, I dredged up the past. To my mum, the way to deal with trauma was to never talk about it again. Dad was quieter, but I sensed he had a similar attitude. That was how their generation dealt with the messy, difficult, and painful things—by putting them in a box and hoping the box never opened again.

But the fact I understood how they felt didn't make it any easier, and as time went on, a chasm opened. I stood on one side, my parents stood on the other. Weeks went by, and I continued to see Maddie even though they disapproved. I took her gifts; she told me about the other children and her favourite members of staff. She carried around a stuffed bunny toy and drew me pictures that I stuck on my fridge.

Even after I rented a house closer to my parents, even when I saw them weekly, and I tried to put into words exactly what Maddie meant to me, they were resistant.

One exasperated day, I said to Mum, "Why don't you come with me to visit?"

"Why would I do that?" she asked, standing in front of a chopping board covered in carrots.

"Because she's part of my life," I said.

"Oh, and for how long?"

Dad walked in, saw the tense expressions on our faces, and walked back out again, muttering about his newspaper. The fact he was so unwilling to step in had started to annoy me.

"Forever, Mum. She's going to be in my life forever."

She dropped her knife onto the chopping board. "Don't be so ridiculous. What are you talking about?"

And it was at that moment I said the words out loud. I'd been thinking about it for some time, but I'd never truly admitted it to myself before. "I'm going to look into ways to foster Maddie. Maybe eventually adopt her."

The blood drained from my mother's face. "You can't."

"Why not? I've always wanted children, but it was never going to happen with Simon. All the staff at Marigold House talk about the special bond I have with Maddie. No one else understands what it was like at that farm."

Mum sighed. "Oh, would you move on, Zoe. It's been two months, and you don't talk about anything else—"

She carried on, but I didn't hear her. I walked straight out of the house. I got in my car, and I drove away, while Mum stood in the kitchen window, her mouth wide open in shock.

Later that day, Dad called to try to smooth things over, but Mum had crossed a line she could never take back. She was bored of my problems. There was a time limit on me talking about almost dying at the hands of a sadistic killer. But she didn't get to dictate how and when I healed.

"I'm sorry, love," he said. "I know she said some hurtful things, but she's sorry."

I pursed my lips because she wasn't sorry enough to call me.

"You should know I don't completely disagree with your mum," he continued. "About the child, I mean. It does seem like a... a risky venture. Are you absolutely sure you want to be connected to that girl for the rest of your life?" He sighed. "Zoe, I know you've been through a lot, but adopting a child is a huge decision. Especially right now."

"I've thought it through," I said. "Believe me, I've thought of every possible outcome, including her murdering me in my sleep. She's five years old, Dad. I have to believe that a five-year-old has a future no matter what they've been through."

He sighed. "And you're sure then?"

"I'm not going to change my mind, Dad. Knowing Maddie is the one good thing that came out of what happened to me. I have night-mares every night. I can't concentrate on my job anymore. Going to see Maddie every week is the only thing keeping me going."

"Oh, Zo," he said. "I'm so sorry. I hope she brings you a lot of joy, I really do. And... I can't speak for your mother, but I know I'll always be there for you, no matter what. But just think about this, okay? What if this feeling you have towards Maddie is temporary? What if taking care of her becomes too much for you? Because she's a damaged child, and damaged children are unpredictable. They have the kind of prob-lems it takes an extraordinary person to handle."

"I know all of that, Dad." My voice sounded quiet and shaky even to my own ears. "I can do this."

I wanted to believe it. More than anything, I wanted to believe I could do it.

CHAPTER EIGHTEEN
NOW

We return from the funeral to an empty house. No arguing over games consoles comes from the living room. No noisy cartoons or Mario Kart music. My heart leaps up into my throat because we told them not to go out, and now they aren't here. I dash through to Maddie's room. Then Gabe's. I slide the patio doors open and hurry out into the garden with Justin following me.

"We told her not to leave the house!" Justin's skin grows tomato red. He rubs the bridge of his nose.

"Maybe they're in the back yard," I suggest, though already knowing we would have seen them through one of the windows.

We check the perimeter of the house, the front and back, including the garage. I call Maddie's phone, and there's no answer.

"Call one of her friends," Justin says, snatching his car keys from the kitchen table.

"She doesn't have any," I reply, the realisation hitting hard.

"Jesus. Where've they gone? What the *fuck* are they doing?"

"Maybe she took him into Penry? Or down to the beach?"

"You take the car into Penry," he says, "and I'll head down to the beach."

"All right." I pluck my keys from the bowl, concerned with the way Justin's eyes are wide and bulging. I've never seen him have this kind of reaction before. Yes, he gets stressed at times, but it's usually him calming me down. I'm worried, too, but even though my heart races, I know deep down Maddie probably just succumbed to Gabe's whinging and took him for ice cream. Justin believes she's a threat to Gabe.

Am I kidding myself? Is my daughter capable of hurting her brother? I think back to Cecilia's words as we sat together, gazing out at the sea. Blinding myself to who Maddie is doesn't help her or me. *Am I doing that now?*

We split up, me in the Volvo and Justin in his Mercedes. As I put the car into gear, I have to fight the tiredness creeping up through my body. The last few days have taken a toll.

I drive along the cliff road, heading towards the town. Holiday-makers in floppy hats and beach cover-ups shoulder their tote bags filled with towels. Driving these roads always requires extra concentration. People lose their inhibitions during holiday season. They wander from the footpath and scuttle across the road in flip-flops, dangerously close to tripping in front of my car. By the time I reach the row of cafés and trinket shops, my heart is in my mouth.

The silence breaks with the cheery squawk of my ringtone. I pull over outside a fish-and-chip shop to answer.

"I've got them," Justin says. "They were on the beach."

"Okay. I'm coming home. Everything all right?"

His voice tightens when he answers, "Yeah," before hanging up.

I'm baffled again. I've never seen him so furious. Perhaps Phoebe Thompson's death has rattled him more than he's letting on. I know I have my own complex feelings about it. I drive away from the shop, heading through a pedestrian crossing back towards the house.

Susannah would tell me to sit down and talk to him. Communication is always the answer. But when it comes to talking to each other... we avoid it. Maybe we don't want to admit our vulnerabilities, or maybe we can't. I know something keeps me blocked most of the time.

My fingers tremble against the steering wheel as I pull into our garage. By the time I'm through the garage door and into the house, I can hear raised voices and crying. I speed up, feet skipping across the hallway.

"If you're going to live in this house, you're going to do what I say. You're going to behave yourself. Is that clear?"

"Then maybe I'll move out."

I find my daughter sitting on the living room sofa, staring up at Justin, her expression sharpened by fury. Justin leans over her, his face still flushed and angry. Gabe is crying in the armchair, a large plaster on his thumb. I'm not sure which to deal with first.

"Someone tell me what's going on," I say, heading to Gabe first. "What happened, sweetie?"

"They were in the rock pools," Justin says before anyone else has time to speak. "Gabe fell and sliced his thumb. *Anything* could've happened. What if a strong tide came in, and you lost your footing? It's dangerous down there. I *told* you to stay in the house."

"Are you okay, sweetie?" I ask Gabe, kissing his thumb.

He nods.

"He's fine," Maddie snaps. "He wanted to go. He complained all morning because he wanted to go to the rock pools. He was fucking bored. I can babysit my kid brother, for God's sake."

"Don't you dare use that language." I didn't think Justin's skin could develop a deeper shade vermillion, but it does.

I step between the two of them. "All right, that's enough. I know everyone's stressed, and some mistakes have been made, but let's stop, shall we? We're okay. No one got washed away by the tide or eaten by a bloody shark. We survived. So let's be happy, okay? Let's just be happy that we're all here as a family."

Justin walks away, his shoulders slumped. "Whatever, Zo."

Maddie smirks.

"Don't smirk at me," I snap. "What do you think you're playing at? We said not to leave."

"He wanted to—"

"I don't care. He's a kid. You're sixteen. You should know what's right and what's wrong." My skin tingles all over as I say those words. I hadn't meant to, and now I can't stop thinking about the warm parenting I'm supposed to show Maddie. I'm too angry for that right now.

"Fine," she says, directing her head away.

"I'm going to go speak to your dad. Wait here."

"He's not my dad," Maddie whispers. "My dad is dead."

I stand there in the middle of the room, staring at her, noticing the depth of earth-brown in her irises that are exactly like Peter's. There's a weight behind her muscular frame that strikes me as like him too, as well as in the breadth of her shoulders. I want to blink it away.

"Okay," I say softly. "I'm going to talk to Justin."

"You'll take his side, won't you?"

"I'm not taking anyone's side."

"Yeah, right."

"Maddie, I'm *always* on the side of my children."

She glances at Gabe. "But how many children do you have?"

"Two. I have two children. You know that."

I hesitate, waiting for her to react, but she doesn't. And when I can't think of another word to say, I walk through to the bedroom to where Justin is standing at the window, his arms crossed tightly.

"I've talked to Maddie and told her what she did was wrong."

"Wow, great punishment. You really pushed the boat out. She put *our son* in danger, but you gave her a good talking-to, so everything's good."

"What the hell is going on?" I ask. "This isn't you. I don't understand it. You can't speak to her like that. You know that."

"You're wrong," he says. "You need to toughen up, because you're letting her get away with whatever she wants, and that has consequences. You know who she is and *where* she came from. And you're giving her too much freedom. Enough freedom so she can go around pushing people off..." He hesitates. "Off of rock pools."

"Gabe told you she pushed him?"

"Not in so many words," he says.

"Tell me the exact words." I slump down on the bed, exhausted. Maddie and Gabe had a tentative relationship in the beginning. And, yes, when he was a baby, I worried, in the same way I worried about Maddie around animals when she was a child. But she grew out of that behaviour. Now they're like a normal brother and sister. I've never, not once, caught her trying to hurt him.

"He said Maddie was right next to him when he slipped."

"If he slipped, she didn't push him," I say, becoming more and more frustrated with my husband.

Justin drops onto the bed next to me. "Don't dismiss this, Zoe. Gabe came back from the beach shaken up and not his usual self. You saw how upset he was. And even if Maddie didn't push him, she was standing right next to him. Couldn't she have caught him?" His face softens. He reaches out and touches my hand. "I didn't mean to get so worked up. I guess the funeral hit me harder than I thought it would."

"I know." I sigh. "I get it. But... I don't know. I think it's easy to say she should've caught him when we weren't there to see what happened. Perhaps it all happened too fast. She's a young girl, Justin. She's not superhuman."

He shrugs. "Well, by the time I found them, Gabe was crying his eyes out and had blood all over his hand. It was horrible, Zo. I walked them both to the car, and Maddie was so *disconnected* and unmoved by his tears, like she was out for a walk. I know... I know I've been a dick today, okay? But I'm seeing Maddie in a whole new light since..." He shakes his head. He means since Phoebe Thompson died, but he won't say it. "And then she seemed so nonchalant about her brother, and I saw red."

I pull him into a hug. "I think maybe Maddie needs an extra session of therapy a week. I hear what you're saying. I have my worries too."

He nods. "That's a start. And to be honest, I don't think Maddie should babysit until we feel more confident in her behaviour."

"I agree."

I consider telling him my fears, but I swallow them down. I don't want to argue anymore. I want to peel the funeral clothes from my body and crawl into bed. And I want to eradicate the mental image of Peter McKenna's face staring back at me from my daughter.

CHAPTER NINETEEN
THEN

I watched DCI Cooper's thin moustache bob up and down as he spoke. He'd placed photographs down on my dining room table. Photographs of women.

"I thought you might want to see them. And I didn't want the first time you saw them to be in a newspaper."

He was right, but I couldn't open my mouth to say it because my throat felt clogged. My gaze travelled over the faces of the six women in front of me. Aside from their smiles and the life in their eyes, I noticed no similarities between them. The women were different races, sizes, and ages. Peter McKenna truly worked on convenience and availability.

Finally, I forced myself to speak. "Do you know their names?"

"We do. Would you like me to tell you?"

"Of course I do," I said, more sharply than intended.

"Denise Godwin, Tracey Sanderson, Zuri Abebe, Yasmin Lakhani, Lili Nowak, Susie Hannah."

"Six," I whispered. "Six."

"There's more than six victims," Cooper said. "These are the women we've identified so far."

"What?" I tore my gaze away from the photographs and examined his face. There was no shine to his skin. It appeared flat, almost matte.

Tight without a hint of lustre to it. I imagined he was working long hours, and if so, at least it showed he cared, that he wanted to give all the families closure. "How many bodies are there?"

"Ten bodies. We were able to match belongings and mobile phones to these six women. The rest, we're working on identifying now. It's going to take time."

My finger rested on Yasmin Lakhani's photograph then moved to Tracy before landing on Zuri. I wondered how many of them Maddie tried to help.

"Two bodies contained DNA matching Maddie's."

"Her mother?" I asked. "And what... a sister?" Then I realised... "Oh. He buried his mother with the women."

"That's right. We think he killed her first."

"And the other body that matched Maddie's DNA. Is it...?"

"The percentage match fits the profile of an aunt, based on these results. But there were some issues with the condition of the body that made the test more difficult to run than usual. McKenna buried most of his victims in the paddock behind the farm, but it appears as though a couple were displaced a year or two ago. We think they may have been buried elsewhere and dug up after a flood. The flood damage makes it harder for us to obtain conclusive results."

I found myself relieved I'd decided to skip breakfast before DCI Cooper's visit.

"So, are you sure this woman is Maddie's aunt? Could the test be inaccurate? I mean... could the woman be Maddie's mother? Maybe the results indicate an aunt because they'd been skewed by the flood damage?"

"It's tricky," he replied. "We're being cautious about making that assumption based on these results. But the woman *is* related to Maddie, and we think she's given birth to at least one child at some point."

"Then it has to be the mother. Surely?"

"It's not conclusive enough to know," he insisted. "Like I said, the tests suggest an aunt, not a mother, and in my experience, the tests are usually right."

"Okay," I said, disappointed. I'd wanted a definitive answer, and there was none. "Do you know her name?"

"Not yet. We're having problems identifying her. She doesn't match anyone in our system, and we've been through missing person reports around the time, but we're coming up cold. There's no one matching her age range or basic description. Obviously, it's difficult to get a description due to the age and condition of the body. But we have estimated her death to have occurred around four to five years ago."

"Around the same time Maddie was born."

"That's right."

"Then the timeline fits for Maddie's mother! Surely it's just that the DNA test is wrong."

He hesitated before answering, as though choosing his words very carefully. "We're staying cautious. This information won't be released publicly because of that caution."

I nodded my head, but I couldn't help still believing my first assumption. It seemed like too much of a coincidence for this body not to be Maddie's mother. And yet I also trusted DCI Cooper to be straight with me. Perhaps I was clinging to false hope.

"Sorry," I said. "I didn't mean to jump to conclusions."

He waved a hand as though to dismiss my apology. "You didn't. Those were fair questions. There's something else, too. I think I should warn you about another detail that will be reported in the press. It's particularly unpleasant, I'm afraid."

"What is it?"

"We found a baby."

My face burned red hot. I smelled the sour tang of rancid breath, taking me back to the barn, but a moment later, it was gone. "What?"

"We think the same woman might have given birth to a stillborn baby. McKenna buried the body on the farm."

I let the words sink in. "And this baby... is it... was it related to Maddie?"

"We haven't run that test yet. Again, there are some issues with the condition of the remains."

My stomach lurched. I rested a hand against my abdomen and let out a shaky breath. The unfairness hit me hardest. Peter McKenna's vile existence had robbed so many young lives and destroyed Maddie's childhood. He'd annihilated her family and buried them unceremoniously at his farm. I hated him. I raged inside, the taste of it as bitter as bile.

"Are you okay, Zoe? Shall I get you some water?"

I balled my hands into fists. "I'm fine. Tell me about these women."

"Well, Denise, Tracey and Zuri had a history with substance abuse. They all have records for possession as well as hospital records consistent with heroin use. We know from Maddie's statements that McKenna preyed on homeless women."

I closed my eyes and pictured him strolling towards them while holding Maddie's hand. A nice man with a daughter. I thought of Maddie as a toddler, experiencing side streets and back alleys as McKenna preyed on the vulnerable, homeless women without families. What had McKenna promised these broken people? Sanctuary? Drugs? Food?

"Is there anything else you know about them?" I asked.

"They were all murdered in the last ten years."

"No, I mean about them. Their personalities. Their home life."

"Denise was raised by her grandmother and left home at eighteen to live with her boyfriend. It sounds as though he got her into drugs. Before that she was a good student; she took piano lessons and loved musicals. Tracey had a difficult childhood. She was in foster care for most of her life and ran away when she was fifteen. Zuri lost her mother when she was ten. She lived with her father, who worked a lot. I found out from her father than she was good at maths and volunteered at their church. We don't know as much about the other three victims, but as soon as I do, I'll let you know."

"Thank you," I said. "I needed to know them as people."

Cooper nodded. We let the situation wash over us for a moment. The lives taken, the fact that I could have been found in a shallow grave just like the others.

I pulled in a deep breath. "So, these six women, Maddie's grandmother, and a possible aunt. That leaves one other body you haven't identified."

"Yes," he said.

Unknown. Unnamed. Unwanted? It twisted my heart. No, I hoped not. I hoped she'd been wanted at some point in her life.

"And that's everything we know." Cooper began to gather up the photographs. "It's going to take time to piece everything together. If you think of anything, doesn't matter how small, let me know. It could help us identify those two bodies."

"Okay. I will. I promise."

"I'll let you know if we find an identity for Maddie's mysterious relation. Perhaps we can track down living family members, though if no one ever reported the woman missing, I wonder if they'd even be worth tracking down."

The thought made me shiver. "A living relative could come forward and claim custody of Maddie, couldn't they?"

"You'd have to check with social services about that. But in theory, I would imagine so."

"Surely a family like that wouldn't want to take Maddie?" I couldn't stand the idea that Maddie could be thrown to predatory or apathetic relatives.

"Unfortunately, this is a high-profile case, with lots of media attention. You don't know what kind of leeches are going to crawl out of whatever dark corners they live in. Maddie could one day tell her story and make a lot of money. And as Peter McKenna's next of kin, she owns the farm too."

I blinked. I hadn't even thought of that. "The farm can't be worth much, can it? Not now."

"It's a decent spot of land." He shrugged. "Though it would be wise to bulldoze the house and start from scratch."

I couldn't imagine anyone wanting to live there. Not with the memory of those restless bones, the blood spilled.

"Anyway," he said with a sigh. "I'll keep you updated. The bulldozers are still finding remains, but the rest appear to be animal bones."

"Animal bones?"

"It's not unusual on a farm. They have lots of working animals, of course. But there are... more than expected, and some are... well, baby animals. Domestic animals."

"Oh my God."

"I think McKenna's tendencies began at a young age. Let's put it that way." He rubbed his eyes, and his voice dropped to barely above a whisper. "What a monster."

When I saw that modicum of vulnerability, I knew I needed to know more. "Can I ask you a question, DCI Cooper?"

"Absolutely. Ask away."

"In your opinion, could someone like Peter McKenna have been saved before he started murdering people?"

He laughed.

"What's funny about that?"

"Nothing, but you're not the first person to ask me this. The thing is, I'm not a psychologist, I'm a copper. But what I can tell you is that I see the same faces coming back to the station. I arrest the same people over and over again. There are exceptions, obviously. You've got your people who make mistakes, do their time, and move on. Then there's criminals who've had a tough lot and feel trapped enough to keep doing what they're doing. Some of them manage to break that cycle, but it's rare. If I'm honest, those people are failed by the system as much as anything. But when it comes to your question—no. I don't. Not in regards to men like Peter McKenna. You've got your career criminals, addicts, and chancers, and then you've got Ted Bundy. You know? Some psychopaths are born. Some people are plain evil, and that's that."

His words didn't surprise me. In fact, they echoed the feelings of many people I knew; I was sure of that. Including my parents. Perhaps admitting this makes me arrogant, but I believed he was wrong, and I still do. I didn't believe anyone was born evil. I didn't think evil, in the form of demons or pure malice, existed. I might have been an optimist or a fool, but it remained a belief deep down in my core: any child could be saved.

IN THE WEEKS that followed DCI Cooper's visit, I spent most of my time researching fostering, visiting Maddie, and reading about the grisly discoveries at Ivycross Farm in the newspapers. I quickly discovered that Cooper had shielded me from some of the most horrific details.

All of the women had been tortured and raped over a sustained period of time. I found myself reading every detail in the trashy tabloids, then eating chocolate or drinking three or four glasses of wine to dull the terror of it all. The six-inch nail embedded in flesh, the shackles, the desk, the blood-soaked straw. It was all too real. It brought back too many memories: the hot pain of my wound; the sharp searing agony as it drew back through my skin. I stroked my scar and kept reading.

According to the papers, he'd talked to them for hours. They'd screamed and screamed. Young Maddie would run away from the farm when she was scared and walk around the countryside on her own. I wasn't sure where they'd got their information from. It sounded either made-up or pulled from Maddie's witness statements.

At night I dreamed about her—a tiny child, lost in a field, the long grass stalks almost as tall as her body. She wore daisies in her hair, and the spring sunshine turned her skin light pink. The scent of wildflowers, buttercups, and chamomile lingered around her. I saw her fingers stroke the white cow parsley flowerheads as she danced. Then a scream pierced the calm, tugging me back to reality.

A severed finger lay in the grass.

Every single one of Peter McKenna's victims was missing the little finger on her right hand. He'd kept the bones in a drawer in his bedside table. He would've chopped off my finger at some point. No doubt he had some dramatic way of removing it, maybe with a meat cleaver or an axe. And a part of me would've lived in that dark drawer next to him as he slept.

When I didn't dream of Maddie, I heard the ghosts of the women begging him to stop. They might very well have been in my room, watching me sleep, wondering why I got to live when they didn't. That was a valid question without an answer. Why me? I asked myself the same question every morning. I hadn't done anything spectacular with my life, and I didn't consider myself to be anything other than ordinary. But I'd lived while my fallen sisters' cries for help were ignored. Now I had a chance to do something good.

CHAPTER TWENTY
NOW

I wanted so much for our week to go back to normal after the events following Phoebe's funeral. Instead, I find myself pacing around the garden, trying to calm my nerves. Maddie sits by the window with Justin, the two of them talking. I'm glad to see them talking again, but Maddie isn't looking at Justin—she's looking at me.

In the days following the funeral, Justin's angry outbursts towards Maddie meant I had to play mediator between them. And in that time, I forgot about the rest of the town. I forgot about the Shahs, still hurting, still without a daughter, still pushing me away. I forgot all about the sick sourness lying at the pit of my stomach whenever I noticed distrust emanating from the Penry community.

Maddie returned to school yesterday, and I didn't think much about it. Today, she came home with a black eye, and when I asked her what happened, she said, "Katherine Sutton threw a rock at me."

And now I'm pacing the garden because my blood is boiling. In the window, Maddie holds a bag of ice to her face. She waves, her fingers dancing lamely, and an incredible sense of sadness cools my hot temper. After telling me about Katherine Sutton, she closed down and wouldn't answer any of my questions. Justin stepped in when I began to lose my cool. And in truth, I'm glad he did. This time, I'm the one red-faced and full of vinegar. I want Katherine Sutton here right now so I can... *Do what? Throw rocks at her? Yes, that would be a start.*

I march back to the house, waving to Gabe through the window, trying to convey some sort of normalcy. Thankfully, he's on his Nintendo Switch, ignoring all the drama. I hate to think what all of this is doing to him. Moving here was supposed to take us away from the craziness in my life. And it worked, for a time, until Riya Shah went missing. Then Phoebe Thompson died, and now I don't know what's going on in sleepy Penry. I researched this place for months, and it came up with nothing in recent history. No high-profile murders and barely any street crime. At least, until we came here.

When I stride into the room, Maddie stands up and walks out.

"Mads?" I call, confused.

"Let her go," Justin says.

I take a step as though to follow Maddie, but then I stop.

"Did she talk to you?" I ask.

"A little. But I think there's a lot she isn't saying. It sounds like after school, she and Katherine got into a fight, and Katherine threw the rock. Katherine and her friends ran off."

"She hasn't told a teacher?"

"No. She came straight home. I didn't see her on the way, otherwise I might've been able to stop this. We should call the school." He glances at me then away. "Unless..." He trails off, turning towards Maddie's room. He places his hands on his hips, which he tends to do while thinking.

"What?" I prompt.

"Well, we know she's not telling us everything. And we know that Maddie can handle herself, right?"

"Yes." My voice sounds defensive. Clipped.

"Then it stands to reason that Maddie had a larger role in all of this than she's letting on. What if Maddie did something, you know... *horrible* to Katherine. We know what she said to Ellie at the sleepover, right? We know how cruel Maddie can be. Maybe Maddie even started the fight. We don't know how injured Katherine is. She could be in hospital for all we know."

"Justin!"

He shrugs. "Sorry, but it's true."

"I think someone would have told us if our daughter put another girl in hospital." I glance guiltily over at Gabe, who's still engrossed in Animal Crossing. I lower my voice. "Why are we speculating about our own daughter? We're supposed to be on her side, aren't we?"

Justin clasps my shoulders with both of his hands. "I am on her side, Zo. But I'm also realistic. You're a sensitive person, and I think you're letting that interfere with the facts."

I pull away. "We don't know the facts. Did she tell you what the argument was about?"

"No," he says. "Though I think I can guess."

"Phoebe," I whisper. I step around my husband and head towards Maddie's door.

He catches me on the arm, stopping me in my tracks. "I think she wants to be left alone."

"I don't care what she wants. I need to get to the bottom of this. Justin, our daughter is in pain, and I need to make her better."

His eyebrows bunch together. He lets go of my arm so that I can carry on, but before I leave, he adds, "You know you can't take her pain away, right? Maddie is a grown person now. She's not a child anymore. She's sixteen years old. She has to work through her problems by herself."

His words surprise me. As a school counsellor, I didn't expect him to dismiss the parent's role so quickly.

"Don't forget I see kids at the school all the time. Once they hit sixteen, they don't listen to their parents anymore."

"That's not true," I say. "Maybe it comes across that way, but—"

"Trust me," he says. "Whoever someone is at sixteen, they'll be that way for the rest of their life. They're basically adults. And pushy parents don't do anything to help matters. They just make everything worse. You don't want to make things worse for her. Do you?"

"What are you talking about? I'm not going to make things worse."

"Are you sure about that?"

I shake my head and leave, despising the expression on his face—

the sincerity, like he's doing me a favour by explaining my own daughter to me. And yet I hesitate outside Maddie's door. I raise my hand to knock, and his words echo in my mind. Should parents back off when their child reaches their mid-teens?

No, I think. I'll never back off. She could be forty and in trouble, and I'd still knock on her door and listen to her. "Maddie, hun. Can I come in?"

She leaves it so long before she answers that I actually back away. But when the door edges open, she stands there in velour loungewear and bare feet, her long hair pulled up into a messy topknot. She's vulnerable Maddie again, the wood nymph I found by the oak tree.

"How's the eye?"

She thuds over to the bed and sits, throwing her weight around as only a teenager can. The icebag is on her bedside table, condensation collecting on the wood. I decide not to chide her about it. Over on her desk, her laptop is open, and a TikTok video of a girl dancing plays on a loop, the sound on mute. I briefly wonder why she's using her computer for TikTok and try to examine the other open tabs, but I can't read them from where I sit on the bed.

"Maddie, I need you to tell me about this fight with Katherine. I know you don't want to talk about it. I understand why. You know I respect your privacy. But sometimes, parents need to know so they can help."

"I don't need your help."

I take a note of her choice of words. She could have said I don't *want* your help. Instead, she chose *need*.

"Great," I say. "Good for you, tough girl. The thing is, I have to deal with other parents and teachers and whole host of people connected to the girls you go to school with. So when one of those girls throws a rock at my child, I need to know why. For one thing, you could go to the police about this."

Her face tilts up to mine. "God no. I'm not going to the police. Don't be ridiculous. They think I killed someone, for fuck's sake."

I sigh. "All right, enough with the language. I get it—you're grown up. And we don't know what the police think. They asked you some questions, and that's it. But if you don't want to go to the police, we won't. Okay?"

"Fine."

I fold my arms and cross my legs, lotus style, showing her I'm settling in and waiting. Then I raise my eyebrows and nod in a "go on then" gesture.

"It was about Phoebe. Katherine made this dumb comment about me murdering her because I'm a psycho."

"Okay, and then what happened?"

But before Maddie can answer, my phone rings. I figure it could be the school, or even the police about Phoebe, so I jump off the bed and step out into the corridor.

"Is that Zoe Osbourne?" a woman's voice asks.

"Yes."

"This is Diana Sutton. I think we need to talk about our daughters." I picture Katherine's mother speaking to me between two tight lips, one hand resting on her hip. Agitated, twitchy. Maybe a vein bulging somewhere.

"Yes, I think you're right. Maddie told us what Katherine did."

Diana continues in the same aggressive tone. "Did she tell you what she did to my Katherine?"

Her words catch me off guard. "N-no," I stammer. I screw my eyes closed, hoping it won't be devastatingly awful.

"She pushed her into the road," Diana says.

I gasp. "What?"

"She pushed her into oncoming traffic," Diana's voice increases in volume and pitch. "They were outside school, they had an argument, and your daughter shoved mine. A driver in a car going towards *my* child had to perform an emergency stop to avoid knocking her down. My daughter almost died because of yours. If that car had been going any faster..." A sob vibrates down the line.

I lean against the wall. "I'm sure... I'm sure she didn't see the car, or..." My voice sounds thin and weak even to my own ears. I dig deep, trying to find a valid explanation for it all. I come up with nothing.

"Your daughter tried to kill mine."

The words hang there for a moment.

"No," I say. "Wait. We don't know that. Katherine threw a rock that hit Maddie's eye. Her vision was... She probably didn't see... I'm sure she just lashed out—"

"I'm going to call the police," Diana interrupts. "They can figure out whether Maddie tried to murder my daughter. But until then, keep that psycho away from my child."

She hangs up. I press my palm against the cold wall, my stomach contorted into knots. Grounding myself with the cool surface, I try to figure out what to do next, but I'm lost.

And in that moment, Maddie pokes her head out of the room. With a voice as innocent as a child's, she asks, "Is everything okay?"

CHAPTER TWENTY-ONE
THEN

S ade was on my side. That was important in the world of
fostering. I'd won the first battle. After three months, no family
members stepped forward to claim Maddie. She continued to
live at Marigold House, and with each visit, she changed. She with-
drew, shrinking like a flower without light. Even though she smiled
when I walked into the visitor's room, she came across as listless,
nothing like the chatty, confident girl at the farm. The capable child
who'd made me toast and saved my life shrivelled before my eyes. It
hurt me. It especially hurt me to think that Maddie blossomed at the
murder farm but wasted away in care.

Sade told me the best course of action would be fostering to adopt.
That way, they could monitor Maddie's progress before making
anything permanent. It also meant that Maddie wouldn't be uprooted
more than once, which the local authority preferred. There were, of
course, a multitude of caveats. Firstly, Maddie had special needs due to
her traumatic childhood. I couldn't go into this blind, and I needed to
be prepared. She was disruptive at the home. She started fights with the
other children. She sometimes had to be restrained by staff. She could
throw a loud tantrum one minute then refuse to speak the next. This
behaviour escalated after my visits because she always wanted me to

stay. Even I could see we'd developed a bit of a co-dependent relationship after our time at the farm. If we wanted to heal from what had happened there, we needed to work on that relationship. But Maddie didn't understand co-dependency. She simply knew what she wanted and what she didn't want.

According to Sade, my job could be a problem. Local authorities preferred at least one person at home full time. A working single mother was unlikely to be accepted. But seeing as I still worked part time hours following my ordeal, the balance of work and home could be negotiated. And that meant I needed a second source of income because my part-time wage wasn't going to stretch to two people. To make money quickly, I agreed to something I'd said I never would— one interview with a journalist. It paid ten thousand pounds to sit and talk about the horrors at Ivycross Farm. The thought made my skin crawl. In my mind, I was selling my soul, but the practicalities outweighed the negatives.

I sat there and watched the journalist's beady eyes glow with excitement when I told him all the juicy details. He seemed far too fascinated about whether I'd been raped or not, but aside from that, it wasn't too painful. My mum bought the newspaper, but I never read it.

To ensure I knew what I was in for, I took online courses on fostering: Childhood Trauma and How to Deal With the Aftermath, Paperwork and Panel Hearings, Adapting Your Parenting Styles. I learned a lot about warm parenting. I met with Sade every week to visit Maddie, but I also met with her separately to talk about every aspect of my life. My childhood, my touchy relationship with my parents, my even-touchier relationship with my ex-husband, my job, my hobbies, my mental state and so on. Those questions probed deep, and had it been anyone other than Sade, I would have grown more and more defensive as time went on. I'd come to like and respect Sade, though. As it was, I still had to grit my teeth or bite my tongue a couple of times to get through it.

In between work, meetings with Sade, and visits with Maddie, I scoured Mumsnet and other forums, hunting for threads about fostering. I read horror stories and success stories, finding that advice varied wildly. Some recommended getting a sweet family pet that was good with children; others said never to get a pet. I decided not to get a pet.

"Zoe, we've spent all the time we need to spend with you," Sade said one day. "Now we need to speak to your family."

"What? My parents?"

She was driving me up to Marigold House to see Maddie again. I watched her in profile as we travelled up an A road, the sunlight bouncing off the soft angles of her face.

"They'll be in Maddie's life too," she said. "We need to talk to them and find out if they're supportive or not. You're going to need help. You'll need childcare at times. I'm sure your parents will be the ones to step in."

I bit my thumbnail and stared out at the boxy beige bungalows dotted along the side of the road. "Okay, no problem. When do you need to speak to them?" I didn't tell her that my mum thought I was making the biggest mistake of my life by adopting Maddie. I couldn't.

"How about next Tuesday?"

"That should be fine."

"And we might need to speak to your ex-husband too."

I snorted. "He definitely won't be helping me with childcare."

"That's fine. It's mostly to check for potential issues."

"No issues. Just an arsehole." I covered my mouth with my hand. "I shouldn't have said that, should I?"

She laughed. "I won't include it in my report. Seriously, don't worry about it. As long as he's not going to be trouble, it'll be fine."

"Trust me, he's not in the slightest bit interested in me or what I do, so he won't factor in at all." It felt strange to think that Simon, a man I hadn't spoken to since signing the divorce papers, could affect my ability to foster a child. But I understood why they were being thorough.

We had our best visit to date. Maddie cried when we left, but apart from that, she remained well-behaved and sweet throughout. We took her for a walk around the grounds, picked daisies and put them behind our ears, and raced each other up and down the lawn. I found myself glancing at Sade as though to say, "See? Look how good we are together. No one else could adopt her. She's mine."

Maddie giggled through the hour. It brightened my heart to see her smile. But then, in the last few minutes, the atmosphere changed.

"Be Dad, Zoe," she shouted, running up and down the lawn. "Pretend you're bad, and I'll stab you."

At first, I wasn't sure what to say, and I noticed Sade's neutral but penetrating expression as she waited to see how I handled the situation.

"No, honey," I said. "That wouldn't be a fun game."

She pouted. "Why not?"

"Because it's a very serious situation, and there are some serious situations that aren't appropriate to laugh about."

"But I think it's funny," she said. She stopped running and stood in the middle of the lawn, her messy tendrils of hair slanted across her nose.

"But why do you think it's funny, Maddie?"

She shrugged, her eyes brimming with tears.

"It's okay," I said. "You've not done anything wrong." I pulled her into a hug. "It's okay, sweetheart."

* * *

I WORRIED MORE about the interview with my parents than the rest of the process combined. Mum had made her feelings perfectly clear, and she didn't tend to hold back when it came to sharing her opinions with anyone. I wasn't going to be with them during the interview, which meant I had no control over what they might say. I woke up in a cold sweat most nights, worrying about how she might mess up this opportunity for me.

The day before the scheduled meeting with Sade, I went to my parents' house. We sat in the bay window, sipping tea out of Mum's favourite pink teacups, our conversation skirting around the difficult subject matter I'd come to discuss. Scarlet poppies brightened the borders of my parents' front garden, and occasionally, Mum waved at a neighbour walking their dog. I'd always loved this bay window. As a child, I'd tuck my feet under my legs and read a book, my back resting against the curtain.

Once the teapot was empty, I built up the courage to ask, "What are you going to say to Sade tomorrow?"

Mum sighed. Her foot kicked back and forth, the shape of her long toenails visible through her pop socks. "Honestly, Zoe, I haven't decided, and I shan't be deciding until I hear the questions."

"You know I really want this, don't you?"

She shook her head as though she couldn't fathom why. "Yes, I know you do. And nothing I've said or done has managed to talk you out of this ridiculous idea. I suppose that's worth something, the fact that you haven't given up." To my surprise, she started to cry.

"Mum?" We were never very good at comforting each other. I reached over and tugged on the sleeve of her top. "Don't. You'll set me off."

She sniffed deeply, blinked rapidly, and pushed the tears upwards so as not to smudge her eye makeup. "Your father and I never asked to be put in this situation. You're bringing a traumatised child into our world while we're settling into our retirement years, and I think that's very selfish."

I thought about her words for a moment and realised she was right. It didn't make me want to not adopt Maddie, but for once, I understood where she was coming from. "Well, perhaps Maddie doesn't need to be in your life all the time, at least not at the start. We'll take it slow."

Her features relaxed, and I saw the shape of her youth. She hadn't always been this stern when I was a child. I'd known her laughing and carefree once.

"I'm not going to be calling on you to babysit every week or force you to come to the park with us. Throwing Maddie into a new relationship will be hard too. We'll take it very, very slowly. But you don't *know*, Mum. You don't know that this is going to go badly. I think you've convinced yourself that it will. What if bringing Maddie into the family becomes something wonderful? I want you to be part of that."

"Oh, Zoe," she replied. "Being a mother is hard enough when the

child is your own flesh and blood. I'm sorry to say that, but it's true."
She sighed. "I'm not going to stop you. I know you're stubborn. I still
remember telling you not to pluck your eyebrows thin, and you did
anyway." She cast me a quick sideways glance, knowing full well I'd
never managed to grow back the lush, dark brows I'd once had. "I truly
hope it works out, for all of us. I do."

The next day, I received a phone call from Sade to say the interview
had gone very well and that my parents sounded supportive but realistic about me fostering to adopt Maddie. She was happy to make her
recommendation, with the next step being the panel.

"At that point, it's basically a formality. I don't see any reason why
you shouldn't foster Maddie. It's going to be a long, slow process, but
I'm ready to move forward," she said. "I'm happy for you, Zoe. And
most of all, I'm happy for Maddie, that's she's found someone who
cares for her after everything she's been through."

It started to sink in then. I was going to be a mother.

CHAPTER TWENTY-TWO
NOW

I follow Maddie back into her room and shut the door. She sits on the bed, lightly this time, and pulls her legs up.

"That was Katherine's mum." I take Maddie's desk chair. The browser on the laptop is now closed, and the dancing TikTok girl is gone. "And she put quite a different spin on the event."

"What did she say?"

"That you pushed Katherine into oncoming traffic."

Maddie's small mouth tightens, her lips disappearing back into her face. She leans forward and places her chin on her hand. "Well, that's an exaggeration."

"Tell me what happened."

She sighs. "Katherine has a squad. Idiotic groupies who hang on her every word. They jumped me after school, started calling me psycho and murderer and everything. Then they threw these pebbles at me. Small ones. One of them—maybe Katherine, I don't know—threw a rock. I'd turned around to tell them to fuck off when it hit me in the eye. I couldn't see shit. I ran at her and pushed her away. I didn't know the car was coming. And for God's sake, it was outside the school, so the car was going like ten miles an hour."

"All right," I say, relief flooding through me. "I can see you didn't intend to hurt her. Unfortunately, I think Diana wants to inform the police."

"That's typical of everyone around here," she says, her bottom lip sticking out.

I sense she has more to say, so I prompt, "What do you mean?"

"They can't stand it, that I'm alive and existing. I'm scum because of where I came from, and I don't fit into their beige middle-class lives. They want to tear me down and always have. Phoebe Thompson's death is an excuse for them to do that. I hate it here." Her face hardens.

"You are fantastically, brilliantly different, and I wouldn't change you. But other people are afraid of what they don't understand." I walk over to her and sit by her side. She leans into me, and I wrap an arm over her shoulders. Her hair smells like coconut. Her fleecy top is soft under my fingers. With her bowed head and her worries hanging in the air, she's as simple as any teenage girl can be. Peter McKenna is a million miles away. "We'll get through this together, okay?" I kiss her head. "And we'll speak to the headteacher—"

"No." She pulls out of my arms. "Are you stupid? That's the worst thing you could possibly do."

"Maddie! Don't speak to me like that." I keep my voice calm, careful not to escalate the situation.

"It is, though. You *can't* go to the teachers. I can handle Katherine Sutton and her squad, okay? Let me deal with it."

"If that's what you want. But at least let us speak to Katherine's mother and see if we can stop her going to the police."

After a pause, Maddie agrees.

I leave her alone in her room.

I DON'T KNOW how he does it, but Justin manages to convince Diana Sutton not to go to the police. We joke about his silver tongue, then for a few days, normality resumes.

Phoebe Thompson's death is ruled an accident. Apparently, the autopsy didn't find any evidence of a struggle. There was nothing on

Phoebe's phone to suggest someone wanted to meet with her late at night, and there were no witnesses. In the end, they couldn't find enough evidence to suggest she was pushed. Remarkably, it emerged that Phoebe had a tendency to sleepwalk. A weight lifted from my shoulders as soon as I saw the news article. Now, no matter what, at least my daughter wasn't going to be charged with murder.

But every time I stared into her hazelnut eyes, I thought about Phoebe and Katherine. I pictured hands on Phoebe's back. I saw Katherine stagger into the road in a hundred different ways. Maddie's explanation for what happened to Katherine made it sound as though she'd lost herself for a moment. That she hadn't even been thinking about the road or the fact that there were any cars around. Someone hurt her, and she'd lashed out. Perhaps that was reasonable.

I pictured Maddie afraid, her arms flying out to protect herself, shoving instinctively. But if Katherine had thrown a rock, that meant distance between her and Maddie. How much distance did Maddie need to cover before she knew exactly what she was doing?

In my mind, I saw Maddie as innocent, and I saw her as guilty. Sometimes I imagined it playing out in between innocence and guilt, with both girls running at each other, but Maddie getting the upper hand and taking advantage.

How do you even discipline a child with dulled conscience? Have I failed as a parent?

In the car on our way to Maddie's second therapy session of the week, we sit in silence. Gabe is with Justin, probably playing football in the garden. Dads and sons always seem so easy together, like nothing could ever break their bond. My experience as a mother to a daughter felt infinitely more fragile, like the slightest pressure could cause an implosion. That pains me to admit given what we'd been through together.

Dr Boateng wears her hair in a short crop of tight curls. She's around forty, petite, and always smiling when we arrived at her office. I'm not sure whether she's a naturally bubbly person or if the bright smile is there to put her clients—the children and their parents—at ease.

"Good morning," she says, gesturing for Maddie to take a seat.

"I'll be back in an hour." I give them both a wave on the way out. Every time I leave her there, my stomach fills with butterflies.

To fill the time, I wander around the town, the whole time picturing Maddie and Dr Boateng sitting opposite each other. Does Maddie mention me in her sessions? Does she blame me? Or does she talk about our family life? Perhaps her friends or lack thereof? Riya's disappearance, which she doesn't talk about with me? What about sex? I've never known Maddie show interest in another person sexually. There have been no boyfriends or girlfriends, and she's never discussed her sexuality with me.

As I do every week, I grab a flat white to go and do some window-shopping. Penry isn't great for clothes, so I like to make a note of anything I might want to come back and try when I have more time.

"Zoe?"

I'm at a loss for a moment. When I turn around, a pretty woman in her early thirties stands behind me. It takes me a moment to remember who she is. Then it comes to me. I met her on a night out with Justin's colleagues.

She lifts her hand for me to shake. "Angie. I work with your husband." I obviously took too long to respond, and she realised I'd forgotten who she is. But I remember her name now—Angie Starling, a teaching assistant who started with the new term.

"Oh hi, how are you?"

"Great," she says, smiling.

I remember the shape of her grin from the night out. Four or five teachers smooshed together around a table and Angie laughing at all of Justin's jokes. My body had pulled taut at the sight of those dazzling, perfect teeth and the way her eyes crinkled in the sweet unassuming way men like. I'm not usually a jealous person, nor am I competitive with women, but something about her rubbed me the wrong way that night.

"Are you shopping?"

"Actually, no," I reply. "I just dropped Maddie off at her therapy session and came for a wander."

"Oh, how is she?"

"She's okay." Then I add, almost as an afterthought, and more because I feel I should, "Obviously, she's upset about what happened to Phoebe. And..." I stop myself before I blurt out any more. Gossip spreads pretty quickly around our small town.

"I never believed any of it, even for a minute." Angie takes a step forward, a lock of brown hair falling across her petite nose. She has one of those faces that always seems familiar, and I think it's because she's pretty but not beautiful. She has a girl-next-door quality about her. "She's a good girl, Maddie. What those sixth formers did to her was horrible."

My eyebrows scrunch together in surprise. "What do you mean?"

Her expression freezes. "Oh, I guess she didn't tell you." She shuffles her feet awkwardly. "Maybe it isn't my place to say."

"Please do. You know what teenagers are like. She doesn't tell me anything. If it's important, I can help her." I try to sound nonchalant but hit desperate instead.

"Okay, well... Her locker was vandalised. We don't actually know which kids did it, though all the teachers have their suspicions."

Someone bumps into my shoulder as they hurry past me on the pavement. I hardly notice. "Vandalised? How?"

"They filled her locker with bloodied Barbies and scrawled 'murderer' all over it in red paint."

"Fuck," I blurt out. "Sorry." My hand flies to my mouth. "Jesus. I forgot how cruel teenagers are." I shake my head. There I was, worrying about Maddie being a sociopath, when every other teenager around her behaved jaw-droppingly awful. "I can't believe she didn't tell us." I wonder if this is related to the incident with Katherine Sutton.

Angie places a hand on my forearm, long fingers wrapping around my flesh. "These kids are tricky. You know, I swear, the parents of the teenagers I teach are the loneliest people in the world."

I nod my head, my heart thrumming beneath my ribs, and back away from her intense stare. "Speaking of teenagers, I should go and pick up Maddie. It's almost been an hour now."

She relinquishes her grip. "It was lovely seeing you, Zoe. Ask Justin when we're next going for a drink. I fancy a night out. You'll come, won't you?"

"Sounds lovely."

She begins to walk away, glances at her phone, then stops in the middle of the pavement. I notice her hand fly up to her mouth. Her body is so still and stiff that I know instinctively something awful has happened.

"Are you okay?" I take a cautious step towards her.

She shakes her head. "I can't believe it. I just got a text message from the headteacher. Riya Shah's body was found today."

My knees almost sink in on themselves, and I keel forward slightly before righting myself. "What? Where?"

"I don't know the details." She sniffs, holding back tears. "I thought she'd run away."

I step away from her, my jaw slack, and watch the people on the street walking up and down, holding their coffees, and chatting on their phones. It's like I'm trapped in a glass box, watching them.

"Was she... Was she murdered?" I whisper.

"I don't know." Angie takes a step back. "I should get to the school. I might be able to find out more there." She slides her phone into her trouser pocket and walks away, leaving me standing there alone. In shock.

I turn my head, and she's there, Riya, staring at me, smiling underneath a plastic coating. Several weeks ago, I placed the poster there myself, on the village noticeboard. There's a watermark running down her nose from where the rain has seeped beneath the plastic. But there she is—honest, gentle, warm-hearted Riya. My daughter's only friend. The one person Maddie couldn't manipulate. She respected Riya instead. I've never seen that dynamic with Maddie and her school friends before. But along with the warmth of her, she had a steely side.

And now... Well, now I knew deep down in my heart that pretty, kind Riya Shah was murdered. Perhaps I'd always known, because why would a girl like Riya want to run away? But who could do such a thing? Who would want to extinguish her bright flame? I know exactly the kind of man who would want to do that. A man like Peter McKenna.

DR BOATENG ASKS me if I'm okay as soon as I step into her office to collect Maddie. When I catch a glimpse of my reflection in her computer monitor, I realise why she asked. A waxy sheen coats the makeup I applied this morning. Smudges of mascara stain the skin beneath my eyes despite my best attempts not to cry during the walk back. I tell her I'm fine and then forget to even ask how the session went before leading Maddie out of the office.

"What's going on?" Maddie asks as soon as we reach the carpark.

Warm, midday summer sun beats down on the back of my neck. I can't stand it. I want to drive somewhere cold.

"I haven't seen you look like that since the farm," she says.

"You remember what I looked like back then?"

"Sure, I remember everything from that week."

We climb into the car, and I try to calm my trembling hands.

"I have some horrible news, Maddie." I glance at her, and she gazes up at me with a neutral expression on her face. It horrifies me, and I have no idea why. "Riya Shah has died. The police found her body today. I don't know anything more than that, but I thought you should know straight away."

Maddie jams her thumbnail into a ridge running along the car door. She's quiet for a moment, thoughtful. "We all knew she was dead."

"That's not true," I say, though I think perhaps she's right.

"Was she murdered?" She shakes her head. "Of course she was murdered. That's what happens to girls, isn't it? They get murdered."

"No. I know it feels like it, but it's rare—"

"The bodies underneath my dad's farm would say otherwise."

"What your father—your biological father—did was *exceptionally* rare."

She sighs. "Yeah, I guess. But what about all the girls killed by boyfriends and husbands and dads and brothers? And the girls sold to men over the internet?"

"I know. It's awful." I regret telling her in the car, because now I want to hug her, and it's awkward to lean across the seat.

"I guess they were weak," she says.

"No, Maddie, that's not—"

"Riya was weak. That's why she's dead, and we're alive. We escaped from Dad, but she couldn't escape the man who killed her."

"We don't know—"

"We do," she snaps. She pushes her thumbnail harder against the door. "If any man comes for me, I'll kill him."

Her profile remains sharp, with her jaw tense and her mouth set in a straight line. But when she looks at me, I catch a blistering, crackling glow emanating from her gaze. Now her temper shows, and it scares me.

CHAPTER TWENTY-THREE
THEN

It took me five wobbly paces down the stone steps outside the town hall before my knees felt as though they were about to buckle. I sat down on the cold ground and sniffed heavily. Sade sat next to me and handed me a tissue.

"Happy tears," I clarified.

She rubbed my shoulder. "I know. Believe me, I can tell."

I patted her hand. "You made this happen for me. Thank you so much."

She shook her head. "No, you did it. You got here. You saved that girl." She passed me a piece of paper. "Maddie wanted me to give you this after the hearing."

I wiped away the remnants of tears, unfolded the note, and read. It was scrawled in green crayon, misspelled and messy, and yet the purest, most beautiful possession I'd ever owned.

DEAR ZOE,
I want to sea my bedrum. I luv you. You are pritty.
Maddie

· · ·

UNDERNEATH THE NOTE, Maddie had drawn a bunny rabbit, along with a love heart. Next to the love heart, she'd drawn a hand with a tiny hole in the centre. It was the one part of the letter that seemed out of place, and the sight of it made me shudder. But in a way, it made sense. Maddie wanted to reference what bonded us. Maddie had pulled the nail from my hand, which ended up saving me. We'd moved on since the farm, but did our relationship always go back to that place? Did it even matter?

I carefully folded the note and placed it in my handbag. I said goodbye to Sade in the carpark, called my mum to let her know the outcome, received the muted response I'd expected, and went home to my quiet house that wouldn't be quiet for much longer.

At the panel, I'd been told that it'd be around six weeks before Maddie could move in. That meant I had time to decorate her room. Over those weeks, during my visits to Marigold House, I showed her photographs of wallpaper and bedding. She pointed at the ones she wanted, her choices delighting and surprising me. She wanted wallpaper with a galaxy print, a deep blue spattered with white dots. She requested a stuffed rabbit toy, of course. I chose one that made me laugh because I thought it would make her laugh. It was far too big and carried its own carrot. She liked a small white bookcase and a pastel-blue bedspread covered in baby-pink cherry blossom. Using money I'd made from the newspaper interview, I bought her everything she wanted, adding in a small desk, a chest of drawers, and a gorgeous doll-house that I couldn't resist even though it cost considerably more than the rest of her toys.

When the day came, I woke at five in the morning and struggled to keep my breakfast down. The house was stocked with Disney DVDs. I'd bought her favourite yoghurts and mini-chocolates and arranged the doll house. Sade brought her to the house with a backpack and a box. She hid halfway behind Sade's legs, peeking out nervously. I'd never seen her this apprehensive before. I wondered if she worried about things not working out too or that she might go back to the care home.

"Come on in, Maddie. Let me show you your new home!" I'd

decided not to make it a big deal. At one point, I'd thought about buying a cake and balloons, but decided to be cautious.

I bent my knees and dropped to her level, reaching out a hand for her to take if she wanted. She'd never been shy with me before, but everything was new to her now—the house, the concept of having a mother, and a safe place to call her own.

"Good girl," Sade said as Maddie took my hand.

We walked around the room together, and she trailed her hand over the furniture, the walls, and the television, like she was claiming it all. Sade and I exchanged a glance, both happy to see her exploring.

"Well, I'm going to let you two adjust," Sade said. "You have my number if you need anything."

Maddie lifted a photograph of me with my parents, staring intently.

I stepped across to stand next to Sade. "Thank you so much for everything. None of this would have happened without your support."

"It was my pleasure," the social worker said. She pointed to the door. "I'll let myself out. You two carry on."

An hour later, we were alone, sitting together on Maddie's bedroom floor with all the dolls pulled out of the dollhouse.

"Shall we give the dolls names?" I asked, watching her as she made her own choices, enjoying how I could give her the freedom to explore and be herself. So far, we'd walked through every room in the house, and she'd asked me questions about photographs and furniture.

"This is the mummy doll," Maddie said, lifting a dark-haired female doll wearing a blue dress. She made the mummy lie on the bed. "This is Daddy." She put the boy doll on top of the girl doll.

I tried not to overreact, even though the sight of the dolls lying on top of each other made my insides squirm with discomfort.

"Are they asleep, Maddie?" I asked cautiously.

She shook her head. "Not yet. But the mummy will be asleep soon."

I remained very still, not wanting to make her feel bad, though obviously I knew what she'd recreated in the dollhouse wasn't normal. "Perhaps we should have the mummy and daddy sitting in the garden."

I picked up the dolls. "The daddy is mowing the lawn, and the mummy is growing herbs."

"Okay," she said eagerly. "Is there a stream?"

The word took me by surprise. It felt beyond her normal vocabulary, but she did grow up roaming the countryside, so it made sense she'd at some point learned the word *stream*.

"Would you like one?"

"Yes please," she said.

"Okay, wait here."

I got a blue scarf from my bedroom and created a stream outside the house. Maddie placed the little girl doll with the mummy doll by the stream.

"What are they doing, Maddie?"

"Washing their hands," she said.

It seemed a bit odd, but I went with it. Afterwards, the mummy and daughter dolls walked through fields of flowers, for which we used the bedspread, then sipped tea in the garden. At one point, Maddie made the daughter doll hide in the cellar away from Daddy, and it took me a while to coax her out.

"You'll never have to hide in the cellar again, Maddie. I promise you that."

WE HAD A TUMULTUOUS FIRST NIGHT. Maddie woke up screaming, her tiny faced screwed tight and flushed red. It took me a few moments to calm her, during which she beat me with her fists, but I let her, even though I suffered bruises the next day. Then we went downstairs for a glass of water and watched late-night TV until I saw her eyelids drooping. I managed to carry her to bed and set her up with the stuffed rabbit, but about an hour after that, she crawled into my bed with me. I couldn't bring myself to make her leave.

I'd arranged even more leave from work to settle Maddie into the home. During that time, we went to a garden centre to choose plants for the herb garden. She'd liked the mention of it during our dollhouse play, and I decided to create it for real. One thing I soon loved about Maddie was how much she loved to be outside. She'd spent her first few years on this earth roaming the countryside alone, and a small garden at the back of a terraced house was quite an adjustment for her.

At the garden centre she ran wild, her jaw dropping at all the colourful flowers. She had such confidence that she walked straight up to strangers and start chatting with them, charming even the frowniest of shoppers. But it was exhausting keeping her from picking up every flower. She tried to take things out of people's baskets and didn't understand why she couldn't do that.

A few days later, in the park, she was she same again—chatty with strangers. This time, though, she was extremely cold towards anyone her own age. When a little boy asked if he could go on the swing after her, she yelled, "No," and made him cry. I had to apologise to the boy and his mother before taking Maddie out of the swing. She ended up in tears. She fought me when I picked her up, kicking out her feet and knocking me squarely on the chin. All the while, I sensed eyeballs boring into my back, as half a dozen mothers experienced second-hand embarrassment.

I tried not to let it faze me, because in all honesty, I'd expected worse. Though I still found it challenging. Clingy one minute, she would refuse to let go of my hand when I tried to do an everyday task like put laundry in the washing machine. Then she'd switch gears and run from me the next. Sometimes she stayed in her bedroom and stared out of the window, ignoring my pleas for her to talk to me.

The two weeks went by in a blink. I'd never been so tired. I was sure newborn babies were as hard, if not harder, and I wasn't the first mother to go to bed exhausted every night, but those weeks were tough. She tested everything—boundaries, pressure points, and my absolute limits. And through it all, I had to remember the warm parenting. Disciplining Maddie wouldn't do much. I had to explain right and wrong over and over again. I had to ensure she saw the consequences to her actions, like asking shop staff to come and talk to her when she pulled tins of beans from the shelves.

When it was time for her to start at a new school, I woke up with a stomach cramp. It felt too soon. She'd socialised with children at the residential home, and she'd lived with me for two weeks, but deep down, I couldn't quell the sensation that I was making a big mistake. I had no other choice but to go with it. I needed to go back to work, and Maddie needed education.

She cried when I dropped her off at school. Not the sweet tears of most nervous children, she wailed. A teacher dragged her away from me. I sat in my car for fifteen minutes, knowing I was going to be late, but finding it impossible to stop the tsunami of tears from pouring out of me. And despite how horrible it felt, I knew then and there that I loved her with every part of me and that I would do anything to keep her safe.

Later that day, when I collected Maddie from school, she came running out from the building with a huge grin on her face.

"Zoe, look," she said. "We drew pictures."

A short woman with bright red-lipstick and strawberry-blonde hair followed her out, walking over to me as Maddie shoved her crayon drawing into my hands.

"Maddie did really well today. Nice to meet you. I'm Rita, Maddie's teacher."

"Oh, hi. We spoke on the phone, didn't we?" I'd called the school ahead of time to give them some information about Maddie's background.

"That's right. I'm happy to report that she was no trouble at all today."

I had to admit I was surprised by that, so much so, that I rocked back on my heels. "Wow, that's great. Well done, Mads. Ice cream later?"

She cheered.

"She was a bit quiet with the other children, but we'll keep an eye on that and encourage her to join in more. I just wanted to let you know how well she did because I know you must be anxious."

"I was," I admitted, letting out a long breath. "This morning was..."

"I know." She nodded. "I saw. But don't worry. We're going to be very accommodating to Maddie's needs. I promise."

"Thank you so much." Then I glanced down at Maddie's drawing. "Wow, Maddie, this is so good! Is this our house?"

"No," Maddie said.

When the realisation hit, the smile faded from my face. She hadn't drawn our home. She'd drawn the farm, with the barn standing adjacent to the white farmhouse. Stick figures stood in a row outside the house. Maddie and I were there, or at least a woman with brown hair like mine. But out in the distance, near the barn, another set of stick figures lay on their backs.

"Are you all right?" Rita asked.

"Um..." I glanced up from the picture, my trail of thought gone. "Yes. It's just..."

Rita examined the picture more closely. Her eyes narrowed before opening wide. "Does Maddie have a psychologist?"

"She has a child therapist, yes."

Rita nodded. "That's good."

Suddenly, I noticed Maddie watching us both, and I bent down to her level. "This is a beautiful picture, Maddie."

"Is it?"

She knew. She'd read our faces. Maddie's upbringing had been difficult, but she knew enough about people to recognise emotions.

"Yes." I hugged her close to me.

CHAPTER TWENTY-FOUR
NOW

The heavy air of the garage settles around us. Maddie shuffles in her seat, raising one knee to rest against the dashboard. I lift a heavy arm and tap the ignition switch. Next to me, I sense Maddie watching almost curiously. She knows I'm close to tears, and she isn't good with emotion. She doesn't know how to give comfort. But soon, her hand rests softly on my shoulder.

"It's okay, Mum."

Mum. God, what that word does to me. It tears my heart in half and pulverises my insides. The most exquisite ecstasy and the most exquisite pain in three letters.

I regard my daughter, truly scrutinise her, every inch of her face. She's beautiful. Perhaps not classically beautiful, but the strength of her features and that penetrating stare make her striking.

She attempts to read my thoughts. "It's not going to happen to me, you know. No one could hurt me. I'm too strong. Like I said, I'd kill anyone who tries."

"Maddie, don't say things like that." I sigh.

"I won't." She shrugs. "Not to anyone else anyway. But you know. You've killed someone. You know what it takes to survive."

"No, that's not... That's not what the world is like. I know what I did to your father happened when you were very young, and I know you think about it a lot, but what I did wasn't normal—"

"I'm not an idiot, Mum. I do know that. Every single therapist likes to remind me of what's normal and what isn't." She juts out her chin, back to teenage sullenness.

"Then why do you keep talking about life like it's a fight to the death?" I squeeze her hand. "Tell me about your therapy session today."

"All right. Dr Boateng asked me about my week. I told her I missed hanging out with Riya. Then we talked about Katherine Sutton and how I shouldn't have pushed her into the road. Then, you know... Phoebe's death and everything going on at school."

"You mean the bullying," I prompt, remembering what Angie Starling told me outside the shop.

"Yeah, I guess so."

"Why didn't you tell me about your locker?"

She scowls. "How do *you* know about my locker?"

"I bumped into Miss Starling while you were in therapy. She mentioned it."

"Oh." Maddie's voice quietens. She shakes her head, as though shaking a thought out of her mind. "Yeah, I guess she was around when it happened. She, like, talked to me and stuff."

"What do you mean?"

"She helped me clean it up and told me not to worry about the people who did it." Her gaze drifts to the window, directed, pointedly, away from me. That's not like Maddie, she's usually extremely direct.

"Do you know Miss Starling well?" I ask.

She turns back to me, her eyebrows lifted. "No. She just helped me this one time."

NEWS OF RIYA's fate ripples through Penry, and I think many of us hug our children tighter in the days that follow. I pull on my big girl's pants and take flowers, a card, and a casserole to the Shahs' house. They don't open the door, and I end up leaving it all on the doorstep. I don't blame them, but I hope they at least eat the food. I leave what I hope is a heartfelt note that Parvati won't take the wrong way. I miss her so much and want nothing more than to talk to her. But I can't break into her house and force her to let me comfort her.

We keep the kids home and don't watch the news. The hot weather breaks, and a blistering storm whips up along the coast, waves gnashing against the rocks and churning up white foam. We make our own pizza and take duvets to the sofa. Justin and I hug our children. Maddie avoids Justin as much as possible, but she's at least civil and lets me hug her.

But I find I can't escape from the news. Whenever the kids are asleep or distracted, I relentlessly doom-scroll social media, feeding on whatever morsels of unpleasant knowledge I can find. I'm morbidly curious, comparing my experience with Peter McKenna to news about Riya.

She'd been stuffed in a suitcase and taken to the dump. One of the workers found her by chance when he noticed a cloud of flies circling it. Then he noticed the weight and called the police. The night I read about how she was found, I dreamed about her inside that suitcase, and in my dream, she was still smiling.

We barely leave the house for three days. I keep the kids off from school, though there is a day when the school closes out of respect. But I decide to let Maddie attend the memorial service planned on a Wednesday morning. Justin promises to stay with her and make sure she isn't bullied.

On my own for the first time, I head over to my group therapy. Most of them already know Riya has been found, but I still see shocked faces as I talk about her case and how it's hit Maddie. But Cecilia sits next to me and gives me encouraging smiles and shoulder rubs.

"I think the police are holding back information," I say. "I don't even know how she died. All I know is that they're investigating it as a murder. Someone shoved her in that suitcase. Someone did that! This world is so dark, sometimes I can't stand it."

The group is quiet enough to hear a pin drop.

After therapy, I stop and have coffee with Cecilia. She buys me a chocolate muffin to cheer me up.

"How has Maddie taken the news?" Cecilia rips the top off her muffin and takes a large bite. "In her stride again?"

"Actually, no. She's genuinely subdued. She liked Riya a lot, and I think she misses her."

"You don't think she..." Cecilia raises her eyebrows as though I should infer what she means from her tone. It takes me a moment to understand.

"No!" I blurt out, louder than intended. I lower my voice when I notice staring faces. "No. Not at all. She wouldn't." My skin crawls, and I tug at my cardigan sleeve. Believing Maddie is capable of an impulsive push after being bullied by a mean girl is one thing. Murdering a friend, stuffing her in a suitcase, and dumping her in a bin is another.

"It's okay. I believe you. I'm not suggesting she's... you know," she whispers, "a murderer. I thought maybe you'd want to talk about it again. I know how lonely it is being the mother to a troubled teenager."

"It is," I reply, Angie Starling's words on my mind, "but I'm fine. And Maddie's fine too. They actually closed Phoebe's case. They couldn't find any evidence of it being anything other than an accident."

"That's great," she says.

The moment stretches, and in it I'm convinced that Cecilia believes Maddie got away with murder. Perhaps Cecilia thinks Maddie *is* capable of anything. Perhaps I gave her that impression with my verbal diarrhoea during our meetings.

"You know, I keep having these strange dreams," Cecilia says. "This is weird and quite disturbing, so..." She stares out of the window. "Ah, maybe I shouldn't say anything."

"No, go on. God, if anyone understands weird and disturbing, it's me!" I laugh.

"I keep dreaming that I'm going to jump off the cliff. Is that weird?" She lifts her hand and wafts it as though trying to cool down.

"It's not as weird as you might think. There's definitely a call-of-the-void aspect to this place," I say. "I've had similar dreams. That and a tidal wave coming to wipe us all out."

"Wow, we're so gloomy." She laughs. She takes another bite of muffin, then adds, "We should go for drinks one night."

I immediately think about Riya and start to shake my head. "I don't know. I used to be good friends with Riya's mum, and it feels wrong somehow."

"You can't grieve for them," Cecilia says. "They're not yours to grieve. People aren't going to think less of you if you actually have some fun for a change."

"I know, but—"

"But what?"

"Well, things have been pretty rocky with Justin lately. Maybe I should stay in with him. Talk more."

"Perhaps," she says. "But what makes you think that? Maybe you need time apart."

I shrug. "It would be nice. I'm hardly ever out of the house these days."

"I bet he goes out all the time."

"Not lately," I say. "But he was out a lot before all this happened."

"More than you, I bet," she says.

I agree, because it's true. Justin's football team and golf weekends do mean he takes more time away from home than I do. For some reason, I hadn't even thought about Justin's team recently. They must've decided to put a hold on matches after Phoebe's death. A lot of the players were dads, after all.

"Come on, Zo," Cecilia says. "I want to see you in the evenings when you can relax. I'm sober, so it's not like I'm going to be a bad influence."

In the end, she convinces me.

CHAPTER TWENTY-FIVE
THEN

Dropping off a five-year-old girl at her therapy session always felt weird. I never stayed in the room during those sessions, but sometimes I watched through the glass window as Maddie played on the floor while Dr Wilkinson sat on a chair with his legs crossed, either taking notes or asking questions. I had regular meetings with him to discuss Maddie's progress. Dr Wilkinson never sugar-coated a single thing, and I was grateful for that.

"She's quite open about her father," he told me one day. "She discusses the murders willingly, but with a sense of emotional detachment. I'm afraid to say that she saw a lot more than any child should be subjected to. She saw him raping the women. Hurting them." He removed his glasses and massaged the thin skin next to his large nose. I noticed the beginnings of age spots dappling his cheek bones, and while his hair was thick and shiny, it was almost completely snow-white. "Now, she might forget a lot of this as she grows up. Childhood amnesia is common. She might remember it all. I can't predict the future. But what I do know is that her sense of right and wrong is off." He replaced his glasses. "I've heard she's been getting into trouble at school."

"Yes," I admitted. "She's been in a few fights. I've been trying to teach her how to share, but if she wants something from another kid, she just takes it."

"She's impulsive, and she doesn't know how to be anything different. It's going to take time. A lot of patience. But I think you're doing a good job, and your bond is undeniable. Maddie loves you." He lets out a breath through his nose, which whistles through the quiet room. "But be careful. You're both in a bubble right now, and you have been since Maddie moved in with you. We know life isn't a bubble. It bursts eventually, and then things start to change. Routine is great, but keep an eye on Maddie when you have to break that routine. Life often throws us curveballs, doesn't it?"

I agreed, having no idea what he was insinuating then. Later, I suspected he was talking about my single status and how it would probably change in the future. Of course, any lover I brought into my life would alter Maddie's life too, and we had no idea how she might react to that. But before I had a chance to find out, life threw me a completely different curveball. Around six months after Maddie moved into my home, Dad found out he was ill.

At this point, my relationship with Mum and Dad wasn't a close one. They visited, and they did their best to interact with Maddie. Dad even played with her, and Mum asked her questions about school. They never stayed more than a few hours, and Maddie acted like they were my friends rather than her grandparents, but I saw them gradually warming to her. On one of those days Mum gestured for me to follow her into the kitchen while Maddie showed Dad her new dolls.

I wasn't surprised when she pulled me into the kitchen. She'd seemed agitated all morning and yet at the same time oddly quiet. I braced myself for bad news.

She gritted her teeth, and she whispered, "Dad's ill."

I almost dropped the mug I was holding. "What? How ill?"

"Very ill. He has Alzheimer's." She pressed two fingers to each eye, stemming the tears. "It took me a while to clock it. You know how forgetful he is. Then one day, he..." She inhaled, her breath shuddering, then cleared her throat. "He looked me in the eye, and he said, 'Who are you?' The floor dropped out from beneath my feet."

"Oh, Mum." I gripped the counter edge as it washed over me.

"The next day, we went to the doctors, and he had some tests done." She sighed and sank down into a chair. "He's... It's quite advanced already. He could have years, but then again, he might not. And who knows how long we have until he forgets us completely?"

I sat on the chair beside her and pulled her into a rare mother-daughter hug, picturing Mum coping with Dad as he deteriorated. The thought took my breath away with fear and grief and worry. "Well, you have my help, now. I can come round whenever you want."

She made a scoffing sound. "You have Maddie to think about. You won't be able to help at all, will you?"

"That's not true," I said. "I can come any weekend or in the daytime when I'm off work and Maddie's at school. Or I can find a child-minder."

Mum dried her tears and stood. "She'll run rings around a child-minder. Madam mustard."

"She's not that bad." I heard the defensiveness in my voice. I stood, too, edging towards the door, already wanting out.

"That girl can charm the birds out of the trees when she wants to. And when she doesn't..." Mum raised her eyebrows.

"You don't really know her, though." It irritated me that seconds after a moment of vulnerability, she chose to push me away. And, yes, I didn't want to admit that perhaps there was some truth to her words. That Maddie could be manipulative when she wanted to get her way. And maybe I had a tendency to indulge that from time to time.

"Neither do you," Mum snapped.

"She's a child!" I snapped back.

We faced each other, both red-eyed and drained. Neither of us wanted to admit we were taking out our pain on each other. Perhaps we didn't realise. Why couldn't we find some middle ground? Why couldn't we ever support each other?

I walked back into the living room, completely forgetting that I was supposed to make Dad a cup of tea. Instead, I got down onto the carpet and played dolls with Dad and Maddie.

"She's showing me her favourites," he said, his gaze fixed on my daughter.

"This is you, Mummy." Maddie lifted a brown-haired doll with exaggerated purple makeup. It was the first time she'd called me Mummy.

"It is? Let me see." I took the doll out of her hands and tried not to cry. My entire body felt hot all over. "Thank you, Maddie. She's so pretty."

"Mmhmm," Maddie said. "And she likes reading and drinking wine and eating chocolate."

Dad laughed. "Sounds like our Zo."

I sensed Mum walk out of the room. Instinctively, I reached out and grabbed my dad's hand, holding him tight. Neither of us spoke, only Maddie, who chatted to us about her other dolls.

I think about this moment a lot. The first time she'd ever called me Mummy. The dolls. The feeling of my dad's thin skin beneath my fingers. The itchy carpet against my knees. Sunlight slanting through the room. Why couldn't time have stood still? Not forever, but for longer. Give me more than a few seconds to hold on to every emotion running through my body. Memories of Dad when I was a child mixed with the present of my daughter and her dolls. But it was fleeting. Our lives changed in so many ways after that day. And there were times I wondered if I was even supposed to be Maddie's mother, especially when two months later, as I tried to help Mum deal with Dad's decline, someone came forward claiming to be Maddie's birth mother.

CHAPTER TWENTY-SIX
NOW

I drive home feeling lighter. Not only did therapy help, but I've also made a friend. Two coffees and a night out is definitely friend territory, and it's been a while since I've had that experience with another woman. The last friend I made was Parvati. Before that, I had school friends who fizzled out post abduction. Fair-weather friends who were easily bored by any kind of drain on their fun, like trauma from escaping a serial killer.

On the way into the house, I call out a breezy hello to my family, dump my keys into the bowl, and burst into the living room. It's four o'clock, and I expect the kids to be home. And they are, but sitting on the sofa near them are two police officers. Justin's face is as white as milk. Maddie sits opposite the officers, her arms folded, her face angled down. Her expression is unreadable, but her body language tells me all I need to know.

DS Rosen and PC Morton say hello as I settle into the armchair near the living room window. DS Rosen takes a sip of his tea, which I assume Justin made him. He's using the mug that says, "I'd rather be reading." I bought it for Maddie three years ago, around the same time she and Riya became friends.

"Sorry to drop in unannounced like this." Rosen's pale-blue eyes rest on me, and I notice his carefulness. An ambiguous smile that is not too wide, not too sarcastic. His eyebrows rise a touch for approachability. Yet none of it hides a face that always observes and analyses. "But I am grateful for the cuppa." He lifts the mug as though to toast me.

I cross one leg over the other, not saying a word.

PC Morton flips open her notebook, pen poised.

"How can we help you?" I ask.

Rosen places Maddie's mug on the coffee table. "I'm not here for a very happy reason, I'm afraid. As you know, Riya Shah has sadly died."

"Yes, we heard. We're heartbroken. She was Maddie's best friend."

Rosen glances sideways at Maddie. "I'm sorry for your loss. Is it okay if I ask you all a couple of quick questions? It won't take up too much of your time."

"Okay," I say. "We're happy to answer any questions. Riya meant a lot to us, and whatever we can do to help the Shah family, we'll do it."

"Thank you, that's very kind." He turns to Maddie. "Maddie, could you tell me about the last time you saw Riya?"

"I saw her at school, as usual," Maddie mumbles.

"The day before she disappeared?"

She nods.

PC Morton scribbles this down.

"How did she seem to you?" he asks.

"Upset. She'd broken up with her boyfriend." Maddie frowns and meets my gaze.

I nod grimly, encouraging her to continue. As protective as I feel of her, the sooner this is over the better.

"I told the police this when Riya first went missing," Maddie says.

"We won't be long, Maddie, I promise," he says. "Now, could you let me know the name of Riya's boyfriend?"

"No," Maddie replies, her tone sharper than I'd like. "I don't know his name."

"You don't?"

She shakes her head. "He didn't go to our school."

"Okay," Rosen says, "but I don't understand why she wouldn't mention his name."

"She wouldn't tell me." Maddie shrugs.

"You weren't curious?" he presses.

"She had her reasons. I wasn't going to force her, was I?"

One good thing about Maddie's forthrightness is that she genuinely doesn't care about gossip, and she doesn't force anyone to reveal secrets. Maddie is the kind of person to take a secret seriously *if* —and it's a big if—she thinks it's worthwhile keeping.

"Do you know *anything* about Riya's boyfriend? Think very carefully, because any small detail would be useful."

Shuffling in her seat, she unfolds and refolds her arms. I can tell she's weighing up her options.

"He was older, but I don't know how old. He owned a car and used to give her a lift sometimes. She said..." Maddie trails off and regards me.

"What is it?" I blurt out.

She speaks to DS Rosen. "He was married, and he had children."

I gasp. Rosen straightens his back, and PC Morton writes everything down.

"Do you know how old this man was?" Rosen asks.

Maddie shakes her head. "She never said."

"Do you know how old his children were?" he asks.

"No. All I know is he had kids, and she said it was why he never picked her up from school and why they never had dates in public."

"Where did they go for dates?" DS Rosen asks.

"Sometimes he booked a hotel room. She'd put on lots of makeup to look over eighteen, and they'd go to a city to spend the night." Maddie glances at me again. "They didn't meet that often. She always wanted to see him more than he wanted to see her. Sometimes I thought she was making it all up to get attention."

"It's okay," I tell her. "You weren't to know."

"Is it okay?" Justin's voice made me start. He'd been so quiet since I'd arrived. In fact, he'd barely moved, and I'd almost forgotten he was there. "You should've told someone, Maddie. Why didn't you? Were you jealous?"

"No," Maddie says. "Why would I be? I didn't even know who it was. I didn't even know it was true."

"I mean it probably wasn't," Justin continues. "Married men don't have affairs with teenagers."

"Justin, let Maddie speak!" I snap.

DS Rosen adds, "Unfortunately, some men do manipulate teenage girls into relationships with them. And if that happened here, I need to know about it. So, she was sad about her relationship ending, but what about before then?"

"Fine. Happy with the arrangement, I guess," Maddie says. "I mean, I think she got frustrated sometimes. Like she hated it when she wanted to meet him, but he had to do family stuff."

"Do you know why she broke up with this man?" Rosen asks.

"She said they didn't have much in common, and she liked Felix."

"Who's Felix?"

"A boy at school."

"Do you know his last name?" Rosen glances at PC Morton to indicate she should keep a note of everything.

"Henderson."

"Great. Thank you, Maddie."

"Was it him?" Maddie leans forward, placing her hands on her bony knees. "Did the man kill her? The one she dumped?"

"We don't know that yet." He fixes her with a firm but neutral expression, ending the conversation before it can begin. Most teenagers would back down, but not Maddie.

"He might not have taken it well," she suggests. "Or maybe his wife found out. Maybe it was his wife. How did Riya die?"

"I can't tell you that—"

"She was murdered, though, wasn't she?"

Rosen's lips close together tightly, and he clasps his hands. "Maddie, I have one final question for you. Where were you that Friday night when Riya went missing?" He checks his notes. "The third of April, between seven p.m. and eleven p.m.?"

"In my bedroom, doing homework."

"That's right," I say, without thinking about it. "She was here all night. I watched a movie with Gabe that night, and Maddie was in her room."

Rosen glances at me. "Okay, and did you stay in your bedroom most of the night or join Mum?"

"Bedroom," Maddie says.

Fuck. Did I see any of her that night? After dinner, which is usually about six o'clock, I tend to leave Maddie to her own devices. Sometimes I pop my head in and see if she'd like some ice cream or to chat about anything, but not every single time. What about the night Riya went missing? Did I see Maddie getting a snack or a glass of water? I can't remember, and Justin was out at football practice, so he wouldn't have seen her either.

"And what about you, Ms Osbourne? Do you remember seeing Maddie?"

"Yes," I say, without hesitation. "I saw her wander through to the kitchen. Once at about eight, and again about nine thirty."

PC Morton scribbles all of this down.

"Same," Justin says. "I saw Maddie making a sandwich and a cup of tea in the kitchen. We had a chat about her English coursework."

"You weren't at footie practice that night?" I blurt out.

"It was cancelled," Justin says. "Don't you remember?"

"Oh yeah," I reply. "That's right—it was."

PC Morton scribbles in her notebook again. The questions come to an end, and DS Rosen makes sure to tell us we need to contact him if we remember anything. But as he's speaking, my mind drifts. *Did I forget about football being cancelled? Or is Justin lying?*

LATER THAT NIGHT, after Maddie and Gabe are both in bed, I pour two glasses of wine and take them out to the garden. Justin sits with his back to me, and I take a moment to appreciate the man I married, with his broad back and long neck. Then I step forward and place the glass down on the patio table next to him, pulling him from whatever thoughts kept him from noticing me approach.

"Thanks, babe," he says, flashing me one of his easy smiles.

I pull my cardigan tightly around my shoulders and curl myself into the chair, lifting my knees to my chin. It's a beautiful evening. The sky is clear of clouds, and a midnight blue chases the last remnants of the cherry sunset.

"Just," I say, tapping the wine glass with my nail as I hunt for the words. "You didn't lie to the police, did you?"

"What? About footie? No. Don't you remember it getting cancelled?"

"No. I don't. I thought I spent the night at home with the kids. I thought you came home late that night."

"But I didn't," he says. "We watched *Cruella* before dinner, and then you and I watched a thriller once Gabe went to bed. Remember?"

I try to imagine him sitting next to me on the sofa, but I can't picture it. Obviously, we have watched movies together many, many times, but I can't remember that night. "Which thriller did we watch?"

He takes a gulp of his wine. "I dunno, something old with Robert De Niro in it, I think. Zo, why are you being weird about this? I wouldn't lie to you, would I? It's not like you'd dob me in to the police for trying to protect our daughter. I was there."

"And you saw Maddie making a sandwich?"

He sips his wine again. "No."

"I didn't see her either."

"That bit, I did lie about. See? I tell you everything." He reaches over and squeezes my knee. "You know you're my person. You know I'm a total blabbermouth, and you know I tell you every damn thought that goes through my mind, including how much I fucking love you."

I take his hand, the knot in my stomach gently unwinding. "I know."

He leans over to kiss me, and my worries melt away, at least for the seconds our lips touch.

Then, as we settle back in our chairs to listen to the waves so many feet below and watch the stars emerge from the dark, I find my thoughts drifting in another direction. "Do you think Maddie could have left the house that night? Do you think we should've been honest with the police?"

Justin pushes a thumbnail against the arm of his chair. "I don't know. Maybe."

"It's too late now." I don't want to think about it anymore. I want the wine to warm my blood and for murder and secrets to be somewhere else. Anywhere but here.

I find myself thinking about the first time Maddie called me Mummy. I even consider calling Mum. But it's Dad I want to talk to. I can't anymore, though, because he's not the same as he was.

"Do you think our lives will ever be normal?" I mutter.

"Huh?" Justin's eyes come back into focus as though he was lost in his thoughts.

I shake my head. "Never mind."

CHAPTER TWENTY-SEVEN
THEN

The first time I saw a picture of Lucinda Garth, I knew she was all wrong. Maddie had wide-set eyes around a small nose. This woman's eyes and nose crowded together inside a thin face. Maddie's straight chocolate hair in no way matched Lucinda's bottle-dyed black curls. I researched her on social media and discovered she was in her mid-forties and lived about fifteen miles away from McKenna's farm of horrors. The location was somewhat plausible, but the resemblance wasn't there.

Lucinda came to the police first and told them she'd been one of McKenna's victims. She described how he'd tortured and raped her, kept her chained in the barn, and ripped Maddie from between her legs when she was born. She'd described the barn well. I would give her that. But most of those details were available online anyway.

I kept digging, trying to find evidence of her lies. A Facebook or Twitter post would help. Anything to prove she was elsewhere when she claimed to have been imprisoned by McKenna. But there were gaps in her posts corresponding with her story. She could easily have gone back and deleted them before coming to the police, though.

The police didn't take her seriously, and neither did I. For one thing, she refused to take a DNA test. We all knew why—she was lying.

But Lucinda Garth decided she wasn't going to go away, effectively making my life hell.

First, she took her sob story to a daytime television outlet who cared more about creating entertainment than uncovering the truth.

When asked why she wouldn't consent to a DNA test, she dabbed at tears with a tissue and said, "I did. They took hair, saliva, and blood, and then they lost every single sample." She waved her hand dramatically, as though swatting a fly. "And I said to them, 'That's it. That's all I'm giving.' I spent a year with that monster as he tortured me, and I'm not letting anyone else put their hands on me. You don't understand how *monstrous* it feels to have hands on you, a needle in your vein..." She sobbed.

"But wouldn't this clear everything up?" the host, a woman with shrewd blue eyes, asked. "Wouldn't another test result in access to your daughter?"

Lucinda descended into a blubbering mess, spitting out her words mid-sob. "I can't... I wish I could, but I can't... I have a phobia now, of people touching me, trying to take things from me."

"Why didn't you go to the police after you escaped from Peter McKenna?"

"He said he'd find me and kill me," she spluttered. "I was too scared. I'd been homeless most of my life, addicted to heroin and meth. When I got away, I... Well, I went on a bender. So I wasn't in any position to be a mother, no matter how hard I wanted to be. And then I forced myself to get clean. For Maddie."

I watched most of the interviews while shaking my head. There were times she almost convinced *me*, and I knew she was faking it. For one thing, she hadn't even mentioned the female relative of hers buried beneath Peter McKenna's farm.

She took her story to various other outlets, and it ended up printed in every tabloid under the headline: *My Story*. Even the broadsheets wrote tentatively sceptical articles. One well-regarded journalist suggested the public wasn't taking her story seriously because of classism and that Lucinda's working-class origins were to blame for the fact she hadn't been granted any access to Maddie.

Meanwhile, I tried to keep the articles away from Maddie. I watched the interviews on my phone when she was in bed. I kept away from the paper stands in shops. I didn't mention Lucinda to her at all, because I simply didn't believe Lucinda's story. I didn't want Maddie to start believing her birth mother was alive and out there or that she'd need to stop living with me. But carrying all that stress trickled down, and she started getting into trouble at her new school.

Two months into the Lucinda Garth saga, I had a meeting with the headteacher to discuss Maddie's violent outbursts. She'd punched a girl for stealing her red crayon, slapped a teacher on the hand when the teacher tried to lead her out of the classroom, and repeatedly banged her own head against a wall while throwing a tantrum.

"I think we should book in a few meetings with Maddie's teacher present," the headteacher said. "It might be time to consider a functional behaviour assessment, and from there, we can put together a behavioural support plan to help Maddie move forward with her education."

"I don't know what any of that is," I said.

"Don't worry. It's nothing scary. We put together a formal document with some reasons why Maddie is acting the way she is and how to support or intervene in a way that helps her."

"Okay," I said, relieved. "Then I think we should do that. Whatever helps her."

At home, in between searches about Lucinda Garth, I researched educational plans for children with behavioural issues. The idea centred around figuring out what set off the behaviour then teaching the child to behave more appropriately when that situation occurred. That was good in theory, perhaps, but I worried about the teachers putting it into practice with Maddie.

Being the foster mum to a child still processing her trauma began to weigh on me emotionally. Of course, I loved Maddie, and that was perhaps why it weighed quite so heavily. I cared. Deeply. Someone who didn't care wouldn't feel that way. But the constant meetings, the therapy, my part-time job, the rift between me and Mum, Lucinda Garth's outrageous claims, and my dad's illness were all getting to me, not to mention my night terrors about Peter McKenna's barn.

I didn't use alcohol or drugs, but I ate my feelings. But even as I binged, I never purged. It started small, with biscuits and treats, then the convenience food slipped in when I was too stressed to cook. Then I realised I was feeding Maddie crappy food lacking nutrition too. Something had to give. One of those incredibly stressful situations needed to end. Then I had an idea. This whole thing with Lucinda had begun with a TV interview. I could end it with the same thing. It was time the world found out that Lucinda Garth was a lying fraud trying to steal Maddie's inheritance. And if I could earn enough money from the interview, I could quit my job and focus on being a mum for the next few months. It seemed like the perfect plan. Every tabloid would contain *my story*, the real story. Not hers.

Not long after my escape from Ivycross, I'd ignored a PR company who'd promised me an opportunity to tell the world my story. I got in touch with them, and they set up an interview with Delia Grisham, a reporter renowned for her personal hour-long deep dives into her interviewees' psyches. The deal was, I got ten thousand pounds for the interview, which was less than I'd hoped, but with the promise of further opportunities that could prove lucrative. The most interesting part of it all came as a consequence from the PR company putting feelers out—a potential book deal. I'd receive a six-figure advance, perhaps larger if the interview was a success, and all I had to do was write about my experience at Ivycross, along with my relationship with Maddie following the escape. People wanted to know why I'd chosen to adopt the child of the man who tried to murder me.

I didn't say yes right away. First, I wanted to set the record straight once and for all. I needed to shut Lucinda Garth up. I accepted the money, booked the interview, quit my job so I had more time for Maddie, and prepared.

Four nerve-wracking days passed before the interview was scheduled to shoot. Of course, Mum tried to talk me out of it. She didn't approve of people "sharing their dirty underwear in public," as she put it. I think she was afraid she wouldn't come out of the story in a good light. Perhaps she knew deep down that she hadn't handled any of this well. Perhaps she felt guilty.

The day before the interview, Lucinda wrote a blog post, which gained some traction on Twitter, garnering over ten thousand retweets.

It has come to my attention that the woman fostering my baby is going to try and slander me. She is a LIAR. I don't believe any part of her story. Was she even at Ivycross Farm? Did she really kill McKenna the Monster? There are whisperings that Zoe Osbourne is nothing but an opportunist. After running away from her responsibilities for a week, she came across Peter McKenna DEAD and took Maddie to the police. Who does that? Remember, guys, DON'T TRUST WHAT YOU HEAR!!! I am being slandered for TELLING THE TRUTH! You know what is in my heart is real. You know the agony I've been through. When has she ever even cried?? She's a stone woman. A robot!! And now she's going to go on TV and tell lies about ME!

I want to thank every last person for supporting me. I'll keep fighting to win my baby girl back. I called her Maddie after my grandmother Elsie Madeleine Garth. I am Maddie's mother. Not her! And I'll prove it.

I snapped. Underneath her post, I wrote, logged in as myself: *Then take the DNA test.*

It was visible for around five minutes before it was deleted, and Lucinda blocked me. But I didn't care. I had plenty to say in the interview.

CHAPTER TWENTY-EIGHT
NOW

On my way to the Black Swan to meet Cecilia, I can't help but miss the swanky nightlife of a larger city. Back in the Peaks, I was a taxi ride or short train journey to Leeds, York, or Sheffield. Penry has plenty of nice pubs, family pubs with outdoor seating, and a couple of nightclubs to accommodate hen and stag parties, but no thriving cocktail bars. I can't help thinking about putting on a slinky dress to sit at the bar with a martini. I met Simon in a bar fresh out of university. Back then, I had shorter hair, but once we were together, he asked me to grow it longer. Stupidly, I did. My hand drifts up to my hair, and I allow my fingers to comb through the dark tresses. I never did cut it short again. Maybe I should.

Simon wanted me slim and pretty, in a dress, wearing makeup, and with shoulder-length hair. Justin wanted me however I looked. But he also encouraged me to be healthy. Not in a mean-spirited, controlling way like Simon. He saw the way I sheltered myself indoors and encouraged me to go back out there. So, I started walking, and it helped, a lot. I never obsessed about running again like I did with Simon. Instead, I found a happy medium.

Having someone in my life ready and willing to accept and support me alleviated some of the stress that caused my binge eating in the first place. I'm still a stress eater. I still get severe situational anxiety. Those things will probably never go away, but I've mostly found a way to cope with them.

Nerves tickle my stomach as I take a seat by the window. It jars me to realise I haven't been out with a girlfriend since I last met Parvati for dinner. It was here, in the Black Swan, and we sat three tables over, sharing a bottle of Rosé. I miss her, and that fills me with the black tar of true sadness, not only for Parvati and her murdered daughter, but also for the realisation that I'll probably never get that friendship back with her.

I sip my white wine spritzer and try to concentrate on the present instead.

Cecilia arrives ten minutes late, carrying a plastic bag. She dumps it on the table, along with her handbag, which I note appears to be YSL. She's wearing a cream-coloured pencil skirt and a white silk blouse. On the other hand, I'm dressed in black in case I spill my spritzer.

"Oh shit," I suddenly blurt out. "I ordered myself a drink and completely forgot that..." I trail off, my heart sinking that I could be so thoughtless. Of course, Cecilia is tee total. But she casually waves her hand.

"Drink whatever you like, hun. You need it. You've earned it with the last few weeks you've had." She plonks herself down on the chair and thrusts the plastic bag towards me. "Go on. Open it."

She's incredibly pretty when she smiles. It lights up her tawny-brown eyes.

Tentatively, I open up the bag. "I didn't know we were doing gifts! I would've got you something." My hand comes across a squidgy brown paper package. I remove it, quickly fold the bag, and unwrap the gift. Inside is a similar bag to Cecilia's, quilted, cream and luxurious. There's a YSL logo on the side. "Cecilia... But... This is too much!"

She raises one palm. "Before you panic, you should know it's a knock-off." She lifts her own bag and lowers her voice. "I found a guy selling them near the seafront. I wouldn't normally, but feel it. This fake is amazing. You'd never know!"

I find her enthusiasm intoxicating. Soon, we're both giggling like schoolgirls bunking off PE. Then I open up the flap and check inside the bag. I can absolutely tell it's fake from the flimsy lining and the dodgy zip. *But from a distance...* I smile to myself. I can actually afford to buy myself a YSL bag if I wanted one. Designer items had never been my thing. This, however, is more fun. There's something delicious about the camaraderie of sharing bargains with another woman.

"I love it. Thank you! What do I owe you?"

"Absolutely nothing." She raises her eyebrows. "It's a gift."

As Cecilia heads to the bar to order a Coke, I place the bag down on the floor next to my own rather plain brown leather bag that I bought on holiday in Italy.

"I got you a top up," Cecilia says, placing a wine glass next to my half-empty one. "As a sorry for being late."

"Oh, don't be silly, but thank you." I pour the remnants of my first drink into the second.

"I got a call from my ex before I came out."

"Your ex-husband?"

"The one and the same," she says. "He's been released from prison, and... to tell you the truth, I'm scared of him. He's..." She sips her Coke. "You've seen the Halloween movies, right?"

I shudder. "That bad?"

She shifts her weight in her seat. "Pretty much, but without the mask. I have a restraining order against him, but it's never stopped him before."

Her skin is pale. I didn't notice it when she walked in, but I see it as clear as day now, and her fingernails are a bluish-white tint where she holds her glass tightly.

"I'm so sorry, that's awful," I say. "What did he say on the phone?"

"Nothing. He said nothing, but I know it was him. Who else would call and breathe down the line like a fucking psychopath?" She shakes her head. "What I don't understand is how he found me. I moved across the country to get away from him. I thought I'd done everything I could to stay anonymous. But he's still found me." She wraps her arms around her body and regards my glass of wine for a second or two too long. "It's relentless. You can't choose who you fall in love with. And when they turn out to be a psycho, you can't get away from them. Ever. You end up running and running, knowing they'll catch you up eventually, wondering if today could be your last day because they've decided it will be."

I don't know what to say. I dig into my bag and produce a tissue when her eyes water up. "God, Cecilia. I'm so sorry. If you need anything. If you need a safe place to stay, I live in a house with a security system. We have a spare room. We can put you up for a few days, or a week."

"God, no, I couldn't!" She dabs away tears. "Don't be so silly. But *thank you*." She squeezes my hand.

"Is your daughter going to be okay with him coming out of prison?"

"Gary's a bastard, but he'd never lay a hand on Lily. That's one thing I'm sure of. In the twelve years we were together, he never touched her. But she saw way more than she should've seen."

"I'm so sorry. It must've been awful."

She nods. "You know, I think the lies and the manipulation were worse than the physical stuff. You heal from a bruise, don't you? You actually see your skin mending. Some wounds leave scars. A fading reminder, I guess. It gets blurrier as time goes on. But when you're programmed into thinking that this man loves you, that you're his whole world and your value comes from his love... that takes longer to heal. You know?"

"Yeah."

Then she says, hesitantly, "Do you know? Have you been through it yourself?"

"No, well, I... umm..." I stumble. "My ex wasn't exactly abusive, just self-involved and controlling. An arsehole, basically."

"I bet you're glad to have Justin now then."

"I am. He's one of the good ones."

"What's that like?" she asks, laughing.

I open my mouth to tell her, but then pause, and it drags on, and the atmosphere shifts. Unspoken words hang between us.

"Is everything okay? Between you and Justin?"

I shake my head. "I think we've hit a rough patch. He's been different lately."

"How so?"

"Stressed." I laugh. "I guess that's to be expected. I've never known him stressed before."

"How long have you two been together?"

"Just over ten years."

"Wow," she says. "And he's never been stressed before."

I shrug. "I'm the worrier. He's the rock. Until recently." What I don't tell her is how this new side to Justin feels like a complete stranger at times but horrifyingly familiar at others. Instead, I say, "Honestly, I'm not sure who I'm more worried about right now—Maddie or Justin."

She leans in. "Spill. Get it off your chest."

I didn't realise how much I need to talk until that moment. I tell her everything.

WE STAY LATE, chatting about everything and nothing. I even tell her about Peter McKenna, which I never do. It's nice. I relax and unload. She's patient and a good listener.

On the taxi ride home, I think about Mum again. I even consider calling to check in. It's past midnight, though, and she wouldn't be happy.

Moving to Penry wasn't a decision I made lightly. Unfortunately, my relationship with her deteriorated to the point where I decided it'd be better to simply leave. I occasionally take Gabe to see her, or I go to visit Dad and see her there, but aside from that, we're estranged.

In the hallway, I slide the red pumps from my numb feet and stagger through to the living room, where Justin is still awake. He lifts a crystal glass filled with amber liquid and winks. My muscles clench, and I don't know why.

"You're up late." My voice sounds tight. I clear my throat in an attempt to sound normal again. "Did you wait up for me?"

He gets to his feet and moves closer. "Hey, baby." He pulls me into a hug and plants a kiss on my lips. His breath smells sour, and I pull away. "You okay?"

"Yeah, I'm good."

"How was your night?" he asks.

"It was great."

"Did you get a new bag?" He gestures to the fake YSL in my hand.

"Cecilia bought it for me. She found a guy selling knock-off designer stuff." I lift it and grin, still tickled by the idea of a girlfriend buying me a counterfeit bag.

Justin frowns. "Not really your style, though, is it?"

"What do you mean?"

"Fake designer stuff?" He scrunched up his face as though in disgust.

"It's a bit of fun."

His expression lightens. "Oh, yeah, totally. I'm just not used to seeing you with stuff like that, I guess. Plus, you're loaded. You could buy yourself real one."

I shake my head. He misses the point. Maybe it's too much of a girl thing to explain. We wander through to the lounge, and I sink into the sofa. "The kids okay?"

"Yeah. Maddie went to a sleepover."

"What?" I straighten. "A sleepover? With who?"

"Some girl called Annabel."

"Who the hell is Annabel? Did you check? Did you call her parents?" Maddie hasn't been at another girl's house since Riya went missing. *Died*, I remind myself. *Riya is dead.*

"Jesus, calm down, won't you?" he snaps.

I balk. I lean away from him, watching him messily swig whisky, a dribble of it escaping from the corner of his mouth. There's a flush of red skin worming its way up his neck. He's drunk. I have a sudden urge to run into Gabe's room, take him in my arms, and lock the door, and I'm not sure whether that's my past trauma speaking or something new.

"What the hell has got into you?" I whisper. "Why are you being like this?"

To my surprise, he crumples. He puts the whisky down on the coffee table and places his head in his hands. "I don't know. All I know is that I feel angry and scared all the time." He lifts his head, grabs my hand, and places it against his chest. "Can you feel my heart pounding? It does that all the time now."

"How long have you felt like this?"

"Weeks," he admits, letting my hand drop. "I guess it's all the worry about Maddie."

I soften, moving closer to him. It makes sense that the events of the last few weeks have unsettled him. I'm unsettled too. "You should've said. I'm sorry. I've been preoccupied with everything and never thought to check in with you."

"It's fine," he says. "I knew what I was letting myself in for. I need to handle it better."

"What do you mean you knew what you were letting yourself in for?"

He swigs the whisky one more time then wipes his mouth with the back of his hand. "I knew this kind of thing was going to happen eventually. Maddie's obviously a sociopath."

I'm too shocked to speak at first. "I can't believe you said it like that."

"I know you think the same thing."

I get up from the sofa and start to pace. "That's not... I... Look, I'm not a psychologist. I don't get to diagnose her. Labels like that aren't going to help, are they?"

"Zoe, for the first time in God knows how long, we're alone together, and *she* isn't in the house. Just admit it. Admit that Maddie is a sociopath without a conscience."

I shake my head. "It isn't that simple. There's a spectrum—"

"Do you think she murdered Riya Shah?"

"No!"

"What about Phoebe Thompson?"

I scratch my arm and turn my face away. "No."

"Yes, you do."

I shake my head. "I can't believe you let her leave the house."

"She's nearly seventeen. What was I supposed to do?"

"Not let her leave!" I shout.

"And have her murder me too?" He lifts his eyebrows. "You need to wake up, Zoe. You protect her no matter what, and it's sick. You're both sick. You're both fucked in the head." He jabs a finger at me. "You have survivor guilt, and you've invested every bit of your emotion into a serial killer's daughter. You're blinded by the fact she saved your life. It's not that you *can't* see it—you *won't*."

"No, I see it," I say. "But I don't care. You're right about one thing. I owe her my life, and I'll always fight for her."

Justin lifts his arms and lets them drop to his sides. "This is pointless. I'm going to bed."

He storms out, leaving me standing there in the middle of the room. I hear the slight shuffling of small feet and notice Gabe in the doorway, rubbing his eyes. I hurry over to him and stroke his hair.

"Is Maddie going to kill us?" he asks.

"Gabe, why would you say that?"

"You're scared of her." He sounds so matter-of-fact, as though it's normal to be afraid of someone you live with.

"She would never hurt us." I pull him into my arms and hold him tight. "Never, ever."

CHAPTER TWENTY-NINE
THEN

The *Delia Grisham Show* producers wanted all the juiciest details, as grisly as possible. A bald-headed man with a clipboard made it clear, even though he didn't explicitly say those words.

"We air after the watershed," he told me. "Which means you can say whatever you like. We can always edit things out if we feel viewers will be shocked. But, honestly, you can't shock Delia Grisham fans, so don't hold back. Okay?"

I followed him through the maze of backstage. People buzzed around me. Disconnected voices echoed eerily through walkie-talkies and headsets. Finally, sitting in the makeup chair, I wondered whether to describe the pop and squelch of the nail driving through his eyeball or begin with the urine-soaked clothes I sat in for hours. What would satiate the people? How much blood did they want me to spill?

The thought of saying those things nauseated me to the point where I worried I might vomit on set. Also, I wasn't stupid. If I wanted that six-figure book advance, I needed to withhold some details. Who would buy the book if I told them everything in this interview? That advance was going to change mine and Maddie's lives. It would give me *options*. I'd been born with a certain amount of privilege, being from a typical middle-class home, but I'd never truly known freedom. Not like the rich did. And while I'd never been a greedy opportunist, the idea of being able to buy the security and space I needed was enough to convince me to pursue the money offered.

"We're ready for you now, love," someone said, another headset person but not the bald man. They'd introduced themselves to me, but I'd forgotten their names. I found it difficult to concentrate on anything these people said to me. I kept thinking about Maddie. I'd dropped her off at an early-morning school group before coming to the Manchester recording studios, and she'd been bleary-eyed that morning, confused by the change in routine.

The Grisham show sometimes had a studio audience, but not today. I followed Headset Man to a small closed set decorated to resemble a hotel room, with a maroon patterned carpet and colourful but non-descript modern art on the walls. I sat down on a striped chair, and Delia sat opposite me in an identical chair with a stack of question prompts on her lap. Up close, her skin appeared too taut, like it'd been pulled back. Perhaps it had. After all, she was a fifty-year-old woman without crow's feet.

"Hello," she said. "It's nice to meet you. I'm Delia. Thank you for coming." After a brief smile, her eyes flicked down to the cards.

Message received, I thought. She didn't want small talk between takes. I was fine with that.

The lights warmed my skin. My pores were clogged with heavy foundation and powder, my lips greased up with pink lipstick. I'd never been one to wear a lot of makeup, and now I felt like a show pony pushed out into the limelight, worrying about lipstick on my teeth.

Someone counted down from five, and before I knew it, the interview started.

"Do you believe Lucinda Garth's story?" Delia asked, keeping her voice neutral.

"No, I don't." My voice had a note of finality, showing I was done with Lucinda Garth. "I don't believe her because I *know* she's lying."

"Why would she lie?"

I cleared my throat and took my time. "As Peter McKenna's next of kin, Maddie is set to inherit Ivycross Farm. Now, the farm itself isn't going to be easily sold. Many superstitious people would not want to live there. I know I wouldn't. But the farm includes a lot of land, which will be worth some money. Lucinda Garth is attempting to capitalise on that."

"Some might claim you are too," Delia said.

"I know." I clasped my hands together to steady my nerves. "But it's not the case. Maddie and I have a special bond, and I simply want to take care of her. I don't care about the farm at all. When Maddie is eighteen, she can decide what she'd like to do with it."

"What else makes you think Lucinda is lying?"

"Well, for one thing, she never took a DNA test. She claims that the police lost the samples. That isn't true. She refused one right from the start. If she was telling the truth, she'd take the test. It's that simple. Unfortunately, she's a good actress, and she's managed to convince a small minority of people that she's being victimised. Those people are so lost in her tangled web of lies, I'm not sure I'll ever manage to convince them otherwise." I paused, trying to steady my breathing. I focussed on the scar on the back of my hand. "There's something else that was never reported by the media."

Delia leaned forward eagerly. "What wasn't reported?"

"The police found two bodies beneath the farm with DNA that matches Maddie's DNA. One was Peter McKenna's mother, so Maddie's grandmother. The other was a young woman. Unfortunately, this young woman's body suffered damage from a flood and relocation. The police were unable to confirm *exactly* what relation she was to Maddie, but the results suggested she was an aunt. So if Lucinda is Maddie's mother, then her sister was murdered by Peter McKenna. Why hasn't she mentioned this in any of her stories? She didn't know about her—that's why. I wasn't going to say anything about this, because it helps to keep this information back in case Maddie's *real* mother ever shows up, but Lucinda Garth refuses to go away. It's time to stop this right now. She is not Maddie's mother."

"That certainly seems to be the case," Delia said, "if what you're saying is true."

"It is. Obviously, the police have been taking their time to catalogue all the evidence. When they've completed this, I'm sure it will be public knowledge. They can confirm everything I've just said." My blood ran hot, pumping hard through my veins, making me feel simultaneously powerful and weak, almost exactly how I'd felt fighting Peter McKenna in his torture barn.

For the rest of the hour, I told Delia about everything I'd seen in McKenna's house. The neat piles of women's clothing. The trinkets he kept in boxes. The photographs on the walls. I described the barn in intricate detail, making sure to point out the places where Lucinda had got it wrong. She'd described the barn as wide and open, when in fact, there were several animal stalls inside. I even told Delia about hiding in one of the stalls to surprise McKenna during my escape.

"I want to say their names. Denise Godwin, Tracey Sanderson, Zuri Abebe, Yasmin Lakhani, Lili Nowak, Susie Hannah. The six identified women murdered by Peter McKenna. We say his name a lot, don't we? But we don't say theirs. And they deserve to be remembered. Nothing but luck and the kindness of a five-year-old child helped me escape that day. If Maddie hadn't loosened the screws on my shackles, I wouldn't be here. I'd be dead, in the ground, with Denise, Tracey, Zuri, Yasmin, Lili, Susie, and two other unidentified victims. And Maddie would still be at the farm, watching her father kill women."

"I think you're doing yourself a disservice, Zoe," Delia said. "You fought. Without your fighting spirit, you'd be dead. But you're not. You're a very brave person, and so is that little girl. It sounds as though you belong together." She smiled. And with that, the interview concluded.

Physically exhausted, I drove to Maddie's school in a daze. She buzzed with excitement as I tried to muster up the energy to listen to her rambling.

"George let me play football with him today," she said. "He's nice."

"That's great, sweetheart."

"You look funny today." She climbed into the car, and I clipped her into the car seat.

"I had my interview today. They put makeup on me."

"I don't like it." She screwed up her nose. "Mummy, George said there's a lady who is my real mum."

I froze. It was the first time she'd mentioned anything about Lucinda. "What did he say?"

"Well, he said his mummy told him I'd be going to live with my real mum soon. Is that true?"

"No, sweetheart. You're stuck with me."

"Good," Then a moment later, she added, "I don't want her to come back."

In my exhausted haze, I asked, "Who, honey?"

Maddie stared out of the window. I'd never seen such a wistful child. Then it hit me. She was talking about her mother. I pressed my knee against the back seat and waited.

"My other mummy."

"When was the last time you saw your other mummy?"

"Long time ago."

I decided not to push. She probably wouldn't be able to tell me anyway. "Maddie, if I show you a picture, will you tell me if that person is your mummy?"

"Okay."

I reached into the front of the car, grabbed my phone, and tapped "Lucinda Garth" into the search engine. When her face popped up on the image search, I passed the phone to Maddie.

"Is that her?"

"No," Maddie said. "My other mummy was much prettier than her." She made a face and passed the phone back to me. I almost laughed at how offended she was. "Will you make sure my other mummy doesn't come back? I don't want her to. I like living with you."

"I'll make sure, sweetheart."

I checked the cat seat one more time and closed the car door. Despite the afternoon sun, cold had seeped into my blood. Maddie remembered her mother.

CHAPTER THIRTY
NOW

Gabe's feet are jammed against the small of my back when I wake up, still wearing my dress from the night before. They're two tiny bricks against my spine. I drifted off while putting him back to bed, and when I check the clock, it's six in the morning. On a Sunday. I'm not sure whether it's the remnants of alcohol in my blood, but I woke with a snap, as though a hypnotist brought me back from unconsciousness. I can't go back to sleep now.

When I swing my legs over the side of Gabe's bed, my feet find his Darth Vader figurine, and I cringe when its sharp angles press into my flesh. I hobble through to the kitchen and fill the kettle. The sunrise blooms over the sea, rippling streaks of magenta across the surface of the water. I take a mug of hot tea into the garden, shivering in my dress, but enjoying the cool bite of the morning.

I'm sure my makeup is smudged, and the soft fabric of my dress is creased, but I can't face heading through to the bedroom I share with Justin to shower and change. I sit there watching the pinks morph into a clear blue sky, the salty air caressing my skin. At about seven thirty, Maddie strolls up, her overnight bag slung over her shoulder. Wordlessly, she sits next to me on a rattan chair.

"Who's Annabel?" I ask.

"Hello to you too." She pushes her hair behind her ears and lets out an exasperated breath.

"I'm not in the mood for small talk."

Maddie notices me properly for the first time, and her penetrating gaze takes in my odd attire. "Why do you look like you've had a drunken one-night stand?" She grins. "Oh, shit, did you cheat on Justin? Are you booting him out? Have you had enough?"

"No!"

She tuts, disappointed.

"Don't call him Justin. He's your dad. And he's done a lot for you recently."

"He's not my dad. And..."

"What?"

"Nothing." She sighs. "Annabel is a friend I made online."

"What?"

She holds up a hand. "Don't have a heart attack, Mum. Okay? She's nice. She lives in Penry, but her mum home-schooled her, so she doesn't have many friends. We chilled at her place and watched a film. That's it."

"I want to talk to her parents."

"Nope."

"Maddie."

She stares me down. "Mum, I'm nearly seventeen. I could move out if I wanted. Next year, I'm going to leave whether you like it or not. You can't keep micro-managing my life."

"Micro-managing?"

"Yeah."

"God, you're weird sometimes." I throw an arm over her shoulder, and she lets me. "Fine. I'll stop being a nosey bitch. But you have to stop pushing your parents away, okay?"

"Fine," she says, in her exaggerated teenage voice. She's quiet for a moment, leaning into my shoulder, which is awkward with the gap between our chairs. "Mum. You do know that no matter how we met, you'll always be my mum, right? I know we're not related, but you're *my* mum, and that's all I care about."

I glance away before she pokes fun at the tears gathering in my eyes. "Okay. You know I feel the same way. No matter what."

She bobs her head up and down once, firmly. The gesture is almost grim in its earnestness. "And I know I'm difficult or whatever. I know I probably have some... problematic traits and that you have to defend me when people accuse me of murder." She says it so casually, like it's an everyday occurrence. Maybe it is at this point. "I'm going to do better, I swear."

"What do you mean 'do better'?"

"Like, not get myself into all these weird situations, for one thing. Maybe I'll try and keep away from teenage girls who seem likely to die."

I sigh this time. "That makes our lives sound so morbid."

"We do have morbid lives," she says. "But we're alive, and those suckers are dead, so..."

"Maddie!"

"I know... I know. Bad taste. Anyway, what I want to say is you'll always be my mum, no matter what." She pauses. "But Justin will never be my dad."

I finally ask, "Why is that, Mads?"

The air hangs heavily between us, laden with anticipation. I'm aware of every drop of tea lying in the pit of my stomach and how it could lurch at any second. I'm convinced then that I've missed an essential piece of the puzzle and that Maddie holds it. But what? Why won't she tell me?

"I don't trust him, and I don't think you should trust him either," she says.

We both sense movement behind us at the same time, twisting our torsos in the direction of the sound. Justin waves at us from the window, a sheepish grin on his face. I know that smile. He wants to talk about our argument.

Maddie stands and walks away, a quiet, dejected sigh coming from her as she moves. It's obvious now, how much she dislikes him. I'd always assumed it came from jealousy and from some of the attachment issues she'd had as a child. But now I think otherwise. She truly does not like him. And I wonder if I should've picked up on that sooner, so that I could re-evaluate the way I see my husband.

Over the years, I've had to ask myself: is it my trauma response, or am I in danger? Is this person bad, or am I projecting my fears onto them?

There's my husband in the window. He's either the safe, protective, and loving man I believed him to be or a person I don't know. Am I capable of recognising an abuser standing right in front of me?

I think of his drunk hands on my body, the convenient way he sometimes ignores every sign that I'm not interested in sex. Why do I let out nervous giggles around my own husband? Why does he make me uncomfortable at times? Why is it okay that he puts his own hobbies first? I don't stay out overnight because we have kids, but *he* does. Would he stay in for me? The situation never comes up because I don't tend to be invited anywhere. I don't have many friends, and even that makes my mind swirl and swirl. Does Justin ever encourage me to have hobbies outside the house, or does he wait up for me every time I go out with a girlfriend because he doesn't like it?

Is there an art to picking and choosing the parts I love about him, deftly ignoring the parts that aren't so good? These last few weeks have transformed him into someone I don't recognise. Someone angry. Someone argumentative. And why is that? I'd forgive him if it were his stress response. I know I've not always been a ray of sunshine since my abduction. Perhaps stress corrupts people into the worst of themselves? Or does it reveal the truth?

Why doesn't Maddie trust him? Why did he lie to me about his cancelled football practice? I stand up and move towards the house. My muscles are tense again. This has all happened so quickly. I love him, don't I? I've always loved him. He's my rock, my gentle man.

"You okay, babe?" he asks as I walk into the house.

"Yeah," I lie. "I'm fine. Tired. Woke up with Gabe kicking me."

He nods. "Cuppa?"

I agree. I examine his face, searching his features. I think of how gently our relationship began. We took it slowly, me, him and Maddie meeting in a café near Maddie's primary school. Secret glances above hot chocolates. I'd been cautious about Justin. Not like with Simon. But then Simon was great at playing a character. He adapted his personality to whoever interested him at the time. I loved running, so he told me he was training for the London marathon. I loved Italian food, so he took me to his "favourite" Italian restaurants, all of which turned out to be places he'd researched online. Justin never came across in that way. He had a genuine down-to-earth personality. He liked walks, disliked pets, preferred Thai food, and loved the sports I hated.

"Shall we talk?" he asks, handing me the tea.

I pull myself back to the present. "I think it's time."

CHAPTER THIRTY-ONE
THEN

Lucinda Garth retaliated, taking to Facebook, Twitter and Tumblr to spout vitriol about me.

Do NOT listen to this liar. She was never even at Ivycross Farm. She has the police in her pocket because she sleeps with them all. My heart breaks because while this lying cheat gets away with it, my Maddie is being abused. Someone sent me photos of her BRUISES! Do not believe Zoe Osbourne, she is a LIAR.

She posted similar messages to her social media accounts and personal blog. And with every post, there would be dozens of comments egging her on to reveal more.

Around this time, I started to receive death threats: *You're a waste of air. Just kill yourself. If you don't, I'll finish the job for you.* I closed my Twitter and Facebook accounts. I urged my mum to do the same, as these people were targeting my family too.

I reached the point where I came close to hunting down Lucinda Garth myself. I dreamed about shoving that rusty nail through her eyeball instead of Peter's. I'd wake up tense. Only Maddie, therapy, and writing helped my muscles uncoil.

I thought about suing her for defamation. I had a case for it. But I thought it might put Lucinda in the spotlight and that she would actually enjoy the process. So I waited for her to get bored and move on. I focused on three things: Maddie's education, helping Mum with Dad's ongoing illness, and writing my book.

I had plenty of time to write after leaving work. Oddly, I barely cared about quitting the job I'd held for years. My colleagues gave me a card and some chocolates, and that was that. The last part of my old life peeled away, like an onion skin, leaving the new Zoe, the fleshy centre. Just my parents and the occasional text from an old friend tethered me to the "before."

The publisher suggested some ghost writers to me, but I decided I wanted to tell my story my way. After sending them sample chapters to prove I could string a sentence together, they agreed.

A week after the interview aired, I went into the school for a meeting about Maddie's education assessment with Maddie's teacher, Sade, Dr Wilkinson, and the headteacher.

Rita, Maddie's teacher, took the lead in the meeting. "We've made some observations, and we feel like Maddie tends to become aggressive when she wants something. If she wants a crayon, she takes it. She sees the world as competitive. Like a race. She thinks winning is... well, winning. And she doesn't see cheating as a problem. We'd like you to work on this at home as much as you can."

"I do my best," I said. "I try hard not to give in at home. She's really not so bad, you know?"

"Oh, we don't mean that she's bad," Rita added. "These are trigger points we've noticed at school. I bet you've seen them at home too."

"Don't feel disheartened," Sade added. "We always knew school would be a big adjustment period for her."

I agreed with them. Of course I did. I saw the same problems with Maddie that they did, and I knew it was all down to her father. He took lives because that was what he wanted. So for the next few weeks, I spent a lot of time trying to make helping others seem like a good thing to do.

"Is it better to give presents or receive them, Maddie?" I'd ask.

"Get presents!" she'd reply.

"Presents are fun. But what about making someone else happy?" I'd prompt.

She'd think about it. "No, I want presents. Can I have one?"

"Only if you're a good girl at school today. Are you going to share your crayons?"

Sometimes shadows passed over her features. "S'pose so."

And so it went on. I never quite felt like she understood the reasoning behind being "good," but she at least learned that if she behaved herself, she'd be rewarded. It was better than nothing.

After those chats, we watched television or played with her doll-house. Sometimes the chats led to rebellion, and she screamed or threw her dolls at me. Other times, it brought us closer. In moments of contentment, when we cuddled up on the sofa, I'd ask her gentle questions about her "other mother," as she called her birth mother.

"Do you remember what happened to your other mummy?"

"She left," Maddie said.

"Left the farm?"

Her small face angled up towards me, her eyes large, a lovely nut-brown shade. "One day, she wasn't there anymore."

Maddie never offered up too much information about her mother, and after a few minutes, she'd tell me she was too tired to keep talking about it. But I assumed she meant that she never saw her mother again because her father had killed her mother. I started to believe that the body found by police was in fact Maddie's mother, and no one was ever going to take her away from me.

It was an odd sort of fairy tale where the monster killed the queen, leaving the princess to live with her fairy godmother. But it brought me comfort at night. It made me believe we'd have a happy ending. I needed to believe that. Otherwise, I wouldn't sleep.

MADDIE WENT through cycles of good behaviour followed by frustration and tantrums. At the end of the school year, the head-teacher, filled with genuine regret, told me that the parents were complaining and it was time to find another school. I was devastated. We had a rhythm. Everything about that school was convenient. We walked there together. I'd built up a relationship with her teacher. We stopped at a nice café on the way home, and I bought her a hot chocolate or a muffin.

It didn't hit us at first, because we spent the summer holidays in a bubble. I ignored Dr Wilkinson's warnings and leaned into it—my life with Maddie became my everything. We'd get up, eat breakfast, water and prune the herb garden, go to the park, watch movies, and read stories. After Maddie went to bed, I opened share bags of chocolate and worked on the book. I was in the throes of my unhealthy eating habits, binging at night then starving myself before travelling anywhere, scared of my digestive system playing up at the worst moment.

When September rolled around, the bubble burst, and Maddie had to attend a new school. It wasn't as pretty. There weren't as many colourful drawings in the windows, and the carpark was full of potholes. But this school hired teaching assistants for kids in need of support in the classroom. That was a big draw for me. Having someone in the room keeping an eye on Maddie could potentially stop any of her aggression before it even occurred.

A blond-haired man jogged over to my car on Maddie's first day. He crackled with energy, and his cobalt eyes twinkled in the autumn sun. His hand lifted towards me, and I took it, surprised by the jolt of electricity that shot up my arm.

"You must be Zoe and Maddie," he said, his voice lilting with warmth, a hint of Yorkshire accent. He had that kind of "pleasant young man" energy that made older women stop to chat at bus stops.

"Guilty as charged," I said.

"Hi, Maddie." He got down on his haunches so they were eye to eye. "It's nice to meet you. I'm Justin. I'm Miss Staveley's assistant. I'll be helping you settle in today. Is that okay?"

"No." Maddie folded her arms, still cross about moving schools.

"I get it," he said, stretching his legs back up to full height. "Guess what! My parents moved when I was ten. And I had to make a whole new set of friends. I didn't like it either."

"So?" Maddie stuck out her bottom lip. She had her face angled down, one of the tell-tale signs of an incoming tantrum.

"That's rude, Maddie," I said, keeping my voice light. "We've talked about rudeness. What did I say about it?"

"Don't remember."

"Yes, you do, because you repeated it to me this morning. I said that we should all be kind to each other. The world is a much better place with kindness."

She remained sullen.

"Plus, you get ice cream after dinner if you've been a good girl." I relented.

Maddie pointed one toe in Justin's direction, then she glanced up at me and unfolded her arms. Finally, she let me place a bookbag over her shoulder and a lunchbox in her hand, and she followed Justin into the school. He waved at me, the sunlight catching the natural high-lights in his hair.

OVER THE NEXT FEW WEEKS, I heard a lot about Justin from Maddie. Apparently, Justin helped her make a papier-mâché sword when the class was learning about the Romans. He told another little girl—Carlie—to share her PVA glue, and she did. Maddie found this remarkable, because she always had problems asking other children to share their things. Justin made school brighter for Maddie, and every day, he walked her back to the car, and we learned more about each other.

I learned about his degree and that he hoped to become a fully qualified child psychologist one day. He liked hiking on the moors, though that made my heart skip a beat. I didn't want to tell him who I was and what had happened to me. But he never pried, even when I gave vague answers to questions like "What are you doing this week-end?" I didn't want to tell him I was meeting a solicitor to see if I could sue the woman pretending to be my child's birth mother because she kept telling lies about me.

Our first coffee together happened because Maddie insisted on it. She wanted Justin to come for hot chocolate after school. He agreed after I indicated it would be okay. Maddie and I went on ahead and waited for Justin to meet us at about five o'clock, after he'd finished at the school. We ate paninis as we waited. Maddie jiggled around in her seat, singing softly as she transformed her sandwich into an aeroplane and made it fly through the air. To me, she would always be a miracle. Having her next to me was a wonderful fluke of fate.

Then Justin walked in, and I noticed his slim figure and mop of untidy hair. A few other women watched him enter, but his eyes found me before he noticed them. For the first time in years, I saw a man, and I wanted him. And that made me... conflicted.

"Hey," he said. "Nice panini, Maddie. Want a hot chocolate to go with it?"

"Yes!" she said, grinning at him with half-chewed food between her teeth.

"What about you, Zoe?"

"Oh, you don't have to." Even to my own ears, my voice sounded clipped. "Actually, I still have half a cappuccino here."

"You sure? It's my treat."

"Honestly, I should be the one to—"

"Please, I'd like to," he said.

I still didn't accept a drink. I'd clammed up. That moment of lust led to insecurity. It led to me imagining Peter McKenna's breath on my neck. I hated to admit it, but I didn't trust men, not anymore. And yet, this man might, possibly, be different. I couldn't give him my trust, which meant I didn't deserve his sweetness. Insecurities seeped into my thoughts. He wouldn't want me anyway, I decided. I'd changed in appearance since the farm, and not just because I'd gained weight. I never had time for a professional haircut, and I hadn't bothered with makeup. Why would he find me attractive? Worse, there was the invisible stain that lingered—battle scars from the past.

I barely spoke for the hour we spent together. Instead, I watched

Maddie as she chattered on about our house and the herbs we'd been growing in the garden. We'd put together a petite greenhouse to keep them safe during the winter months. When she veered into some dangerous territories—like her father, her social worker, and the residential house she'd stayed at—Justin never even blinked. He talked to her like she was a person.

He met us again two weeks later. This time, I warmed up slightly. I allowed him to buy me a Bakewell tart to go along with my latte. He'd brought a game with him. We each got a piece of plasticine and had to sculpt an item out of the clay. Then the other two would have to guess what it was. Maddie made animals, flowers, and, hilariously, one of her teacher Miss Staveley, which Justin even guessed. He teased my poor representation of a high-heeled shoe and my misshapen horse.

Quietly, as we left the café, he said to me, "When can I take you out on a proper date?"

I blushed. "Not yet."

"Okay," he said, without missing a beat. Some men might have become defensive at even a sniff of rejection, but not Justin. "Whenever you're ready. Do you want to let me know? Or should I ask again sometime?"

"Maybe ask again." I'd never been particularly forthcoming with men. "But this is nice." I gestured to us and Maddie, who was playing with the plasticine.

"It is," he said.

We carried on like that, meeting in the café after school every Friday. We felt like a family each time. Before him, I hadn't known I'd been searching for a missing piece, and yet when he arrived, I knew I had.

CHAPTER THIRTY-TWO
NOW

"I love you, Zo," Justin says. "You know that, right?" And I'm immediately transported to our wedding day, staring at him in the registry office with his open, emotional, sensitive eyes gazing back at me.

"I know," I reply.

Yes, I believe he does love me. I do. But I look at him, and I see two realities. The one I thought I was living in, with a great, supportive, and gentle man. The other is a distorted version of the same thing, obscured by my own bias, my projection of who Justin is and who we are together. Which one of these realities is true? If it's the latter, there's another truth beneath the surface, one I don't want to unearth.

He grabs my hand and pulls me out of the room back out into the garden. He's filled with urgency, tears brimming. "I shouldn't have said any of that shit last night. I'm so sorry. I didn't mean it."

My gaze locks on his hand on top of mine. His skin is soft against mine. I wonder what my dad would've made of Justin. They met once, but Dad was too poorly to be himself by then. He hadn't liked Simon, even though I could tell he tried to like him. He never told me why either. Perhaps he saw in Simon what I hadn't seen myself: the latent narcissism waiting to drain me emotionally during our marriage.

It could be the thought of Simon, but sudden heat surges through my blood. "Don't lie to me. Show me enough respect to tell me the truth. You do think I have survivor guilt, and you think I'm blinded to who Maddie is. But I see her. Every part. I'm not going to walk around calling her a sociopath, though. What good would that do?" I sigh and take a step back. "There's a part of me that will always wonder whether she..."

"Say it, Zoe." He folds his arms across his chest, waiting.

"Whether she pushed Phoebe Thompson. But even if she did, I'd still love her. I'd fight for both of my kids if they are in trouble. I'd do anything for them."

"What about Riya?" he asks. "If Maddie killed one, then she must have killed the other."

"Don't be ridiculous. Maddie and Riya were best friends. Riya's death is... different. Someone carefully planned her murder. She was found in a suitcase, for God's sake. Maddie couldn't have done that. But with Phoebe, it's different." I run my fingers through my tangled hair, searching for the right words. "I could understand that. They had a fight, she seethed, she followed Phoebe out there, and it happened... spontaneously. Maybe she pushed her harder than she expected. An awful thing, obviously, but—"

"Zoe, you sound insane."

"What?"

"You sound completely insane." His hands fly up to his head, where he gestures wildly to mimic insanity. "You're saying one murder is okay and the other isn't. And you're saying Maddie is capable of one not the other. Do you even hear yourself? You just admitted that you think your adopted daughter is a murderer."

"No, I didn't. I said I could forgive one and not the other. I don't even think she *did* kill Phoebe. I'm just saying I could—"

"You'd *forgive* her for killing someone? Even if she never received any justice?"

My voice comes out shakily. "Yes."

"That's sick. You're sick. *She's* sick."

"I can help her," I say. "I'm the only one who can."

"She'll never learn the consequences of her actions if you don't force her to suffer them." He lets out a fast, whistling breath through his nose.

"Consequences of what? The police investigated Phoebe's death and ruled it accidental. They have no proof Maddie did anything, and neither do we."

"What about Riya?"

"You tell me," I snap. "Because you're the one who lied about where you were that night. And you're the one who lied about seeing Maddie."

"Yeah, well, I wanted to help her too. She's my daughter too."

My jaw smacks shut, teeth clicking together. A few weeks ago, I would've believed him. Not now. Maddie doesn't consider Justin to be a father to her. Everything Justin says sounds like he doesn't think of Maddie as a daughter.

Before I can say anything else, I notice movement at the house. Gabe wanders out onto the patio in his PJs.

"Maddie told me to tell you she's gone to see Annabel."

"Okay, thanks, honey." I smile widely at him, hoping he didn't hear our fight.

Before I can walk away, Justin grabs my arm one more time and spins me towards him.

He lowers his voice to a whisper, smiling so that Gabe doesn't sense anything is wrong. "You'd better hope this Annabel doesn't end up dead too." But then he jabs a finger towards my face, so fast I know I'll wonder later if it even happened. The words come out through his teeth, low and snake-like. "Because teenage girls are dropping like flies. And our daughter is in the middle of that shitstorm."

And with that, my easy-going husband becomes a stranger to me. Barely a heartbeat after his pale finger jabbed towards my face, he scoops Gabe up into his arms and asks my son what he'd like to do today.

"Let's go to the beach!" Gabe says.

THE TWO OF them leave about thirty minutes later while I remain sitting in the garden, still in my crumpled clothes from the night before, sweat beading across my forehead in the mid-morning heat.

I call Maddie's mobile phone, but it goes straight to voicemail. Then I remember her word of warning, her request not to be "micro-managed," and I refrain from calling again. This new friend seems highly suspect to me. But the more I push, the more Maddie will pull away.

My mind buzzes with negative thoughts about the new friend. I conjure up a psychopathic Annabel tutoring Maddie to embrace her dark side. Shivering, I see the shadow of Peter McKenna standing behind my daughter with this faceless teenage girl at her side.

"Get a grip, Zoe," I mumble to myself.

I head inside the house and close the sliding patio door. Before I dive into the mystery of who Annabel is, I need to figure out what's going on with my husband. It's time to investigate the whopping lie he told me and the police.

Justin has always been the kind of man to pick up and quit hobbies fairly quickly. There's a box in the garage filled with archery equipment and more boxes full of paints, brushes, and canvasses. At one point, he decided to go vegan but lasted two weeks. However, despite his tendency to quit everything else, his commitment to the football team has been consistent. Until, that is, this lie about the cancelled practice. And, come to think of it, he hasn't been to any practices since Phoebe died. We haven't mentioned it. Perhaps the dads haven't felt like playing since two teenage girls died, which is understandable. Either way, I need to find out.

The first thing I do is call Mikayla, the wife of Billy, one of Justin's football teammates. We met once, at a parents' evening. We exchanged phone numbers that day because Maddie and her daughter, Philippa, both had work experience at the same place for a week, and we wanted to carpool.

"Hi, Mikayla. It's Zoe Osbourne."

"Oh, hi, Zoe. Actually, I'm on my way—"

"That's okay. I actually wanted to talk to Billy. Is he there? I have a question about football team stuff. I'm trying to organise the household; you know how it is. Can I check the schedule—"

"Why?"

Her response takes me aback. "Well, because of the reasons I just said."

"No, I mean... Okay, this is awkward. Justin quit the football team six months ago."

My first reaction is that Mikayla has it wrong. She must be thinking of someone else. But after a moment of silence, she carries on.

"Justin quit, and Sam's dad, Robert, took his place." Her voice softens. "Sorry, Zoe, but it's not a mistake. I've been out for drinks with the whole team. It's common knowledge that Justin quit a long time ago."

"Are you sure?" I still feel like she has it wrong. How could I miss this?

"I'm sure, Zoe." Her voice is soft with pity.

I can hardly stand it. I clear my throat. "Right. Thanks, Mikayla. Could you do me a favour and not mention to anyone that I called you?"

"I won't. I promise."

"Thanks."

"Zoe, what are you going to do?"

"Find out where he's been going, I guess."

"Try not to jump to conclusions. You never know—it might be a nice surprise."

I almost laugh. There is no way my husband has been lying and staying out late or even overnight because he's planning a surprise birthday party. No, there's more to it. I'm certain of it.

"Hey, does Billy still go on the golf trips?"

"What golf trips?"

Fuck. "Never mind. Thanks, Mikayla."

"No problem."

I tap my phone screen and drop it onto the sofa. No football. No golf. I storm through the house and into the garage, not bothering to put on shoes. My bare feet slap the cold garage floor. I step around my car and head over to the back, where we store our outdoor gear.

He knows I don't socialise with the mothers at school. Parvati is my only mum friend, and Dev isn't interested in sport. So how would I find out? Who would tell me he didn't go on these trips? Aside from that week I sent Mikayla a few messages to arrange the carpool, I never saw or contacted anyone from Justin's team or their wives. He relied on my lack of social interaction. Maybe he even encouraged it. Maddie never liked school dances or parent events, so sometimes we didn't go. Other times, Justin volunteered.

I stop. There they are: his golf clubs. I've never paid much attention to them before, but now they are essential. One by one, I yank the clubs from the case, examining them, and one by one, I find clean, smooth metal. Next, I empty out every compartment, searching for the remnants of a trip. I'd expect to find receipts maybe, food wrappers, golf balls... *anything*. Every single compartment is empty. I stare down at the clubs by my feet. Every time he goes away, I watch him pack these clubs into the back of the car. But they've never even been used.

CHAPTER THIRTY-THREE
THEN

Maddie had never frightened me before Justin came into our lives. She had behavioural issues, and some of the odd things she said made me uncomfortable. But she never focused her aggression on me or any other member of my family. All of that changed when she was seven.

I'd thrown two birthday parties for her already. For the first one, I'd taken her to the zoo and watched carefully as she fed parrots, stared wide-eyed at the penguins, and listened to the zookeeper talk about chimpanzees. For her seventh birthday, Maddie, Justin, and I went on a day trip. Maddie had chosen her own birthday, and she'd decided on July the thirteenth because it'd been her dog Chalkie's birthday. We took her to Scarborough and ran along the beach, greasy with sunscreen.

In this year, she officially became my daughter—the local authority authorised an official adoption since no credible family members had come forward with any evidence of being related to her. Lucinda Garth and her fans had finally backed off. I was in love. My book was a few months away from being published. Things had never been better.

It happened gradually. Maddie grew frosty with Justin when I started spending time with him alone. Arranging a date with Justin proved to be a tricky manoeuvre involving expensive childcare, which meant we didn't spend time alone together often. Mum still flat out refused to babysit Maddie at night, though she did watch her for an hour or two here and there. We were in the process of finding a care home for my dad, which also complicated things and tinged much of that time with sadness. I loved my life, but I hated that my dad was deteriorating so quickly. I wanted him to spend more time with Maddie, but Mum often stepped in and put a stop to it.

After dating for months and discussing the future at length, Justin decided it'd be best if he moved into my house with Maddie rather than ask Maddie to move. By this point, I'd used some of my book advance to buy the house I was renting. We spent time on Pinterest researching ways to extend into the garden to accommodate us both. By selling Justin's house and two of us paying the mortgage, we could combine our savings to make our home big enough for the three of us—or possibly four of us in the future. I'd never known the kick of a growing baby. I wanted to experience pregnancy, to hold my baby in my arms.

I couldn't blame Maddie at first. She knew her life would never be the same. Guilt gnawed at me when she began wetting the bed. She hadn't wet the bed since leaving the residential home. But when I talked to her, she either acted as though nothing was wrong, or she shut down defensively and refused to speak. I had many a one-sided conversation with a frustrated little girl scowling at her feet.

Since Justin and I had become a couple, it'd been arranged at school for Justin to work in a different classroom, and an older woman called Rachel helped out in Maddie's class instead. Unfortunately, Maddie's behaviour at school deteriorated, leading to Rachel isolating Maddie from most of her classmates for their protection. I found other children's schoolbooks in Maddie's bag then a stuffed toy I didn't recognise. Pens mysteriously appeared. She even took Miss Staveley's watch once. I returned it the next day, red-faced with contrition. The stealing continued outside school too. She grabbed items from the supermarket shelves and tucked them into her clothes, especially if Justin was there. I caught her stuffing a Galaxy bar into the waistband of her leggings, the hard glint of determination in her eye challenging me. When I made her put it back, she pushed over a display of tins. Again, I had to apologise profusely.

Justin bore the brunt. Whenever he took care of Maddie on his own, I'd arrive back at the house to see him on the verge of tears. The charming but difficult girl he'd known at school became a whole other beast at home.

"She threw my cycle helmet so hard, it smashed against the bathroom door!" he said once as I came home from therapy.

Another time, he held up his hands, exasperated, and said, "I went to the toilet, and when I came out, she was gone. She'd been drawing, right there at the table. I searched the whole house for her. Every damn room and every wardrobe. I even went through the kitchen cupboards! She was gone for half an hour. I was about to call the police. Then I went back out into the garden... I'd already checked the garden, and she wasn't there, but she was now. I found her burying my mum's antique brooch out there in the dirt."

"No, oh no, I'm so sorry." I pulled him into a hug. His mother had died of breast cancer the year before I met him, and that brooch meant the world to him. "Is it all right?"

"It'll be fine after a good wash. Thank God. I found her crouched right down by the wall. She'd placed a stone right by where she'd dug. It was like she wanted to know where my brooch was, but me never know. Like she wanted that power over me."

Disciplining Maddie never came easily to me, and there were limits regarding what I considered appropriate, given her background. But this time, she'd gone too far. Maddie had been excited for her first-ever school trip. Miss Staveley's class was heading to Alton Towers at the end of term, and I'd told Maddie that with good behaviour and Rachel's supervision, she could go. After what she did to Justin, I sat her down and explained that her consequences had actions, and that she could no longer go to Alton Towers.

Her gaze sharpened until her eyes resembled shiny little beads. She tilted her head down so that shadows filled the hollows of her skull. "I *hate* you. You're the worst mummy in the world!"

She threw herself on the floor and thrashed around, slamming her head against the chair leg.

"Maddie, stop!"

I sank to the ground and grabbed her shoulders. But she squirmed and wriggled out from my grip. I gritted my teeth and clutched her forearm. The battle escalated, and she twisted her body, letting out a grunt, then clutched my hand. Before I had time to stop her, she buried her head down to my flesh and bit hard and deep into my arm.

I yelped. She stopped. She scuttled back away from me, and in that moment, I realised I'd lifted my free arm with the intention of slapping her. She sat there, fixated on the raised hand, and my gaze travelled over to it too. I dropped my hand. She'd seen it. She knew what I'd intended to do. I'd almost changed my mind about Alton Towers after that moment, simply to assuage my guilt.

"I'm sorry, Maddie. I didn't mean to—"

She leapt to her feet and ran away. After a few hours in her room, she came back downstairs and wrapped her arms around my waist.

***

SIX MONTHS LATER, a couple of weeks after my book, *Maddie and Me*, was published, I'd just finished up answering questions for news article when Justin called me from school.

"Babe," he said. "You'll never guess what."

"You forgot your wallet?"

"Nope."

"Your school swipe card?"

"Nope."

"Umm, sanity?"

"Have you given up yet?"

"Yeah." I laughed. "I've given up. What is it?"

"My dissertation won an award."

"What? Oh my God, Justin. That's amazing! What award did you win?"

"Well, it's like a rising-star award for research in education."

He'd been working on a dissertation about child behaviour in the classroom. I'd read some of it, amazed by his astute observations. And while reading it, I recognised Maddie in there as an anonymous case study. Not that I minded. I knew she was important to him both personally and professionally.

"That's incredible! I'm so happy for you."

"And there's an awards ceremony too. It's in Edinburgh. Zo, we should go. You haven't celebrated your book release yet, and now I have this award."

My heart sank. It meant an overnight stay, maybe even two, and I'd never be able to find childcare. Maddie couldn't come with us, not when we'd be out late at night.

"Of course," I said. "As long as we can find childcare for Maddie."

Justin was quiet then, a slow breath exhaling down the line. "This is important, Zo. We *have* to go."

"All right," I said. "I'll make it happen."

I tried our regular childminder, Maryam, first, but she didn't do overnight babysitting, plus she was reluctant to watch Maddie again. Last time, Maddie had thrown spaghetti at the wall then kicked poor Maryam in the shin. We had a few other places to try, but they couldn't accommodate us on the weekend we needed to go. Justin was an only child like me, and his dad lived in New Zealand. I tried a few of the mums I was friendly with from Maddie's school, but her reputation preceded her to the point where none of them were willing to take her in. I heard about a lot of swimming lessons and camping weekends and birthday parties on those calls. I didn't believe a single one of them.

"It leaves my mum," I said to Justin later that day at home. We'd settled Maddie in her bed, giving us precious time to be alone with each other. It gave us time to breathe.

"You've never asked before," he reminded me. "She's Maddie's grandmother. Surely she'll allow you this one time."

"Yeah, but she's not Maddie's grandmother by choice, is she? I forced her into this." I bit my lower lip and stared idly at the television, neither listening nor watching the programme playing. "Plus, she's not particularly happy about the book."

I'd tried to keep my mother out of the book, but I couldn't help adding her in here and there. Judging by some of the reviews, readers took a dislike to Mum based on her attitudes towards Maddie. I hadn't intended for that to happen, and the guilt weighed heavily. "You know, she might do it for this. She *might*. If not, I'm so sorry, but you'll have to go alone."

"No," he said with a forcefulness that took me by surprise. "No, you're coming. We'll sort this, Zo. I know we will."

IT TOOK us all by surprise when Mum said yes. Even Maddie asked me twice if she was really going to stay overnight with Grandma and Grandad.

"But I don't want to go," she said, sitting herself down on the carpet as though we were about to make her go right then and there, even though it was a full week until our night away.

"Why don't you want to go?"

"I don't like them." She shrugged like an adult. When not in the middle of a screaming tantrum, Maddie maintained an air of calm that unnerved everyone in the room. I mostly ignored it. I knew she had a manipulative side.

"Why don't you like them? They're your grandparents."

"So?" she asked.

I sighed. "I know this is weird, sweetie. I know you don't know them very well, but it's just for two days. You can play in their garden and watch cartoons, and then you get to come home."

She acquiesced in the end. I suspected that her curiosity got the better of her. She wanted to know more about these people and what they did at night when she usually left. In fact, the morning we left, she had her Pikachu suitcase packed and ready. Before getting her settled in the car, I checked that she'd included enough clothes and toys.

"Hello, Julia," Dad said brightly as he opened the door.

I stood there with my mouth gaping open until Mum manoeuvred him away from the door. "Oh, you silly goose. It's Zoe. Remember!"

"Mum, are you sure this is okay?" I asked as she took the suitcase from my hand.

She didn't look at me. She made an *mmhmm* sound and told me to have a nice time in Edinburgh before pushing me out of the door.

"What the hell?" I muttered to Justin as we got back in the car.

"She wouldn't have agreed to this if she didn't think she could handle it." He leaned across the space in the car and kissed my cheek. "This weekend is going to be so special. I can feel it. I love you, Zo. I really love you."

The warmth of his words chased away my concerns. But I should've listened to my instinct.

CHAPTER THIRTY-FOUR
NOW

How long does it take for a marriage to fall apart? Years? Days? Hours?

While Justin and Gabe are at the beach, I rummage through my husband's clothes, riffling through every pocket, uncertain what I'm searching for. Receipts, notes, discarded garments belonging to another woman? But paper doesn't really exist anymore. What I need is access to his phone or his laptop.

Justin left with his phone, of course, but I have his laptop here at the house. Fingers shaking, I lift the lid. Then I hesitate, hands hovering above the keyboard. I've never liked a snoop. They came across as paranoid and slightly unhinged to me. But there was one simple truth here: Justin lied. If I confront him, I'll be faced with more lies.

"Mum?"

I spin around. Maddie stands in the door to our bedroom. She's flushed, like she's been running. Or is she upset? It's hard to tell with Maddie at times.

"Isn't that Justin's laptop?"

"Maddie, what did you mean when you said not to trust him?"

"Oh," she replies. "Are you sure you want to know? You're not going to like it." She leans against the doorframe and lifts her eyebrows.

"Tell me."

She shrugs. "He threatened me."

I stand immediately, crossing the space between us. "When?"

"When he was drunk one night. I went to get a glass of water, and he was washing his shirt in the sink."

"Why?" I ask.

"There was a stain on it, and I guess he didn't want you to see it?"

I close my hands into fists, anger rising. "What kind of stain?"

"I dunno, like maybe lipstick? I think it was sticky and reddish."

"When was this?"

She shuffles from one foot to the other, my quickfire questions making her uncomfortable. "I can't remember. About a month ago."

"And when you saw him, what did he say?"

She sighs. "He said, if I told you about the shirt, he'd tell you about me cheating on my English exam." She shifts her weight away from the doorframe and steps closer. "He found my cheat sheets in my bag. I know, okay, before you go off. I kept his stupid secret because I didn't think it was that bad. Now I guess it probably means he did something worse than I'd thought."

"What did you think was going on?" I ask.

"That maybe he'd hooked up with someone in a club. Some of the girls at school have seen him drunk around town."

"What? Maddie, why the hell didn't you tell me?"

"Because I knew you'd flip about the exam!"

I press fingers to my temples, not sure which thread to pull first. Maddie cheating at school. Justin's possible infidelity. His drunkenness in pubs.

"Fuck," I blurt.

Maddie laughs.

I glare at her. "Why is this funny to you?"

She shrugs.

Her nonchalance enrages me, and before I know it, I'm directing a tirade at her. "Is that it? You keep this from me and then shrug about it after seeing that I'm upset? You're not a kid anymore, Maddie, and I'm sick of treating you like you are. I am sick of your callous immaturity. I've been trying so hard not to call you a sociopath, and not to believe the nasty things other people say about you, but I am *sick*. To. Death. Of the way you laugh at other people's misfortunes. Will you get out of my sight? Please? I have a cheating husband and a mean daughter, and I'm done. I've reached my limit. I can't... Get out, Maddie, for God's sake."

But she doesn't move. She stands there watching as my body vibrates with anger.

"I'm not the psychopath in the family." And with that, she walks away.

As Maddie leaves the home, Justin enters with Gabe. I slam the laptop cover closed, wave to them, and walk through to the en suite to shower. At least in there, I can finally let out the tears I've been holding back. In the shower, I admit to myself that my husband is a cheating liar and that I took it all out on someone who didn't deserve it.

JUSTIN IS IN THE KITCHEN, making Gabe lunch, when I get out of the shower. I can't stomach food. I try calling Maddie to apologise, but she isn't answering her phone. My long wet hair drips on the kitchen table as I sit with my son and try to pretend everything is normal. He tells me all about the beach, how they went wading in the rock pools and even saw a crab. I make interested *mmhmm* noises, while Justin's eyes narrow. He knows something is wrong.

And, of course, there is. My stomach is full of sour acid that churns and churns. My thoughts race through my mind. I nurse a cup of coffee because each sip makes me jittery.

"It was *enormous*," Gabe gushes. "Claws like..." He mimics crab claws with his fingers as he bounces around in his chair.

Is Justin having an affair?

He hasn't been to football in six months. He's stayed away from home *overnight* three or four times in those six months. Even teenagers at school have seen him out partying. He hasn't even been subtle. Maddie saw him washing lipstick out of his shirt. He's having an affair. But who with?

My thoughts go straight to Angie Starling, the pretty young teacher at Maddie's school. I remember how chatty she was with Justin during that night out. I've never warmed to her. I didn't understand why until this moment. It's because she's screwing my husband. I'm convinced. It takes barely a moment for it all to settle into place.

My fingers tighten around the mug as anger flashes through me. I could throw this hot coffee in his face. But no. I want to do this right for the sake of my children. I need to be calm and find the proof first.

"You okay, babe?" Justin asks.

I could throat-punch him right now, but I simply say, "This hangover is kicking my arse."

Gabe laughs. "You said *arse*."

"I did, didn't I? What a bad mum!"

He continues laughing and starts calling me a bad mum. I frown to myself and wonder if I should try calling Maddie again. I said such unforgiveable things to her. *I'm not the psychopath in the family.* Did she mean me? I'm the one who violently murdered a man. It was self-defence, but there are still times I gaze down at my hands and imagine them stained by Peter McKenna's blood.

Or did she mean Justin?

"What are you doing for the rest of the day?" Justin asks, bringing my thoughts back to the present.

"I'm not feeling great." I angle my chin down so he can't see my expression. "So I think I might stay home."

Unexpectedly, he reaches over and threads his fingers between mine. It takes all my willpower not to pull away. He gives me a sheepish grin, which I know I'm supposed to take as atonement for our argument. Between us, Gabe is quiet, observing our body language.

"Sorry I lost my temper earlier, love." He squeezes my fingers and releases. I relax. He grabs a newspaper and starts flicking through it. "Do you mind if I meet the footie lads for a pint this afternoon? Sorry it's short notice."

My heart flutters. "Of course not." *Where will he truly be going? To see Angie Starling?*

"Jesus," he says, lifting the newspaper closer to his face. "Have you read this?"

I shake my head.

"Riya Shah's body was found with the little finger missing from her right hand. It'd been chopped off." Justin casts a guilty glance at Gabe, who makes a loud *yuck* noise.

The light from the sun streaming in through the window is unbearably bright, and my stomach lurches. I taste pennies in my mouth, imagine the sour rag between my teeth, and feel the throbbing of the wound on my hand.

"Are you okay?" Justin asks.

"Yes," I lie, already picturing the photograph on Peter McKenna's wall. His smiling mother, her hands on his shoulders, one finger missing. I think of Maddie standing next to me on the stairs. I wonder how many times she saw McKenna chop off fingers with a meat cleaver. Then I'm running, huddled over, through to the downstairs toilet. I reach the sink and vomit up coffee.

A warm hand touches my back. God help me, that warm hand, familiar, strong but light, it gives me comfort. And it shouldn't. I should never feel comfort from those hands ever again.

"I'm so sorry," Justin says. "I'm such an idiot. I should've thought..."

I run the taps and rinse out my mouth before staggering away from him and the smell of my sick. The backs of my thighs hit the toilet seat, and I perch there, trying to catch my breath.

"It's what Peter McKenna did, isn't it?" he asks. "He took their little fingers."

"He did. From their right hands."

Justin rubs his hands over his stubble. "And we gave her an alibi."

My head snaps up. "Maddie didn't do this!"

"Yes, she did, Zoe. Yes, she did. I'm going to go to the police to tell them we lied about that night. That we didn't see her come out of her room all night."

"And what about what you were doing? Because you weren't in the house, and you weren't at football practice."

"I was here. You misremembered. We've been over this." He walks away.

He strides quickly through the house, but I'm right behind him.

"Don't go to the police," I call. "Not yet. I need to find her first. I need to talk to her." I reach out for his arm, but he dodges my touch.

He grabs his keys. "This is bigger than us protecting her now." He glances at Gabe. "She's dangerous, Zoe. We have to tell them the truth. Maddie is a murderer and a psychopath, and they need to arrest her."

He swings the door open, and standing there are DS Rosen and PC Morton. Rosen's arm is raised as though he's about to press the doorbell.

"Good timing." He rocks back on his feet, pushing his hands into his pockets, still exuding that unnerving natural calm. "Mr Shelton. Justin, is it?"

"Yes," Justin says.

"We'd like to talk to you if that's all right."

"Okay," Justin says. "Come in if you'd like."

"We'd actually like to talk to you at the police station, Mr Shelton. We'd like that very much."

I take a step away from the door, glancing back inside the house, searching for Gabe. I don't want him to hear or see this.

"Is there something the matter?" Justin asks.

"You're a person of interest, Mr Shelton. Right now, we would like to ask some questions about the night Riya Shah was murdered." He smiles thinly, without any trace of warmth. "I don't want to have to arrest you, Mr Shelton. Not yet."

Numbness spreads over me as my husband steps out of the house and follows the police officers.

CHAPTER THIRTY-FIVE
THEN

Streetlights glanced off the cobbles. My heels clicked and clacked, skidding over the uneven stones. I stumbled, and Justin held my arm, staying my course. It was eleven thirty, and in Justin's free hand, he clutched a hunk of glass—his award.

"Rising star," I said, stroking the stubble along his chin. "My star."

"Are you drunk, Miss Osbourne?" He laughed, pulling me closer.

We found a table outside an old pub, the castle looming somewhere behind us, and sat shivering in our evening wear, sipping whisky and watching noisy revellers in the midst of their pub crawl. Justin slipped out of his jacket and placed it around my shoulders.

"I love you, Zoe. I love our family—me, you, and Maddie."

"I love you too," I said, watching the way the streetlights danced in his eyes, placing my hands on his chest and leaning into him.

After a slow, lazy kiss, he gestured to his award. "I couldn't have done this without you or Maddie. You both mean so much to me."

The thing I loved the most about Justin was how genuine he sounded when he talked. Everything he said came across as though it'd just occurred to him. He lived in the moment in a way I struggled to do. While I disconnected, he soaked in every last second, and yet he remained calm and even at all times.

"I'm sorry it's been so difficult with Maddie recently. She's taking a while to adjust."

"It's all right," he said. "I know what she's been through. Both of you. I'm so proud of you, Zo. Look what you've achieved. A bestselling book!"

"My agent says there's a film producer interested." I shook my head, curls sashaying across the nape of my neck.

"Are you serious? Wow, that's incredible."

"And scary." I sipped my whisky, feeling the warmth travel through my body.

"What are you going to do?"

"I honestly don't know. The money has the potential to set us up for life. How would you feel about that?"

He shrugged. "Depends on who plays me in the movie."

We laughed together. Then I added, "You have your own glittering career to think about." I picked up the award and brought it closer to us. "Rising star. On the way to becoming a *big* star. What's next?"

"Honestly, I don't know. I want to work in schools. I want to make a difference. I'm not even sure research is for me anymore."

"Really?"

"Yeah, maybe at some point down the line. Right now, I want to work with the students."

"You're so good with people."

"Why don't we get married, and I can be a kept husband?" he joked. "We can live off your book royalties."

I flicked him playfully on the elbow.

After our giggles died down, he gently cradled my hands with his own. "Let's do it. Seriously. Let's get married. I love you. I love Maddie. I want us to be a family."

My heart thundered against my ribs. I realised I wasn't cold anymore, not with his touch on my hands. And most of all, I wasn't afraid of the future, knowing he'd be in it, because he was my anchor, always.

"Okay," I said, excitement bubbling like champagne in my throat. "Let's get married."

"Shit. I don't have a ring. I'm sorry."

"I don't care."

We ordered champagne and sat outside the pub chatting until the early hours of the morning, making quick decisions. I decided I'd keep my maiden name because I'd already changed Maddie's to Osbourne.

"Okay," he said. "But how would you feel about double-barrelled for our next kid?"

"Sure." It felt modern. "And Maddie can decide if she wants to change hers when she's older."

"Deal," he said. "Now, big or small wedding?"

"Easy. Small."

"My preference too."

We floated back to our hotel, where we drank more and fell into bed together. I was so drunk that I wondered if I'd imagined it all. But, no. The next morning, we ordered room service while recovering from our hangovers.

After plenty of grease and caffeine, Justin persuaded me to shower and get dressed.

"We still have a few hours," he said. "Plenty of time to find a ring."

We browsed ring shops together but didn't settle on anything perfect. I decided that I wanted Maddie to help me choose. Then the reality started to settle. I began to wonder how Maddie was going to react to the news.

"Babe." Justin emerged from the back of a jewellery shop, clutching a heavy marble bust of Shakespeare. "We have to get this."

"Why?"

"Because you deserve an award too. Here!" He thrust the statue at me, and I quickly adjusted my grip to keep hold of it.

"You're crazy!" But I laughed, and it washed away the worries in my mind.

For the rest of the day, we lugged the impractical statue around Edinburgh before boarding the train home. I kept it on the floor between my feet, worried it'd topple over and hurt someone. My hangover intensified as the train chugged along, and my head throbbed.

Justin disappeared to the snack bar and returned with a bottle of water and a packet of ibuprofen. "I think you might need these."

"Have I mentioned that I love you?" I asked, smiling.

I fell asleep with my head resting against his shoulder, safe in his arms.

That evening, we drove back from the train station to collect Maddie at my parents' house. Despite the utter exhaustion from the late night of drinking and the long journey home, I couldn't stop smiling. And when Mum opened the door, I found myself bursting to tell her the news. But I never got the opportunity. She hustled into the hallway, red-faced and mean, dragging Maddie by one arm.

"Take your spawn of Satan and get out," she screamed.

I stood there completely stunned, my jaw practically hitting the ground. A moment later, Mum shoved Maddie's suitcase through the door, then it slammed in our faces. As I stood there, flabbergasted, Maddie laughed.

MUM IGNORED my phone calls for a week. In the end, I arrived at the house with a coffee and walnut cake, leaving Maddie with Justin for the afternoon. It was Sunday, and I knew they'd be in, because they always spent their Sundays pottering around the house, doing bits of DIY or gardening. She saw the cake, said nothing, but let me into the house.

Mum managed to inject an aggressive impatience into her every move that afternoon. She slammed the kettle down, stirred my tea so hard the spoon rattled against the ceramic rim, and cut into the cake like a butcher chopping meat.

"Your father's asleep, so don't make too much noise."

I wanted to point out the racket she was making on her own, but I kept my lips firmly shut, knowing exactly when not to antagonise my mother.

We sat on the sofa in the living, room making small talk and praising the cake, which was moist and sweet. I examined her face, noticing the tell-tale signs of exhaustion—the dark circles, the dry skin, and her mussed hair. Worry tightened my chest. How was I going to support this stubborn woman? Would she ever let me in?

"Mum, are we going to talk about it?"

She slapped her plate down on the coffee table as I braced myself for it to break into pieces. Somehow, it survived. "Well, I didn't want to. But perhaps you should know exactly what you're dealing with."

"For God's sake, just tell me what she did!" I hadn't meant to snap, but I couldn't stand the mystery any longer.

"All right, give me a minute, will you? I'll tell you." She crossed one slim leg over the other, her cigar-cut trousers riding up at the ankle. "She was fine at first. Quiet. I've never liked quiet children particularly, because you don't know what they're thinking. Though you were fairly quiet, and I didn't mind that. But she seemed bored. She kept playing on that... that screen thing you gave her." She meant a Nintendo DS, but I didn't want to interrupt her flow to tell her. "Your dad was in a silly mood. He kept calling her Nancy. He went to school with a girl called Nancy, you see. And I saw Maddie looking at him a bit. I didn't want him to scare her. I know how it is with old people and children. So, I nipped next door and asked Samantha if Maddie could play with their golden retriever puppy."

I tried not to let my concern show, but every muscle in my body tightened. I'd made the decision early on in the adoption process to never, ever own a pet. It might be awful to worry my own daughter was capable of animal abuse, but her father might have abused his pets in front of her. I'd taken her to petting zoos to teach her how to be gentle around animals in a controlled environment as a way to counter that experience, but, still, I didn't want to risk it.

"Samantha said yes, to drop Maddie round. She has a little girl too, about three years old, called Daisy." She made a face. "I've never cared for those flower names. Whatever next? Buttercup?"

"Mum," I said softly.

"I took Maddie round and told Samantha I'd pick her up in an hour. But twenty minutes later, she asked me to collect her already. I said, 'Well, what's the matter?' Apparently, the puppy bit Maddie on the arm. Not hard, but Maddie got very angry and stormed off."

Relief flooded through my body. At least she hadn't harmed the dog. "I don't remember seeing a bruise."

"There wasn't one. I checked. Once I'd coaxed her out of Samantha's garden anyway. Samantha had this odd expression on her face. Distrust. That's what it was, like she couldn't believe I'd brought this strange child to her. And she was holding Daisy like she didn't want Daisy anywhere near her. I asked her if everything was okay, whether Maddie had behaved herself, and she said she was fine, but that Daisy was overtired and needed a nap. I found Maddie in the garden, sitting on the grass. She'd been crying, which I thought was normal for a child her age. Her hands were all muddy like she'd been digging. At first, she wouldn't talk to me, but when I asked her to come with me, she did.

"Outside the house, on the front garden, she asked, 'What's wrong with Grandad?' I didn't know what to say. I told him he had a poorly mind. That he kept forgetting things he used to know. She said, 'My dad had a poorly mind too.'" Mum sighed and shook her head. "What was I supposed to say to that?"

"She's been through a lot, Mum," I reminded her.

"I know. She went back to playing her game. Your dad felt a bit better, so he did some pruning in the garden. After a while, Maddie went out there to help. I watched from the kitchen to make sure nothing went awry, but they seemed to be enjoying themselves. Your dad let her push the lawn mower around for a bit. They cleared out some weeds and pruned the roses. I think they were out there a couple of hours or so. Afterwards, I made sure Maddie had a bath because she was filthy. We had chicken for dinner, and I put her to bed."

I frowned. I'd expected more drama. So far, Maddie hadn't done anything wrong, merely spooked the neighbour, probably because she didn't always react to things in the same way other children did.

"It was after she went to bed the problems started. First, she woke up screaming about an hour later. So I went up and talked to her. She said she'd had a bad dream, that Grandad had hurt someone because he forgot he wasn't supposed to. I told her that Grandad wasn't going to hurt anyone and that she should go back to sleep. She did. Nothing else happened. Your dad and I went to bed. He was tired from all the gardening, so he slept right away." She wrapped her arms around her body. I saw the change in her posture, the straightening of her back. "When I next woke up, Maddie stood over our bed, holding her pillow."

Mum's words chilled me. Electricity shot up my spine. "Another nightmare?"

"No," Mum said. "I don't think so. She was standing right by your dad's head, and she held the pillow up, like she was... like she was about to..." Mum's arms had risen, as though she, too, were holding up a pillow. Her eyes were glazed, fearful.

"No," I said. "Why would she?"

"I think she got into her head that your dad was going to hurt people and she had to stop him."

A cold fist formed around my chest, squeezing and squeezing. "God. No. She wouldn't."

"I didn't give her the opportunity. After I put her back to bed, I stayed awake all night, making sure she didn't come back into the room. That child... she has a warped sense of morality. She thought after one bad dream that your dad needed to be... euthanised."

"We don't know that," I insisted. "Maybe she wanted to sleep in your bed. She sometimes sleeps in mine."

"Oh, I couldn't let her that close to me at night. Not knowing where she came from."

"Mum! Stop it! She's a little kid. Have you ever stopped to think that she acts like this in front of you because you don't treat her like she's an actual human child? Have you ever considered that? I'm so fed up with the way you treat her. And me!" I stood, anger coursing through me.

"All right, maybe I am different around her. But there's some truth to what I'm saying. She'll never be normal. She's too broken. One day, she's going to kill someone because it's in her genes."

"You're wrong," I said, on my feet, heading towards the door. I didn't want to be around my mother for one more second.

"I hope I am," she called after me, not bothering to get up from the sofa. "I sincerely hope I am, Zoe."

After leaving my parents' house, I sat in my car parked across the street for a few minutes, trying to compose myself. I could see how Mum had come to the conclusion she had, given Maddie's nightmare, but at the same time, I didn't believe that Maddie would attempt to murder my father. I couldn't bring myself to believe it. Maybe she'd thought about it for a moment.

But, no. I shook my head. *No.*

I thought it might be a good idea to speak to Samantha, Mum's neighbour, so I walked around to the house and pressed the doorbell. I rubbed my arms against the cold, ready to be home with my family. I'd never met Samantha, so when she answered, I quickly explained who I was. Samantha invited me in. She had Daisy on her hip, who waved at me, beaming, her pretty blonde curls framing her face. Samantha had one of those enviable figures, with a narrow waist and full hips. She plopped Daisy down on an armchair, and their puppy bounded up to me, its ears flopping around.

"I'm sorry if my daughter, Maddie, made you feel uncomfortable the other week. She had a troubled childhood, and she doesn't always behave the same way other children do."

Samantha smiled. "Oh, that's fine."

I carried on petting the puppy. "What's his name?"

"Dexter," she said.

"Oh, he's lovely. Mum said he bit Maddie. Did she do something to antagonise him?"

Samantha rubbed her hands on her jeans and shifted her weight as though she were uncomfortable. "Nothing bad. It's just..." She paused again, and I wanted her to spit it out. "I think she wanted to test Dexter. She stroked him at first and then lifted his paws. I saw her lifting his ears. I mean, it was pure curiosity, nothing more. I don't think she intended to hurt Dexter. She poked him in the belly, and he snapped at her. We're going to behaviour training now, so he doesn't do it again."

"Right. That's good. And after the bite? How did she react?"

"Well, she didn't lash out at Dexter, if you're worried about that. Some kids do, don't they? They escalate the situation. Actually, she..."

she grabbed Daisy and tried to make her go out into the garden with her. She was a little rough, so I took Daisy away and let Maddie go into the garden. She kind of sat there, digging in the earth with her hands, talking to herself."

I could understand why Samantha had called my mum. In her shoes, I'm sure I would've done the same. Maddie needed special care at times, and she hadn't been prepared. What happened wasn't her fault, Dexter's, or Maddie's. It was Mum's. "Like I said, she doesn't always do what other kids do in a similar situation. It probably came across as strange."

Samantha nodded. "I wasn't sure if maybe she was autistic."

"No," I said. "But she has been through trauma."

"I'm sorry."

"It's okay." I stood up, giving Dexter one last pat.

"She could probably come round again sometime," Samantha said. "If maybe you stayed in case anything happened again."

"Maddie would love that," I said, but I sensed the offer had been made out of politeness rather than any desire to spend time with my daughter.

I left the neighbourhood with a heavy stone of sadness resting in the pit of my stomach. Even a night over with my parents had proved too much for both Maddie and my parents. I couldn't blame Mum for being scared when Maddie stood in their room with a pillow, but I still hated the way she was with my daughter. The whole situation felt like such a mess. Part of me never wanted to see my mum again, part of me sided with Mum about Maddie's behaviour, and all of me wanted to help them with Dad's deteriorating health.

That night, I fell asleep picturing Maddie standing over the bed with her pillow raised. And I wondered, for a moment, whether Maddie had believed she needed to euthanise her grandad. After all, she'd known when her own father needed to die.

CHAPTER THIRTY-SIX
NOW

I stagger back into the kitchen. *Person of interest. What does that mean?*

Gabe starts to cry. I rush over to hold his small head in my hands. He leans into my shoulder. I take in the smell of him. Saltwater, sand, and jam from his sandwiches.

"What's going on?" he asks.

"Nothing, sweetie. Dad went to talk to the police."

"About Riya?"

"Yes," I say.

"But why?"

I swallow. *How am I supposed to answer that?* "Well, I'm not sure yet. I think they'll tell us soon, though. Come on, let's go and put some cartoons on."

I settle him down on the sofa while I send Maddie a quick text message: *We need to talk. It's about Riya. It's urgent.*

This time, she replies straight away. *What about her?*

I type: *The murderer removed her finger like McKenna used to.*

I hesitate then add: *Justin is a person of interest. The police have taken him in for questioning.*

She replies. *Holy crap, mum.*

I type. *Come home, Mads. We need to talk.*

Not right now. But soon. I don't think Justin killed Riya. But I think I know who did.

Who? Maddie, tell me!

The blue dots dance across the screen. *I can't tell you.*

Maddie, talk to me! What do you know?

Give me time, okay? I'm figuring things out.

When I try to call, her phone goes straight to voicemail. She sent me the message then turned it off so I can't speak to her.

I'm not sure how long I sit next to Gabe, as still as a statue, the shock of it all running through me like tiny bolts of lightning. Five minutes, maybe more. Colours and shapes blur across the TV screen. Gabe puts his thumb in his mouth, which he hasn't done for years, and cuddles my side. His tears are gone, but he knows. Perhaps he's known longer than I have. Perhaps he saw the slow disintegration I missed.

Then it hits me. It hits me so hard, a hand flies up to my chest, presses hard against my sternum.

"No," I muttered. "He can't..."

"Mummy?"

"I'm okay, sweetheart," I mutter, barely noticing that he called me "Mummy," which is something else he hasn't done for a while.

No, I'm thinking of Maddie sitting on the other side of this room, politely answering DS Rosen's questions about Riya's mystery boyfriend.

He's older.

He's married.

He has children.

They go to hotels.

Justin works at Maddie's school. He's popular and well-liked among the students, especially the girls. I've seen them wave to him when we're out in Penry together. I've seen them walk away giggling, like teenage girls tend to do. I've never, not once, seen Justin look at those girls in anything other than what I considered a normal gaze, but now I know he can lie. Now I know he can pretend.

Are the thoughts in my head real? I filter through every memory I have of Riya. She was a beautiful girl, with a gorgeous smile and silky long hair. I see her laughing at one of Justin's goofy jokes when she comes to visit Maddie. I see Justin offering to drop her off at home after coming over for tea. I see it all in a way I've never seen before. Then I picture her nuzzling into his neck, smearing lip gloss across his collar. I see him whispering in her ear, warning her not to tell anyone their secret. I see his hands wrapping around her throat... She's dead and lifeless beneath him. He takes a sharp knife to her lifeless finger...

The television comes into focus. Finally, the colours and shapes morph into cartoon characters, and the brain fog of shock sharpens into a purpose. Sitting around doing nothing isn't going to help anyone.

"Do you want to go for a drive, honey?" I ask.

Gabe stares up at me, hesitant and full of fear. But he smiles sweetly. "Okay, Mum."

BENEATH ME, the car rumbles, the juddering chug of the engine waiting for me to release the handbrake and drive away. But I haven't decided where I'm going yet. I want to find Maddie, but I have no idea where Annabel lives. I can't drive around Penry, knocking on doors. If only I had one of those tracking apps installed for the whole family. But Justin and Maddie were against it. Now I know why.

I glance at the rearview mirror, where Gabe stares out at the garage beyond the car. "You okay, bud?"

He nods. He's quiet.

I place my hands on the steering wheel. I need to go to the police. I need to know what's going on. I can warn them about Justin's lies before he implicates Maddie. I can tell them he wasn't home the night Riya Shah was murdered. No matter how many times he tries to make me believe I've forgotten, I know the truth. I point a control pad at the garage door and watch it rattle open. Letting out a shaky breath, I put the car in first gear and make my way out of the drive.

As I'm driving, I try to connect the dots in my mind. My husband was having an affair with a sixteen-year-old girl. He was twice her age. He worked at her school. He was in a position of power, and while she may have been *barely* over the legal age of consent, that set of circumstances is undeniably paedophilic. And when I messaged Maddie to tell her Justin was a person of interest, she replied back that she didn't think Justin is the murderer. Why would she say that? Has Maddie been conducting her own personal investigation all this time? And if so, how does this Annabel fit in?

I try calling her using the hands-free controls on my dashboard but get her voicemail again. "For God's sake, Maddie! Pick up!" In frustration, I swerve around a tight corner, drifting dangerously close to the right-hand lane. A lorry driver toots his horn.

"Mum, are you okay? Where are we going?"

Gabe's high-pitched voice sounds terrified. I take a left and get off the main road, choosing a less direct route while I calm my nerves.

"I'm fine, sweetheart. Everything's fine."

A few minutes later, I finally pull into the carpark next to the police station and glance back at my son. He's so like his father, with boyish, overgrown curls and sweet blue eyes. Am I jumping to conclusions? Just weeks ago, I still considered my husband to be a gentle, caring man, someone I loved as much as my children. A protector, in his own way. A man who maintained a calm equilibrium in the household.

Lies, Zoe. So many lies. Don't dismiss this. Don't ignore your gut instinct.

I think of his rage-tensed, smiling face and the index finger he jabbed towards my face.

"Okay, we need to pop inside here for a moment," I say to Gabe.

"Why?" Even in his youth, he must recognise the police station for what it is.

"I need to speak to the detective." Now that I'm here, I don't know what I'm going to do with Gabe. He'll overhear everything I need to say about Justin. Am I prepared to let that happen?

A light film of sweat spreads over my forehead as we walk into the building. I hold Gabe's hand as we step up to the counter and ask for DS Rosen.

"Zoe, it's good to see you." Rosen approaches and raises a hand. "Did you want to chat?" I notice him taking in my demeanour—my damp hair, my sweaty face, and the small child in my clutches.

"Can... could someone take my son? I don't want him with me when..."

Rosen understands immediately. "Absolutely." He steps through to another room and returns a moment later with a middle-aged woman dressed in a suit. "Sue's going to show this young man where we question suspects."

"Cool," Gabe says.

Sue bends down and asks Gabe his name. She's smiley and pleasant. I relax slightly.

"Come with me to an interview room." Rosen gestures for me to follow him. "Can I get you a glass of water? A tea maybe?"

"Water would be good." My throat itches with dryness.

A few moments later, I'm sitting opposite Detective Rosen with a glass of water resting by my hand. He smiles politely, the grey wall stretching out behind him, his hands folded together on the table.

"What brought you here today, Ms Osbourne?"

I sip the water. "I know you're questioning my husband right now. Have... Have you released him yet?"

"No," he says.

"Is that because you're going to arrest him?"

Rosen raises an eyebrow. "What makes you think we're going to arrest him?"

"Well, you said he was a person of interest."

He unfolds his hands and leans back. "That's right." His mouth becomes a tight line. I can already tell he doesn't want to give me more details. Every part of my body feels the weight of his patient, observational gaze.

I brush a lock of hair away from my forehead. "I think my husband is going to lie to you, and that's why I'm here."

"What do you think he's going to lie about?"

"Well," I say, "I... I realised something today. I discovered it, rather. Justin has been lying to me. For the last six months, every week, Justin was supposed to be at football practice for a local team. But he quit the team months ago. And every so often, he goes on a golf weekend. Another lie. The night Riya died, Justin told two lies. He told me he was at football practice. He told you he was home. Since then, he's been trying to convince me that we sat on the sofa together and watched a movie. We didn't. He wasn't there. I don't know where he was, but I'm beginning to believe..." My voice cracks. There's a sharp sensation in my nose as tears threaten.

"Take your time," Rosen says.

I sniff and clear my throat, willing myself not to cry. Not now. "When it comes to repeated lies like this, there's usually one explanation, isn't there? He's having an affair. Riya told Maddie she was in a relationship with a married man. Justin works at Maddie and Riya's school. He wanted to work with teenagers. It all adds up, doesn't it?"

Rosen lets out a long exhale through his nose. "Riya Shah spent some time at your house, didn't she?"

"Yes. She and Maddie were friends. Riya came to dinner every couple of weeks. Sometimes she came with us to the beach and once on a holiday."

"Did you notice anything out of the ordinary between your husband and Riya?"

"No," I say. "Nothing. He talked to her like he talked to Maddie. I never noticed him looking at her. I didn't see anything strange. Justin is good with teenagers. He talks to them like adults. So, no, I didn't notice anything, but that doesn't mean it wasn't there." I shove a thumbnail between my teeth, thinking. "But the holiday and the beach trips all happened years ago. Over the last six months, Maddie spent more time with the Shahs than Riya did here at our house. Maybe... Maybe Justin kept it that way so that they didn't trip up."

"Thank you, Ms Osbourne. That's useful information."

"Well, thank God I've been useful," I snap. Then I sigh. "I need to know what's going on. Have you arrested my husband?"

"No." He pulls in a deep breath. "We have a witness who saw Riya in your husband's car the night she was murdered."

My hand flies up to my mouth. "Oh God. And to think I actually felt guilty for thinking he was capable of murder. I nearly didn't come. I had no proof. It seemed like a hunch rather than... than anything real." Numbness spreads over my body, along with a prickling sensation. I'd experienced it before passing out once, so I pinch my elbow sharply to bring myself back. "A few months ago, I would never have suspected a thing. But... recently he's been so *angry*. He was never angry. Never. He kept talking about Maddie like she was the problem, and all this time, it was him." My hands ball into fists. "That's why he removed Riya's finger. He wanted to implicate Maddie. He wants the world to believe it was her!"

Rosen remains calm. Neutral. "Try not to jump to any conclusions. We've got an investigation to go through, and it's going to take some time to obtain the answers we need. You've had a shock, Ms Osbourne. Is there someone I can call? Family you can stay with?"

I shake my head. "How long will he stay here at the station?"

"He hasn't been charged for Riya's murder, which means we can't hold him here against his will. Like I said, we have a process to go through. DNA collection, CCTV footage to examine, and witnesses to question. I'll be sure to let you know when there are any updates. I'll keep you as involved as I can."

"I appreciate that." I let out a sigh of relief. Rosen's questions left me concerned I'd be shut out, that they wouldn't tell me anything about the investigation. "What happens tonight? Will you have to let him go soon?"

"Yes."

"And he can come home?"

Rosen raises his eyebrows. "Unless you stop him from coming home. Do you own your house?"

"We both own it."

"Do you feel he could be a danger to you or your children? Perhaps you could apply for a restraining order? I'd imagine a court would agree to that, as long as we find evidence of the affair with Riya. He's a person of interest in connection to the murder of a teenage girl. You have a teenage girl in the house you need to protect."

"How long will that take?"

"You can get an injunction today if you believe yourself to be in immediate danger. Though Mr Shelton will be given an opportunity to tell his side of the story in a courtroom after he's given notice of the injunction. Would you like to do that?"

"Yes," I say. "I would like to do that."

CHAPTER THIRTY-SEVEN
THEN

I lied to Justin. We were so happy, newly engaged, that I didn't want to frighten him. So when he asked me why my mum had reacted so badly after we returned from Edinburgh, I lied. I told him Maddie had spooked the neighbour by playing rough with her toddler and frightened Mum by having nightmares. As far as I knew, he never found out about Maddie, the pillow, or what my mum thought she'd intended to do. And with that, life went on. I never brought up the incident again. I didn't ask Maddie why she'd done what she did. The reason for that was very simple—I didn't want to know.

Though I had to admit that the story Mum told me changed the way I thought about my daughter. I searched for signs of a warped sense of justice. I began to notice that her frequent petty thievery applied to the children in class she didn't like, especially those who had wronged her or others. For instance, Thomas had a tendency to bully Mohammed, and Maddie stole Thomas's Spiderman action figure. Miss Staveley, Maddie's teacher, once told me about how she found Maddie flushing pieces of Lego down the toilet because Mei refused to share them with her. Knowing all of this taught me patience and perseverance. I took every opportunity to teach her kindness. I wracked my brain, thinking of ways to spin an example, trying to explain the law, authority, and how we were supposed to go to those in authority to allow them to give out justice. That it wasn't our place to judge guilt. But was it working? I never could quite tell. She said, "Yes, Mummy, I understand." But did she?

We lived as a complicated but happy family in the years that followed. Sales for my book shocked even my agent and publisher, who sent me a framed book to commemorate them. The movie rights went into a bidding war, with a top Hollywood producer acquiring the rights. Suddenly, we had money. We had options.

After Dad moved into the residential home, I had nothing tethering me to the place where I'd grown up. My relationship with Mum had taken a nosedive to the point where we tolerated each other, nothing more. Now Dad's mind had faded, he rarely recognised me, which more often than not left me in tears. One day, I sat in his new bedroom in the care home and cried as he called me Julie.

"Oh, stop your whining, Julie. Get a life! You've always been a bitch!"

Mum told me not to visit if I was going to upset him. She'd turned away from me, her shoulders set. I think it was that exact moment I realised she'd moved on from me. Like all of her unspoken pain, she folded me up, put me in a box, and closed the lid, trapping in it all the good memories, the playgrounds, the birthdays, and the trips to the seaside. I could try my best to claw my way out, but I'd also closed myself down. I wanted to move on.

Dad would've stopped it. If he'd been well, he would've forced us to talk. But he couldn't, and I couldn't deny the freedom I suddenly felt. Responsibility lifted, making my whole body feel lighter. Justin and I started scouting for places to live on the coast. He wanted to work in a secondary school rather than primary, but somewhere quiet. Not an inner-city school.

"A secondary school is going to be so much more rewarding, Zo. That's where you find the kids with problems," he'd said. "I want to listen to their problems. I want to make a difference. I love the littlies, but you can't have a proper conversation with them. It's all about playtime and colouring. I want to have conversations with troubled kids."

I admired him. He yearned to make a difference. He grew a foot taller in my estimation. Here was this tender man willing to listen to teenagers and their problems. I couldn't do it. I had one child to worry about. I couldn't worry about dozens more too.

We found Penry. We fell in love with the bay. I liked the sea breeze on my face and the faint scent of salt and vinegar filtering out from the fish and chip shops. The house stood tall and industrial on the cliff edge, with those impenetrable shutters and the panic room in the basement. We left the north and followed our hearts south to Penry.

Not long later, there was a wedding, a quiet day. Us. Maddie as bridesmaid. Two teachers from the school as our witnesses. Then there was Gabe. A beautiful day. A beautiful boy.

I finally had my pregnancy, complete with feet kicking my organs, swollen ankles, back pain, and all the lovely aspects of pregnancy that I won't go into because I'd rather forget them. But I had my experience, and at the end, Gabe greeted us with a red screaming face.

Maddie watched my body grow with interest. She was nine and finally grown out of her bed-wetting and petty-thievery stage. We made cards for Gabe, bought presents from Maddie, and also lavished as much attention on her as possible. We listened to Maddie's therapist and made her feel special, emphasising her role as big sister. I was nervous, for Maddie, for me and Justin, and for baby Gabe. How would Maddie react?

For the first few months, I barely breathed. I walked a fine line of trying to trust Maddie, dreaming about her standing over my parents' bed with the pillow lifted, and also keeping all of those fears from Justin, whose relationship with Maddie had improved but remained somewhat distant.

But, while Maddie had a few tantrums, Gabe's arrival brought us closer together if anything. She adored him as a baby, found him mildly infuriating as a toddler, grew cautiously protective of him as she approached her teen years, then found him mildly infuriating again. I learned to trust her with him because she never hurt him, not once. I relaxed. I put the past behind us. I concentrated on life. I'd never known such happiness. I loved my family.

I still had nightmares about Peter McKenna, but now my husband held me in the middle of the night. I felt safe in his arms. There was no other man I trusted like him. I still feared aspects of my daughter and the paths she could take as she grew into a young woman. But all these things were shadows on a hot day, pushed to the edges of my mind.

CHAPTER THIRTY-EIGHT
NOW

I complete an occupation order with Gabe at my side. It's like I'm in a dream. He's playing with a toy police car. Sue, the police-woman, let me borrow a laptop so I could apply online. She's kind, offering advice as I make my way through the forms. Every time Justin's name comes up, I glance guiltily at my son, who has no idea what's going on. He spent the morning playing in rock pools with his dad, and now I'm getting an injunction that will separate him from the man he considers his hero.

The form includes a witness statement, which Sue tells me is to detail any abuse I may have suffered from my husband.

"But there hasn't been any," I say.

"Are you sure about that?"

That one question sends my mind into a spiral. There has been gaslighting. So much of it. From the lies, the affair—with a teenage girl—and the way he's been subtly manipulating me about Maddie. And, of course, there's the fact that *he* may have killed the teenage girl he'd preyed upon.

I keep thinking about Justin and Riya. Didn't Maddie say that Riya wanted more from the relationship? That she wanted to see him more, and when he couldn't give her that, she ended things between them. Poor Riya. At sixteen years old, she'd entered into a relationship and trusted a man without thinking about her own powerlessness. Their relationship could never *be* a *relationship*. He used his power to get what he wanted. And when she expressed what she wanted, he killed her to shut her up.

"Okay, now send it to this email address," Sue says then reads it out for me. "There you go. That's done. This will last until your court hearing. But you do need to tell your husband. So email him now."

I do as she says then close the laptop. "What do I do now?"

"Well, you could stay with family. Or a friend. Or you could go home. It's up to you. We'll call you as soon as we release him from questioning."

"Okay. Thank you so much for all your help."

"It was no bother," she says. "You've got a great kid there."

"Gabe, say thank you to Sue for watching you."

"Thanks, Sue," he says. His voice sounds quieter than usual.

I'm going to have to explain everything when we get home. I can't quite believe it.

He lifts the toy car up to her, but she waves her hand. "Oh, no, you keep that, sweetheart."

"Thanks," Gabe says.

He stays silent for the journey home, idly pushing the car up and down his leg. I try calling Maddie several more times, but there's no answer. But I do have a missed call from Cecilia, which I return.

"Hey, hun," Cecilia says. "How's the hangover from last night?"

Instead of answering, I start to cry, my tears blurring the road in front of me.

"What's happened?" she asks.

"It's Justin," I blurt out through tears.

"Can I come over?"

I tell her the address.

IT's dark by the time we get home. The two of us traipse into the house, dragging our feet. Gabe hasn't asked about Justin yet, but I know he understands something is going on.

"You must be hungry, monkey," I say. "Want some toast and jam?"

He shakes his head.

"Do you want to talk?"

He nods.

I pull him onto my lap on the sofa and stroke his hair. "Your dad has made a huge mistake." I breathe in, trying to find the words. "Now, this is going to be hard, sweetie, but we'll get through it. Your dad is being questioned about the murder of Riya Shah."

He gazes up at me, his small face red and scrunched. "No!"

"It's true. Dad and Riya were special friends, and the police—"

He climbs down from me, his legs and arms flailing. "No! No, no, no, no. He wouldn't! Daddy wouldn't!"

"I know you love him, and he loves you too, very much. That won't change—"

"I hate you!" he screams, running from the room.

I'm about to go after him when the doorbell rings. I hurry through the house to the door and throw my arms around Cecilia. "I'm so sorry for dragging you out here. Come in."

She's clutching a bottle of vodka. *Good. I need it.*

"That's okay. God, you sounded awful on the phone. Are you all right?"

"I filed a restraining order against my husband."

"What? When?"

I unscrew the cap on the vodka bottle and take a swig. "The police took him in for questioning. He's a person of interest. He's been having an affair with a teenage girl." I take a breath, realising it all came out garbled. "Justin was in a relationship, if you can call it that, with Riya Shah, and the police pulled him in for questioning."

Her expression freezes. "Jesus."

"They have a witness who saw them together."

"Oh, Zoe. I'm so sorry. Do you know who the witness is?"

I shake my head and take another swig, enjoying the warmth from the spirit as it circulates through my bloodstream. Then I remember Cecilia's sobriety, cap the vodka bottle, and push it far back on the kitchen counter. "No. I have no idea. Maybe it's someone from school. I should check on Gabe. He ran into his room in tears. It's been an awful day for him."

"You do that," she says. "I'll make some coffee. You'll need it after the three shots of vodka you downed."

"Sorry," I say. "I didn't mean to—"

"No need to apologise. I bought it because I knew you'd need it."

But I notice how she takes the bottle and puts it in a cupboard, as though she doesn't want the temptation.

Gabe is in bed, fast asleep, when I check on him. Gently, I pull his duvet around his body, still clothed, and back out of the room. Poor kid. The events of the day must have wiped him out.

On the way back, I hesitate outside Maddie's room, remembering the day I noticed her secretively closing a browser on her laptop. Impulsively, I grab it and take it back with me to the living room.

Cecilia hands me a black coffee and gestures for me to sit on the sofa. "Come on, you need to rest."

I place the coffee down on the side table but shake my head. "I need to find Maddie. I've done everything I can about Justin, but Maddie is out there, and I need to find her."

"Okay, well, let's try and find her," Cecilia says. "I'll help you."

It's a relief to have a friend. To have someone here. She smiles warmly and gestures for me to go on.

I open Maddie's laptop and am faced with the lock screen. An eye symbol blinks, and the facial recognition programme prompts me for the passcode.

"Shit. I don't know her code."

"Is there a date that's important to her?" Cecilia asks.

I think of us both sitting in Peter McKenna's corridor, me in the throes of pneumonia, my chest rattling, my lungs on the brink of collapse, and the freezing cold set into my bones.

"The day we met," I murmur and type the date into the box.

The lock screen flashes away, giving me access to her computer. I let out a shaky breath. "God, I can't believe it. I'm actually in." I flex my fingers, not sure where to start.

I double-click on the email icon and bring open her personal inbox. I'm not sure what I'm expecting. Teenagers communicate on Snapchat and WhatsApp instead of email. But I scan her inbox, finding nothing strange. Most of her emails are spam, online shopping orders, or communication with her school. Then I head over to the storage settings, because what I need is access to her phone. If she backs up her messages, then maybe I can learn more about this Annabel girl.

"How's it going?" Cecilia sips her coffee. "Have you found anything?"

I click into iCloud, and there they all are—backups for WhatsApp, Instagram, Snapchat and more. "Not yet, but I've found her files. I feel like such a terrible person doing this."

"Hun, you are so far from a terrible person," she says, shaking her head. "I mean, these are extenuating circumstances. Like, seriously extenuating. You need your kid back, so get your kid back."

She's right. I click through Snapchat first. Although there's a shocking number of unpleasant messages from Katherine Sutton, the girl Maddie pushed, there's nothing from anyone called Annabel. Then I open the backed-up WhatsApp messages and let out a gasp.

"What is it?" Cecilia leans over my shoulder. A few strands of her hair hit my collarbone. "Angie Starling. Does that name mean anything to you?"

"Yes. It does." I open the chat. "Oh my God."

The thread is long, going back months. There are hundreds of messages, photographs, and even a few calls logged. My skin prickles as I skim read through them, a nauseating sensation lying in the pit of my stomach as I notice how Angie calls Maddie "my sweet girl."

"What the hell is going on?" I whisper.

"Look." Cecilia points to a message halfway up the screen. "She refers to Maddie as her daughter."

No. No no no no no.

Cecilia turns to me. "Is that possible?"

"Yes," I breathe. "It's possible. The police never found Maddie's birth mother." I scroll farther up the screen, where I find a selfie of the two of them together. Every part of my body turns freezing cold, like I'm back in that farmhouse with pneumonia, in sodden clothing and soaked skin. The resemblance is glaring. They're more like sisters than mother and daughter, but Angie could have been young at the time of Maddie's birth.

Both are staring at the camera with warm chestnut eyes, slightly hooded, more rounded than oval and set wide apart above a petite nose. Some of Maddie's features are sharper, inherited from her father, while Angie has the soft girl-next-door appearance I noted the first time we met.

Angie is Annabel. Maddie hasn't been seeing a friend she met on the internet; she's been in contact with her birth mother.

CHAPTER THIRTY-NINE
NOW

I t doesn't take long for me to find Angie Starling's address within the messages, and I scribble it down on a scrap of paper. My heart hammers against my chest. Maddie's mother is the one woman in this world I dread.

"Are you okay?" Cecilia asks.

"Not really. I'm not sure what other revelations I can take tonight."

"This woman works at Maddie's school, right? When did she start?"

"Oh, I don't know. About six months ago, I think. I actually... When I realised Justin was lying to me, I briefly thought he must be having an affair with her. She came here about six months ago. He quit the football team six months ago." I rub my temple. "If only it was that simple, right?"

"Six months," Cecilia says. "Not long ago. Do you think she sought you out? It can't be a coincidence, can it? She moved here to get closer to Maddie."

"She planned this."

"Sure seems like it," Cecilia says. "Come on, let's go and find Maddie. We have the address. I can drive."

"I can't leave Gabe."

"Bring him with us," she says. "You need to get your daughter back."

She's right. I close Maddie's laptop and get to my feet. My legs and arms feel heavy, but at the same time, my body is primed and ready to go. The need to find my daughter outweighs everything else.

Gabe stays asleep in my arms as I scoop him up from his bed. I carry him all the way to the car and clip him into the seat. He's going to wake up en route, or maybe when we get home, disorientated and afraid. I can't leave him here, though, and I don't have anyone to call to babysit.

I pass Cecilia the car keys and climb into the passenger seat. The garage remains dark and still. My thoughts drift to the police station. Perhaps Justin has been released already. He might come here and find the house empty. He might assume we've gone to a hotel.

Cecilia parks the car outside a small bungalow about a five-minute drive from the school. Peering through the car window, I see a perfectly ordinary house in an ordinary street. The lights are on, but the curtains are closed. She has lined curtains, so I can't even make out the colour. My adrenaline spikes, my pulse echoing in my ears, like the sound of the sea inside a shell. I hear Maddie saying, "I know we're not related, but you're my mum, and that's all I care about."

She's known for a while, and she chose not to tell me.

"Mum?" Gabe's sleep-softened voice comes from the backseat. "What's going on?"

"You wait here, sweetie," I say to Gabe. "I need to go inside."

He stares at the bungalow, his face drawn and tired. For once, I see myself in his features, and it saddens me that it's now I notice them, because surely that means I'm emotional and worried more than I am happy.

"I won't be long, I promise. I need to find Maddie."

But before we get out of the car, Cecilia places a hand on my arm. She glances back at Gabe and lowers her voice. "Listen, I have pepper spray in my handbag. I carry it with me always in case my ex jumps out from behind a bush. You know nothing about this woman, except for the fact she moved here to get closer to your daughter. And if she is

Maddie's mother, that means she spent time with Peter McKenna. What if she wasn't a victim? What if she was his girlfriend? She could be dangerous."

In the eleven years since I escaped Ivycross Farm, I have, of course, considered this. I've always wanted to believe that Maddie's mother was forced to give birth, that she was incarcerated by that man, which is an awful wish. But the alternative is that Maddie's mother cared for a monster. That she willingly lived with him, knowing what he did to his victims.

"You're right," I say. "I'm going to call the police before we go in." We left in such a hurry that I didn't think to do it before we left. I want to call DCI Cooper, the detective from the McKenna case all those years ago, but Rosen seems like a better choice, given the circumstances. I dial the number on the business card he gave me, but it's late, and he doesn't answer. I leave a garbled message explaining the circumstances, adding Angie's address at the end.

"Are you sure you want to go in there?"

My fingers hesitate on the door handle. "Give me the pepper spray." I hold out my hand, waiting. "Watch Gabe for me."

She digs through her bag and hands over the small canister. "Are you sure about going in alone?"

"I can't take my son in there. I won't be long. But you know what to do if I am."

"Mum?" Gabe observes me through his long eyelashes.

"I'll be back in a minute, bud. You be good for Cecilia."

I'm out of the car, striding up the driveway, my nerves as taut as stretched wire, stomach like a washing machine. But I dealt with Peter McKenna once, so I can deal with whatever ghoulish girlfriend he might have once had. The doorbell chimes. I wait, counting my heartbeats. *One, two, three.* Maddie said in her message to me that she knew who killed Riya. *Four, five, six. Did she mean Angie?*

The door opens.

"Zoe, hi," she says.

"Is Maddie here?"

"Why would Maddie be here?"

"I've figured it out, Angie. I know who you are."

Her expression never changes, and that scares me. I expected shock or concern. I wait for her face to crumple, for her to show some sort of emotion, but she maintains the same sickly sweet grin on her face, one that crinkles her eyes just so. She pulls the door wider.

"Come in," she says.

I follow her, noting the plain white walls along the hallway. No photographs. No travel trinkets or wall art. We step into a neat kitchen, where she flicks the switch on a kettle.

"I don't want a cup of tea, Angie. I want my daughter. Is she here?"

"She left a few minutes ago," she says. "I think she was going home to you. I'm sure your paths crossed without realising. How funny."

My thumbs hook through my belt loops, the fingers on my right hand brushing the bulge where the canister of pepper spray sits in my pocket. "You should know I told the police I was coming," I say. "I gave them your address."

She shrugs. Her nonchalance reminds me of Maddie, which pains me to admit. "That's fine. Though I don't know what you're expecting me to do." She smiles again, and her tongue pokes playfully through her teeth.

"How long have you both been talking?"

"Not long. A few weeks."

That strikes me as odd, considering how long Angie has been in Penry.

"But you've been watching her for a long time. Biding your time. Haven't you?"

"Is it a crime to want to be close to your own daughter?" she asks.

Behind her, the kettle boils. I instinctively take a step back when she reaches out to grab it.

"I hadn't seen her for so long. Can you blame me?"

"Yes," I say. "Because you left her with that man. And you never went back for her."

Angie grabs a mug and tosses a teabag in it. Mint tea, I notice. She doesn't bother asking me if I want one. Instead, she pours the water into the mug and idly plays with the teabag string.

"You don't know my circumstances, so don't judge me."

I stay silent, but inside, I think about how I fought to get out from Ivycross Farm and how determined I was to take Maddie with me. I'd known her for barely a day, and I wanted to protect her. Angie gave birth to Maddie and still left without her.

"Will you let me search your house? I need to know Maddie isn't here."

"She's not. I've already told you." She holds the mug with both hands as though clasping it for warmth.

"And you could be lying." My gaze fixes on that mug. She could use it as a weapon at any moment.

"Fine. Search the house. You won't find her."

I don't want to turn my back on Angie, so I move quickly out of the kitchen. I keep my hand near the pepper spray throughout my entire search. Each room is practically identical to the last. White walls and beige furniture. No photographs. No sign of life. Why has she come to find Maddie now? Where has she been? I have so many questions, but I can't ask a single one until I've found my daughter.

When I try the wardrobe and find nothing, I'm forced to conclude that Angie was telling the truth. Back in the kitchen, I check for signs of a cellar door, the last place she could be hiding. There isn't one.

"Happy now?" she asks, sipping her tea.

"Once Maddie is safe and sound, we need to talk."

"Gladly," she replies.

"If you see Maddie before me, can you tell her that I've take out a restraining order against Justin? Her phone is switched off."

"The stepdad?"

"Adoptive dad, but yes."

"Oh," she says. "Is this because he was seeing that girl?"

"You knew about that?" I take a step towards her. "You knew, and you said nothing?"

"I've been watching," she says, making the words sound like a threat. "I've noticed some of your husband's habits. It's a shame, because you seem pretty decent."

I don't like her. The sound of her voice makes my skin crawl. I can't stay in her company for another second. But as I start to leave, I notice something about her hand that I didn't see before. Two scars, one in the centre of her left hand, and the other across her right little finger.

Angie lifts her left hand. "You noticed. I usually use makeup to cover it. We're scar twins." She grins.

"McKenna did that to you."

"Yes."

"He tried to remove your finger."

She places her left hand back on the cup and holds up her right hand. Now I see how the joint doesn't bend properly. "He broke it. This was before he started removing the fingers." She sighs. "I guess I was one of the first. He wasn't quite as... dramatic then." She grips the mug with both hands again. "And you were the final girl. The good one."

"No," I say. "When there's a final girl, there's one survivor. Three of us survived Peter McKenna. You. Me. Maddie."

"Lucky us."

My phone rings. It's DS Rosen. Angie makes a hand gesture to suggest I answer it.

"Hello."

"Hi, Ms Osbourne. I'm calling because there's been a development regarding your husband. He has an alibi. He saw Riya Shah that night, the witness told the truth, but we have CCTV footage of him going somewhere else before the time of Riya's death. He spent about an hour with Riya before she left to catch a bus, and he drove somewhere else."

"Where did he go?"

Rosen hesitates. "He went to visit another student."

"Who?" I ask.

"Phoebe Thompson. We have CCTV of his car driving out to a park close to the Thompsons' house, then more CCTV of them checking into a hotel. Room service went up about an hour after they checked in. Then there's CCTV footage of them leaving the hotel about an hour after that. We caught his car driving through Penry about twenty minutes later. It wasn't him, Zoe. I thought you should know. He couldn't possibly have abducted and murdered Riya Shah in that timeframe."

Instead of relief, all I can think about are practicalities. What does this mean for me and my family?

"Have you let him go?" I ask.

"Yes," Rosen says. "But he knows about the injunction. He knows he can't go home. However, if he ignores the restraining order and shows up at the house, call 999 immediately."

"I will."

"And your message. Did I hear that right? You've found Maddie's birth mother."

"Long story," I say. "But everything seems fine on that front."

"Okay," he says. "Remember, call 999 if you're in trouble. You can call me too, but they'll be quicker."

When I hang up the phone, Angie is two steps closer to me than before. I stepped away to speak to the detective, giving her an opportunity to close the gap between us. Did she intend to hurt me? Or was she eavesdropping?

"I have to go," I say.

"Trouble at home?"

"Something like that."

"I hope you find Maddie," she says. "We should meet up and talk things through. There's a lot to talk about."

"Yes, there is."

"Bye for now then." She stands at the door, waving like a Stepford Wife. Every part of my body shivers with repulsion.

CHAPTER FORTY
NOW

The house is quiet—and dark—when we return. Everything is as I left it. It takes me two attempts to punch in the code on the keypad, my hands shake so violently. As we rush inside, I hurry through the corridor into the kitchen, flicking every light switch, calling Maddie's name. No one answers.

Cecilia grabs hold of my shoulder before I venture any deeper into the house. "Let's go together. Pass me that pepper spray."

I reach into my pocket and give her the canister. Then I take Gabe's small hand in my own, and we make our way slowly, room by room. We linger in Maddie's bedroom. I never spend much time here. Everything is as it should be. There's a photograph of me and her on her bedside table. She's around ten years old in it, and we're at the zoo. We fed goats together. She beams out from the centre of the frame, grinning from ear to ear. I'm pregnant, my face and body rounder than usual.

On the wall above her dressing table, there are a couple of photographs of her and Riya attached to the yellow walls with Blu Tack. Next to them are two photographs of Maddie and Gabe, hair wet with seawater, blankets tossed over their shoulders. I remember taking the pictures and marvelling at their happy, round faces. None of Maddie's chosen photographs include Justin.

"He hit on me."

The sudden sound of her voice makes me clutch my chest. I let out a gasp, half shock, half relief, and spin to face the door. Next to me, I sense Gabe and Cecilia do the same.

"Maddie!" Gabe dashes forward and throws his arms around her waist.

Maddie ruffles his hair. "Good to see you too, little bro."

"Where did you...? How...? We didn't even hear you," I stutter.

"I was in the panic room," she says.

"Why?"

"In case you were him." She lets go of Gabe then gazes down at him with a frown on her face.

"Daddy?" Gabe asks.

"I'm sorry, bro," Maddie says. "I know what it's like to have a bad daddy." Her words make me flinch.

"What did you say when you came in?" I ask.

Maddie places her hands over Gabe's ears. "He hit on me last year."

I close my eyes, wanting the ground to swallow me whole. "Oh, Mads. No." When I open my eyes again, she's as she was, as though saying the words didn't touch her emotionally. "I'm so sorry." I wrap my arms around her. "You should've told me."

"He pretended like he thought I was you because he was so drunk," Maddie says. "And I guess I believed him at first. But then..." She places her hands over Gabe's ears again. "I never wanted to go swimming around him again. And... he lied about stuff. Like the day I took Gabe to the beach when you said I shouldn't. He made out like I wanted to hurt Gabe. That wasn't true. I tried to grab him, but I couldn't reach." She lets go of Gabe's ears and stands straighter.

"I never thought you wanted to hurt him," I say. "Why didn't you tell me about Justin?"

"I dunno. I thought it'd ruin things. I didn't like him, but I knew you did. I didn't know what else he was doing at that point. And then he figured out I'd been cheating on my exams, and he held it over me."

"Oh, Maddie." I brush her hair away from her face. "I don't care about your exams. Not right now, anyway. Always tell me. Okay? No matter what."

I can tell she isn't convinced, but she nods anyway. Then she looks across at Cecilia. "Who's this?"

"My friend from group therapy."

Maddie scrunches up her nose. "Friend. You sure about that?"

"You might need me tonight," Cecilia says, ignoring Maddie's rude response. "What with your adoptive father just released from the police station."

Maddie turns to me.

"He didn't kill Riya," I explain. "The police have proof. But there's no fucking way he's staying with us tonight. So let's go and put all the shutters down and lock up this fortress."

MADDIE TAKES Gabe to bed as Cecilia and I work through the house, lowering shutters, changing passcodes, and checking each of the exits. I'm quiet, saying nothing except numbers for the new codes. They have to be completely original and unrelated to anything Justin might guess. Birthdays are out of the question. We use random numbers, which I scribble down on a Post-it note and shove into the pocket of my jeans.

"It's not your fault, you know," Cecilia says. "I've seen the lengths men will go to in order to cover up their second lives. There are people out there who present themselves as one person, only to reveal a whole other side to them. Whoever said people can't hide their true selves is full of shit. Humans have been doing it for centuries. They have this canny knack of compartmentalising or justifying things to themselves to allow them to be the perfect husband by day and total bastard by night."

"But how could I miss the fact that he hit on my fifteen-year-old daughter?"

She leans against the corridor wall. "Because you didn't see it. Because he hid it all from you."

I shake my head. "Not quite all of it." I think about his greedy hands when he's drunk. Even now, at this point in our marriage, I sometimes don't like saying no to him in bed, because the silent treatment he gives me in return makes me feel so shitty that I usually allow him to do what he wants to do. "It crept up on me. He's so lovely in other ways."

"People are capable of the ultimate kindness and the ultimate cruelty."

"I guess I've experienced more of the latter." I idly lift my hand and touch the scar in the centre of my hand.

"But wasn't what you did for Maddie the ultimate kindness?"

"No," I say almost immediately. "Because it was selfish. I needed her as much as she needed me."

"It was still kind, Zoe," Cecilia says. "Don't miss that part out."

I scoff. "I'm so sorry I've dragged you into all of this. You don't need this. Not with your ex out of prison."

"Actually, this is exactly what I need," she says. "Being alone right now doesn't feel good. Having a friend to be around—I need that."

I reach out and slip my hand into hers. "Same. Thank you for everything."

Before we hunker down for the night, we check on the panic room and quickly change the code, scribbling it down on the Post-it. Then we head to Gabe's room.

"He's scared," Maddie says, stroking Gabe's hair.

He cries on Maddie's shoulder, his eyes red-rimmed and bloodshot.

I bend down and rub his arms. "It's going to be all right, monkey. Okay? Everything is going to be all right."

"I thought Daddy loved me," he whimpers.

My heart breaks. He sounds so young. Even his voice is higher, more babyish, as all the fear and uncertainty scares him.

"He still loves you, sweetheart. He's done some bad things, but that doesn't change how much he loves you."

I mean my words, but they taste sour on my tongue. The man I married seduced two teenage girls and made a pass at his own adopted daughter. Even his alibi for not killing one girl involved another dead teenager.

Did Justin kill Phoebe Thompson? He was out that night and arrived home a few minutes before I got the call about Phoebe's death. I hug Gabe tighter, wondering. I hadn't had a chance to allow my mind to wander, what with Maddie's disappearance and Justin's arrest. I hadn't even mentioned Angie Starling to Maddie yet. Then there was the matter of Riya's death. Who murdered Riya?

Once Gabe is asleep, Cecilia informs us she's going to stay on the sofa and keep watch. Maddie and I head to my bedroom. I want to clean the sheets, to scrub away the scent of my husband, but I'm too tired.

In our pyjamas, we collapse onto the duvet. The day over, finally. Possibly the worst day of my life, because at least escaping Ivycross farm meant I got to meet Maddie. I turn to face my daughter, noticing the way her dark hair spreads out on the pillow, and I finally say it.

"I know about your birth mother. I went to Angie Starling's house, trying to find you."

Her eyebrows shoot up, and I'm partly offended by her shock. "You figured it out?"

"I hacked into your laptop. I saw your messages. Are you mad?"

"More like impressed." She smiles. I suppose this is one benefit to having an unemotional, slightly sociopathic daughter.

"I saw the selfie of you two."

"Yeah," Maddie says. "I guess we look alike."

I reach across and take her hand. "I'm glad you've found her. But be careful."

Maddie raises her eyebrows. "Believe me, I am being careful." She stares up at the ceiling, a pensive expression on her face. "I trust her about as much as I trust Justin. You and Gabe are the only people in this world that I trust at all."

CHAPTER FORTY-ONE
NOW

Cecilia wakes me with a fresh cup of coffee. She sits in the armchair near the bed, cross-legged. Wearing the same clothes as the night before, she's still as neat and tidy as always. I wonder if she even slept.

She sips her coffee. "Well, he didn't show up here. I guess that's a good thing."

"The restraining order must have got the message across." I grab my phone and check for messages. None are from him, but there is a missed call from my mother. I guess news of Justin's questioning has made the national press.

Maddie sleeps while I shower and change. As I head back into the bedroom, she sits up in bed with her knees pulled to her chest. "Are you sure you can trust her?"

"Who? Cecilia? Why not?"

Maddie shrugs. "What if she sought you out? She could be a stalker obsessed with your book, one of those true-crime nutters. Or she could be Lucinda Garth's minion."

I haven't heard the name Lucinda Garth for a long time, and it dredges up an old feeling of pity mixed with fury. "Hun, not everyone has an agenda. Some people are just nice."

She rolls her eyes. "Yeah, right."

"It's true. I get why you're cautious, and believe me, I am too. But Cecilia wouldn't be helping us if she wanted to hurt us. She's already had plenty of opportunities, and she hasn't taken those opportunities."

Maddie glances down at her phone, frowning.

"What is it?" I ask.

"Angie wants to meet. She wants to see both of us."

"When?"

"Today." Maddie regards me. I can tell she's hiding her excitement. Despite the neutral expression on her face, her fingers twitch around the edge of the duvet.

I consider it for a moment. Does it feel safe to meet this woman while Justin is out there? Or am I being paranoid? He'd be pretty stupid to try anything right now. But I have to consider Gabe. If Justin is going to do anything, I believe it'd be trying to take Gabe away from me. Perhaps Cecilia could take Gabe to her apartment in case Justin turns up at the house.

"All right," I say. "We could meet in the park."

Maddie types the message out on her phone. "Eleven?"

I nod.

We eat breakfast and Cecilia agrees to take Gabe to her place. My mum calls again, but I switch my phone off so I can pretend it ran out of battery. I don't want to hear her voice right now.

We leave the house at ten thirty. Maddie wears a sundress, and I notice that her shoulders are golden. She's caught the sun, as Mum always used to say. There's a faint trail of freckles dotted along her nose and cheeks. What a beautiful young woman. A fierce sense of protectiveness surges through my blood. No teenage girl should have to deal with a man in his early forties making a pass at her. She trusted Justin. She knew him when she was six years old. I feel sick, angry, and raw, but mostly angry. Anyone who wishes her harm will need to come through me first.

Our drive is short—around fifteen minutes—and we're early. But Angie Starling is already there. Dressed in a mid-length skirt and a floral blouse, she sits primly on a bench. Every part of her appearance is perfect, from the neutral makeup to the way her smooth, naked legs are tucked beneath the seat. Maddie speeds up to get closer, but I find myself dragging my feet. I don't want this to happen.

Angie throws her arms around Maddie, and my fingers tighten against the shoulder strap of my handbag.

Once she lets Maddie go, she holds out a hand for me to shake. "Thank you so much for meeting me, Zoe."

"That's all right. I suppose we have a few things to iron out."

"That's right." She gestures to a picnic basket. "I brought a blanket and some nibbles. It's too lovely a day to sit on benches."

Maddie helps her birth mother spread the blanket over the grass, and we all sit down in an irregular triangle. I can't help but notice the way Angie stares at Maddie as though not believing she's real. Every time she looks at my daughter, I want to reach out and push Angie away.

"I have a lot of explaining to do, don't I?" Angie says. "Where to start?" She sighs. "Well, I've told Maddie some of this, but it's time for you to know, Zoe." Her hands clasp together. She reminds me of a fifties housewife in a sitcom. Every movement appears contrived. But perhaps I'm judging her too harshly.

"When I was sixteen, my sister and I ran away from home. We hadn't had the best start in life. Our dad went out for cigarettes when I was seven and never came home. Mum used whatever drug she could buy that day. If she wasn't out of it, she didn't want to live. But somehow, I always got Lisa and me to school.

"But when Lisa turned fifteen, I saw the way my mother's dirty boyfriends looked at her. I'd dealt with them myself, and I didn't want her going through that. I'd already left school and was working in a newsagent. One day, I started walking Lisa to school, and we just carried on walking." She pauses, her voice cracking with emotion. "We couldn't take it anymore." She balls the material of her skirt in her hands.

"I guess Mum didn't bother reporting us missing. Lisa had a year left at school, but I wonder if Mum told them we were moving away or something. I found out later that she died from an overdose not long after we left." Her expression darkens. She begins to unbutton the cuff of her blouse. "We had nowhere to go and no plan to follow. I felt awful. I'd talked Lisa into leaving and everything got worse, not better."

Angie rolls up her sleeve to reveal the track marks on her arm. "We found ourselves dulling the pain like Mum. We slept in alleyways on cardboard boxes." She shudders. "I won't talk much about that time, because it was bad. But then a man appeared and gave us blankets. A tall, friendly man. He said his name was Peter and he'd be back to bring us food."

She laughs. Her laugh sounds exactly like Maddie's. "I didn't believe him. I knew he'd be back, but I figured he wanted sex. And I would've given it to him at that point, as long as he gave me drugs in return."

I glance at Maddie, with the sinking realisation that I couldn't shield her from any of this.

"He came back with food the next day," Angie continued. "And a couple of days after that, he came back with heroin. Well, by then, Lisa and I were willing to go with anyone anywhere as long as they had smack." She sighs. Her voice speeds up as though she wants to get the rest of the story over with. "We got into his car. We went back to his farm. He set us up in a comfortable room. We couldn't believe our luck. At first." She shakes her head and sighs. "I think the police have guessed the rest. Both Lisa and I fell pregnant pretty quickly. Lisa didn't make it."

Her fingers tighten, the silky material of her skirt tangled between them. Her gaze drops to the blanket beneath us. "After Lisa died and Maddie was born, I... I was such a mess. He kept me like... like an animal." She glances at Maddie. "I'm so sorry I ran. I didn't see a future for me. I saw nothing but the streets again, and I couldn't... I didn't think either of us would survive if I took you with me. I wasn't much older than you are now, sweetheart. Could you imagine it? The... the pressure." She brushes tears from her cheeks.

A shadow passes across Maddie's face. The tiniest ripple of... What? Disbelief? Sadness? She's hard to read, my daughter.

"What happened after you left?" I ask. "You're clearly doing much better now."

"I got clean," she says. "I found a place in a hostel, and then I was accepted into an addiction programme. Bit by bit, I improved. I worked about five jobs. Waitress, cleaner, sales assistant, courier, anything to earn a bit of money for rent. Then I got a promotion at a warehouse, to supervisor. It wasn't much, but the extra cash and regular hours meant I had time to study online. I wanted to be a teacher. I got a job in a school as a teaching assistant, and I moved here to Penry. Now I have my own house and my own job, and I'm finally free from the past."

I can't help myself when I say, "And you chose a job at Maddie's school. You came here on purpose to watch her from afar. That was sneaky."

"I never thought I'd get the job when I applied. These positions are always competitive, especially in nice areas like this. But I hit it off with the head teacher in the interview. And before I knew it, I was watching Maddie come to school every day. I couldn't believe my luck." She hooks an arm over Maddie's shoulder and pulls her towards her.

Maddie resists at first, but then leans in.

"We're going to have to go to the police," I say. "DCI Cooper, the detective on the Ivycross Farm case, will need to know who you are. It's only right that Lisa is identified as one of Peter's victims."

"Sure," she says, rocking her and Maddie from side to side as she holds her.

I watch them, that same repulsion spreading through me. I want to believe her story, I do. But I can't shake the feeling that something feels off.

A few hours later, after sausage rolls, lemonade, and more conversation, when I'm back in the car with Maddie, I keep opening my mouth to speak before closing it again. I can't quite find the words. Angie spent a lot of the time telling Maddie what a beautiful baby she'd been. She even talked about the birth in the barn without painkillers, a towel underneath her, and Peter McKenna pacing back and forth, screaming at her to be quiet.

"I thought I'd die like Lisa," she said in a quiet voice.

Now, I find myself glancing at Maddie, a hundred worries in my mind that I'm too afraid to voice. Angie's transformation is too easy. Could a woman with such a work ethic, who has shown such determination to turn her life around, leave her infant daughter with a serial killer? Why didn't she go to the police? Why didn't she drop Maddie off at a hospital, a fire station, or anywhere instead of leaving her with Peter McKenna?

"You okay, hun?" I ask, and it's pretty much all I ask.

"I'm fine."

"It's okay if you're not."

"I know," she says.

"Shall we call DCI Cooper when we get home?"

"Not yet," she says.

"Why not?"

"I think I want more time with her first," Maddie says. "Calling the police is going to change everything."

"You think so?" I ask.

"Yeah," she says. "It's just a hunch, I guess."

I head to Cecilia's apartment to pick up Gabe while Maddie waits in the car. I briefly tell her about the meeting with Angie.

"I need to know more about her," I say. "I don't know where to start."

"Social media," Cecilia says. "That's always the best place. You need to know who this woman is."

"I could try the school," I say.

"Yes, do that. Shall I come back with you? I can, but I actually start a job tomorrow so I could do with being home."

"You do? That's amazing!"

As Cecilia tells me about her new job at the Penry art gallery, I realise how much of her time I've consumed with my own drama. Then Gabe asks to go home.

"Zoe, be careful, won't you?" Cecilia grasps hold of my forearm. "If you need anything, let me know."

I tell her I will and make my way downstairs to the car, where Maddie waits for us. From outside the car, I can see her texting. Angie Starling again, I bet. My stomach flips. This isn't going to end well. I can feel it.

CHAPTER FORTY-TWO
NOW

Not since the moment Peter McKenna wrapped his arms around my neck have I had a more eventful week. I've learned the man I shared my bed with has a predilection for teenage girls. My adopted daughter's birth mother emerged with a story I struggled to believe. Somehow, I know there is more to come.

I prepare myself for the calls I need to make by starting the day with a large mug of coffee. Slightly jittery after draining half of it, I sit down at the kitchen table and pick up my mobile phone. DCI Cooper first. I call through to South Yorkshire police, relieved to find him still at the same unit in the same position.

He listens patiently as I relay Angie Starling's story, giving no opinion on Angie herself, simply interjecting every now and then to clarify certain points. My fingernails tap lightly on the surface of the table.

"I'd like to get a sample of her DNA. Could you take her to your local police station? I'll be in touch with them to coordinate this," he says. In the background, I hear the rustle of a page turning.

"I'll see if she agrees. I think she will. She... Well, she looks exactly like Maddie. This isn't Lucinda Garth all over again. It's real. I can feel it."

"I trust your instincts, Zoe."

"Thank you." Then I laugh. "I'm not sure if I trust my own instincts right now. Not considering who I married."

"I'm sorry to hear about your husband," he says. "I hope they'll be pushing for abuse of trust. He can still get prison time."

"Honestly, I hope they throw it all at him." I pause. I want to tell him my suspicions about Phoebe Thompson, but this isn't Cooper's case. Instead, I say, "It was nice talking to you again after all these years."

"And you, Zoe. You take care now."

"I will."

I picture his moustache moving up and down as he speaks, and the image transports me back to another time. After hanging up, I call Mum. She has a right to know what's going on.

"Zoe," she says. "I'm glad you called. I've been trying to get hold of you."

"I know, sorry. Things have been crazy here—"

"I saw it on the news. I can't believe it. I always liked Justin. Is it true? Did he kill that girl?"

"No," I reply. "But he abused his power... He..." My voice cracks. I know what she must be thinking—that I can't choose a man, that I'm weak.

But she doesn't say any of that. There's no judgement in her voice when she speaks, only softness. "It's all right. I understand."

"How's Dad?" I twirl a lock of my hair around one finger. I'm not sure why. It feels comforting. I used to do it at school during exams.

"There's not been much change with your dad. He's still confused and... Listen, Zoe, I wondered if you needed me where you are. I could come and stay with you. I could watch Gabe and Maddie."

"Maddie? Really?"

There's a long pause before she speaks again. "I've done a lot of thinking over the years, and to be honest with you, I have some regrets. I don't think I handled what happened to you very well. I'm sorry."

Her words take my breath away, but I try not to let it show. "It was a stressful time for everyone. I'm sure I could've done better too."

In a quiet voice, she says, "No, I'm sure it was all mostly me. And I'm sorry for that."

"I appreciate you saying that, Mum."

"Why don't you come to stay up here?" she offers. "You'll be away from Justin then."

"I'll think about it."

My last conversation is with DS Rosen, who tells me Justin has been charged with breaking his position of trust.

"Don't worry. He won't be getting off scot-free," Rosen assures me. "But it's going to be a while until his trial. And between now and then, I want you to be careful. Has he come to the house?"

"No," I say. "I've not seen or heard from him."

"That's good."

"Can I say something?" Nervous, I rest a thumbnail against my teeth.

"Of course. What is it, Zoe?"

"Justin came home late the night Phoebe Thompson died. What if she went to meet him, and he pushed her?"

"I've had the exact same thoughts," he says. "But there are witnesses who saw him in the pub that night, watching the football game. I'll be revisiting it to check what time he left, but I don't think he had the opportunity to get up to the campsite, lure Phoebe away from the tents, and murder her before going home to you. Like I said, I'll be checking every detail very carefully now that we know he groomed her. And we'll be speaking to Phoebe's friends too. Perhaps one of them knew about Justin but thought it was best to stay quiet."

I let out a sigh of relief. "Okay." Then I blurt out, "Maddie had no idea about Justin and Riya."

Rosen pauses. "You're sure about that?"

"Yes," I say. "If she'd known, she would've told me."

"Well, if you're sure," he says, though he doesn't sound convinced. "I need to go. There's no real reason to suspect Justin is a violent man, but you're being sensible with the restraining order. Don't forget to call straight away if he tries to come back to the house. Okay?"

"I will."

I hang up the phone, every ounce of energy drained from my body. Gabe and I are handling the unspooling of the family the worst. Poor Gabe, who has loved his father every second of his life, now has to face the reality that his father isn't the hero he thought. And I... Well, I suppose I carry the weight of every decision made since the point of no return in that police station.

For the rest of the day, we close the shutters on the house, watch movies, and eat popcorn. Cecilia arrives in the evening with pizza. Somehow, she's slotted into our lives with ease. I push away my worries about her. I try not to dwell on Maddie's warnings. I can't do this alone. And while Mum's offer was nice, I can't imagine her and Maddie staying in the same house together. Plus, I can't take her away from her birth mother so soon. I want to, but it might drive Maddie away from me. She's sixteen. She can move out and live with Angie at any time.

I watch my kids eat pizza and laugh at Cecilia's stories about her time working in customer service, and quietly, I search for Angie Starling on Facebook, Instagram, and Twitter. There's nothing. Then I try Google. I bite my lip, concerned. Again, very little comes up, only a staff profile on the Penry school website.

Aside from my sleuthing, the night is uneventful, and the next morning almost feels normal. Gabe complains about regular things like the fact that we've run out of milk. He strops around, accusing Maddie of stealing his last Yorkie bar. I dig out a mini Mars bar from the back of the cupboard to cheer him up.

I hold the children back from school. Over a morning coffee in the garden, with Maddie and Gabe watching cartoons, I tell Cecilia what I found on the internet about Angie Starling.

"That's weird," she says. "People leave a trail. I mean, yes, she probably didn't want to be found by Peter McKenna, so I'm sure she's lived a cautious life. But he died eleven years ago. I think she'd crop up somewhere. It's not normal. You're right to be cautious."

"I don't like it," I admit. "This has to be purposeful."

Cecilia nods. "I can't tell you what to do, but... Don't let Maddie out of your sight. And make sure Angie goes to the police to give that DNA sample. They'll be able to figure out who she is."

"You think she might be lying about her name?" I ask.

Cecilia shrugs. "My ex used to invent new identities all the time when he was grifting. But Penry school will have done a background check, so I don't know."

Cecilia leaves after breakfast, and I make a lunchtime call to the school. When the secretary puts me through to the headteacher, Bert Browning answers immediately. I give him my name and his voice lowers.

"Zoe, my God, I can't believe what's happened. I never thought it of him. Never."

"Have you heard from him?" I ask.

"No, nothing. Though he's obviously not welcome back at the school."

"He's not welcome back at home either," I say.

"Stands to reason," he says. "Is that why you called?"

"No," I say. "Actually, Bert, the whole story is much crazier than you know." I go on to explain Angie Starling and who she really is. He lets out a few exclamations of shock, and by the end, I can tell he's reeling.

"We screen all of our new staff members. We check for a criminal history, and we check references. Every new employee has to give us three of their most recent addresses and so on. Nothing came up for Angie. But her references were good."

"Can you tell me the name of the school she worked at before Penry?"

"I wouldn't normally," he says. "But I think I'd best. Give me a minute, Zoe." I hear the sound of tapping on the keyboard. "Yes, here it is. St Anne's Grammar School in Glasgow. It's not a school I'm familiar with. I spoke to the headteacher, Rosie McDonald, and she told me Angie was enthusiastic but young and might need guidance. I've always preferred to hire young teaching assistants because a school needs energy."

"Thank you," I reply. "And what do you think of her?"

"To be honest with you, Zoe, we've had some problems. Part of her job is supervising the children with learning difficulties or behavioural issues. And, well, some of our more vulnerable students are... How do I put it? Well, they're afraid of her. I was actually about to have a meeting with her about it."

"She scares the kids?"

"I'm not sure," he says. "Almost all of the autistic children under her ward have requested a new assistant to help them in class. I've had calls with two sets of parents upset that their kids have come home in tears." He sighs. "I suppose you've confirmed my worries about her character and I'll need to terminate her employment immediately."

"Don't sack her. Not yet. I don't want her to know I called you."

"That's an extraordinary request," he says.

"I know. I'm sorry. Just for a day or two. Let's pretend we never spoke."

He pauses, thinking it through. "All right. I'll do that, Zoe. Good luck with whatever it is you're trying to do."

"Thank you. I appreciate you doing this." I hang up the phone, a tentative plan forming in my mind.

CHAPTER FORTY-THREE
NOW

Rosie McDonald is in a meeting when I first call St Anne's in Glasgow. I call back an hour later, and she sounds surprised to be hearing from a random woman in Cornwall.

"Angie Starling? The name doesn't ring a bell."

"She told her current employer that she worked as a teaching assistant at your school."

"Oh," she says. "I don't think so. We've had the same three teaching assistants for the past five years. We're a small school, you see."

She's a liar. I knew it. My heart soars and sinks simultaneously. *Poor Maddie.* And now I have to tell her. My palms itch. I hate this.

But it has to be done. I make my way through to the living room, where Maddie lounges on the sofa next to Gabe. He has his headphones on, playing a car racing game. Maddie's glued to her phone, as always. Seeing her there makes my muscles tense. I know she's texting Angie. I can feel it.

"Can we talk?"

"What's going on?" she asks, lifting her eyes from the screen.

"Not here," I say, gesturing for her to follow me out into the garden. If I'm going to do this, I need fresh air around me, not the suffocating feeling of being inside the house. She sits next to me on the patio and I take her hand in mine. "Honey, Angie isn't who she says she is."

Maddie tips her head back against the chair, and sunshine falls on her face. She breathes deeply and closes her eyes. Then she lifts her head and pulls her hand from mine. She loops her hair around her fingers.

"I know," she says eventually. "She's been lying about pretty much everything."

"You know?" I shift my body towards her, trying to close the gap between us. "What do you mean? Did she lie to you or just to me?"

"Mum," she says. "I've lied too. I've lied quite a bit, actually."

I try hard not to move. Even with the warm afternoon sun on my skin, my blood is ice cold. "About what?"

She lifts one foot and places it on the seat of her chair. "Well, after you rescued me from Dad... Peter... I made it seem like I didn't remember her. But she left the farm a few months before I met you. Dad didn't keep her chained up like an animal." She shrugs. "Angie didn't want to admit to you that what she did, she did voluntarily."

"What did she do at the farm?"

Her gaze drifts away, towards the sea. "She helped him."

"She helped him? What? She helped him *kill*?"

"I never told anyone," Maddie says. "Before she left, she told me to keep it a secret, and I did. I wanted to protect her, I guess, despite everything. But the thing is, Mum, I'm scared now she's back. I'm scared because I know what she's capable of."

"What is she capable of, Maddie?"

"Everything."

That one word makes my spine shoot up straight. "Torture? Murder?"

"Sometimes she cut off their fingers," Maddie says.

My hand flies up to my mouth. "Oh God. I need to call the police. I need to warn them." I leap to my feet and grab my phone. Maddie continues to lean against her knee, silent and calm. "What's her real name, Maddie?"

"Louisa Madeleine Jones," Maddie says. "Her sister was called Lisa. That part is true."

"Did you recognise her right away?"

"Yes," Maddie says.

"And you've kept it a secret from me all this time?"

"Yes."

No hesitation. No hint of a guilty conscience.

"I told Riya about her," Maddie says. "Riya said you'd take her away. She was right. She was always right."

"Maddie..." I start, but then I don't know how to continue. Instead, I walk into the kitchen to call DS Rosen and tell him everything.

I'm a garbled mess on the phone, regurgitating Maddie's words in broken sentences. It takes a long time because I have to repeat myself several times so that Rosen can take notes. But once he understands, he assures me that a police officer will call Angie in for questioning right away. I give him DCI Cooper's phone number for them to speak to each other, then I go back to my children, feeling somewhat unsteady on my feet.

Maddie glides through the sliding doors and gently places herself on the armchair by the window. She's silent and still, observing me. It's unnerving.

"Did you call the police?" she asks, breaking the silence.

"Yes. They're going to call her in for questioning. Maddie, why wouldn't you tell me all of this? First Justin and now Angie... Louisa. I could've helped you." I glance over at Gabe, who's still playing his game, lost to the world.

I take a seat in the chair opposite Maddie. "Why did you shut me out? Tell me."

"I wanted more time with her," she says. "I know she's a bad person. She left me, didn't she? But... But I'm made of her, and I'm made of him, and sometimes, in this family, I have to pretend I'm not. I have to pretend I'm made of you. I like that kind of pretending. Who wouldn't? Who wants to be made of two sickos? I'd rather be part of you. But I'm not, am I?"

"You don't have to pretend anything with me. I'll love you whatever. Do you know that part of me thought you killed Phoebe? I did.

And I would've lied for you. I would've fought for you. I know who you are. You don't have to hide it."

She stares at me, unblinking. "Are you sure?"

"Yes," I say. "I'm completely sure."

"Then I guess there's something I need to show you."

My body lights up like an electrical grid, ignited by a flood of adrenaline. The cool spread of fear shudders across my skin. That's the dread seizing me. I always knew she'd say those words. I just never knew when. She stands. I stand with her. She walks, and I follow. We both leave Gabe behind with his headphones on, not even waving a goodbye to him. I think he's too engrossed in his game to notice. He's checked out from reality now. I don't blame him. I wish I were too.

I expect her to go into her bedroom. For some reason, I assume she's going to show me a text message or file on her laptop. Instead, we follow the shadowy stairs leading to the cellar. My heart thunders. I watch carefully as Maddie taps in the new code to the panic room.

"How did you find the code?" I ask.

"I watched you type it in on the CCTV system," she says.

Of course, she did, I think. The kids have it installed on their phones. So does Justin, for that matter, but I'd already removed his account from the home hub.

The door opens, and I hear a groan. The hairs on the back of my arms stand on end. I already know what we're going to find, but I'm not willing to face it. Maddie flicks on the light switch.

I don't like it down here. It's bare and cold and reminds me, some-how, of that barn at Ivycross Farm. But it has beds and a few chairs. There's a kitchenette and a toilet. There are floor-to-ceiling shelves full of food, blankets, and first aid supplies. I wanted to be prepared in case one of Lucinda Garth's ardent fans came for us. I never imagined it would be used for this.

Justin is tied to the bed. His legs and arms are secured to the corners of the metal frame with the zip ties I keep in the house for sealing opened bags or tidying cables. There's a gag in his mouth. His head moves slowly from side to side as though he's coming around from unconsciousness. His forehead gleams with a thin sheen of sweat. A stain covers his groin area.

"Maddie," I whisper. "What did you do?"

"I saved our lives," she says. "I caught him sneaking in."

"When?"

"The day before yesterday," she says. "We were in the house. I think you and Cecilia were in the garden. I checked the CCTV and saw him in the garage."

"How did you overpower him?"

"I hit him on the head with that candlestick from the corridor."

I notice the bloodied candlestick on the floor of the panic room, wrapped in a shopping bag. I didn't even notice it was gone. When we moved into the house, I hired an interior decorator, who bought a few expensive pieces, including that candlestick. Made of heavy wrought iron, it wasn't really to my taste, but I kept it anyway.

"How did you get him in here?" I ask.

"Well, I knew he'd come in through the basement," she says. "You changed the passcode on the door between the garage and the house. But there are stairs coming down here, right? And we forgot about that door. So I grabbed the candlestick and waited, and then I hit him when he came into the house. I only had to drag him a few feet into the panic room."

In the dim light, I didn't notice the dried blood above his forehead. Then I saw the Yorkie wrapper on the floor and the remnants of a glass of milk.

"You fed him."

"I held a knife over him and made him eat. He behaved himself." She smirks.

"What are we going to do now?" I glare at her. "You realised you've broken the law."

"He came here to kill us," she says sharply. "I found a way to stop him without killing him. I deserve a fucking medal."

"You're sure he was here to kill us?"

She points to a petrol can on the ground. "He was carrying that."

My heart sinks. I walk over to Justin, scrutinising his expression.

He murmurs and looks away, tears gathering in the corner of his eyes. There's the lingering scent of alcohol in the air around him, stale and sickly, the poison seeping out through his pores. A sorry story. Man makes a mistake. Man loses everything. Man gets drunk. Man wants to incinerate everything he owns, including himself and his family. A typically weak ending to a typically weak man.

I turn away before I start to feel sorry for him, grab Maddie by the hand, and lead her out of the room.

"Okay, so you didn't kill him right away. But what now? What are you planning to do?"

She shrugs. "I guess I didn't get that far."

"You can't keep him here indefinitely. Eventually, the police are going to want to know where he is. There'll be court dates he has to attend." I sigh, trying to calm down long enough to think logically. "How did he get here? Did he drive? Where's his car?"

"Still in the garage," she says. "He never took his car, remember? I guess he walked here."

"Okay, so he walked. But from which direction? He could've been picked up on CCTV heading this way. He'll be on *our* CCTV, for one thing."

"We can sort that out," she says. "Tape over those bits with old footage. Scrub the time stamp using editing software."

I shake my head. "I bet the police have systems to detect that. What if he was dropped off by a taxi nearby?"

"With a can of petrol? I don't think he'd risk it."

I clasp her shoulders with my hands. "Maddie, you saved our lives, and I love you. But you have Gabe's father in there, and I think you were going to kill him eventually, weren't you?"

"I don't know," she admits. "I gave him one of your sleeping pills."

"How did you do that?"

"Crushed it up in some milk."

The innocence and the utter unsettling nature of the things she says makes my stomach flip. What can I do? Back at Ivycross Farm, taking Peter McKenna's life had never been up for debate. That man tortured and murdered women for fun. I had to kill him to get out.

And now, my deeply flawed, destructive husband has been abducted by my troubled, adopted teenager, and it's all my fault. I allowed Justin into our lives. I didn't pick up on the red flags. DCI Cooper told me he trusted my instincts, but he was wrong. I failed.

"Mum, he's a psycho," Maddie says. "He's sick. He shouldn't be with girls my age. It's not right. He needs to be put down."

I stare deeply into my daughter's eyes. Mum had warned me about this. I hadn't wanted to believe that Maddie walked into my parents' bedroom with the intention of euthanising my ill father, but now I know Mum was right.

"That's not our decision to make," I tell her gently.

"It was when it was my dad." Her voice cracks. "Why is this different?"

"Your dad was going to kill me, and I acted in self-defence. This is pre-meditated murder. Don't you see that? You're talking about killing Gabe's father. We can't, Maddie. We either call the police, or we let him go. That can be your decision. We can't keep him here, and we can't kill him."

CHAPTER FORTY-FOUR
NOW

Maddie brushes tears from her cheeks and sniffs. "I don't want to go to some juvenile delinquent centre. I don't want to be apart from you."

For once, I find her devotion terrifying. Maddie is sixteen, and instead of finding someone to fall in love with, she's kidnapping her adoptive father. And even now, she wants to stay with *me*. She isn't thinking about her life outside of me. She doesn't see her own future.

"Are you saying we let him go?"

Her voice comes out as a breathy whisper. "Yes."

"He could go to the police," I say. "You might still end up in a detention centre."

She rubs the tops of her arms, her shoulders hunched forwards, rounded. I've never seen her so unsure of herself, so lost.

"I know. I'm more worried about him coming back." Her eyes glint, a familiar glimpse of her usual steel. "Are we doing the right thing?"

"We can move," I say. "We'll get away from him."

"If the courts let you," she points out. "He's Gabe's father. He has rights."

"Oh, Maddie, I wish you'd called the police." I push open the panic room door and stride over to Justin. I pull the gag down below his chin. "Make a sound, and I'll tell your son you intended to murder us. I'll bring him down here to see you in your piss-stained trousers."

A ripple of tension travels along his jaw. He spits out a "Fine" through gritted teeth.

"We're going to let you go."

He blinks twice and glances over at Maddie in disbelief.

"You claim to have never read my book, so I'll remind you how I killed Peter McKenna. I rammed a six-inch nail through his eyeball." I lean closer. "But that's nothing compared to what I'll do to you if you ever come near us again." I pull the gag back into place, my heart hammering, remembering exactly what it was like to be on the other end of this treatment. Justin thrashes against the restraints, grunting and groaning, the skin on his neck turning red and blotchy. I hurry back to Maddie. "We need to drug him again. Have you still got those sleeping pills?"

She runs out of the panic room and returns out of breath a few moments later.

"Is Gabe still gaming?"

"Yeah. With his headphones on."

I pull the gag away from Justin's mouth, remove a pill from the blister pack, and shove it into his mouth quickly, before he has a chance to bite my fingers. He struggles under my hand, but I keep it clamped shut.

"For God's sake, Justin. Swallow."

Maddie rushes over to the kitchenette and pours a glass of water. She crushes another pill on the counter with the back of a spoon then sprinkles the dust into the water. She returns. I let go of Justin's mouth, which he immediately opens and tries to scream Gabe's name.

As quick as a flash, Maddie starts tipping the water into his open mouth. He chokes, splutters, but swallows too. I grab the spoon, turn it upside down, and use it to search for the pill beneath his tongue. It's gone. Once the water has run out, I shove the gag back between his teeth.

"How are we going to get him out of here without Gabe noticing?" Maddie asks.

"I'll have to take Gabe to Cecilia's. I'll message her now and check it's okay."

After firing off a text, I stare down at Justin. I read about family annihilators once. Mostly men, they collapsed under the pressure of being a husband and father. Those with money problems saw their family as a status symbol, and if they were to tear down their own lives, the lives of their children and wives were an extension of that. Others blamed the mother for the family breaking down.

Justin breathes heavily through his gag. His eyes are full of hate. Yes, he blames me. He blames me for his own weakness. I want to kill him in that moment. And I could do it. I could place my hand over his mouth and nose and watch him squirm, suffer, twitch, and die. I could do that. But his body would be bruised around the wrists and ankles. The police would figure out where those bruises came from. They would find my and Maddie's DNA or traces of the panic room on his skin. We could try our best to be clever, but we would never be quite clever enough. The police will eventually trace evidence back to us.

Unless we make the body disappear. I glance over at the petrol can.

No. Whatever Justin is, he's still Gabe's father.

Cecilia replies: *Of course you can bring him here. What's happened?* *Is it okay if I don't tell you?* I reply.

Yes.

There's no hesitation. I like that.

"I'm going to take Gabe to Cecilia's. He should pass out soon. I think we gave him enough. I won't be long, okay? She lives about ten minutes away."

Maddie nods. "I'll stay with him."

"Maybe you should watch him through the door and not get close," I say. "Be careful."

I hurry upstairs, grab Gabe's coat and shoes, and hurriedly tell him he has to stay with Cecilia tonight.

"But why?"

"You can take your Nintendo Switch with you."

"Why, Mum? What's going on?"

"It's nothing for you to worry about, okay? I need to have a chat with Maddie about grown-up things, and we think it's best you're not here. I promise you everything is fine. I love you. Maddie loves you."

"Mummy."

I pull him into my arms and hold him tight. "Don't worry, monkey. Things will get back to normal soon."

It's a lie. We'll never be able to go back. Never ever.

Fifteen minutes later, I hand Gabe over to Cecilia, who sees the harried expression on my face and says nothing. I let her know I'll be back in the morning. On the drive home, I have ten minutes to decide how to do this. I have no idea where Justin is staying. All I know is that he needs to be asleep when we remove him, so he doesn't try to attack us.

Maybe Maddie's right. Maybe he does deserve to die. But this isn't self-defence, not in the truest sense of it. This is murder. How do I know Justin won't reform one day? Taking his life means eradicating that opportunity. Should I call the police and risk Maddie going to prison? I'm an accomplice now. I helped Maddie drug him. And what would happen to Gabe if I ended up in prison too? He might even end up with his father, the man who broke into my house with a can of petrol, ready to murder us all.

We keep him drugged. We wait until dark. We drive him somewhere not too far away from Penry centre, but somewhere secluded. Then we leave him to sleep off the pills, wake up, and take himself home. Then what? Will that be the end of it?

I doubt it.

There's no real solution to this. None. My guts swarm with anxiety, like I'm full of bees. If we make him swallow all the sleeping pills, he'll die of an overdose. It could look like suicide. But there's a wound on his head and bruises on his wrists and ankles.

Burn the body.

I want to throw up. Could I do it? Am I capable of murdering my husband and going on with my life?

No. We have to stick to the plan. Justin can't go to the police because he knows damn well he came to kill us that night. He might come after us, but would he now that he knows what we can do to him? I can take the kids up to my mum's temporarily then wait it out. He'll end up with a short prison sentence for abusing his position of power at the school. Then we can move far away from him and make a fresh start. A remote Scottish Island. Or somewhere warm in Europe. Gabe could learn a second language. I've always wanted bilingual kids.

Maddie... Well, Maddie still needs help. I didn't realise until tonight how much she's still grieving her real father's death. Perhaps I've never allowed her to grieve. I suppose everyone in Maddie's life figured he was abusive and that he was never much of a father to her. We assumed she'd be glad he was dead. But now I understand her relationship with him was much more complex than I thought. In order to cope with his death, she justified it by thinking of it as me "putting him down" because he was sick. And now she thinks it's okay to do the same thing to other people.

How am I going to deal with that? What if one day she thinks I'm sick too? Or Gabe?

I pull into the garage and hit the ignition button. The car stops rumbling. I have to get out and face what we've done. What we've decided. My legs are stiff and heavy, but I can't put it off any longer. I drag my tired body through the garage.

I'm one foot into the hallway when a loud crash echoes through the house. Somewhere in the house a glass shatters. The heaviness in my legs fades as soon as I break into a sprint. There's a strange cry, like a scream caught in someone's throat. I skid around the corner into the lounge then careen across the rest of the space, throwing myself forward without hesitation or concern for injury.

Two bodies wriggle and writhe like interconnected snakes on my carpet. Next to them, the television is flipped over, and there's broken glass, dead flowers, and a pool of water spreading out from a smashed vase. Justin is on top of Maddie with his hands wrapped around her throat. His face shines bright scarlet, a large, throbbing vein visible across his temple. Maddie lies beneath him, her skin pale, her dark hair a tangle against the cream carpet. She scratches his hands, desperately trying to get out of his grip. I throw my full weight against him, knocking him back, but his hands remain gripped tightly around her throat. He's going to kill her.

The thought is clear in my mind but also muddy, like it isn't real, like it can't possibly be an outcome. I physically can't stand the idea that in moments, my daughter will die. I can't. I have to do more. *He's going to kill her.*

CHAPTER FORTY-FIVE
NOW

I grab the heaviest item closest to me—the marble bust of Shakespeare Justin bought in Edinburgh. I smash it down onto his skull, feeling the dull thud of two heavy objects connecting. He falls away from Maddie, his hands releasing her throat. I'm about to drive the bust down one more time when he grabs hold of my legs, pushing me back. I drop the weapon as I fall backwards on top of Maddie. It rolls away, smearing blood across the carpet.

Justin crawls up my body, one arm raised to strike. I jam my thumbs into his eyes as hard as I can, and he cries out in pain before grabbing my wrist and twisting, harder and harder until I'm the one screaming. Beneath me, Maddie wriggles and squirms. She knocks me in the back with her knee, freeing her legs from under my weight. Her heel kicks up, jabbing into Justin's neck. He lets out a spluttering sound, finally releasing my wrists. I scramble towards the marble bust, ignoring the throbbing pain emanating from my wrist, and let out a low roar as I grab the statue.

When I turn back to my husband, he's crouching low over Maddie, screaming in her face. "Psycho bitch! Why won't you die? It's all your fault!"

I stagger to my feet and swing my arm, aiming for the back of Justin's head. But he ducks. It still catches his skull but doesn't have anywhere near the impact I'd hoped. He drops onto his backside, and I swing one more time.

"Please," he says as I connect with his right temple.

He drops onto his left side, blood gushing from the wound. I stare in horror at the bust in my hand, seeing the bits of hair and skin left on its surface. Then, somehow, Justin pushes himself back up to a sitting position, still alive, still conscious.

"Zoe, please." His eyes are bloodshot. His skin is ashen grey, like a bleached, stormy sky. He sits in a pool of his own blood, which travels down his shirt, seeping through the linen. Even my top is covered in tiny scarlet droplets. I imagine they're all over my face, like crimson freckles.

"Stop, Zoe. Please." Blood dribbles from his ears and nose. "Am I dying?"

I drop the bust to the floor. It doesn't smash, and I whisper, "I don't know."

"Can you help me?" he asks.

I shake my head.

Behind me, I feel Maddie's hands on my back, pushing me towards him. I understand. I remember two small hands pushing me towards the body on the cold barn floor. She wants me to finish him. She wants him gone. Out of our lives forever. Because Justin is the same threat as Peter McKenna. No, he isn't a serial killer. He doesn't torture women. But Justin is dangerous in his own way.

I take a step towards him. Then I stop, and my gaze trails the length of the room. What would a police officer make of this crime scene? Would they be able to discern that I delivered one last fatal blow even though my husband was incapacitated? What constitutes reasonable force?

"I can't, Maddie."

My daughter steps forward to lift the weapon, but I stop her.

"We can't. The police will trace the evidence and know."

"You can't know that," she says. "Stop being stupid. Kill him."

"No. I won't."

"Please," Justin sputters. Blood bubbles across his chin.

I walk through to the kitchen and grab a tea towel. Then I kneel next to my husband and press it to his temple.

"Zoe," he says, lifting a finger to my face. "Lovely Zoe."

From the expression on his face, I can tell that he is dying. He's seeing something we don't.

"Riya," he whispers.

My heart clenches.

"I'm sorry, Riya."

"Did you kill her?" I ask.

Justin studies me then Maddie. "She did."

"Liar," Maddie says.

Justin looks at me one last time. "It wasn't me. And if it wasn't me, who was it?" He slumps forward. I watch him take his last breath, blood sputtering from his mouth. It's over.

There's blood everywhere. I move away from the body, trying not to step in pools of blood. I glance at the marble bust, remembering that day in Edinburgh. Foggy with my hangover, laughing in a jewellery shop, looking at diamond rings, I was so happy.

I stagger over to Maddie. We collapse back onto the sofa, and I cradle her in my arms. She rubs her throat then wraps her arms around me.

"I'm sorry," she says. "I'm sorry you had to do that."

We cry for a while, and I wish the only thoughts going through my mind were of the horrible things he did. But I also think about our wedding day. I think about the surprise flowers, the cuddles during cold nights, the socks he wore to bed, and the way he buttered Gabe's toast just right. I see him running along the beach with Gabe, his hair blowing in the wind, a big grin stretched across his face.

Why did it have to end like this?

I have a sudden urge to make all of this go away. Even though I'm sure that I didn't use excessive force and that what I did was in line with self-defence, I realise Maddie is still going to be in trouble for imprisoning Justin in the first place. We won't be able to hide it. I lift her face with my hands.

"We'll wrap him up, clean the blood away, and take him somewhere in the middle of nowhere," I say. "And then we'll cover him in petrol and set him on fire." I let out an anguished sob and cover my mouth with my hand. I have to bite into my palm to stop myself screaming.

"No," Maddie says. "No. We call the police. We tell them everything." She's quiet. The faint outline of a bruise is already spreading across her neck. She lifts her fingertips and touches it lightly. "You were right before, Mum. I fucked up. I have to face up to what I've done. But we're going to lie. Just a little. It's only right we do this." She takes my hands in hers. "As soon as you found Justin, you took Gabe over to Cecilia's so he wouldn't be here when the police arrive. But while you were out, I gave Justin the pills. I tried to get him out of the house before you came back. He attacked me. You killed him to save my life. That's it. That's the story. It's safer that way. Gabe needs a parent. I'll get some time in juvie or a psychiatric hospital or whatever. They aren't going to lock me up for life, are they? I'll get out before I'm twenty-one and have my whole life ahead of me. Everything's going to be fine, Mum."

She gets up and pours herself a glass of water before making the call.

TWO HOURS LATER, we're both released from the police station after Maddie is charged with false imprisonment and assault. We check into a hotel, seeing as our home is a crime scene. I have a shower and sleep for a few hours before going to pick up Gabe. Before I left the police station, DS Rosen told me that he believes my actions to be lawful, considering I was saving Maddie's life. However, Maddie will be faced with a trial for what she did. We have a long road ahead of us, and first of all, I need to find a solicitor.

Over the phone, I give Cecilia a heads-up about what happened, then I collect Gabe, bring him back to the hotel, and sit him down for the worst conversation I've ever had in my entire life. I tell him that his father, the man who, despite his faults, always encircled Gabe with safety, is now dead. And as he cries in my arms, I try to come to terms with it myself. Justin wasn't Peter McKenna. He wasn't that kind of villain. And yet he still tried to kill. He still did that.

Later that day, DS Rosen calls again. The police went to Angie Starling's house, but there was no answer. I ask Maddie to try calling her.

"It's been disconnected," Maddie says. "The number isn't recognised." She pauses. "I bet she's gone."

"Did you warn her, Maddie?"

She nods.

"You called her?"

"Yes." She presses her hands together, lacing her fingers.

I watch her knuckles pale. "Did you say anything in a text message or email?"

"No," she says. "Mum, there's something else I should tell you. I already told the police earlier, but I haven't told you." She flutters her dark lashes, and the cold grip of fear takes hold of my throat yet again. I wait for her to continue. "She confessed to me. About killing Riya. When I told you I already knew who the killer was, I knew then. I wanted to get her to confess and for me to record it. But I never got the opportunity."

Another blow. Another shock. I shake my head. "I don't get it. Why would she kill your best friend?"

"She thought Riya was bullying me. I told Riya to dump her... boyfriend." She glances downwards, no doubt thinking of Justin. "Riya lost her temper. We were at school, and she hit me. She punched me in the stomach."

"Riya punched you?"

She nods. "Yeah, she had a crazy temper. No one else really knew about it."

"Then what happened?"

"Louisa saw it happen, and she took me into an empty classroom to check I was all right. I was so mad at Riya. I told Louisa how much I hated Riya and all this stuff about Riya being with a married man." She pauses, swiping a lock of hair away from her face. "When Louisa confessed to me a few days ago, she told me how she'd seen Riya and Justin together and she thought Riya was trying to break up my family. Louisa has this warped idea about me and how I deserve a real family with a mum and a dad, and I guess she thought if she killed Riya, I'd get to keep my family." She bites her lip.

"She told you all of this?"

"Yes."

"But what about Justin? Why didn't she go after him?"

"I didn't tell her about how Justin hit on me," she says. "If I had, she would've killed him. She thought eliminating Riya would solve the problem. Mum, I know this is all crazy, but crazy is what she knows. This is all small shit for her. She's done way worse with my dad. I'm guessing her last ten years have been a rollercoaster too, but she hasn't told me about those years."

"I don't understand. You don't let other people get away with less than this. You wanted to kill Justin after what he did. Why did you protect her? She's a murderer."

Maddie does not smile or roll her eyes or do any of the things she usually does. Her expression is filled with earnestness. "Because she's my mum. I'd do the same for you. You and her and Gabe are the only people I love. That's the problem. Even with Riya. I cared about her once, but she kept making these stupid mistakes. Like being with a married man. Why would anyone want to do that? I did get it. I guess I lost my patience with her. I probably could've helped her more, but I felt like it wasn't my responsibility. Is that bad?"

"Yes," I whisper. "It is. People aren't designed to be alone. We have to help each other. All of us. If someone is drowning, you help them. That's what we do." I stroke her hair and hold her face. "We're going to get you help so that you can see that. Okay?"

"There's no help for me. Nothing is going to work," she says. "I'm a lost cause."

"No, that's not true. I don't believe that. If you can love me and Gabe, then you can love. We're going to figure this out. I promise."

ONCE THE POLICE obtained a warrant and accessed Angie Starling/Louisa Jones's home, they found Riya Shah's little finger. But they did not find Louisa. After collecting samples of DNA found in her rented home, they confirmed that Louisa Jones is Maddie's biological mother. They also match her DNA with that found all over Ivycross Farm, including on some of the murder weapons owned by Peter McKenna, something that had stumped the detectives for a while. They'd assumed one of the victims had fought back, getting their hands on the weapons.

After I have the place cleaned and the carpet removed, we move back into our home. My empty casserole dish is waiting on the doorstep. I open it and find a note: *I miss you.*

I call Parvati as soon as I'm inside the house. When she answers, I blurt, "I've wanted to call you since the police found her. I'm so sorry. I miss you. I miss Riya. I miss Riya and Maddie together—"

"I'm sorry, too. Everything got so..." I hear her tears, the croak at the back of her throat. "I want you to know that none of this is your fault."

"Are you kidding?" I reply. "It's all my fault. Not knowing that Justin is... was... Maddie's birth mother following her—"

"It's not your fault. You didn't do anything. Justin took advantage of Riya, and Louisa Jones killed her." Parvati gets through the words, but her voice shakes with pain.

"I'll never forgive myself."

"Then I'll do it for you," she says. "Let's meet. Okay? Soon. I need someone to talk to. I'm going crazy in this house."

"All right," I reply, my shoulders lightening. "Call me any time you like. Day or night. Okay?"

"Okay."

The call reminds me that I have a life here in Penry. It's a smaller now, perhaps, but it still exists. And, granted, it's an extremely complicated life, but it's one I want to live.

The house is full of Justin. His smell, his clothes, evidence of his abandoned hobbies—old cameras, pencils, a stained-glass window starter kit. All the painful memories mixed with the happy ones. Despite all of it, I can't bring myself to leave this place.

CHAPTER FORTY-SIX
NOW

Maddie's trial date looms. Our solicitor is confident that the judge will be lenient, given the extraordinary stress she was under at the time and the fact that she saved the family from Justin's rampage. But in the meantime, we try to make the best of things.

We spend our weekends at the beach. Sometimes Cecilia joins us. Other times, Parvati brings Sadiq so the kids can play. Gabe still loves it there. I was worried the place would be tainted for him, given that it was his dad's favourite spot. But he still loves it. And I do too. I love watching my children's great-big grins, drying Gabe's hair with a sandy towel. In July, I broke my pet-buying ban and bought a golden retriever puppy for Maddie's seventeenth birthday. The kids called him Goldie. Now, as the weather cools, we wear puffer jackets and drink hot chocolate from a Thermos flask as we watch the pull and push of the sea. Goldie, already big, bounds happily along, getting his paws wet.

Maddie isn't sadistic. She isn't one step away from murder as my mum always thought. She has a damaged sense of right and wrong; I know that. But if I've learned anything over the last several months, it's that Maddie protects her family.

We don't visit Mum in the end; she comes to us for a week. That was a tense week, but one filled with talk, tea in the garden, late evenings watching the sun set over the Celtic Sea, the occasional argument, and a modicum of tentative progress. She hugged Maddie before boarding the train to go back. They'd never hugged before.

My house still feels like my house. I'd worried it never would again. There are times when I catch Maddie staring at the new carpet in the lounge and the spot on the bookshelves where the Shakespeare bust used to sit. But she tells me that we can't move because then Justin and her father win for making us scared. Besides, I can't do it to Gabe. I can't eradicate Justin from our memories. While I take the wedding photographs down from the walls, I don't burn them. I don't cut him out. I place them inside photograph albums. His clothes go to charity. We sell his car and golf clubs and anything else of value and donate all the money to a local women's shelter. But I keep his rising star award, packing it away in the same storage box where I keep the wedding photos. The house is my house, and because it's mine, I can choose the memories I wish to remember and pack everything else away to never be opened again.

I WALK into the house to find a white envelope on the doormat. Maddie and Gabe aren't home. I dropped Gabe off at Parvati's house so he could play with Sadiq while I was at group therapy, and Maddie is at her driving lesson.

The envelope is addressed to me. It's printed, not handwritten. There's no return address, but the postmark is international. I tear it open and spread the paper out on the kitchen table.

DEAR ZOE,

DON'T COME LOOKING for me. I'm gone already. This isn't one of those threatening letters trying to scare you into leaving me alone. I don't *think you'd find me anyway. And to be honest, once you read this letter, I doubt you'd even take this to the police. You'll understand why.*

First, I want to thank you for allowing me to see my daughter. You're a good person, Zoe. I know that because I've met a lot of bad people in my life. Only one of them was worse than me, and I'm scum, but you know that.

I read in the newspaper about what was found in my house. I also read that Maddie told you I confessed. The thing is, I didn't confess, and I didn't keep that finger in my house. Maddie and I talked about a lot of things, but I never told her I killed Riya Shah, because I didn't. But I know who did.

What did Maddie tell you about her childhood? That she doesn't remember? That I never existed?

If she did, she lied.

I wasn't one of Peter's victims, not in that sense. I wasn't kept chained up in his barn until I gave birth. Peter was my boyfriend. We met in Blackpool when I was homeless. He bought me. Sort of. He paid for me and my sister's company that weekend—he was on holiday—and afterwards we moved back with him onto the farm. The part about me being a teenage drug addict is true. I was addicted to heroin. He could've been the devil asking me to sell my soul, and I would've done it. Well, I suppose I did. He's as close to the devil as anyone's going to get.

I didn't know what he was into at first. Not until he came home one day with an unconscious woman under his arm. I was pregnant with Maddie and trying not to use. I wasn't well. My sister was worse. Her pregnancy was tough. I thought the baby was eating her from the inside out. And Peter wouldn't let us go to the hospital. We had worse problems than worrying about some other woman.

I hardly noticed her screams. Everything in me was numb. Peter was an evil man. He beat me, manipulated me, used me. And I stayed because that was where I thought I belonged, in the dirt with him.

As time went on, my sister died. The birth was brutal. After fifteen hours of me begging Peter to take her to the hospital, I staggered away from the bodies, my arms and chest covered in blood. I can't write it even now. Two bodies, one tiny, still attached to my sister through the umbilical cord. It changed me.

I was terrified of giving birth. I thought constantly about ways to kill my baby before it came out of me, but I knew I was too far gone. In the end, my labour couldn't have been more different. Maddie came out tiny and screaming after five hours. Peter gave me a belt to bite down on as the baby tore out of me. I was weak for days. I couldn't feed her. I'd lost so much blood. Peter had to stitch me up and bandage me. That bastard didn't have a clue what he was doing, and he wouldn't let me in the house with all the blood. I gave birth in the barn. In the same place he killed them.

Peter gave me smack for the pain. Whatever Maddie nursed from me contained that drug. We were empty shells of people. Eventually he bought formula for her, so at least we weaned it out of her system. I didn't love her at first. She screamed all day and all night. Peter got so mad, he made me take her out into the fields away from him so he couldn't hear her. Sometimes I'd lay her down in the grass next to me, roll away on my side and close my eyes, hoping a fox would come by and take her away.

But eventually, she stopped crying. She developed a personality and become more than the red-faced screaming blob I'd come to resent. She laughed. She wrapped her fingers around mine. She wriggled around when I tickled her feet. She started to crawl, then she said "Mama."

I wanted to be better for her. I cut down on the smack. I collected apples from the orchard and made applesauce. I found a dusty old parenting book in Peter's house, and I used it to check she was developing right. I learned what her different cries meant. When she was teething, we stayed in the barn away from Peter, so he didn't have to listen to her screams. When she started to talk, I spent hours babbling with her. I tried to teach her how to read, but I wasn't patient enough.

Peter grew restless. He hadn't killed a woman for a long time. He wanted me to lure someone in. Women trust other women, he said. Peter was getting older and fatter. He had a mean face. No one would go anywhere with him, and he knew it. Snatching women off the street was *risky. He'd have to go out into a city and find a homeless girl, like me, who wouldn't be missed.*

I won't go into details, but he got physical with me. And that's when I started bringing the women back to the farm for him, so he could kill them.

As soon as Maddie could walk, he made her watch. Then he made us both join in. She remembers every time her father placed a knife in her hand. Maddie was involved in every murder between the ages of three and five.

And, yes, I know she was a child. No, I don't know what it did to her. And yes, I know you probably won't believe me.

Why would you believe the word of a mother who left her child behind? I get it. I told you that you'd judge me. I did a shitty thing. I knew he'd come after me if I took her. I knew I'd make it if I left her. Yes, I chose my own life over hers. Yes, I regret it every day.

But it all worked out, didn't it? Because Maddie found you. I didn't just read your book once. I read it over and over again. I read all about your love for her and how you've taught her how to love in return. I read it because I wanted to believe Maddie was happy. And I think she is, overall. I truly think she is.

When I came to find you, it was because I needed to see her again. You hadn't been on television for a while, and you hadn't written any more books. I guess you'd settled and felt like you didn't need to. I needed it. I needed it more than anything. So, I made some quick cash by means you don't want to know. I bought a new identity. I faked Angie's background. I faked her references. I charmed the fuck out of that headteacher at Penry, not truly believing I'd even get the job (my back-up plan was a bar job in the next town), found a house to rent and settled in.

I watched. First Maddie. Then you.

I'll tell you what, you missed the red flags with your husband. I saw him at the school watching those girls. I saw his eyes roaming to their knees, their chests. A typical middle-class perv. He hides it under smarm. Have others come forward yet? He'll have more victims, I'm sure of it.

I watched Maddie at school being bullied every day. Couldn't you have done more to protect her identity? Did you have to write that book?

I followed Maddie when she went camping. I stayed on the edge of the woods, watching. No one knew I was there. It was the dead of night.

The Thompson girl was a bitch. I know you shouldn't speak ill of the dead, especially not dead children, but she was. Snooty. Entitled. Mean.

She went to the edge of the cliff. I think she was out of it, either drunk or sleepwalking. I saw her shiny hair glinting in the moonlight. And I saw the shadow that followed, the one that leapt out of the dark, put two small hands on the girl's back and shoved, hard.

Swift justice for everything that girl had done to our child. Because, yes, it was Maddie. I know her shape. I'd watched her for so long that I knew how she walked, how she stood. It was her. She murdered that girl.

What do you think, Zoe? Riya Shah is a step too far, isn't it? That's premeditated. But I didn't kill her, so how did that finger end up in my house? Do you think the police planted it? No, me neither.

No doubt you know about my background now. You know I've been in and out of correctional facilities for most of my life. You know I'm a drug abuser, someone who lived with a serial killer, and a terrible mother. But you also know Maddie.

She's not a bad girl. Broken maybe, but I think she can be put back together. I'm sure she never intended to hurt those two girls. But she snapped, didn't she? The finger removal? An inheritance from her father.

Do you believe me?

I promise you that I'll stay away. I know the police want me now. Maybe they'll find me. I'm going to try damn hard to make sure they don't. But the thing is, if they do, I'm going to tell them the truth. If they don't, I won't. Who knows if they'll even believe me? I wouldn't. But at the same time, I like my freedom very much, so I'll do my hardest to keep it.

You need to know this, Zoe, because you're the only one who can save her. She came from me, but that doesn't matter anymore. It doesn't matter if you believe this or not, as long as you spend your life loving her. Protect her, from herself, from the badness Peter left in her, that I left in her.

That's your job now. Make sure she never does this again.

. . .

With warm regards,
  Louisa

I COULD KEEP THIS LETTER, but I don't think I will. Louisa won't come back. She knows she can't. I carry the letter over to the sink and light it on fire, smoke hitting the back of my throat. Louisa Jones spent most of the last ten years in prison for several different assaults, and in one, she broke a woman's little finger on her right hand. I found out a few weeks after Justin's death that Katherine Sutton, one of Maddie's bullies, had been involved in a hit-and-run accident, suffering a broken leg and concussion. The police found evidence linking Louisa's car to the incident. She's a violent, unstable person, and I don't believe a word she says about my daughter. But not even the heat generated by burning the letter can warm my freezing-cold bones.

EPILOGUE
THEN

Maddie knows her mother is not coming back, but she still heads down to their favourite spot by the brook. She sits on the bank and dips her finger into the freezing-cold water. If her mother were here, they might build a dam together and redirect the flow, watching the light bounce along the rippled surface. Maddie likes the sound of running water. She likes the glimmer of pale stones beneath the surface.

The light is changing. It's getting darker. It's three days after Christmas, and she's never wearing enough clothing. To keep warm, she runs everywhere, and as a result, she's skinny like a rake.

Her trainers are too small now. It slows her down, but not too much. She pretends someone is chasing her, maybe her father, and she ducks down into the grass, rolls on her back, and shakes her legs in the air. Then she jumps back onto her feet and pumps her arms to make herself go faster.

In the neighbouring field, a couple of horses watch her. They have blankets fitted around their bodies. They chew, snort, and shake their heads. Once, in summer, she trespassed into one of the farmer's fields and tried to catch a sheep. She wanted to feel the wool, see what it was like. Were they more like clouds or marshmallows? She considers going up to the horses. This time, she doesn't. She doesn't want to be out in the dark.

As she comes closer to the farm, Maddie sees the woman again. This woman has been running along these roads almost every day for about a month. She wants to leap out at the woman and tell her to stop, because he's noticed her. That's a bad thing. The woman shouldn't be out here so late. In the dark, it's easier for bad things to happen. And bad things do happen here.

Maddie drops behind a wall and watches. The woman stops briefly to take a swig of water. She reminds Maddie of her mother. Maybe she is her mother, or she could be at least. One day. That'd be nice, if she had a mother again.

After the woman is gone, Maddie gets to her feet and carries on, walking now. She's tired. She feels tired a lot at the moment. She doesn't want to go back to the farm, but her daddy is the only person she has. And at least he doesn't treat her too badly. He doesn't do to her what he does to those women. He likes to make them scream. Maddie feels very, very tired. She wants it all to stop. Maybe she should have waved her arms at the woman and got her to take her away somewhere.

The gate is close now. Daddy will want her to help with the cooking.

Still, she stops. She turns around and looks back. She thinks about everything that she wants and the things she's lost already. More than anything, more than sweets, toys, and warm clothes, she wants a mother. That's what she wants.

EBOOK EDITION

Copyright © 2022 Sarah A. Denzil

All rights reserved, including the right to reproduce this work, in whole or in part, in any form.

This is a work of fiction. All characters, events, organizations and products depicted herein are either a product of the author's imagination, or are used fictitiously.

Cover Design by Damonza

Also by the Author:

ABOUT THE AUTHOR

Sarah A. Denzil is a British suspense writer from Derbyshire. Her books include SILENT CHILD, which has topped Kindle charts in the UK, US, and Australia. SAVING APRIL and THE BROKEN ONES are both top thirty bestsellers in the US and UK Amazon charts.

Combined, her self-published and published books, along with audiobooks and foreign translations, have sold over one million copies worldwide.

Sarah lives in Yorkshire with her husband, enjoying the scenic countryside and rather unpredictable weather. She loves to write moody, psychological books with plenty of twists and turns.

To stay updated, join the mailing list: http://eepurl.com/hoIPaT for new release announcements and special offers.

www.sarahdenzil.com
Writing as Sarah Dalton - http://www.sarahdaltonbooks.com/

Lightning Source UK Ltd.
Milton Keynes UK
UKHW041923280322
400747UK00003B/13/J